TKEN DARKNESS

FROM INTERNATIONAL AWARD WINNING AUTHOR

KIA CARRINGTON-RUSSELL

Hopeless

This had never been my war.
But as I walk in the darkness, in a crowded room of misfits;
I realize this is my fight now.
I have power.
But I doubt it is enough.
I have blood lust.
But it is out of my control.
I am a monster.
But I am not the only one.
I will do everything in my power to keep you safe;
My love, familiar, and husband.
I will protect you, even when all hope is lost.
Because you gave me the light to start living again, even in the dark.
My hand will always find yours.
Thank you, and I hope we meet again, even in the next life in a
different time and place;
Where all is not so cruel.

Chapter I

’D BEEN HERE before, in the land of frost and snow known as the Antarctic. The moment its rigid chill lavished my skin, I embraced it with a tenderness embodying its harsh nature. For this mission, I’d have to be as cool as the ice and as effective as the wild snowstorm we’d teleported into. I wasn’t affected by the harsh elements, if anything, I found it more soothing in comparison to the frivolous sun that would from time to time appear in the wilderness we currently resided in. Since my awakening as half-vampire, the sun unnaturally irritated my skin. The negative temperature had no hold over my bare skin showing through my sleeveless leather shirt and pants. Nor did it affect Chase whose torso was on full display courtesy of his open leather jacket audibly flapping in the wind.

The snowstorm was wicked in its way, trying to push us back eerily as if sending a message not to step any further into this mission. I couldn’t see past my hand, though I could sense Chase and Tythian by my side. Without hesitation, Tythian began guiding us toward what I imagined to be the direction of Tracey’s Council.

I hovered my mind over Chase’s. We were still connected fluidly like any other time, but I forced myself to become rigid around him. We had a part to play, and although it pained me to deny the bond we shared, I had a duty to uphold in this mission. And it was for us. In the grand scheme of things that Cesar, Tythian, and Chase agreed would benefit us all. I had a role to play and to accomplish that, I had to seemingly renounce my claim on Chase temporarily. I wasn't at all happy about it, but this was my contribution to their ambitions.

It still pained me and left me dejected, thinking of the state Chase was in only days ago and my inability to help or bring him back from that condition. I felt numb, and a part of me, somewhere deep and closed off from Chase, felt broken from what I'd allowed to happen to the others as well. I despised myself for the state I'd left Tori and Dillian in and my inability to save the wolves. I cut my thoughts off. They served me no purpose here and only as a distraction. I had to focus on the mission. But the haggling of my failures never seemed to truly vanish.

My leather boots crunched on the loose snow above the thick ice we walked on. Even if we stepped out onto a thin layer, I doubted we'd fall through. The vampires had a deadly stealth and weight to them, defying natural gravity. It was almost as if physically, they didn't exist at all. The crunch of my shoes was our only giveaway if it could ever be heard over the howling wind.

I followed Tythian and Chase into the blizzard, resisting the urge to let my mind wander over Chase and relish in our co-dependency. Instead, I squared my shoulders, admiring the weight of my Barnett crossbow at my hip and the bows and sword sheathed at my back. Tythian and Chase were dressed similarly with their preferred weapons of choice. Though Tythian and Chase were certain Tracey's Council wouldn't attack us immediately, we were still prepared just for that. They were confident in the likelihood of Tracey agreeing to an alliance. But in the time of war and asking someone to perform an act of betrayal—nothing was guaranteed.

"Do you have any idea where we're going?" I asked after an hour of idly strolling about in the wild storm.

Tythian hissed under his breath at what he'd likely consider to be my imprudence. "The only way you make it into Tracey's Council is by personal escort."

I scoffed at him and crossed my arms mirroring his repugnant attitude. "In other words, you have no idea where it is, and we're going to freeze our asses off before we get anywhere?" I argued.

"Or maybe I've lulled you out here so I can finally put an end to that forever bitching mouth of yours."

"Enough," Chase said in a lowly voice that vibrated through me. He commanded attention even when we couldn't physically see one another. It was enough warning toward Tythian, and he remained silent. Had we been back at the institute who knew how Chase might've reacted, but it wouldn't have simply been with one word. But here, out in the open, even if we were taken to Tracey's Council, we couldn't act so defensively of one another. I looked down, ashamed that he could so easily play the part and act indifferent towards me. And I was already bickering at Tythian.

We fell into silence, allowing Tythian to lead us around aimlessly for hours. We continued pushing through the snowstorm waiting for a member of Tracey's Council to collect us—if ever. Sometimes it would ease, and we could see one another clearly. Chase and I would share the briefest of glances to ensure one another was okay. And then we'd circle back into another snowstorm or perhaps it was the same. We walked aimlessly and irritatingly through the harsh weather. I wondered when they'd give up. For how many hours or days would we circle, waiting to be 'escorted'?

"Tythian, maybe if we stopped in one spot for a few hours," Chase bartered over the gentle breeze. "Perhaps that'll entice them to seek us out if they think we're setting up camp." We'd broken out into a patch of clear sky. The sun was vexatious as it beamed down with harsh precision. I'd give anything to hide from the intensity of its wrath. I almost wished I was wearing one of those stupid cloaks Cesar ordered us to wear to try and take the edge off slightly.

Tythian was becoming frustrated. We all were. Yet neither of them seemed surprised by the audacious wait. How long were they willing to wait? How long was I willing to waste before I'd itch to return to the institute? My shoulders sagged. A part of me didn't want to return and face the others empty-handed—another failure. I could sense Chase side glance me and dropped my gaze to the ground, cowering my feelings into a ball that he wouldn't be able to reach. I didn't want him aware of my distraction nor want these negative feelings to influence him or his mind ever again. I had been the reason for his undoing last time. I had to hide any emotions that could inflict stress on him ever again.

I mentally armored myself again, these thoughts and emotions were only distracting my focus. I almost wished that while Chase and I played the part of non-lovers there was a way to remove the emotion and feelings that were oppressed onto me because of our bond. If I had to deny my connection to him, surely such a thing was possible.

"We'll give it two hours. If nothing happens, then we'll continue walking however long it takes. They'll come for us eventually. They won't be able to let such a prize slip through their fingers," Tythian gloated.

"We are after all traitors to the Council," Chase said, bemused. Despite his efforts in trying to make a joke, it wasn't funny. It was the truth and a deadly existence they were exploiting and gambling on.

"I saw a small cave a while back," Chase shouted over the breeze that picked up and began to howl spookily. Surrounding us was nothing but blinding white and sun. The ice looked as if it went on endlessly. "This way." Chase's coat and hair stiffened from the extremity of the weather. Small icicles formed on his thick eyelashes and coat. Had it not been for my vampire part, I imagined it would've only been a few hours until the cold seeped into my bones and became life-threatening. And yet, walking with these two aimlessly for hours felt more like an inconvenient excursion.

We paced back and forth in a cave, agitated by the small space we inhabited together. I was irritated by Tythian standing so close to me because I despised him and anguished over not being able to reach out to Chase so naturally.

We kept a lookout for those who might come and find us. No fires or bedding had to be made. No plan of sorts, simply a counting of time until we were approached. Patience and inaction had never been my forte. Though I understood its importance, it didn't make me less agitated when I so strongly believed my time and focus were better spent elsewhere. We spent hours in the cave keeping to our best manners— which equated to no idle chit chat.

"They'd be aware of our presence. They're hoping we simply move on," Tythian presumed. "They're fully aware of who we are and that we've purposefully stepped into their territory. Perhaps we should go toward the human camp close to here. If they have anything to do with them or are in ownership of those humans, then they'll be forced to come out to protect their resources."

I chewed on my disgust. The way he and all the other vampires so flatly spoke about humans irked me. I'd never given humans much empathy even in my station as a Token Huntress, but still, the thought of being lined up as mere food sources disdained me. Especially now that I'd become the predator, they almost made it too easy.

"That actually might work to lure them out. We'll hover for a while. If they don't come, then we'll walk for a bit and then circle back. If they notice a consistent interest, they'll indefinitely approach us," Chase remarked. I brushed away the small layer of ice that had formed on my thighs, impatient with this game. "They will come, Esmore," Chase added confidently. I sighed but softened my expression. Chase so thoroughly believed that this was the only way, so I had to have faith in him, even if the stiff clothes and sun were making me frustrated and sapping my energy.

After an hour of deliberate slow walking, hoping that someone would intervene in our path, we stood atop a snowy peak where we could look down at the human camp. It was the same one Chase and I had spotted the last time we were here. No one was outside during the horrific weather, and their thick defensive doors were closed.

This had been the place I'd wanted to bring Dillian and Julia to. And now the likelihood of that ever coming into fruition was near impossible. I looked over at Tythian whose cool blue eyes rested on the entrance of the camp. His black dress shirt had begun to solidify against his body and tanned skin. His blond slicken hair was a frozen mass, which I imagined infuriated him a great deal. He was looking everything but his usually composed self. So finally, I found slight joy and amusement in this journey and at Tythian's expense.

As planned, we circled back another two times. I was tired, parched, and thirsted for blood after being dragged through snowstorms and then clear skies with blasting sun that prickled at my skin. We were in the mainstream of the snow blizzard once again. My frozen eyelashes were heavy, and my face had become eerily numb despite my inability to feel the temperature difference. How many days would we be forced to surrender to this tiresome expedition?

Tythian stopped, and at his unforeseeable signal so did we. A small team of vampires circled us. I couldn't make out their silhouettes but arched my arm over my shoulder reaching for my sword, waiting for their attack.

"We've come to have an audience with Tracey," Tythian boasted over the loud snowstorm. They stirred amongst themselves.

A deep voice called out from the nothingness of blanketing snow. "And what makes you so sure she'd want an audience with the likes of *you*? I should kill you both on sight."

"But you haven't, and I'm sure your lady can make that decision once she's heard us out herself," Tythian announced tentatively. His tone was often condescending, and already his tone sounded certain that the negotiations had already begun and were working in his favor. He always acted as if he were the center of any room he walked into, and it would always bend to his will. That those in the room would do as he said and if they dared argue … well, that's when they'd see the side of Tythian I too often clashed with.

There was a contemplative pause. My hand was only a mere inch from the handle of my sword. I couldn't see them, but I could sense where they were positioned. After great deliberation, they seemed to pool away into the snow, and Tythian continued marching on. The others divided around us, escorting us to follow his lead. Chase was acting his usual robust self. The only thing that gave away his tension was when I brushed my mind against his and reprimanded myself for doing so. I had to stop our co-dependency, or I'd become dependent on it even during this mission which could give our lie away.

An hour of suspense later, and being tortured at a ridiculously slow pace to fight through the savage snowstorm with the expectation of being ambushed, we came to a stop against a giant ice wall. I looked up into billowing white where the storm spluttered fresh flakes of snow on the icy landscape. There was no end to its sheer height and size. We'd come to a completely dead end.

"This way," the deep voice instructed. I could make out his thick, dark fingers dragging across the considerable wall. Tythian followed with little indifference. Chase naturally walked in front of me, absentmindedly using his larger frame as a shield if a scuffle were to break out. I remained acutely aware of the two who followed me as we were guided along the great icy wall. The leader and Tythian dipped into a crevasse that seemed to appear from nowhere. As soon as I followed through the narrow slit, I was stimulated by the beauty of the narrow, iced hallway. I looked up, now able to fully appreciate the size of the wall I'd just been admiring from the outside. It was a buffer, a screen to hide the entrance of their Council.

I looked over my shoulder at the still billowing snow that crept in on the edges of the entrance. The two men behind me were wearing thick blue coats. The odd material worked well enough to keep the snow from soaking through to their underclothing. I, on the other hand, though wearing leather and didn't feel the cold, looked like I'd lost the battle against the snowstorm. I contemplated the edge of my golden plait that had frozen tips.

Chase's grunt forced me to look back his way. He raised his eyebrows in his usually bemused state, even when we were in enemy territory. I huffed at him, flinging back my hair and taking on my 'role.' The others had walked slightly ahead, and I still couldn't see the man who had escorted us here. His back was turned to me, tightly fitted with the same blue garment that the others wore. What grabbed my attention was the sheer size and width of his sword. It looked like an oversized hatchet with a leather sheath that did nothing to take away its intimidating presence. He was a giant in size, I estimated at six foot eight. I'd never seen someone so tall and broad. So, it begged the question, would his size make it easier to take him down, or was he a perfectly aged and competent warrior? In the way that he held himself, I'd gathered it was the latter.

Stop gawking, Chase interjected, bemused. The sound of his velvety voice in my mind rolled along my spine, raising me into a peaked awareness. My nipples hardened, and I willed my body to stop reacting to his tone. I could feel him chuckle down the line at my response.

Chase, this isn't funny. Don't distract me, I lectured back. He shrugged slightly as he tucked his hand in the front pocket of his pants—the audacity.

Tracey's Council was grand in scale. Layers of thick iced walls were symmetrically aligned on either side of us. They served no purpose other than confusingly mirroring us at all different angles like an optical illusion. No one and nothing stood within the many sheeted layers. The long straight hallway we walked was stark with only a few lit fires. Unlike Fier's Council where electricity had been adopted once again from the technology era, Tracey's Council had taken on a primitive appeal. It was beautiful in a way. I could only compare it to Fier's Council because it was the only other one I'd ventured into. His, comparatively, was white marble and catered more toward personal entertainment and was aesthetically pleasing for the supercilious vampires. Tracey's was content and designed for their true nature—cold and empty.

The guards escorted us down the hollow entrance where at the end I could see mass lighting appear. I kept an eye on the two at my back, still ready at any notice if we were to be ambushed. I could sense others watching us, but saw no one as I looked through the mirrored iced walls.

A draft slipped in, a small howling noise cooing from no direction in particular. There was a ghostly atmosphere that danced along my skin. The halls of which we passed felt empty. Outside had been nothing but a wild storm, however within it was filled with silence and suspense. I was certain the smallest pinprick of water would be heard throughout the chambers.

Two guards were stationed outside the grand opening of the great hall we were being led to. The arched entrance was detailed in carvings of flowers perfectly articulated in the ice. Over Chase's shoulder and past the guards, I could sense a slow commotion stir. The guards didn't wear the blue hoods like the members who escorted us. They were unified in tight leather that accentuated their very masculine frame. The clothes were too tight in my opinion.

They didn't so much as look at us and were easily waved to the side by the giant vampire who led us into the belly of their lair. Once they divided, giving us access to the main chamber, I was awe-struck by the beauty of the iced pillars and balcony that overlooked with an audience. I scanned the numerous bays of vampires who looked down on us, noticing with startling clarity how many of them were men—beautiful men who looked down with transfixing gazes of curiosity. None bore weapons or looked on in an aggressive manner. When I did spot a few women clustered amongst them, I realized that the majority of them were humans. They were dressed prettily, at ease in their company, and looked down at us with the same form of unrequited snobbery, as if mimicking their owners.

Sectioned in the center on the ground level were two thrones both of which were occupied by captivating women. The vampire who sat on the larger blue fabric and gold-plated throne was an exceptionally beautiful woman with dark mocha skin. Her unnaturally bronze-colored eyes studied me with that predatory gaze most aged vampires had. She wore a long blue silk dress that clung to her curvaceous figure. The tight silk around her chest pushed her bountiful breasts up, and the split on the side exposed her luscious skin as she crossed one leg over the other. She looked no older than thirty, but I knew her physical appearance had nothing to do with her actual age. Assumedly sitting before me, was Tracey.

The younger woman by her side looked no older than twenty. She paled in comparison to the beauty sitting beside her. Not because she lacked in an unworldly beauty herself, but because she was staring at Chase so deliciously that I imagined what her face would look like after I made it not so pretty.

Unlike the woman beside her, the younger vampire had less material to cover her matching mocha skin. The yellow transparent dress that draped over her hard nipples and breasts left little to the imagination. I almost considered the silver glistening laced underwear she wore beneath simply an ornament. She wasn't as curvaceous as the woman beside her, but in the shape of their oval eyes and pointed nose, I suspected they were related. And I knew without much speculation that this was the sister, the one who so very much desired Chase.

"You have a lot of nerve walking the outskirts of *my* Council," Tracey ordained, confirming her identity. Her beauty was as perfectly carved as the ice surrounding her. What I found astonishing was the lack of weapons or soldiers around her. Everyone else was raised on a higher level, as an audience simply to watch. I still wasn't foolish enough to drop my guard.

"We're so humbled to see you too, Tracey." Tythian charmed a tentative smile and bowed insincerely. "It's been a long time."

The colossal vampire who'd escorted us took his position beside Tracey's throne. He shadowed over her figuratively, his sheer size overpowering, yet it took nothing away from her presence. My eyebrows furrowed as he turned, and I could see his face for the first time. Like the two ladies, everything about him was handsome, striking, and beautiful. His green eyes reminded me of a rich forest, his skin so smooth, lips so plump, and cheekbones so high that I was shocked.

Gawking, Chase chimed in. I internally slapped him. He didn't flinch as he stood beside me, as we were in the physical world. But I could tell he found bemusement from my not so discreet stare. I scanned the room once again. They were all beautiful.

"You dare come into my home, armored and with a mere three bodies, how you offend me. Do you know how much I could gain from offering you over? Fier has made it amicably clear how much he wants both of your heads after your high treason and embarrassing his order. Two of his greatest warriors—traitors—both in union with their own *covens* of all things. And one of course, being like a mere son to him." She glanced over to Chase as she took on a theatrical tone. "And then you bring me a child. What, a human? Perhaps a new little vampire friend? Or could it be the elusive rumors I've heard so much about, a fleeting golden bird, a huntress of all things who fell from the sky after surviving her encounter with Oppollo, and lives to tell such a tale?"

I didn't like that she mirrored the same nickname that Fier had adopted when addressing me, 'Golden Bird.'

"Attentive as always," Chase charmed with a bewitching smile. The younger sister lapped that up, smirking and licking her lips like he was a delicacy. She swept back her long caramel curls in a flirtatious manner. My tongue brushed over my teeth as I reined in my desire to claim my familiar in front of her. "And something like that." He winked. I found every will in my fiber not to roll my eyes. This was the part we had to play, but I still didn't enjoy the game.

Tracey scoffed. "And the last I heard that little golden nuisance had been taken care of, her head on its way to Oppollo as we speak." I said nothing, but was disconcerted by how quickly such information had already been spread in the matter of a day. Her gaze swept over me from head to toe. "It does have a somewhat beautiful element to it, doesn't it?" she said, watching me like a prized 'it.' "Allow me to introduce myself personally. I am Tracey, but I assume you are very well aware of who I am. And this here is my sister, Patricia."

Patricia's top lip pulled back as if the thought of greeting me displeased her. I realized it wasn't because of who I was or even what I represented. It was because I was another woman. Jealousy rolled from her in waves. I was an infringement on their sickly male-orientated buffet. I stared down the snooty vampire, my lips slowly twisting into a provocative smile as I delighted in the thought of her approaching me. At least then I could claim everything that happened thereafter as self-defense. Only wicked delight sparkled in my eyes, imagining all the things I could do to her. In the way that she sneered, I knew she understood as well.

Tracey watched the tension between us before snapping in twisted irritation. "And is she so rude she can't speak or simply mute?"

"Oh no, I speak," I said, cutting Tythian off before he could speak on my behalf. I could feel his gaze snap on me, silently reprimanding me and reminding me that we were here for negotiations and to ask for their help. This all too joyous part of me wanting to stir havoc out of recklessness had to be put away. I all but gritted my teeth as I took a step back, allowing Tythian to take over the conversation once again. I was too easily provoked and tired of being spoken down to. But that was the reality of my position, whether within the Guild or even here. Maybe I spited it more now because they were vampires and that was something I could still never truly respect.

I felt Chase reaching out to me within my mind, calming me. I was all too aware of my vampire self's prickly sensations wanting to surface to exemplify to them that I wasn't some little golden bird but their worst nightmare. I shunned away that side of me, the one that wanted to dive into ego and challenge. To be a rightful winner in what others might consider a pointless fight.

"Her name is Esmore, and we came here today to speak with you in private about a matter we feel might benefit you," Tythian bartered.

Tracey scoffed. "I highly doubt that. The longer I entertain your intrusion allows a larger window of time where I might be deemed unfit and fraternizing with the Council's enemy."

"The Council's or Oppollo's?" Chase asked directly. Tracey's sharp gaze slid onto Chase like a viper tracking her prey. "It's no secret your Council is weakening, Tracey. Word is, the last group you sent out in search of a new location, were taken out. Now I don't want to speculate as to who might've done that or which Council might've had ulterior motives, but I doubt a few more minutes of speaking with us will affect your current predicament."

Tracey's bronze eyes bore into him. Her long black polished nails clawed into the gold plating of her throne. Patricia pressed back into her seat watching the tension between Chase and Tracey. And Tythian was concerned about me sabotaging the negotiations? They seemed to be doing no better than me.

I noticed a few vampires above dip into the crevasse of their booth as if shying from Tracey's soon-to-be wrath. I was prepared for Tracey to attack and wouldn't let her any closer to my familiar if she so dared. If they attacked the ruse was up, and I'd protect him with my life.

With slow delicacy, Patricia placed her hand over her sister's. Tracey's gaze slid from Chase to her sister's hand as she seriously studied it, contemplating what her next move should be. I had no doubt Patricia didn't particularly want us alive, but I now understood why Chase was here. Her little infatuation with him was already playing in our favor, even if only to make it past the first few minutes of this conversation.

From the profile I'd been given on the two vampires, I doubted Tracey wanted to ruin her baby sister's expectations. And there was another thing I'd noticed as Tracey's gaze swept over her audience.

Unlike other Council leaders who might've put their underlings on the front line to guard them, she was addressing us personally while the rest of her members were at a safer distance. *She cared for them.* Chase's words hit their target and focused on her greatest weakness and insecurity. Her Council, where it was now, was dying.

Her gaze fastened on me and a small smile swept over her unmarred face. "Let's play a little wager. If your little golden bird is as powerful as some have said, to even oppose Oppollo himself, I will offer one of my finest warriors in this room to test her 'skills.' If she survives a minute against him, I will hear you out privately. The rule, no gifts permitted. Weapons however are by choice."

I could feel resistance pool from Chase. He wanted to charge forward and nominate himself instead. And Tracey waited for him to react in such a way. They would've heard rumors of our being together. And we had to prove them otherwise, us being familiars was an easy target on both our backs. In an ideal situation, I wouldn't still be so fatigued from my fight only the day before. But I couldn't help but feel bemused by the challenge. Only a minute? Did she really think her warrior would last that long?

Despite the situation, Chase resumed his role and part to play. He turned to me with a low patronizing whistle.

"I'd hate to see you wound up hurt now, *sweetheart,*" Chase antagonized. And like a moth to the flame, I too would play this part.

"Disappointed you weren't even considered for the challenge?" I threw back. "It must've had something to do with your tiny hands." I could feel Chase's humor inevitably tug on our line. If it weren't for the audience around us, I imagined he would've laughed.

"Oooh, all words, maybe one day you can put that pretty little mouth of yours into some actual use," he charmed back cockily.

"Enough, you two," Tythian interrupted genuinely annoyed. Tracey's eyebrows were furrowed as she studied us. We had to make them believe we weren't familiars. And there was no easier way to prove that than a reluctant treaty between our groups.

I twisted a smile at Tracey, allowing my fangs to slip free. My eyesight hazed purple as I took a step forward. The intensity of the room watched me as my minor shift made them uncomfortable. I drew out my sword.

"She's both," I heard someone whisper in the audience.

"It's true," another gasped, shocked.

I could feel their gazes and the confusion ruffle amongst the crowd as I briefly swept my mind over theirs collectively. Some were confused. Others were revolted. Some were even curious. I was nothing but an anomaly in their beautifully crafted disastrous world.

Tracey summoned forward the giant vampire who overshadowed her, and I held in my groan. Of course she'd select the biggest vampire in the room. How shallow of her to think his size intimidated me. Such a ludicrous formality and challenge, and yet I couldn't deny the provocation that stirred within my gleeful vampire self. *The bigger they are, the harder they fall,* I chimed to myself unhinged. My vampire self was careless and a relief from my constant degrading monologue. Here I was liberated, and anything goes.

Be careful, Chase chided. He was acting nonchalant, but I felt the urge to remind him not to intervene. No matter what happened. If he came to my aid our ruse would be obsolete, and we came here with a purpose. The only thing that stepped in between that objective and a private meeting was this oaf of a vampire. And suddenly my huntress and vampire were in unison, finding the appeal of taking down another vampire.

"Maybe this could be fun," I patronized him as he approached me. His brilliant green eyes looked down on me as he unsheathed his oversized hatchet. His muscles unnaturally flexed from the sheer size of them. I'd definitely have to take two maybe even three strikes to amputate one of them. I was certain even his neck was so thick that beheading him would take extra effort. So that made the easiest target his heart.

"Iris, know you'll be rewarded handsomely if you end this in under thirty seconds. I want her head," Tracey cooed out to her champion. The hatchet was the same width as me. Calculating his swing as well, it'd take me some time to maneuver around him to get into close range. But that didn't mean it was impossible. Tracey watched on with anticipation, the silk of her dress falling further down her leg as she leaned forward. "Begin!"

The hefty vampire lunged, his speed surprising. I jumped back leaving the heavy hatchet to plow into the ice where I once stood, flickering shards around its undeniable strength. By the time my feet skidded along the ground, he'd already reefed it out, irritated by his first strike that missed. I shot him a smile to antagonize him further. His green eyes sparkled with life. He'd underestimated me. Though he was an oaf, I could see a cool calculation within his gaze. Some might've even mistaken his first strike as all brawn. But I saw straight through his strategy. I couldn't win by trying to get close to him, I'd never make it unless I already had an advantage. If we had more time, I could tire him out. But even then, a vampire's stamina far outweighed our training as hunters.

My sword was useless. I sheathed it and ran for the blue silk curtain that hung from the ceiling and fell over the audience booths' edge. I jumped, grabbing hold of it and bunching it into a tight-knotted grip. I raised my legs as his hatchet swung beneath me, slicing across the wall with shattering precision. The wall didn't so much as shake though those who were above were startled.

I wrapped the bottom of the curtain around my thigh and ankle before he could grab at the end and swing me from side to side. He jumped, narrowly missing the bottom of it once again. I maneuvered myself in the silk strategically as I heaved myself up in seconds. I twisted the silk under my shoulder enough for it to sustain my weight as I pulled out my Barnett crossbow and gathered a nicely fastened arrow.

He used the blade of his hatchet as a shield, easily flicking away the first two arrows. Out of irritation, he left himself open as he jumped and swung for me. My third arrow whistled into his left shoulder. He wasn't so stupid as to leave his chest exposed to me. I hoisted and rolled myself over the iced edge of the balcony as the tip of his blade sliced past where I'd once hung. The vampires scampered away from me like I was some kind of disease drawing toward them impending doom.

I tisked as I flicked my hair out of my face, wishing I didn't have to do this with stiffened bones. I could play this cat and mouse game for another thirty seconds, but all I was proving was that I could merely escape. I untangled myself from the blue silk, irritated.

"You can't stay up there forever," his voice was velvety smooth, coaxing, and venomous all the same. I looked over the edge, swerving to the side as he harpooned an arrow back at me.

"Would you like to come up?" I offered, throwing the silk back over the balcony to patronize him. I jumped on the edge and leaped for the next audience box. Vampires scampered back, horrified that I stood so close to them. He followed me, almost bemused as he gave chase. I continued drawing back my Barnett crossbow as I leaped from ledge to slippery ledge.

"Enough!" he screamed. As I feigned to jump to the next one, he drew back his arms. And I knew I had him. When he let go of his hatchet in anticipation to strike me mid-air, I skidded to a halt and flipped to the ground. My knees cringed at the impact, but I exploded into action. I reefed the hand blade from the garter strapped to my thigh as I burst into a run. He wasn't entirely left exposed and met me head-on. As he swung his fist toward my face, I shifted my smaller frame around him, gliding my blade with the security and strength of both my hands. Black blood pooled from his arm as I trailed along his thick vein and slashed at his eye.

He smacked me away from his face, the sheer force plummeting me back into the iced wall. I flipped myself in time to land on my feet against the ice with a narrowing crunch of my knees. Defying gravity, I used the momentum to pounce back at him. His beautiful face that I'd struck already healing and his bloodied arm almost completely stitched up. He twisted out of my range, collecting the back of my braid and jarring me back. I wrapped my legs around his waist as I stapled the blade toward his chest.

"Time!" Tracey bellowed as she stood up. His hand was wrapped around my throat, ready to pop my head off my shoulders. And my blade was etching into his chest, readying for one final thrust to end him. "That's enough!" Tracey encouraged slightly desperate. *She did care for her men*, I realized. It snapped me from vengeance to take out all the built-up angst and anger on this vampire. It wasn't his fault I'd let the others die. I internally grimaced. Why was everything coming back to this? My failures were haunting me like never-ending ghosts. His grip loosened on my neck, and in my peripheral I could see that Chase had stepped forward, even when I had willed him not to.

"I could've killed you," Iris said as he slackened his arms and obeyed Tracey.

"And I could've killed you," I said, removing my palm from the hilt of the blade and removing the tip from his chest. A droplet of black blood appeared, and it immediately healed. There was a spark of respect that glistened in his eyes before they returned to a dull soldier-like expression. I unwrapped my legs from around his waist and cautiously stepped back. When I wavered my mind over his, I realized he'd adopted a fondness toward me. It wasn't of the romantic nature, but something else I couldn't quite put my finger on.

When I turned to look back at the others, Tythian seemed bored. Chase, however, looked tight-lipped and unimpressed. But when we made eye contact, he broke out an antagonizing smile.

That was too close, he lectured me.

Maybe, I cooed back. *But keep your eye on that one. There's something different about him.* Chase drew his attention to the vampire who shadowed Tracey once again. She briefed a glance over him, taking in every detail to ensure he was left unharmed. And I was certain, by my count, she called it six seconds too early.

Iris has been with her for as long as I can remember, Chase informed me.

Familiars?

I don't think so.

"Well then," Tracey said with a fake smile. Patricia rolled her eyes in annoyance. Oh, how she wished I'd been taken down. She revered me with spiteful vengeance. I retracted my fangs, relinquishing my purple huntress eyes. Tracey stood up, the silk of her dress contently resting on her hips. "Shall we take this somewhere more private then?"

She suggested the direction toward a tall, narrowed hallway to the left of the room. Patricia took stride beside her sister, but slowly pulled back until she was at Chase's side. She linked her elbows with his in giddy delight. I swallowed my bitterness. I felt Tracey's keen eye on me, watching how I'd react.

"I missed you," Patricia seductively said as she looked up at Chase with delicious delight.

"I bet you say that to all the handsome criminal vampires you come across," Chase flirted.

She giggled, pressing her breasts against his arm. I licked my tongue over the back of my teeth, desensitizing my natural reaction of making a bloody scene.

"When we last met you were in a powerful position already, but I think I like the idea of you being a bad boy," she chimed. I wanted to vomit. Tythian was watching us coolly as well, and I wasn't at all surprised that he thought we lacked such discipline that we couldn't play our roles. Those who had watched us whispered amongst themselves. They scattered from their entertainment boxes and into the iced tunnels of Tracey's Council.

We were led into a private room where the next conversation and negotiation would impact the future of our ambitions in this war. We had to convince Tracey to betray the Vampire Council.

CHAPTER 2

THE HALLWAYS WITHIN the Council were a spectacle in themselves with iced pinnacles and pillars that could've only been crafted and carved by nature at its finest. I was still awe-struck by the icy element that was so foreign to the lands in which I was raised. Large icicles hung from the ceiling, mirroring and disorientating our reflection as we walked beneath. It was beautiful, but it was also a harsh element that the vampires of Tracey's Council had become accustomed to.

I searched the empty archways and uneven terrain, waiting for someone or something to jump out in the dire dark with few flames lighting the icy halls. A small trial in exchange for a hearing seemed too easy. But then again, Tythian and Chase knew her personally; they'd worked with her while in Fier's Council. Their reasoning for being here was calculated which meant she held more incentive to betray the Council than any other Council leader.

Vampires were guided by the desire for power in their own delicious way, but I'd never considered the possibility of one of their own betraying them. That's why they hunted the covens because they showed indifference to their rule. But apparently, after all these years, even the members of the Council might lust for change.

Tracey led us into a quaint room that was lavished in silks and couches. In the center of the room was an iced table with a gold-plated tray, stacked with brilliant crystal glasses and a bottle of some foreign molten beverage. She took the largest and singular red velvet couch, sinking into it with little regard to the enemies at her back. Though I doubted she'd let her guard down, it was all in the feigned sense of control. We were in her territory.

Iris, her champion as she so liked to sport him, walked over to the edge of the room where a pit had been chiseled out of the icy ground. It had been specifically crafted as a fire pit. On the edges of its metal base was a bottle of oil. He grabbed it and drenched the already waiting kindle. He bent down over it and rubbed his two index fingers together, sparks erupted between them, and an electrical current much like a mini bolt of lightning erupted. He collected small pieces of wood on the side, starting the fire. It seemed lavish considering they didn't require fire for warmth.

"We import dry wood from another Council, you can imagine the difficulty we harbor in ensuring it remains dry," Tracey said, watching me. "We don't necessarily need fires, but as you can tell from how stiff your hair and clothing is, it takes things a little while to thaw out around here. Plus, I find the flames mesmerizing."

But it wasn't the flames she stared at, it was Iris who continued fostering the fire's growth.

"It's been common knowledge for a while about your lack and loss of imports. It must make it rather difficult to sustain with very few resources yourself," Tythian said speculatively. It earned him a scornful look from Tracey. Somehow, everyone seemed to have eyes and ears everywhere, or perhaps this was information easily obtained when they were ranked in Fier's Council.

I took the seat closest to the fireplace. I caught Iris's stare, sizing him up once again. That gift he harbored was rather deadly, and I wondered how I would've faired if gifts were available to use in the minute trial.

Chase sat across from me with Patricia who flopped into the seat beside him, latching on to his arm pretentiously. She rested her hand on his knee, gawking at him as if she'd never seen a finer man. In her defense, I bet she hadn't. It surprised even me how quickly I was able to compact my jealousy and rage. This was our part to play, so I thrived in the discipline that I often lost to. I could prove to both Tythian and Chase that I was in control. And besides, I knew where Chase's heart lay and whose bed he would only ever venture into. No matter how much she tried to coax him, she didn't hold a hair to what I meant to him. That righteous thought made me smug.

Tythian remained standing as he nonchalantly surveyed the room. Numerous bookshelves encompassed the walls. He looked impressed as he scanned over the titles. Without a word, Iris collected one of the glasses and poured the malt liquid. He offered it to Tracey who accepted it poised. Her blue silk split slithering further down as she shuffled to reach for the glass.

"Would anyone like some whiskey?" She asked host-like. The only one who threw their hand up was Chase. She sported an insincere smile.

Patricia jumped up, barging Iris out of the way. "I can pour his drink," she snarled as she fumbled for the glass and bottle. I'd doubted her beautifully manicured fingers had poured a drink in years. Tracey rolled her eyes at the transparency of her sister's actions.

"Patty, though he might be charming and to your taste, please do remember that he's a sworn enemy," Tracey chastised, taking a polite sip of the freshly poured beverage.

Patricia clicked her tongue. "It's Chase. C'mon, we've known them for long enough. And besides, I've always been far fonder of them than Fier himself. He's such a prick." She rolled her eyes.

"For once, we will agree on something," Chase said, bemused as he accepted the glass and took an indulgent sip.

Tracey turned her gaze to me. "Ah yes, I heard of your desperate measures to retrieve these two from Fier's Council once he'd captured them for treason. From the intel I'd gathered, you two were claimed, familiars." She looked industriously between us. Patricia's grip tightened around Chase's arm. She looked past her nose at me with a gleaming challenge in her gaze. I had to twist my spiteful vampire into not laughing in her face. As if she truly had a chance to come between our bond.

Chase chuckled to himself as I grimaced in disgust. "Over my dead body," I gritted out with as much acid in my tone as possible. I channeled my hatred for all those who'd done me wrong and were on my to kill list. Seething hate came all too naturally, and I cultivated to play my part now.

"Let's just say prim and proper over here's a little pissed because I coaxed and dropped her," Chase said nonchalantly.

"I wouldn't say your efforts were coaxing in the slightest, and they were certainly in vain. You think too highly of yourself," I spat.

"Oh, but how you *wish* you could experience what it's like to be within my sheets," he purred.

"If only to hold a knife pointedly to your heart," I cooed with a slow, predatory smile.

"Enough, you two!" Tythian barked back, clearly frustrated as he rubbed his temples. "Let me put it simply. Familiars they are not, though I wish they'd just fuck and get it over with. I'm sick of playing babysitter to make sure they play nice." He looked at the ceiling in exasperation. It was a little farfetched even for Tythian.

Tracey and Iris watched us carefully. Patricia then spoke up, pressing her peaked breasts against Chase's arm. "I've seen the women and men Chase has courted, and I highly doubt you would be up to his standard. A pity fuck perhaps, but I doubt he'd like to dip his dick into something so tainted and vulgar."

"Pattyyy …" Tracey growled. My smile was slow and sensual. Every part of my imagination flying through the ways I could torture her. She seemed to dip into Chase further, and I could tell she saw all the delightful ways I'd string her up. My silence seemed to only unsettle her further. Perhaps I would've retaliated to the childish remarks any other day, simply because she was a vampire and I so enjoyed killing their kind. But I reined in my personal desire for satisfaction, though I would certainly not forget her comment any time soon. "So then tell me, Tythian, how did you two end up working together and finding a rare creature that could oppose Oppollo? Well, so says the rumors."

I wondered what rumors she'd heard and how accurate they might've been. Maybe my once-off with Oppollo was considered a fluke or it held some kind of intrigue and resembled power, just as it had to Cesar and his aligned covens.

"I'm intrigued to hear about such rumors," Chase said splendidly. Tracey's smile stretched over her fangs, and I had the impression she wasn't at all fond of Chase in the same way her sister was.

"You're in my home, Chase Bourne, and I am asking the questions. As beautiful as you may be, you've come to my Council and put me and my people under threat just by association. *Don't* waste the little time I've afforded you by getting cocky."

Tythian adjusted his dress shirt which was still stiff and frozen in parts. He rounded the chair across from Tracey with feline grace and took a seat. Iris contently watched over the conversation, a constant shadow behind Tracey. His oversized hatchet was equipped back in its sheath. His forest green eyes inspected me in the same way that I did him, with curiosity and challenge. There was something about him that I couldn't quite put my finger on.

Tythian spoke, cutting off any smart-ass remark Chase was about to spiel. He lazily lounged on the couch, and Patricia cozied further into him, all but dry-humping his leg. I looked back to Tythian more interested in what he had to say than putting up with the show on display across from me.

I'm sorry, Chase chimed down the line.

Don't be. Just make sure you scrub yourself clean when we return home, I chided back. *Home.* If that's what we could truly consider the institute as.

"I come from a coven, of which you're probably already aware. I belong to Cesar's coven who is a descendant of Oppollo himself. In short, let's just say it didn't end well between them. I was appointed to infiltrate Fier's Council. There I met Chase. Though I hadn't made my intentions known until …"

"I heard of your familiar's death," Tracey said with little sincerity. "My condolences." Her empty words were the most I assumed one could offer when she didn't trust or have any reason to believe us. It was also her way of telling Tythian she was well informed with the finer details even those which affected him most personally. "What I'm most curious about is why a former Token Huntress decided to betray her own, and suddenly Mr. Bourne here claimed his coven when he had for so many hundreds of years outrun his duty. The only reason I could conclude was because of a matching. For love—a familiar."

Tracey still wasn't convinced, and explaining our personal motives was crucial if we were to gain her trust. We had to separate Chase and me as best as we could, not only for the favor her sister would have toward our request but also branding ourselves as familiars would backfire as an easy target. We had to remove the leverage they could hold over our heads. If Tracey were to deny us, then there was no doubt she'd not only turn on us but also turn to Oppollo and inform him of our intrusion. He would then know that I wasn't truly dead and the time we thought we'd bought would be null and void. We had to convince her or else we'd have to turn to drastic measures and silence them, and I wasn't so certain about how powerful our manpower was. She might've been the weakest of the Councils, but Tracey was the twelfth member for a reason.

Tythian continued smoothly as if her insincerity about Whitney didn't bother him in the slightest, but I knew what lingered beneath was still a fresh wound, one of which might never heal. Even now, *I* was seeing Whitney's lingering ghost. Something I wasn't willing to admit to anyone in case they committed me as insane.

"A familiar perhaps, but not between these two. With complete transparency, Esmore's mother, a huntress, is the familiar of Cesar. Unbeknownst, because of her gift, she was able to conceive, and the birth of a daughter, half-vampire and half-huntress came into being." I held in my growl not comfortable with the knowledge he was providing. He might've not alienated Chase and my relationship as a targeted weakness, but he'd just thrown an unknown bit of information to Tracey. My mother had much been in the shadows with very little to do with Cesar's reign, which jeopardized her.

"And if I'm being honest," Chase said, placing his half-empty glass on the iced table. "After Fier failed to protect my mother and continued ruling as he does, which you are all too familiar with, I couldn't stand by the ridiculous rules of the Council any longer. And that's when Tythian and Cesar extended a temporary treaty if I was able to claim my coven and numbers, and brought value to their play."

A small presence at the entrance interrupted us. Tracey whipped her head in the direction of the handsome vampire who guided a human woman into the room. Tracey hissed at his intrusion, and he flinched, staring at the floor from intimidation. "Leave the human and go," She growled. The frail woman looked to be in her thirties. She looked up at me under her thick eyelashes with heavy bags under her eyes. She shuffled forward somewhat reluctantly.

She didn't act in the same manner that the humans from Fier's Council did where I was informed it was a mutual agreement and the humans came willingly. She was hesitant to come forward to Tracey who flagged her over.

"She has a gray hair," Patricia commented and looked away in disgust. "Such ugliness."

"Patty, dear, do you feel the need to comment on everything. This is something that can easily be fixed, though they know my particular taste for the younger blood. I don't understand why they would've thought this one appropriate," she said to Iris as if he would be forced to deal with the situation afterward. "Come here, woman."

The human looked back toward the door where her vampire escort abandoned her. Slowly, she took one step in front of the other toward Tracey who held out her hand. The woman's fists were clenched, showing white knuckles. Unlike the vampires here who wore very little, she wore thick fur-like fabric. But it did nothing to keep the chill away from her skin. She was pale and fatigued, as I would expect any human who was constantly fed from.

"Come closer," Tracey drawled. The woman did, closing her dark brown eyes out of fear. Tracey reached out to touch her cheek. The moment she did, color and life seemed to thread into her skin. The once pale skin plumped into a rosy complexion. Her dry and crisped long tangled hair lavished thickly, the few strands of grey slowly drawing to a complete jet black like the rest of her head. Her breathing became easier, and all but the bags under her eyes looked renewed. *Beautiful,* I thought, disgusted. Tracey had a gift to create beautiful things to please her aesthetically. But as I honed my hearing onto the human whose rapid heartbeat continued, I realized it still rattled with a sickly beat.

Tracey was only changing her appearance. "Here," she said, pushing the woman toward Patricia.

Patricia pounced on the woman and dragged her into her lap. The woman whimpered as Patricia wiped the hair from her forehead. "It's okay," she cooed. "I'm not going to kill you. I'm sure we've played this game before. You know how this works." She looked at Chase expectantly. "Do you want some?"

"I'll stick with my whiskey for the time being," he said with a devilish smile as he collected the glass once again. "But bon appetit." She smiled with delight and plunged into the neck of the woman who hardly made a noise. I twisted my gaze back to Tracey, forcing my vampire down with absolute control. The smell and intoxication of the human flared my nostrils and senses. And I had no desire to fight with Patricia over a human when I couldn't even claim the right to my familiar. Since Dillian and Tori had turned, I'd oddly found an ounce of control I'd never known before around humans. I thrived in the thought of starving my monster from within, forcing it to be uncomfortable and desperate. The self-punishment brought me self-satisfaction in what I thought I most deserved for failing them.

"And so, you've come to me with this trinket of a thing," Tracey said, waving her hand at me. "And ask what of me exactly? Patty, show some restraint in front of the guests." She clicked her tongue at her spoilt younger sister. We absolutely had a brat in the room. Patricia threw her head back, not a single drop wasted, but the woman was near faint. Iris collected her as Patricia threw her away disgusted and wiped her lips euphorically. She watched me as she did so sensually as if trying to make some kind of pass.

"It goes without saying, Tracey," Tythian spoke up. "I think you very well know why we're here. You've made your intentions very clear in your attempt to leave this forsaken region for centuries. Even so desperately going behind Cesar's back with a group of scouts in the hope of finding another place, which from what *we've* heard, was wiped out, no doubt from dissatisfaction for going against Council rules. We want to join hands with you and overthrow the Council. More specifically, Oppollo."

Tracey released a wicked laugh. "You expect me to believe that a handful of covens can overthrow the Council and Oppollo? You and I both know he comes from a different time completely. There is no way. How foolish I would be to agree. A dangerous game you were playing, and now you're on my doorstep, for what? Negotiations? Please, between a coven and Council? I should have killed you the moment you stepped on my doorstep."

"But you haven't," Chase pointed out charismatically. "Because you've run out of options. And you're curious about her." His gaze drifted to me as did everyone else's in the room.

Tracey's humor subsided, and Tythian spoke up. "Even if Oppollo is removed, it's highly possible someone else will outrank and try to lead the collective. Fier is certainly a member to be taken seriously, and I have no doubt that he has his own intentions of swooping in on Oppollo's demise. Everyone knows at the next Council meeting, Oppollo is going to push for utter syncretizing under his rule. Once that happens, and he spreads his own members amongst the separate Councils you won't have such freedom. Your chance of ever getting out of here will be vanquished. And from the looks of your Council, your fatigued humans, and resources, you're running out of time. You can't afford to sit back."

Her gaze bore into Tythian with hatred. But she didn't deny her struggles that were all too transparent. Patricia looked between Tythian and Tracey seemingly an innocent bystander, and placed her hand on Chase's knee as if searching for comfort or silently pushing her favor.

"We want to be at the next Council meeting," Tythian continued.

Tracey barked another maddening laugh. "Are you utterly mad? You will condemn us all. Even speaking to you now endangers everything I've built and more. I barely kept my reign after my last mishap," she whispered harshly as if someone might overhear. A fragile and desperate woman she was. "And you want me to lay it all on the line, simply because you ask it of me. Because you show me a pretty little girl, who only knows how to run and flee. What gift does she even have that is so great, so mighty that she can vanquish Oppollo?" Her words came out in hushed whispers.

Iris spoke up. "How do Cesar and her mother feel about letting a child enter their battle and creating a war far greater than we've already known. Though I doubt there would be any maternal attachment from the mother's side, Cesar would surely prize her. A naturally born vampire has never been heard of."

"You know nothing of my mother," I said with a growl in the back of my throat.

"I know too well the customs of the Hunter Guilds, little one, and that doesn't deter from your presentation that brings us a greater problem. You'll not only draw the attention of opposing Council members but also hunters. We live peacefully out here. Hunters haven't reached so far out for over fifty years. With your involvement, you're suggesting my lady risk it all, on what, a child?"

Tracey nodded as he spoke. There was a desperate spark in her eyes as she agreed with his every word. In what way could he possibly be accustomed with the hunters' ways? And it riled me to be condescended to as 'a child'—a child who almost kicked his ass.

"Let us remind you that this isn't hinging on simply one mutant," Tythian spoke up. I snapped my gaze on him with a snarl that grumbled from my core as he adopted their word, 'mutant.' "With or without her, we've been planning this for some time. It's just convenient that her gift derives similarly to that of which Chase harbors. The difference being she can control it. And that was what Oppollo found most challenging. That, and also she's inexplicably immortal."

"We're all immortal," Patricia spoke up. Iris led the human woman out toward the exit. She'd gained a faint consciousness and scurried out of Iris's grip, who seemed to handle her too gently.

"Well, not quite," Chase said, putting his hand over hers. "We all know we have our weakness. Any one of us can be killed—even Oppollo."

"Prove it," Tracey commanded. I looked at Tythian. Great, how was I supposed to truthfully objectify myself as an immortal when I was certain if I was beheaded there was no coming back from that—even for me. Tythian offered me no way of suggestion as I should've expected from him.

I stood up with a wave of gusto. We had to convince them that they needed us more than we needed them. I curled my hand around the handle of the blade gartered to my thigh. Iris unsheathed his hatchet in warning.

"Calm down." I deliberately waved him off. It had only been once that someone or something aimed for my heart. And that was the cold and dire day Oppollo reached into my chest and tried to pull it out. That didn't mean this was going to hurt any less, and even then I still resided doubt and hesitation. What if this time stabbing into my chest did end me? I hid the feelings and thought away from Chase as I considered it. I'd oddly found an inner peace at the thought but could only mock myself for it. As if it'd be that easy to put myself out of my own misery.

I flipped the handle around and positioned the tip toward my chest, ready to exemplify my, oh so immortal ways. Even I wasn't fond of the thought of self-mutilation, especially just to be made an example of.

"Wait!" Tracey exclaimed. I looked at her expectantly. "How do I know you aren't tricking me?"

"By shoving a blade through my heart?" I asked sarcastically.

"Then have your own soldier do it," Tythian suggested, shrugging his shoulder. He all too easily wanted to watch me suffer by someone else's hand. He always tried to mute the little control I possessed. My vampire's temperament snapped.

"Why don't you try, Tythian?" I said, flipping the handle over my fingers and lunging for him. Chase caught me in time, his arms wrapped around my waist to hold me back as I kicked forth. Tythian hadn't so much as flinched, his distaste for me dancing in his eyes as I struggled against Chase's firm hold. He couldn't care less what form of mutilation was to occur to me or who did it, in fact, I imagined he was infuriated he couldn't do it himself.

"So much for a secure alliance," Patricia scoffed. My gaze snapped on her. Iris was in front of the two women, his arm outstretched behind him to pull the blade from his back if I were to turn on them as well. I could feel Chase washing waves of serenity over me and fought against it as I tried to fight against the way it made me feel. I wanted to relish in this fury.

"Get off me," I snapped, shoving him back and feeling the wind come out of me as I did. I hated every moment we played this part. I hated myself more for losing control when I'd told Tythian I wouldn't. I should've known he'd purposefully push me to prove that he was right and superior in his way of control. Did his hatred for me overshadow his desire for these negotiations to go well?

Chase whistled and raised his hands with a twisted grin. But I could feel him scanning my mind and ensuring I was okay. I pushed down on my irritated and savage self that was too quickly attracted to coming forth. But it made me feel powerful and in control. Entirely separate from the desperation I'd been feeling days before—alienated by my loss and grief. I pushed those mournful oppressive feelings away.

"Hey, Bruiser," I said to Iris, offering him the blade in my hand. "You want a stab?" Chase flinched beside me. It was a gamble like it had always been. And at this point, I simply didn't care what happened to me anymore. It was better to feel this feisty temper with no regard to consequences than what was actually breaking me inside.

"No," Tracey purred from behind. "I want him to do it." And she pointed directly at Chase.

CHAPTER 3

"Me?" Chase asked, baffled. "You want me to stab Cesar's daughter in the chest? You're utterly mad." He whistled. He brushed his fingers through his stiff, shoulder-length black hair as if pushing away the request just as easily. I could feel the waves of panic roll from him at the thought of the blade piercing into my chest, no matter who the handler was.

I cooed back to him, wishing direly that I could reach out to him and let him know it was okay. Well, it wasn't, but it had to be. Tracey had chosen Chase for only one reason, and that was to prove our separation.

"Please," I jokingly scoffed. "As if you haven't wanted to do it since the day we met." *It's okay, Chase. I'd rather you do it than anyone else.*

Our conversation internally was much different from the way we expressed ourselves in front of the others all in the art of acting.

You can't ask this of me, he desperately pleaded. He looked at me longingly with a challenge in his eye. As if the words I'd spoken out loud were some kind of trickery. Like he was debating whether there would be consequences if his superficial desire were to be met. But he knew as well as I that we couldn't hesitate around one another.

I refuse, he shot back. *This plan is—*

It has a purpose. We're here for a reason. You told me that, I fired back. *I will not die.* I could feel his reluctance and the stress it was anguishing over his mind. And that only ruptured the beginning of panic through me. He'd only just come out of his saber-like state. It'd been the second time he'd tumbled into the drop, unable to handle the amounted trauma that continued to build. I sent him a graphic image, reversing our roles. I hated threading through this kind of graphic imagination down the line. But I permitted him that if I knew there was a guarantee he wouldn't die … if I could cut off that unrelenting emotion that attached us together, I would do it. I could slip the knife within his breastplates and imagine it was someone else if he asked it of me, and if I were forced to do it. And oddly enough, I felt more comforted if it were him doing it over the others.

I hid my true feelings because the savagery of it would break him. I almost sought out the possibility of this not being fail-proof. Maybe just like that, this world would be behind me. The visual shot at him hard and fast. The graphic intent of me piercing the same blade into his chest with little acknowledgment. I felt immobilized by the intent behind being a Token Huntress in the way in which I was raised. Don't ask questions. Just do. Even he could do that.

We had vowed never to hurt one another. But, we also respected one another as warriors. His hesitation mirrored a lack of trust, not in the act of doing something heinous, but because he wasn't entirely sure if I was speaking the truth. And the gamble was my life.

"You hesitate," Tracey purred over Iris's shoulder.

"Let me do it," Patricia sniped with excitement as she tried to intertwine her fingers with Chase. I could feel Tythian's cool gaze on us, expectantly warranting us not to screw this up.

Chase pulled his fingers from Patricia's grasp. "You would too if you saw how crazy protective Cesar was over his princess daughter," Chase snipped back and took two stalking steps before me. "This might hurt," he said, and I could see the change in his demeanor. There was a detachment of emotion, and I felt the familiarity of being devoid of feeling. Once he'd made the switch it became easier for me to follow suit. The link between us threading through the divide of our love and segregating into focusing on the task at hand.

With quick ease, his hand wrapped around the handle of the blade, angled it, and his palm slammed on its top puncturing it down. He didn't see me, only the target. The blade went in sharp, piercing an unruly breath from me. I choked over the blade, and from reflex my vampire erupted forward, and I slashed my nails across Chase's face in defense. He barely flinched as I stumbled back and sagged into the chair. Pain erupted throughout my entire body, reminding me of the possibility of death. That a knife implanted in my chest should be a quick and palpable ending. As I looked down at the handle sticking out of my chest, I wondered if I would rot like other vampires or if by mercy, my body would decay naturally in honor of being born a huntress.

I took a shallow breath, my breasts rising as my body sparked from its shocked and stupor state. My vampire prowled along the surface in fighting spirit to survive. Delicately and uncomfortably, I wrapped my fingers around the handle of the blade and, inch by inch, pulled it out.

Every second felt like I was frozen in time, the reality that this could've gone wrong. The truth that I should be dead. My blade clattered to the floor with the unholy realization that I truly was a monster. This wasn't just a trick anymore, a one-off fluke that kept me alive once. This was what my parents had birthed, and my mother fiddled with by removing my heart. I was hideous.

The gaping hole in my chest very tiredly weaved together, so slow was my healing abilities, still on the offense from my fight with Oppollo and then his assassins.

I craned my head to the side in an obscure way to look at the others. My purple vision pinned on them one by one as they watched me disturbed. All of their jaws were firm as they studied me, the undead shaken and unsettled by something completely foreign to them.

"What the actual fuck?" Patricia said, receiving a quick and effective look from her sister. My gaze landed on Chase. His eyes scurried over me as he realized what he'd done. This was also the first time he'd seen it himself, this curse of mine that my mother had set upon me, replacing the true evil of my gift. My heart was hidden and concealed, truly suffocating the taint of my power until one day ... if ever she'd put it back in. *You could destroy entire species,* I recalled her saying.

His stormy gray eyes shadowed with the same emotional clamp, and I felt him concave on himself like a bricked wall, separating me from the target he'd honed in on. It allowed me to breathe in my own right. This was best for both of us while on this mission. Our emotional switch impaired before it started, having a negative consequence on Chase especially.

"And her gift?" Tracey stumbled for words. I wondered what rumors had spread. Maybe the truth of my birth-given gift had been revealed publicly, it certainly had been amongst the Hunter Guilds thanks to Campture. But in the world of vampires, none of them had seen it, no one besides my mother. And so, my fight with Oppollo had been limited down to a few factors, one of which being my heart that knew no death. And large black wings that sprouted from my back that I'd used to ensnare him in our fight.

"Do you have a spare shirt?" I sassily requested with an unnerving smile. In the way that Patricia took a step back, I knew my sinister ambiance affected them in the way I'd hope. I wasn't just a rumor nor was I a plaything. I wanted them to fear me in every way that my prey as a huntress had found out.

I called forth the Descendant. Bone and large muscle mass rapidly grew beneath my skin and pierced through my shoulder blades. The surging hot pain was like a desirable elixir to me now. Black wings pushed the sofa back, slamming it against the bookshelves as I stood as if it were offended by its very audacity to stifle their introduction.

Iris pushed back Tracey protectively from my sudden movement. My black wings flexed in appreciation of being free and admired. I ruffled them slightly, washing my gaze over them as well. When I'd first brought forth the Descendant, my wings had been white. In only a matter of time they'd now hastened to obsidian black. I had no doubt that was an indication of the losing battle I'd been struggling with from within. And it *was* a battle already lost. I scarcely hung on to the old principles and former life as my huntress in the hope that one day it would guide me back to some kind of redemption. But even I contemplated I was too far gone.

"Is this not the same power as the Descendant?" Tracey asked in admiration as she pushed Iris to the side to take a better look. She was skeptical of their appearance, but the way she watched on as Chase pierced my chest unflinchingly, it was apparent our unraveling to convince them of our indifference toward one another had already begun to take hold. After all, who would truly be willing to murder their own familiar? I thought of Lincon. Only a madman, that was who. And Chase and I had not yet spiraled into complete insanity. If anything, that only made us more dangerous.

"I've never watched the Descendant at work. Though I imagine if a certain vampire were actually able to control his gift, then I'd like to challenge his might against my own," I spited Chase in the humor that we were acting out. His gift and lack of control of it was general knowledge. And neither of us had time to question how offensive our words might be against one another. We had to play our savage part, and once he'd switched off that side of him that cared, it made it easier for the both of us.

He curled a vicious smile that piqued my interest as if I was looking at his predator-like gaze for the first time. And how it turned me on. "I wouldn't need it, *sweetheart.* I've told you before. I'll take you on any day. I don't need an impressive wingspan to help me win a fight." He batted his eyelids with bemused resolve.

"If only you didn't have to take such a cheap route to put a blade to my chest and had the actual balls to fight me," I said with a provocative smile.

"Enough," Tythian growled. "Pull your heads in. The both of you."

Tracey watched her sister with interest who had wrapped her arm around Chase with claiming possession. She hissed at me, and the smile I flashed her with baring teeth provoked her further. I reeled myself from extending a challenge to the little brat. Coming into her home and offering a throw down just to appease my own selfish satisfaction would be frowned upon. Not that I seemed to care much at this point. But my huntress self reminded me of order and control. A miserable stake that grounded me. I began to count as my father had once taught me. *One. Two. Three.*

Iris turned his head toward Tracey, never letting his gaze drop away from the immediate threat in the room. Me. "I've heard of few gifts from hunters over the years which included body morphing and 'adjustments,' some of which included wings."

My eyebrows shot up in surprise that he made it his personal duty to keep an eye on gifts amongst hunters. It was disconcerting to think how much he might've known in the same way we had tried to gather information about our nearby Council. Tracey hinged on his every word. I wasn't sure what I was to do next to prove some ultimate godly power they were expecting from me.

"Besides pretty wings, how exactly did you better Oppollo?" Tracey asked. I delighted in the question, knowing that my next words had to be careful. It wasn't her trust I needed, there would never be such a thing. But what I did have to do was shine value on myself. For her to feel as if she could only look at our offer seriously, I had to be a Token.

I looked at her in that eerie way that was devoid of anything hunter or human-like. It was the monster below that thrived in darkness I would soon be punished for sinking into. "If I were to do what I did to him in this room …" My voice was lower, scarcely my own. I could feel the intensity with which Tythian and Chase watched me. They were concerned as to where this was leading and what had possessed me. I crooked my head to the side slightly, a part of my hair failing from my braid as I did so. I watched her hauntingly and then Iris, the larger threat at hand. "I fear not much would remain."

It was a truth and a lie, all in one, unnerved by the art of bluff and acting. She would make me perform for her because I would've requested the same. But with her life, or more importantly her brat of a sister in the room, I knew she wouldn't risk it. Not now, and it would buy us more time to be in her graces. To be considered. Iris watched on skeptically as if ready to call out my bluff. But much like Tracey had concerns for her sister, he wouldn't provoke a predator in the room with his lady announced as the sacrifice.

I snapped my wings shut, retracting them as quickly as they sprouted to life. Patricia flinched and clung to Chase tightly, her nails digging into the arm of his leather jacket.

"It's not just what she brings to the table, Tracey," Tythian said, drawing the attention of the room to him once again. "It's what we as a whole can offer. If your efforts were to align with ours, your Council may survive another couple of hundred years. I dare say if you don't, you'll perish."

Tracey's top lip peeled back as an unholy sneer crept from her. Her fangs were impressive in size. Offended. Objectified. Imprudent. But there was one thing that wavered above all else—survival.

"Trace," Patricia tried to pull her sister out of her tornado-washing thoughts. Tracey was reluctant to remove her gaze from Tythian as she contemplated his demise. "Tracey," she snapped again and stomped her foot. This time she did draw her attention. Patricia flinched under the harsh rebuff. She softened it, but allowed no less hatred to fall upon Chase who her sister was so infatuated with. "Think on it," is all Patricia said.

Tracey suddenly found the silk of her attire far more interesting. She smoothed it over as she looked at the damage the couch had caused to her stack of shelves. Some books had fallen and sprawled over the icy floor, barely missing the fire that crackled.

If she were to be found out, she'd be put up for treason. But by the sounds of it, she had no other choice. From this she could save her own tail, but Chase and Tythian were confident in their verdict. If nothing changed now, she'd be dooming them all. And so, I watched on with heightened interest if Chase and Cesar's gamble would win. If a crack in the Council would help us fluidly influence a side game. The times were changing, and everyone had to make a choice. To stick with what they knew, the structure and hierarchy of their already appointed fate, or fight for a new future, in the hope for freedom unbeknownst to their current binding.

"I'd like for you to join me for dinner," Tracey purred as she continued to roll her smooth unaged hands over her silks. "Feel free to make yourself at home until then as my guests," she said with a courteous smile. "But ensure you don't speak about any of this to my people. Though we speak with hushed tones, I am the one to make the decision for them. Their loyalty is absolute, and this is not yet me giving you a favorable answer. But perhaps when you look around, you'll see what the magistrate of the Council has done to my throne."

CHAPTER 4

I N A WAY of speaking, she'd afforded us the freedom to roam the halls of her Council, however all of us would be closely watched and followed. Reluctantly, we'd become divided. Tracey had summoned Tythian to speak with privately. Patricia had dragged Chase away by the arm evidently with all kinds of flirtatious concoctions. And without Tracey even asking him, Iris was portraying a personal guide in retrospect of being another blade at my back.

Separation wasn't ideal, but we kept tabs on one another. I hovered my mind over theirs sporadically, ensuring nothing went awry. The moment it did, more specifically around Chase, I'd drive through iced walls to reach him if I had to, even if it meant taking down half a Council army in my wake. Without that happening though, he was serving punishment enough keeping his ruse up with Patricia. The thought left a vile taste in my mouth.

The person I didn't trust the most was Tythian. Though he represented Cesar, I was always wary of what he might say or organize of his own accord which I knew wouldn't benefit me. But this was ordered by Cesar himself, he knew where we were and who we were with. As much as he despised me, his return and success were measured by whether Chase and I came back with him. It was a great power to uphold knowing I held it over his head. And oh how he seethed it.

"We don't ordinarily receive guests," Iris spoke for the first time since idly walking me through narrow, icy halls. It was grand in size and scale, much like how I often got lost in Fier's Council. But it almost felt empty of inhabitants in comparison to its grand scale glory. I wondered if the Council members' numbers had always felt so small or if over the three hundred years since the Vampire Council dominated, they'd struggled here since placement, slowly dwindling down over time. Or who knew, maybe they'd been here even before then. This Council seemed more like a punishment than a reward to claim a place on the Council table. One of twelve and Tracey had drawn the unfortunate luck of being placed here.

"I can't imagine why," I rhetorically said. From my peripheral, I could see a lazy smile spread on his face. My eyebrows furrowed in confusion by the six-foot-eight vampire who seemed to find amusement in his situation.

"I was wondering how you might've been promoted to Token within your Guild at such a young age, and especially with an attitude like that," he chimed back. I stopped short of my next step and looked at him with an acute awareness. The way he spoke to me was as if he knew me and the expectations that I shouldered in my former Token position. And then it dawned on me—like a spark of lightning.

"You used to be a hunter," I said deliberately slow. I traced the movement of his expression for any tell of his words or story. That maybe he was lying, and I was being bated. When I hovered my mind over his carefully, in case he had any mental gifts, I found no ill intent.

His eyebrows raised with consideration as that lop-sided smile accumulated again. "A very long time ago," he purred. He raised his hand in the direction of a small spiral iced staircase. Questions raced through my mind. I'd never met any hunters turned vampires, besides Dillian and Tori who'd only recently been changed.

I considered him again, looking into those forest green eyes. They once would've been fluorescent, branded as all hunters. When I refused to walk up the stairs with him at my back, he let another smile slip, entirely different from the mask he wore in front of Tracey. He was somewhat ... charming in an elusive way. He barged past me, not at all concerned by my closeness and how quickly I could reach for my knife as he brushed against me to take the lead. After he'd walked up a few steps, he looked back down on me with a challenge, "Well, are you coming?"

I looked back down the dark frozen hallway of which we'd just strolled, no one else followed. The stairs had been worn down after years of use.

When we reached the top, I was mesmerized by the beauty and heart of Tracey's Council. Unlike the dire and darkly lit halls we'd been dragged through, this area thrummed with life. There were numerous layers and balconies to oversee all the different floorings. Each one continued to drill further down, the depths unable to interfere with all the natural light that came in from the shining glazed rooftop. It was a thin layer of ice above that allowed the blasting light to seep through, despite the howling snow above it. Flame sticks were perched around adding to its ambiance.

Vampires and humans alike chatted and went about their daily business as normal. On the level that we'd exited, a few vampires lounged on velvet-lined couches. Small tables had been chiseled out of ice where they played some form of board game I was unfamiliar with. Or any kind of game for that matter. The two men closest to us were chatting amongst themselves, the closest to me with his feet hoisted on the table as he casually threw his hand around in idle chat. Their delicate features were beautiful, fortified by high cheekbones, luscious hair, and entrancing gazes. I'd realized with absolute disgust that Tracey's infatuation with beautiful things was a very real living thing in her Council, even enforced on her members, most of which were men.

I'd only noticed a few sporadic female vampires, which were a rarity as I looked over the populace. All other females had been human. As I dipped over the railing to peer further down, I noticed on the second level, vampires trained. Again, all of those who trained were men. The area's expansion was so different from the glass shielded rooms in Fier's, where they'd torture one another to build tolerance. Each Council had its own ambiance.

On the third level, I was bewildered to find three men, very much enjoying one another's company. Their bodies fractioned over one another as they embraced with masculine grunts and groans in daylight where anyone looking down could see. They didn't care, and as I noticed the few items of choice, such as swings, gags, whips, and weapons on the level, I realized that layer was not one of punishment or training. Well, not in a way that would do them any good on a battlefield.

I looked up, realizing there was only one other level above us. It was like a labyrinth of levels, catering to those who seemed to mostly laze about. No wonder Tracey's Council had dwindled down to nothing with such a blasé attitude.

"I don't even have words," I admitted as I couldn't help but look back toward the third floor. I saw commotion further past that on the other levels but decided to draw my gaze back to Iris who watched me with bemused intent.

"It's a lot to take in at first, I imagine. Tracey's Council is very open to say the least. She is known as the lady of leisure for a reason."

"First I've heard of it," I grumbled under my breath. He chuckled, surprising me. His bravado had changed as soon as we'd been ordained as guests. This place was so foreign to anything I'd seen before. It held such laughter and open nonchalance when a war was brewing outside, and people lost their lives daily. And here, time seemed to have literally stopped. A woman of leisure? Tracey was more so deemed a lady of ignorance, and she was now paying the price.

"Firstly, let's get you some appropriate attire. Though your gift might be impressive, I imagine you shred through many shirts." He hummed and started walking ahead of me. I tried to look over my shoulder to see how badly it'd torn my sleeveless leather shirt. "Are you coming?" he encouraged.

The two vampires closest to us watched me with interest but feigned no more than idle curiosity. The way they so casually acted after Tracey's extension and announcing us as guests was unnerving. It went against all primitive instinct I'd known vampires to have. They should be on their guard. Ready to attack. Ready to kill anything that threatened their structure and home.

Iris came to a stop in front of a small, chiseled-out open arch. Inside the room I could see the various materials and clothing stacked on hanging rows. A human woman was startled by our appearance. Like the woman I'd met today, she was young and beautiful, but the bags and wrinkles of fatigue under her eyes told a story otherwise. She hung the long silk dress and collected an empty welted wooden basket. She scurried past us with her head down.

"The human women here serve, such as the one who just left. We import materials from other covens, and she hand sows and beads the fine material," Iris informed me about her peculiar behavior. "And lower-ranking vampires do so for Tracey and Patricia personally."

I held back the snarl at his suggestion. Women were seen as less here. Or that had been the value of what Tracey and Patricia built her Council upon. They liked beautiful things, and they wanted to be the only beautiful women here. It was practically a reverse harem.

"And what happens to the human men?" Men or women it didn't matter what gender, either way as humans amongst a Vampire Council it was contracted as mutual agreement and protection. Those were the rules of the Council.

Iris led me into the room. Again, I was still wary and prepared for the moment his character turned and ensured I was the one to stay closest to the door and exit. I scanned the minds of those who were chatting outside, gauging what emotion was rumbling through their thoughts and a possible shift in movement. If they began heaping toward the door, I'd know they were working on an orchestrated ambush.

"We have an agreement with the humans who choose to live on their own within our territory. Like the camp you spotted and watched over to entice us out." The depths of my stomach turned. That place, the singular camp I'd fixated on to possibly take Dillian and Julia to, in the hope they could make a new life, away from all I'd dragged them into—had already been claimed by a Vampire Council. "When the women come of age at sixteen, they're brought here. We allow them to choose a select few amongst themselves to remain and continue their populace. As for the men, we take only those who wish to come themselves willingly. You'd be surprised how many do. They're usually young men, some choose to follow the young women who'd been outcast; others to beg to be turned; and some simply hoping for an easier lifestyle, of which they do receive here. They only serve as food and well, other leisurely participations."

"So young women as sacrifices." I hissed as I picked up fine material through my fingers. "And men as revered guests. Why am I not surprised that a Council would think of something so sinister and foul?"

Iris purposefully flicked through garments, and I could sense that all-knowing smile of his flick up. "Would you believe me when I say it wasn't Tracey's choosing? Though the arrangement suits her just fine." He looked over his shoulder at me. "It was the human leader at the time who made the suggestion and offering, a man no less. And would you believe me when I say only men have ever led each of the camps since? We offer them protection from sabers and other vampires in exchange for a handful of humans every year. It was they who decided to haul the women at our feet. It would appear over time, some things would never change." He grimaced with a fiery rage in his eyes. "We receive so little every year that our vampires have no choice but to execute restraint. Or we'd all suffer from starvation in the months to follow. We could take over the humans entirely and bring them all back, but that wasn't on our sworn agreement of which the Council's take seriously."

"But anyone outside of the Council's rule is sacrilege," I rhetorically said. When he didn't reply, I considered that he harbored similar thoughts to myself. If he was once a hunter, I wondered how far his beliefs and ambitions about the Vampire Council had strayed. Much like I was fighting myself for structure and tolerance of my vampire self, I wondered how he'd converted entirely. I didn't expect him to tell me how it'd happened, but I'd gamble on asking the question. The thought of Dillian and Tori came to mind, and I was wondering if there was a stable life for someone who'd been turned against their will. I had Chase to ground me, but even then, sometimes I felt like it wasn't enough. That I was still losing to the darkness, maybe it'd be the same for them.

"How did you become a vampire? Were you dragged into this against your will?" I could feel the vein in my neck protrude as I asked him—the edge of my tone, drawing his attention. I'd slipped up but for only a second. When I thought of him being turned against his will, I thought of Dillian and Tori.

"No," he said, pulling out a light blue silk dress. "I chose this of my own accord. It was so long ago that I can't even recall what the face I'd been born with looked like." My face twisted in revolt. So, he'd let Tracey work her twisted beautification gift on him as well. He seemed only amused by my disgust. I looked away from the blue silk dress he raised to me suggestively. He put it back down and kept looking.

"Do you have any leather?" I asked. He shook his head. I was more attentive to his becoming a vampire than any of these foreign garments. It didn't bother me overly wearing a torn leather shirt, it wasn't as if the temperature affected me. The only ones it seemed to be an issue for were the very shallow vampires within this Council. "You betrayed your Guild?"

"That I did," he said as if a side thought. He was intently looking through the dresses, and I wondered how much he'd elaborate. He was far chattier than I would've pegged his profile for initially. His voice was rough and violent when he next spoke. "I was not the first, nor will I be the last." He looked at me pointedly. "I realized even in my time that we were following the rules and mechanics that bound us by the very humans with the same mindset who would willingly throw their women and children as sacrifices to save their own ass. I could no longer pity the humans, nor could I fight on their behalf for a battle that had long ago been lost. No matter what stories and lies they fed me as a child within my Guild. I was just a number, a warrior amongst their midst that they were willing to so blindly lead into every fight, without the backbone of their own merit. Once I snapped free of the mechanics, with the help of Tracey, I've never looked back, and I've never pitied the humans ever again. We had been designed as mere guinea pigs, and the only upgrade we received was being played as fools. But as children, we were told it was an honor. So brazenly I wondered how bad the other side could be, the monster so to speak."

My hand rested on the coat hanger of a silver garment. I looked over my shoulder at the giant vampire. He and I shared similar thoughts, not that I'd ever admit it. It was so foreign to accept the idea of someone else breaking free of the traditions and mechanics built into us. We had thought we were on top and that we were in control. That we found the humans and were their saviors. But the truth was, we were still stationed and doing what we were told from the very first hunter who birthed breathe in those labs during the technology era. "How old are you?"

His green gaze slid over to meet mine. I wonder, how long had he waited for his judgment day from another hunter. All that he told me was with a fiery passion. How long had it sat on his chest, to the point where even as a vampire he held no filter in telling me his story that I might use against him. Or perhaps he identified with something inside of me that wasn't entirely from this world of vampires. That only a former hunter could judge or understand. Or perhaps it was a lie concocted to trick me into trusting him. Of which I wouldn't fall for. But I could see the sincerity in his eyes and the way he walked and moved, the arrogance of his fighting stance. I knew the air about him all too well. He had been born and trained as a hunter just like me.

"One hundred and nineteen," he admitted reluctantly. I held in my surprise. Vampires' ages didn't surprise me, but the thought of him being a former hunter changed that interpretation. I still had no idea if I would age, and truthfully, I hoped my body would take its natural course.

Something that was impossible for Dillian and Tori. I pushed my revolt down.

"Do you ever regret it?" The words were out before I could refrain them, and it caught me off guard. I rarely spoke so openly with someone, especially an enemy. But the reckless part of my nature seemed to snub the idea of caring for the consequences when it so lavished in the idea of killing or being killed. Whatever lies and truths were told during were only creating a story that was never mine. But I could only reflect his answer on what Dillian and Tori might feel.

"Who knows," he said, deep in thought. His eyebrows furrowed to craft one imperfect line on his forehead that I was certain Tracey would scream to see. He pulled out a long black silk dress, and my gaze fell on its ridiculous details.

"I have no desire to wear something so elaborate. If a shirt can't be found I'll remain as is," I said to the oversized vampire who looked cramped in the iced room.

"It might not be to your liking, but if you are seriously trying to impress Tracey as a guest, I would suggest you honor her hospitality. And as you know, this may draw out for a while. Time around here seems to stop. You might even enjoy the liberation." I held my tongue before I insulted his grand ideal of 'liberation' that was them ignorantly dying out. But I was certain he was already aware of that. "And with an added bonus, I feel a dress such as this would ignite a rather childish reaction from Patricia."

My eyebrows shot up. This whole Council was ridiculous in their maintenance and expectation. I went to walk out of the room, comfortable in the clothing I wore and disturbed by the commotion made over simple attire.

"A word of advice," he said. "You'll offend Tracey greatly if you don't change what you're wearing for dinner."

"I'm not here to make friends," I bitterly said over my shoulder. I wavered my mind over Tythian and Chase checking up on them. Neither seemed disturbed. I certainly hoped I wouldn't be cooped in this Council for too long. And I certainly had no care factor toward wearing specific garments to entertain their leader. This wasn't the focus of our mission.

"But you came here to make allies," he said with a long knowing smile. His superior tone agitated me. Tythian had warned me to be accommodating and pleasing toward Tracy and her Council. But it seemed almost ridiculous to care about such a minor detail of all things we had yet to discuss and agree upon. Why did it matter what I wore? I crossed my arms over my chest and turned to him.

"And why would you offer me something to purposefully piss off your Council leader's little sister?" I asked though the sudden idea of infuriating instead of killing her appealed a certain savage charm. So luxurious was the Council's time to focus on such stupid things. I relished in the day when they'd be vanquished, and these ridiculous settings were burnt out.

"I might have to protect her with my life, but it doesn't mean I like the brat," he said with a sinister sparkle to his green eyes. I didn't trust him. But as I glanced over the dress, I realized he'd collected one of the few that wouldn't tightly bind my legs together. That I'd have free movement to kick and still harbor my weapons.

As hunters within the Guild who fought beside one another, I would've hated Iris's attitude and mischievous twinkle that reminded me far too much of the twins, Kora and Kasey's. But as for now, that conveying part of my vampire self-relished in the idea of showing Patricia up. She might've had her hand around my familiar in a pathetic attempt to claim him, but I knew what drew his eye. It was childish, reckless, and unnecessary. We were here for a mission. It was only an additive to rile Patricia up. A little green monster began surfacing as I was overtaken by the thought of playing with fire and seeing how much I might be burnt.

I pulled back from the idea, fully aware that my thoughts were jeopardizing this very mission and I was rolling into a wave of insanity as I let my inner vampire delight in the game. What was happening to me?

That broken piece of me had let something darker crack through. And when I saw glimpses of it, it reminded me of the craziness that had long ago burrowed into the likes of someone I knew. Someone like Lincon.

But how much trouble could one measly dress create?

CHAPTER 5

THE MOMENT CHASE had finally freed us both from the shackles of our emotional unity, I felt lighter. We'd both been so engrossed within our companionship and life support that I forgot there was another way. That there was a little switch that could be flicked, and his inner emotional workings could be simmered near to nothing. It wasn't that he was no longer aware of them, and he certainly didn't extinguish them. If he had, he'd turn saber. But he'd buried them and glazed over in the same way that I did, united by the idea of our task and how we acted as individual soldiers before our unity.

Chase was acting in the way most knew him—goofy and free, living a contradiction to the power that lay beneath. I'd overheard vampires discussing the two male visitors whose beauty and poise held up to their reputation. I was biased toward Chase, and Tythian I could never ordain any part of him as handsome. Especially his true monster that wasn't far from the surface no matter how much he thought he'd smoothed over it. Perhaps I despised him so much for it because like called to like, and I saw myself slowly eroding into the harsh and cold state of Tythian's existence. I was aware that gradually I was becoming an unhinged version of myself. And that terrified me as much as it fueled the thirsty beast beneath to grow.

What felt like hours of submitting to Iris's undivided attention and lack of conversation in the public eye left me irritated and fatigued. Walking around in enemy territory even when labeled as 'guests' was never comforting. It was different from the last time I'd infiltrated a Vampire Council, though it made me no fonder of the company. Vampires gawked at me, varied in their reactions. Some watched on admirably as I walked past, others curious, and some openly sneered with disgust. I'd become accustomed to this reaction.

Iris said nothing after our divulged conversation, airing about a silent existence. His broodish demeanor was in full swing once again. I wondered if it had something to do with his obligation to Tracey or whether he was perceived in a certain way within his own inherent Council. Maybe despite his long life as a vampire, he was still shunned by others for being born a hunter. He remained tentative as he led me to separate chambers on the fourth level.

I was acutely aware of Chase's presence on this floor level, and a wave of calm swept over me as we steered toward that particular room. Tythian was still on another level by himself and idly making his way through the floors. Despite Tracey no longer being with him, I imagined he was being carefully watched, and he wouldn't be silly enough to jeopardize our mission by escaping the public eye. I still found it alarming how casually they allowed us feigned freedom. But they did have us outnumbered, and it only showcased Tracey's arrogance. I wondered how other Council leaders would've received us if they too were in dire need of help.

Iris led me to one of the open carved archways that acted as an entrance. I could hear Patricia's giggles fluttering about the hallway as we approached it and entered. Her laughter didn't cease though there was venom in her gaze as she expectantly watched me enter. She was standing naked, admiring herself in the reflection. She looked over her shoulder and then at Chase with a promiscuous smile, as if she was egging me on to have some kind of reaction. Chase only briefed a glance of acknowledgment my way before divulging in a sip of whiskey. I ignored him all too aware of everyone's attention—especially Iris's.

The room was beautiful in all its ice-carved structure. Velvet lounges were scattered leisurely amongst the room and ice so pristine circulated it acting as the perfect inbuilt mirror. The numerous angles and versions of myself almost made me nauseous. I very rarely had seen my reflection and being bombarded in such a way was offensive.

Three holes had been carved from the flooring in the ice, filled with icy water. A selection of soaps, liquids, and scents scattered amongst the room. Beside each of them were numerous buckets of water. Two male vampires waited beside the door as if awaiting an order or possibly to go fetch more buckets.

Three human women were busy fluttering amongst the room. One attended Patricia who snapped her fingers in command to fill hers and Chase's glasses with another serving of whiskey. Another attended to her, now holding up numerous dresses in the hope of pleasing her taste. She scoffed at the second choice which evidently wasn't lacking in enough material for her.

"This way," the third woman said to me, unable to look me in the eye. I glanced over to Iris who shrugged his shoulder and took post beside the vampires who stood at the door. Another three vampires loitered around one of the bathing holes, slowly beginning to take up chat once again. But I could feel their focus was now intentionally guided toward me.

"I don't need to bathe," I said to the woman in an attempt to hold back my imprudent tone. It wasn't her fault, but it made me feel no less angry. Their leisurely pace and principles were starting to irritate me. Such nonsense was the customs that I had to abide by when I'd been so used to a less superficial upbringing. Near the blue vase that held dead frozen roses in the corner of the room was a small rack with the dress Iris had chosen for me earlier, hanging.

"Does she not bathe?" Patricia snorted to Chase mockingly. She swiveled the glass in her hand. "Something so filthy attending dinner with *my* sister, and you refuse to attempt to scrub that tainted skin."

Chase swallowed hard. I peeled a sickly smile. "Perhaps you would like to take another two steps closer and say that again."

"And be even closer to your putrid existence, I think not," she scoffed but was still daring to take another step.

Iris's silent footsteps had already made it across the room to mediate. His gaze fell on Patricia. "Please keep in mind she is a guest. If a fight were to break out between the two of you, your sister will not at all be pleased to hear you instigated."

"And who do you think *you* are to tell *me* what to do?" She looked down her nose at him despite the height difference. "In my opinion, anything with hunter in it, before or after death is filthy."

Iris didn't flinch under her harsh bratty tone. He towered over her, remaining where he stood. The human beside me shrunk into the shadows, and the others in the room had now silenced. They watched on with interest. No doubt so they could gossip away once they left.

"And besides, the only reason why she'd care to attack me is because I have something she wants," she said suggestively, looking over at Chase like he was a toy to her new collection. I felt Chase waving over my mind, making sure I wasn't about to implode. It was light in comparison to its usual influential touch, evidence that we were suppressing our emotional attachment. "Or maybe," she said with a snake-like gaze as she padded over to Chase, barefoot and naked, unaffected by the ice on her feet. She danced her feather-light fingers across his shoulder and stroked his jawline. "We should make love in front of you right now, just so you can imagine it being yourself next time. Wouldn't that be kind of me to do?"

Chase pulled her hand away from his face. "Don't use me in your catfight. I have to work with her father remember." She seemed embarrassed by the rejection as she stood naked in front of him, pompously like she'd never been denied.

I snaked a smile. "I still don't want to fuck you," I said to him. "But it brings me so much joy to watch you ignore this little princess here."

Mortified, she snarled at me and leaped. I almost laughed, giddy with the assault. But before I could even flinch into action, Chase had already grabbed her from behind, and Iris stood in front of me, ensuring no such thing happened. I sagged in disappointment, but to still relish in the moment allowed my smile to creep further, antagonizing her only more. My fangs had ejected with delight my vampire self coming to the forefront.

"You're nothing but filth," she spat at me. Iris took the brunt of it.

He glowered at her, "Need I remind you, she is our guest. What would your sister think if she heard of such an ineloquent attitude?"

Patricia sneered at him. I heard the faint humor of Chase's laughter down our line. It was quieter than usual, but I could sense it. Patricia's gaze snapped on the three vampires who suddenly found interest in the floor as they looked away not to match her gaze. "What are you looking at?" She screamed and threw the glass of whiskey at them. "GET OUT!" She squealed. I let out a low whistle in appreciation for the mental breakdown I was watching. Someone was evidently used to getting what she wanted.

The vampires scampered out wisely ushering the humans with them.

"You cannot tell me what to do!" she snapped at Iris, trying to pry out of Chase's grip.

"You are not this Council's leader. You would be wise to remember that," Iris said, towering over her.

"But I'm next in line, perhaps you should be more cautious about that!" she snapped.

"If you last that long." I couldn't help the snide remark leaving my lips. Chase offered me a reprimanding look. I shrugged my shoulder, equally delighted and disgusted that I lacked in the control from it leaving my mouth.

"Maybe we should get ready in another chamber," Chase suggested as he dragged her out. She was kicking and cursing, her beautiful caramel lush hair thrashing back and forth. The two vampires who stood beside the door briefed a glance at one another, and one of them cockily dared to smirk. Though as soon as he caught Iris's attention faltered and looked ahead once again.

"Follow them," Iris instructed. "And bring one of the humans in."

"I can dress myself," I said, jarring my chin up.

"But not to the standard of Tracey, and you'd be a fool to think this little incident doesn't reflect poorly on your negotiations." He began to pace toward the door's entrance to take post instead of the guards.

I crossed my arms over my chest. "Doesn't mean you didn't enjoy the entertainment."

I saw the slightest of twitches on the corner of his lips. He said nothing, but I knew it was the truth. I was starting to suspect not many within the Council enjoyed the little brat. But he'd made a good point. I just needed to stick it out until Tracey agreed to join us. And I'd hoped that would be tonight. To stay within this Council for any longer was most vexing.

I sat in a luscious silk black dress robe while the human had fussed about thawing out and washing my hair, much to my irritation with flowery scents I'd never come across. Iris had lit a small fire inside the chamber room, giving my hair time to dry out before the woman started sweeping my hair into a high ponytail. She tried various styles, none of which I was very pleased with. I'd only ever had my hair in a thick plait. The subtle changes annoyed me. It felt like I was yet again being forced to change for them—the vampires which I felt had already taken so much of my former self.

I pushed down the divulging demand from my vampire to sink my fangs into the sickly human as she focused on her task at hand. It brought me no comfort to know if I did so much as attack her, she'd hardly even attempt to defend herself. I denied my vampire quenching its thirst with that unruly control I'd found ever since Dillian and Tori had been changed.

She tinkered through a small ornamental red box. Her hands had become pale and blueish as she flexed them back and forth trying to force blood flow. She'd taken off her hand mittens just to do my hair. Though she was wrapped in thick woolly material for clothes, it didn't surprise me the humans only came out for a few hours at a time. When they went into their own sector of the Council it was inundated with warmth and fires. It was astonishing enough that they were able to survive here, or maybe Tracey's gift had something to do with that.

The woman sifted through various hairpieces and pulled out a black flowery hairpin that looked like a small comb webbed with little glittery tips. I dipped my head closer toward her so she was able to place it into the top of my hair closest to the band. Her hands were shaking from the cold as she dipped a small brush into a tiny pot of red to apply on my lips. I watched her wearily as her hand drew closer to my lips, torturously slow as she became acutely aware of my predatory intent. More goosebumps rose on her arms. Her breathing became shallow.

"I won't attack you," I promised as I felt my control wavering. I clamped down on it harder, using the image and graphic memory of the wolves rotting blood to deter my heightened interest. My stomach twisted in revolt. Even as I watched the pulse of her throat, I slowly began to count to ten as my father had once taught me.

"Is it because you're more huntress?" she whispered as she looked over at Iris. He would've heard her. Perhaps if it were anyone else, they might've reprimanded her for speaking to me directly. Evidently, gossip spread through here quickly if even their acclaimed food was speaking.

I watched the brave human curiously who dared speak with me even as she was being watched. As I now knew age seemed distorted, but I realized the secret was looking around their eyes for that sickly hollow. "How old are you?" I asked. She looked over to Iris to see if she was about to be chastised. When he looked forward, feigning ignorance, she glanced back over to me and dipped the red to my lips. The smooth cold brush prickled at my lips as she brushed it back and forth elegantly following the blossom of my lips.

"Eighteen," she said with a coarse throat. "Do you like it, being both?" she asked. My lips tightened as she finished with my lips and turned back to her small satchel of foreign items, all of which were used to beautify. I imagined it was a rare thing for them to apply here considering Tracey contorted everyone to appease only her and her sister's aesthetics.

"No one has ever asked me that," I admitted, and for what reason I didn't know why, I was opening up to this human girl. She was the same age as me. I was soon to be nineteen, and yet I felt like our worlds couldn't be more apart. I felt pity for her and the life she was living that was out of her control. And yet with all the power I held and strength to fight off my enemies, I was in no better position than her. I too was shackled by the orders and constitution laid out before me, all in the name of keeping us safe and alive. It was no better in the Guild than it was now, but at least I had naivety then. A year ago, I wasn't yet aware of how cruel this world had come to be or more specifically had always been. "I would say I don't like it very much."

Her eyebrows perked up surprised. The woman found a smaller brush and dipped it in black. "You'll have to close your eyes," she encouraged. My gaze snapped intently on her, and she shuddered into submission. I released my snake-like gaze from her, embarrassed that I'd unleashed all my caution and suspicion on a harmless girl. Of all the things that could kill me in this world, it would never be a human. I slowly closed my eyes, widening my mind and senses to keep tabs on everyone who shifted around me and delicately placed my hand beside the knife at my thigh.

"Do you wish you were back at your human camp?" I asked. I felt the delicate pinprick touch of the brush as if my voice startled her. She began to thickly stroke it over my eyelid, past my eye with a wicked flick.

I could feel her heartbeat increase. She was scared to answer the question. No doubt because it could lead to certain prosecution if she were to answer honestly or seem ungrateful for the life she'd been provided.

"This was my role to take. It doesn't matter if I liked or disliked it. We all have a place to serve, and this is mine," she said somewhat robotically.

She began to apply the second thick black wing. I realized with disdain that it was a lifetime of taught beliefs and stigma regarding her role. I couldn't help but understand the oppressive relatability. We were of two different worlds and upbringing, yet here we sat, not so different at all.

Once she'd finished both of my eyes, I opened them, fixating on her. I studied her as she placed her paintbrush down. She flexed her hands back and forth in an attempt to increase the blood flow once again. A crack in the side of her hand split open, and I watched it with predatory amusement as it slowly began to bleed. She fisted it into a ball and placed it on her lap.

"Wow. Your eyes are so beautiful," she commented. I hadn't even realized she was now looking at me or that my fangs had slipped out. The woman was filtered in brilliant purple, and my mouth began to dry as it studied her main artery and the sickly smell of her fresh blood. *Beautiful? Really?* I wanted to devour every drop in this young woman, and she dared think of me as beautiful. I turned my gaze away from her.

"I suggest you leave," I said, biting back on the remains of my control.

"But your dress—"

"I can put it on myself," I said too anguished. She needed to leave. If she didn't … then I'd be too tempted. It was too easy to fixate my self-reflective hatred on appeasing the vampire instead. It was an easy out and one I was becoming too tempted by.

She scurried about packing her things and making her leave. She'd dropped the red paintbrush at the entrance. Iris leaned over to swiftly pick it up for her. She nodded, surprised, and fled the room. I stared down at the mittens that she'd left behind, too much in a hurry to remember them. I reined in my control, the absence of her scent and smell of her small prick of blood washing over a cool wave of relief. All the while I could feel Iris's gaze on me.

"What are you looking at," I growled under my breath.

"Me, one hundred and so years ago," is all he said before standing on the other side of the door, allowing me privacy. "Now get changed."'

CHAPTER 6

T HE DRESS HAD been fiddly to put on. The sheer black material fitted like a tight corset with elegant straps that I'd nearly ripped apart trying to tie up myself, leaving much of the sides of my stomach exposed. It hardened at the top, swirling into shoulder pads that were tipped with a golden hue. It almost resembled ornamental armor. It dipped into light black transparent material that dyed into gold. The splits on the side gave me ample room to move, and every time I took a step my garter and blade were exposed. I still had my sword and Barnett crossbow, but I appreciated the dress's complexity that although foreign, made me look fierce.

My thick black boots crunched on the ice as I walked. I'd ignored Iris's encouragement to change into some sort of thin-tipped heel. Not only had I never worn them before, but they took away from the practicality of being prepared to fight. And besides, I wasn't willing to offer all of myself over to their ridiculous customs.

It had been the first time I had makeup applied, and I couldn't help but look at my reflection more than once, still surprised by the not-so-subtle difference, especially the red on my lips. Had it been a year ago, I might've considered that I liked its dangerous color, but now it reminded me only of the truth in my nature that I anguished for blood.

Iris and I hadn't spoken since the human left the bathing chambers. I was certain he'd picked up on my momentary slip of control and now silently led me to the others. I'd noticed as we walked throughout the halls that other vampires we passed mostly ignored him, though they were daring enough to gawk at me.

Iris hadn't changed attire, and I wondered if he was permitted to join us as equals or if he was only to stand watch in case an argument erupted. Or perhaps Tracey would make her final decision and demand he try to take off our heads. My stomach swirled with excited anticipation at the thought. We'd had less than a minute to challenge one another. Now seeing his gift, I was curious how I would fare against him. I wanted to become stronger and test my bounds, and if something were to happen to me during that … then I oddly found no hesitation. I wanted to claim it was because of how we were raised as hunters but knew it was something far more unsettling that stirred because of recent events. Dillian's words echoed like a blade running down my chest. *You're reckless, it's like you don't care what happens to you now.*

"Here," Iris instructed as he rounded me up the final staircase. We were heading for the highest level. One I hadn't yet been to. I could feel the others already waiting beyond. I felt Chase's mind graze past mine. The clamp he'd put on his emotions brought me much freedom and relief. It was like an antidote to the desperate struggle I'd been experiencing, and if I'd known it was manageable, I might've offended him by asking him to do it sooner.

I could feel the ice-cold tension radiate from Tythian. It oozed from his presence before I even walked into the room. Or perhaps that was because I'd become so accustomed to his sharp contentment, expecting it, waiting for it around every corner with distaste since we now worked with one another so closely.

Both of them snapped their heads up attentively when Iris led me into the room. Neither Tracey nor Patricia were yet here. I was surprised Patricia allowed Chase a moment by himself, without clawing into his arm with filthy nails and intentions. Chase twisted a smug smile as his gaze trailed from my toes and slowly dragged up, memorizing every inch of my body. He sent me a wicked image of all the things he wanted to do to me in that dress and in what position he wanted me; first starting with me pressed against the thin glass veil that looked over the other levels, my breasts brushing against its cold glass as he bunched the skirt around my hips and pounded me from behind.

My jaw clenched as my body cruelly stood to attention. My stomach fluttered with anticipation as I refrained from crossing the room to pull him in and demand he do exactly that.

"Well, look at that, the princess can look girly-ish," Chase said, covering the filthy thoughts we were sharing. His façade easily wavered the tension as I remembered my role and place here.

"You know it's in bad spirit to piss me off before dinner," I said with feigned agitation.

Chase was well suited and groomed himself. He'd tied back his hair, only a small slip of fringe rounding the right side of his face. His blue gem earing sparkled more iridescently than usual as if it had been recently polished. Instead of his usual open leather jacket that revealed his divine muscles and stomach, it was covered by a dark blue suit that was sprinkled with small sparkling rocks along the cuffs and collar. Again, I had to refrain from openly gawking and running my hands down the sophisticated material. He looked like something that had just come out of a painting, perfect in all his god-like features. And for a split second, I could imagine what he might look like with his great Descendant wings, the vision glorifying.

Tythian wore a deep red dress shirt that was finely buttoned up. It looked no different to his usual attire though it might've been slightly tighter than normal. I wondered if Tracey had helped him pick it out to please herself.

They were both seated at a long iced table with blue velvet lined chairs. The table was catered to sit eight, and I wondered if this was an informal, intimate dinner for Tracey's guests. Closest to the entrance and to my right was a small lounging area much in the same style as the first room Tracey had heard our proposition. It contained a small fireplace, numerous lounges, and a table with an array of colored liquids.

Above us was an unobscured view of the sky that much to my surprise was still bright and pillowed with snow. Time seemed elusive here. I was certain it should've been nightfall, but against my better judgment or some unnatural precedent, it wasn't turning dark anytime soon.

I walked over to the left where the edge of this level, unlike the others, abruptly stopped. From ceiling to floor, a thin layer of ice barricaded the level. I imagined for privacy reasons so others couldn't overhear the conversations being had. The ice however, was crystal clear, and I looked out able to catch glimpses of the other levels as Tracey's Council went about their daily business.

Iris took stride by my side. I could feel him watching me and then the other two men. "The dress suits you." He spoke for the first time in hours. My eyebrows furrowed in confusion at the bizarre compliment until I could feel the flick of tension transfix through Chase. My lip twitched up in a snake-like smile. I understood, he was playing Chase, crafting jealousy and trying to see if he'd react.

"It would appear you have good taste," I replied as I remained watching over the vampires who played chess below us. Iris didn't so much as give in to a smirk. He simply stood there with his hands behind his back, airing stoic pride as I watched over the Council fluttering below. Chase continued idle chat with Tythian. It strangled an odd reaction from me, realizing how long the two had worked with one another and been friends, considering how much Tythian and I now seethed one another. And I very much doubted it'd be a relationship that could ever be refurbished.

Iris shifted to the entrance like a vape in the night and waited patiently for Tracey and Patricia to ascend the stairs. He'd felt their presence before any of us, and it only showed his loyalty and acute awareness of their movement.

Tracey walked in first, imploring the small bow Iris offered her. We turned to watch them walk in. They both seemed to shimmer far more than usual, their mocha skin beautifully sparkling from the light that broke through the ceiling. Tracey wore a deep burnt orange pantsuit and jacket that hung over her shoulders. Her very perky and unmoving breasts were just as much as a feature as her confidence under the sheer white thin material she wore as a shirt.

Patricia wore a pastille violet dress that clung tightly around her waist. The opening to her dress was cut in half, freely showing her breasts as it dragged down past her belly where it clipped by three linked chains. The split then dragged down her right thigh, shimmering her glittery skin that seemed more accentuated than it had when I first met them.

Patricia's gaze hungrily slipped to Chase as she devoured him with her eyes. I reined in any small tell and irritation. Her eyes snaked over my attire which only seemed to rile her. Her fists clamped down over the numerous gold bangles and rings she wore with brilliant gems. My smirk grew larger as I thought about our scuffle only hours before in the bathing chambers. I felt a smugness as those grueling eyes transfixed on Iris accusingly as if knowing he'd selected this dress specifically.

"Patricia," Tracey said in a low warning. "These are our guests. Stop acting like a child," she reprimanded. Patricia seemed taken aback as her sister walked forward and suggested we all sit around the table. I could feel Patricia's gaze bore into my back only further feeding my smugness.

"Sit beside me, Esmore," Tracey instructed. It wasn't an invitation; it was a command. "I truly wish you didn't feel the need to wear your weapons while we have a meal together."

"There are very few places I go without them," I replied. I would never leave myself vulnerable, just as the others had continued wearing their own. And just as Iris was still at her back, phantom-like, ready to move in an instant to use his blade on us if summoned, I considered this fake politeness and idol chat a waste of time. This wasn't about building relationships, it was about solidifying a mutually beneficial alliance. But she seemed to enjoy drawing out the process, convinced her hospitality was enough to compel us toward whatever demands she might have.

Tracey tisked at me as she sat at the head of the table. I took her right side, opposing Patricia and Chase. Begrudgingly Tythian sat to my right. Three tall and unused candles were positioned down the length of the table. Chase pulled a lighter from his pocket, idly carefree as he took it upon himself to light them. Tracey seemed somewhat annoyed but allowed it.

"Bring them in," Tracey commanded. Iris placed his fingers in his mouth and let out a shrill whistle. Five humans were led up the stairs. Three of the women looked devoid of emotion whereas the other two seemed elated to have been chosen. They were all wrapped in warm material, but I couldn't help but drop my gaze to the mittens they wore, much like the ones the girl had left behind in the bathing chambers.

The women waited in a line, fidgeting and not willing to meet any of our gazes. Two male vampires ushered them into the room, one holding a silver platter covered with a pristine silver lid. He waited for instruction by my side as he stood stiffly with the hidden dish. I could smell it from here, and I wanted to barf.

Iris rounded the table, pouring glasses of some strong-smelling liquor. "I acquired something special for you," Tracey chimed with enthusiasm. "Tythian mentioned you thirst for blood but also remain to eat food. I must admit I'm very curious. Though it's a novelty to sometimes watch the humans eat, I've never seen a creature crave both." She looked at the male servant expectantly, and he revealed the silver plate, placing it in front of me. I refrained from gagging at its foul stench, despite being a fresh thick, bloodied piece of cold red meat. It was off-putting like I was being treated as some kind of beast—being rewarded in some lowly way.

"I don't think it exactly works like that," Chase commented. "That looks outright disgusting."

Tracey snapped at me in agitation. "Does this not please you?"

I looked away from the meat catching Iris's disgusted grimace. Surely this was a hoax. "I do crave both. But this is ..." The meat had already begun to freeze. And I could feel the recoiling of both my vampire and huntress self as if this was some kind of compromise for both their desires. And yet it wasn't appetizing at all.

"Very thoughtful," Tythian commented.

"Would you like to try it?" I growled back at his smug expression.

"Well then," Tracey grumbled. "I apologize for the offense. Take a human instead." She flicked her hand to the side, silently ordering the servant to remove my dish. I was irked by the trivial trial and test.

The women shuffled around the table, dropping to their knees beside our chairs in submission. Their hair had been plaited to the side for easy access to their slow pulsing necks. I stared at the blonde-haired woman who dropped to my side. She was beautiful and young, no doubt fiddled with by Tracey's magic. "Or do you not drink from humans either?" Tracey mocked my hesitation.

The thought was tempting. I was thirsty, and my body craved the delicacy for a speedy recovery. It felt like I'd only ever had enough just to take the edge off but the longer we stayed here, with the dire cold and company, the further I grew impatient to feast again. But it wouldn't be in the woods where Chase and I could hunt for animals. It wasn't in my comfort where Chase might've attempted to pull me back into restraint if I lost myself.

Although I didn't like to conform to the Council's way, I didn't want my hesitation to appear as a weakness or vulnerability either.

"I do," I said, trying to marginalize my thirst so I could ensure I was in absolute control. Patricia was first, with very little patience as she jerked back the woman's head and bit into her. The woman squealed in surprise, and Patricia jerked her even further as if in warning.

I could feel Chase's attentiveness toward me. He wasn't watching me but hovering his mind over mine in a lowly manner of support. Tythian lifted the woman's wrist and elegantly dove his fangs in, exploiting the slow euphoric release he offered her. Tracey watched me not delving into her own human until I would. Chase mentally stayed with me for moral support as his fangs sunk into his human's neck. This is what he was. This was what *we* were. The popping of their skin being pierced and the smell of blood eluding the air contracted my fangs and purple eyes.

I constricted my temptation, slowly and controlled. I dipped my head toward the woman, inhaling the floral scent that was masked with her natural odor. My tongue delicately glazed along the neck, feeling the beating pulse beneath. There was a light salt taste that claimed my tongue, making me even thirstier for the treat. I allowed only a small margin for my vampire self to take over and escape. I pierced my fangs into her neck, opening her blood flow and allowing it to race over my tongue and down my throat.

Every inch the blood touched inside felt like a delectable ointment soothing and refurbishing me from the inside. I clung to her tightly, cupping under her jaw to angle her face away so I could better delve my lips over her cool skin. My vampire would try to break free even more to ravish her and take more than it needed. To take every last drop and delve into her essence so it would become my own. But I clamped on it, thinking of the revolting wolf blood and the image of Dillian's body crumpled and unmoving.

I pulled away from the woman, tearing myself out of the frenzy I was skirting along. Once I'd snapped myself free, I could feel Chase's mind pull away, satisfied by my control. I yanked the silk serviette to my lips, covering it over my mouth and nose, in the hope it would deter the strong scent of the woman. It did nothing to deter it, but I managed to push down my vampire reluctantly, far away so it wouldn't come back up and finish its meal.

"Is that all you'll be having this evening?" the vampire servant asked me, and I looked up at him revolted. The woman had paled, and if I dared divulge in a smidge more, I had concerns it would lead to her last breath.

"That's all," I gritted out beneath the serviette. I could feel Tracey's bronze eyes watching me as she feasted. It was off-putting being studied in such a way. I was nothing but a mere amusement to her.

"Patricia," Iris grumbled, reefing back her shoulders. She was savagely latched onto the woman who was turning a ghostly white. She snarled at him, blood spilling down her mouth as she tried to enforce her claim. "Enough," he said, prying her off and skirting her back into her chair. She heaved against him, wildly savage as he pinned her against her seat.

"Patricia," Tracey reprimanded, peeling herself away long enough from her own meal. The low tone of her sister's voice snapped her out of her blood lust, and coherency crept back into her expression.

"Oh, my," Patricia said with a short giggle and reached for her serviette to clean her face. Numerous droplets of blood had landed on her dress. "How indecent of me." But the way she looked at Chase was as if it was a turn-on, that he too should be aroused by her ravaged appetite. Iris helped the woman stand, which she could barely do herself. He offered her over to the vampire servant who caught her before she keeled over on wobbly knees. The others could at least walk back out on their own without assistance. Tracey flicked hers away, the woman nearly falling to the ground if the second servant hadn't caught her in time.

"Now, where were we?" Tracey called forth attention, satisfied after the gulping silence as we sat around an iced table delighting in devouring humans. All five of them were led to the door, and only until they were descending the stairs did they huddle around the woman to reassure her that she would be okay. I despised this new order that I was a part of but also craved. I was no better or worse than them, but I still seethed them for it.

"We were to discuss the involvement of your Council," Tythian began with a shallow sip of his liquor.

"We've been discussing business all day, and I'm awfully tired from it."

"With all due respect, Tracey, this is why we came here in the first place," Chase chimed in. She appraised him with detest. It wasn't until Patricia wrapped her arms around his protectively that her gaze softened if only slightly. She was toying with us and dragging out the inevitable.

"And Tythian has given me the details, and I have not yet decided on an answer. Until then, I feel like dessert. Iris, prepare us for the fourth level. Esmore, there's something I especially want to show *you*."

Tythian slipped a low growl, his patients tiring under the weight of negotiations. How long had we been here? Every second wasted because of her personal leisure was defiling our personal ambitions and strength.

"You will remember that for *now* you are a guest," Tracey reminded him. "But you are still outlawed. Keep in mind that at any time I could so choose to turn you over. Do not test my leniency."

Patricia's sharp nails had begun to produce droplets in Chase's arms from how tightly she clung to him like he was her new toy, and she wasn't willing to offer it so easily to her sister.

"Now, Esmore, come," Tracey said and clicked her fingers. My spine stiffened as I fought against my revolt to pounce on her. How dare she click at me as if I were some dog. Tythian's sharp gaze was on me, and I could feel his mocking presence doubting I had the control to react accordingly.

Chase's mind skirted over mine ensuring I wasn't about to explode. I inwardly frowned, angered that neither believed in my strength, but I couldn't blame them, my history had only ever been unstable.

I rose from my chair, gritting my teeth, and threw the serviette on the table. "Thank you for the meal," was all I said as I followed her lead. Of which a long snake-like smile appeared across her face as she ushered me to her side.

CHAPTER 7

The fourth level was the most heated of all, if only because of the bodies that slowly rubbed against one another sensually with very few bits of material coming in between. The room was a hazed mirage of euphoria as vampires giddily taunted and fucked one another. Some humans were amongst their kind and seemingly enjoying their time. Only a few women speckled the room, and they seemed prized as they chose one lover to the next with a hunger that looked like it could never be quenched.

Men devoured men, the closest pairing to the entrance, tracing the lines of one another's abdomen with their tongues. I was oddly shocked and turned on within the explicit atmosphere. Feeling Chase's presence behind me only heated the situation further and I furled into myself denying my freedom and satisfaction in the thought of making love to him.

"Traceeey, we didn't expect to see you tonight," one of the women vampires purred seductively. She'd previously been occupied with one of the men who wore nothing but chains and was tied down to a bed. I couldn't see his face, but I felt violated by the pure enjoyment that was openly waving from him in waves as he received every lashing. Blood trailed down the bedding from his body caused by the last lash he'd received. Another man leaped over him and trailed the wound with his tongue. Both of them moaned in pleasure and were evidently erect. "What an honor."

Tracey stretched a beckoning smile, and the two hugged like old friends. "You know I like to see a good show. Come here, Esmore," Tracey instructed, leading me to hard beds in the corner of the room somewhat segregated from the crowd. I froze where I stood, disgusted.

"I have no intention of involving myself." Tracey pretended to be confused as she shuffled off her suit jacket and shimmied out of the shirt. Her bare breasts were obnoxiously large.

"Oh, don't be daft, it's just for a massage," she said, clicking over one of the vampire servants. He wore a leather collar and small leather underwear that hardly covered his ass.

"Loosen up, maybe getting laid might help you a bit." Chase nipped my ear as he walked past, and every reflex was to pounce on him and claim him. So, I settled for the second action that would appease me. As he brushed past me, I locked onto his arm and flipped him over my shoulder. He hit the ground with an oomph and Patricia stumbled back.

I looked down at Chase, predatory-like and with great satisfaction both for the persona I was playing and for my own intentions. Handling him in such a way broke some of the tension that was arousing within me just from being in this room, and was probably the only reason why he let me overpower him so quickly. A smile spread across his lips and for a moment I could see the Chase I loved that was often bemused by my quick action.

"Touchy," he teased.

"Don't touch what does not belong to you," I purred. My body heated at the thought. I did belong to him in every way. But not here. Not now.

"How dare you!" Patricia squealed, looking down at one of her nails that broke. I'd reefed Chase so quickly out of her hold that she'd somehow broken her nail. It hastily began growing out. My smile grew, feeling far more rewarded for the crime.

"Get a hold of yourself," Tythian sneered as he walked past and took a seat closest to where Tracey was now on her stomach being massaged by the vampire who she'd instructed earlier.

"Patricia, go sit over there," Tracey grumbled into the small cut-out hole her face rested in. "Esmore, come, sit beside me." She clicked her fingers at me again. I refrained from showing my irritation and sat in the small blue velvet chair beside her. "Tell me, Esmore, what do you think of all of this?"

I looked around the room, this level that was crafted for fetishes, sex, and release. I tried not to watch Chase and Patricia as she tried to coax him into numerous settings staged around the room. Tythian was approached numerous times, but his gaze alone was effective in deterring anyone from taking him seriously. I was curious if I looked over the edge in the center of the room and further down at the other levels what else I might find. This place was a monster's pleasure house frozen in time. And that was why they were dying out.

"I think it's very different to anything I've seen before," I said honestly.

Tracey chuckled. "Well, I find that not so surprising, you don't even seem of age." She looked down on me and treated me as a novelty. Iris stood closest to her table keeping an eye on what Chase and Tythian were doing. Forever the guard.

"And tell me, why does someone so young as you desire to willfully be in this upcoming war. Oppollo thinks you're dead. You could wipe your hands clean of what's to come, and yet your parents drag you into it further. Do you lack an opinion?" She twisted her face to look at me dead on. The mention of my age and it being deemed as inadequate irritated me. I'd already had to overcome this obstacle within the Hunter Guild. But here in the world of vampires, where I had only lived for almost nineteen years, they had been around for hundreds. The difference being, I was still alive, and they were frozen in time. Well, I considered myself still alive.

The gentleman rubbed over Tracey's glowing skin, drawing low moans out from her as he rolled over certain spots in her shoulders.

"Because I have people I need to protect." However, I felt distant from that truth—I'd already failed. So what else did I have to live for, if not that?

"Ah." She clicked her tongue. "We all have something to protect. It's the only way we're still bound to any form of humanity. If not, we'd turn into the likes of those monstrous sabers. You know you do have options. Tythian has requested I join forces with your covens and offer them intel for the upcoming Council meeting. But what if I could offer you something greater? If you were to join me, I could change your face and appearance. Oppollo wouldn't be the wiser to who you were. You could join my Council. Be my friend. Join my rankings if you so desired."

Tythian was listening in to our conversation and scrutinized her obvious poaching. It only made me more suspicious of her motives. To speak of this in front of the others, so carefree, she knew I'd have no choice to deny her, even if I did want to betray them. What game was *she* playing?

"You know I can't accept that. I want no part of the Council, and once all is done, I want no involvement with the covens either."

She chuckled. "Having a father as a coven leader might very well disable you from being allowed anywhere else. And besides, when word gets around about your fake death, you'll have an even larger target on your back. You might be free of it now, maybe years if you're lucky. But don't be fooled into thinking there is anywhere in this world that you are safe. Not when people know what you can do." Her bronze eyes were fixated on me. "You don't have your power right now, do you? That's why you need time. That's why your parents are keeping you safe for now. That's why you need *my* help. And maybe I can do just that for you."

I looked down my nose at her. The fact that she knew about my heart and gift left an unsavory taste in my mouth. How many knew of my ability before I even had the chance to explore it myself. Whether I'd ever be reunited with it was a question in itself. But I did have a pining to be whole once again. My greatest honor as a huntress had been taken away from me, and despite all that had happened, I couldn't deny that I wanted to feel its strength. To taste what I was at my core and being before any of this vampire matter began.

"I think perhaps this conversation should be taken elsewhere." Iris dipped his head toward Tracey's heeding Council. She charmed a smile, full well knowing what she'd openly insinuated. Whether others were listening or not, I knew factually that Tythian and Chase were. The masseuse and Iris included. She was creating another rumor that harbored power if she let it roam free and take a life of its own. It was a threat. She could keep that knowledge within her walls as a secret, or let it spread like wildfire amongst other Councils.

It was a dangerous game we played as we tried to recruit her. "You're right." She sighed and shuffled back to her knees on the bed. "Esmore, would you like to walk with me privately. I'd like to show you my personal gallery."

Tythian stood up as she did. "You aren't invited, Tythian, though I thank you for your services earlier," she suggested promiscuously as she threw her jacket back over her shoulders, flicking out her luminous hair. Was she insinuating something happened between them? Chase was inevitably uncomfortable as Tracey tried to lead me away privately, and he was tired of his own antics trying to keep up with Patricia without engaging in the way she wanted.

"I insist that she can't offer you any more information than I can," Tythian obnoxiously spat. "Our negotiations are led by me."

"And you are but a man in a woman's world right now. And I desire girl talk. Your dick might offer me pleasure, but I trust no man other than Iris," she alluded. "Make sure he doesn't follow us."

"You don't want me to follow?" Iris said, disquieted.

Tracey scoffed. "You think I can't handle a small girl on my own. How you wound me, Iris."

"I meant no insult." He dipped his head, ashamed.

"I know," she purred, placing her hand on his jaw and dragging her nail across it so it left a delicate mark along his cheek. She licked the tip of her nail savoring the taste. "Make sure the others play nice." She walked toward the door before glancing over her shoulder impatiently. "Well, come along." She snapped her fingers at me. I wearily looked back at Chase.

It's not smart to go alone, he said cautiously though both of us knew I had no choice but to entertain her. Tythian straightened his deep red shirt, irritated that his cunning ways and control were not in place. A small smile crept over my face as I felt a small victory which rarely happened. If looks could kill, I'd be dead. His icy blue gaze bore through me, and I wickedly delighted in the win. Even if it wasn't safe or an ideal situation, I looked forward to it.

CHAPTER 8

Despite the pinprick heels of Tracey's shoes, no noise echoed as she led me into the cold depths of her Council. A small draft came from somewhere, and I couldn't quite make out its direction. Since leaving the heart of her Council, we hadn't come across any other members. I suspected these chambers were private or weren't frequented for a reason.

There was an eeriness to the path she led me down. It was near pitch black, and I could only make out enough with my keen sight as a vampire. Where the iced walls were polished in other parts of the Council, they were rigid and unrefined here. She was taking me to a 'gallery,' but I hadn't yet come across any form of fine art. I reached out to Chase telepathically to reassure him I was still okay.

I'm okay. For whatever reason, Tracey wanted to instigate this private discussion, and I could be just as much at an advantage of attacking her.

The moment anything happens or feels off, let me know.

"I often walk this long hall on my own. It reminds me of why I've been entitled a position as a Council Leader and the responsibilities that lay heavily on my shoulders. You said you had others to protect, yes?" I nodded, and despite having her back turned to me, she noticed the motion. "Then you too know the feeling."

She paused in front of a particular jutted-out piece of ice with admiration, hands behind her back as she studied it. I looked up at the hideous beast that was frozen within. Two red beady eyes looked down on us. Its body was twisted into chunks of what looked to be fur and flesh with an abnormally sized body that outgrew its limbs. It looked as if it had derived from some kind of saber. Its fangs were extended out over its mouth that was agape in what looked like a terrified scream. "Hideous, isn't it?"

"What is that?" I asked, looking between the frozen creature and her admiring gaze. Her features seemed to have darkened, devoid of all the sparkle she'd glittered herself with for dinner. Here in the dark, she too lost her shine.

"This is one of my many men that have fallen to the state of being saber. I just never had it in my heart to let them go." She began moving on to the next one which was equally as distorted but jutted one half-broken wing on its back.

"I've never seen sabers look like this," I admitted, revolted they could develop in such a way. It reminded me of the experiments at the Human Compound where they'd frozen vampires in ice capsules. Here, Tracey had simply somehow done it in a natural state. Perhaps the sabers here mutated like the rodents near the Human Compound.

"Oh, they didn't always look like that. I would snag them the moment they started displaying saber-like symptoms, and then I would contort them into the hideous beast I imagined they'd soon turn into. Right now, their minds are frozen in a between state. Not yet fully saber, but very close to the edge of their reckoning. I do this for them. When they're in my Council, I make them beautiful. When they begin to lose their humanity, this damn disease rounds its corner and near ends their life. I distort that beauty so it resembles the hideous rupture of what they'll become. And then we freeze them."

Gone were the days of Tracey's sanity and scarcity in the way she justified her actions. As vampires, their bodies might've preserved for hundreds of years, but it was most apparent that the longer one lived the more twisted they'd become. And most like Tracey acquired a god-like complex thinking that their way was justified. A misconception because they were immortal they would always outrun the clock. But sabers were proof that most didn't.

I stared at the monster with an unreadable expression. Tracey reached her hand out to press against the cool ice, and I could've sworn for the briefest of seconds I saw its eyes move. Its hideous wing seemed broken and snapped into unnatural angles. I recalled the incident of my own horrific fall and crash that destroyed my wings, splintering them into hundreds of bone shards and torn muscle.

Alarmingly, I realized now why Tracey was such a threat. She used her gift to focus on her Council's vanity, but it could be used in so many other ways. It was a weapon that could be used to strengthen her army and also attack any vampire she wanted, pooling them into a puddle if she so desired.

"Can their aesthetic additives be used, such as their wings? Are they functional?" I asked coolly, trying to maintain my revolt in the way that it reminded me of the human experiments. The visual of the werewolves came to mind.

"Who knows?" she said, shrugging her shoulder. "I doubt the wings would work. I don't know how to craft the muscle, weights, and accurate measurements to make them functional. But even if I did, it's been banned that I do so by Oppollo himself." She rolled her eyes, dropping her hand and moving on to the next installment of her 'gallery.'

"I thought Oppollo didn't yet have full reign over the twelve separate Councils?"

She scoffed, holding in oppressed laughter. "My girl, it's a man's world on the table. His power is different. He comes from a different time altogether, and some insinuate he's the oldest of our kind. It's even rumored he didn't originally come from our world at all. Now, I don't know about folklore or scary stories, but what I do know is when Oppollo threatens other Council's on the table, they either abide or within days they'll be forced to.

Now, of course, we aren't to raise a hand against one another considering our unified power, but it doesn't deter any of the leaders from obtaining what they want in secrecy. There are consequences to those who are found guilty, but often such notions are overlooked or outvoted."

The next monster was a twisted mixture of beauty and horror. Sharp features protruded from the woman's face twisted into razor edges on her cheeks. The bottom half of her body seemed to distort into some kind of scaled tail. A small howl of wind tore down the hallway as I unblinkingly stared at her. Tracey's expression seemed to change with this one. This woman, whatever her worth or who she might've been was evidently special to her.

"Is that why you've been so quiet all this time?" I asked. "You've feared the wrath of Oppollo, or consequently, the Council will vote and side with him?"

She considered this. I could see the fast calculation in her mind. How much should she tell me? Was this a portrayal of feigned weakness or had she already accepted that she needed our help? "Many of us have remained quiet and allowed the powers that be. But Oppollo isn't the only one with power. And it's a difficult balance to maintain amongst the others. It's politics. And I am in a location where I must rely on imported resources from other Councils. Ruffling feathers, so to speak, does not benefit me. And even now, these past few years they've been dwindling as if to make a mockery of my situation and my inability to do anything about it." Her sharp nails dragged along the ice. I side glanced her, surprised she was being so open with me about it. And so, I looked for any indication of a lie or manipulation. Every piece of information comes at a cost.

"Why are you telling me all of this?" She'd been coy about any real discussion earlier in our meetings, or perhaps she'd already negotiated her terms with Tythian, and I was a side thought. She did treat me after all as if I was some kind of new trick or toy. Perhaps that's why she had such admiration for my wings earlier because she could utilize the visual in her next experiment. I was beyond the days of anticipating how a vampire's mind worked because they all twisted self-serving in mysterious ways.

"Because I've let it go on for too long," she admitted with a sigh and rolled back her shoulders. "And I do not trust a man's word as far as I can throw him. Broken promises and manipulation," she seethed from a place that had anchored very darkly into her soul. Her opinion of men had festered for years, if not centuries. "And so, I don't care for what Tythian and his master can offer me or that flighty one, Chase."

"Just because I'm a woman it doesn't mean I'm incapable of cheating you."

"Of course not. In this day and age, I would expect nothing less. I was simply curious as to what this monstered huntress thought about fighting on the other side and being used as a pawn by her own parents?" That sharp interrogating gaze of hers placed itself dangerously on me. It was as if we resided once again in the entry room where she sat upon her throne and interrogated me with disgust.

"It would appear you seem to struggle in making friends," I said coldly, trying to bite back the acid in my tone.

She let out a haughty laugh. "Little one, we are not in the business of making friends. I'm familiar with hunters and their customs. They are programmed no differently from how we are manufactured to thirst for blood. I bet the moment they realized your abnormality and what your true gift was, they turned on you. I dare say they probably tried to kill you before they had the smarts to use you as a weapon."

My lack of response twisted a knowing smile on her face. We moved on to the next creature which was much smaller than the others and harbored a square-like profile.

"I was once with child," she said, seemingly staring off into a place far from here. "Before I was turned. When my family was turned into vampires, my unborn baby died in the process." She pressed a hand to her stomach. "Over the years the remains of my family as we fought amongst one another dwindled to only myself and Patricia." Which explained the sister complex she harbored. But I couldn't help but feel a pang of revolt and regret for her. Vampires didn't care about who they targeted, even a pregnant woman was prized. "So, I may not have raised *my* child, but I can certainly understand a maternal touch to a degree as I've raised this Council from nothing." A twisted idealism, I realized. She was in a world that she had control over and she'd been content until her resources dwindled and she wasn't permitted to move.

Her children were starving, and she has nowhere else to go. She needs our help. The question was whether she was willing to put them at risk during the process. "So, then I ask you again, why are your parents, creatures of both evils so willing to throw their child in the midst of this war? What makes it so justifiable, and you so willing to fight for their reasoning?" What she was asking me was how could she justify and ask that of her own kind. Of her children in her twisted fantasy. How could she so willingly throw them into this fight when more than likely most wouldn't come out alive. This is why she called me here. Tythian could never answer her questions because he had already lost the one thing that mattered to him, Whitney. And now, she wanted to know what I had to lose in this gamble besides my life.

She was vulnerable, I realized. Outdated in a time where her power became a trick instead of the magnitude of its former glory. She'd been oppressed, and now she was daring to peek out of the snow blizzard coma she'd swept over her Council.

"My reason to fight?" I repeated. No one had truly asked me this outright. Ever since being exiled from the Hunter Guild and chased down, I'd only been flung into action, for survival and at the request of others. At the request of Cesar and my mother specifically. The rest was of my own accord in a desperate attempt to protect those who I cared for, those who shouldn't have been dragged into this damaging world because of me. "My mother would do anything to protect me, despite Iris's opposing opinion. As unlikeable as Cesar was, I dare say he too had a protective streak regarding my survival." I'd received enough jibes from the brothers about being his 'little princess.' But I was never conceited into thinking it was from some kind of seeded parental love. I was his heir by blood. His only living child in a world where he shouldn't have been able to produce me.

"But first and foremost, I was crafted as a weapon. One that is able to pass judgment and lead as a Token. I have others I need to protect. If Cesar's objectives align with mine, to sustain that protection, then I'll agree to it."

"And also, you like it," she purred and offered me a knowing coy smile. "I've watched you. This darkness and entity that consumes our soul, it's like it snatches our breath away and births a new life of its own, one without fear and wicked delight. You want danger. You actively seek it."

"That's not true," I curtly disagreed.

"But isn't it?" she purred with delight sparkling in her eyes. "That's why I'm interested to see what havoc you can wreak. You might even create more damage than we've ever seen before and that weighs on my wager."

A breeze bristled my skirt, daring to expose my skin in the way I feel Tracey's reading me so openly in a frightful way.

"It must be difficult to be in your position, in truth, I take pity on you."

"Pity on me?" I leered at her through my peripheral. I don't think it should be me in this position that was pitied.

"Absolutely. You've become a figure for some, a new glowing beacon of hope. And yet the rumors they hear and seek out, that *gift* of yours, isn't even apparent."

I felt myself go rigid at the mention of my gift. "I've shown you my gift."

She snorted a laugh. "Oh, the wings are most beautiful. But I'm talking about the gift that dragged you into this mess. You see it only took one person that night to see your mother runoff from the Hunter Guild. For the life of me, I can't remember the name of your Head Huntress, and I really don't care. Once a rumor is spread in-house, no matter how few are told, it always reaches out. There are traitors everywhere. And your gift isn't so secret. It's just a shame you're unwilling to show it or it's simply that you *can't.*" I felt her gaze scrutinizing me. "I'm weakened by the fact that my gift only works when I physically touch someone. Yours is weakened by the fact that you don't even have it."

"I don't know what rumors you've heard," I purred in an eerily sinister tone. My vampire was coming to the surface, delighting in her threatening tone. "But they don't apply to me. The covens and I can end Oppollo's reign, with or without made-up stories of who I am and what I can do. I don't know what rumors Campture spread, but what I do know is that she put a target on my back when I infiltrated Fier's Council, and she deemed me a traitor. The rest is history."

She seemed to mull over this idea, not at all convinced.

"So then let me ask you this? What will you do if this agreement with the covens doesn't align with your better judgment or decree? What will you do then? Go out on your own? Seek refuge elsewhere?"

A shadow fell over my thoughts as if a looming presence had caught up with me. I hadn't yet been able to think about what it would look like outside or after this war. I'd only been barely scraping through. We'd had many disagreements, but overall we seemed unified in our approach. I was able to use the covens to harbor the others in safety—for now. But even I knew that time was wasting away. And after all that I'd done, I still failed in protecting them.

It was unknown what would happen with the werewolves and the approach the covens would decide to take. I wanted their kind to have a chance in this world, to be given a pardon and find a new way of life.

Not to be hunted and destroyed simply because of the unjust that was done to them. I didn't care for the humans, but I felt a protection to overshadow the werewolves. The thought of Titan came to mind if only because I wanted her to remain safe. I wanted Titan to have a full life and one where she knew how to protect herself.

I thought of Dillian and Tori, who'd been changed against their will. I wanted them to be able to shift into this new phase and find some kind of reason to live. Like I had Chase, I hoped they would find something in return. I wanted those who were different and taken from their worlds, much like I was to survive this wild nature.

I could feel Chase's presence stroking along the link we shared as if feeling my inner turmoil that I was still trying to hide from him. I'd already failed all of them in so many ways. But if the covens didn't align in a way that would still offer them protection, what would I do?

"I don't know," I admitted.

Tracey purred to herself, and the corner of her mouth flicked up into a feline smile. "And that's what makes you dangerous." She spun on her heels admiring the length of the gallery. I wondered how many creatures were trapped in here, silent in their bewitched way. "I will join forces with you. I think it's time I became dangerous too."

CHAPTER 9

I PITIED CHASE who was half-stripped of his clothes and being antagonized for pretending to act 'so coy' as Patricia liked to joke. I diverted my gaze swiftly ensuring no one saw the way I studied every muscle of his body. However, I knew all too well every groove of how it was perfectly dipped and shaped.

Tythian appeared to have a sudden affinity for a piece of fluff on his shirt as we made our entrance, apparently uninterested in our arrival. Iris, however, seemed relieved as he welcomed Tracey with a curt nod. There was still so much I wondered about Iris's background. I wondered how he'd conformed and if it was even possible for a hunter-born vampire to find some kind of peace. I was curious as to whether he segregated himself within this Council or if it was the others who'd labeled him as an outsider.

Tracey waved Tythian over to announce her conviction. The unsteadiness that I now often held toward him shadowed me. He still wasn't all that elated that he'd been uninvited to our chat. He looked down on me with so much spite and hatred that it was hard not to respond. And all I could do in reply was antagonize him with a small smile when I thought of his desperate and disgusting ways of sleeping with Tracey. Perhaps he did it thinking it would offer him better negotiations or perhaps they were old lovers. Either way, I held something over his head knowing too well how much he liked to hold grudges.

A small growl escaped Chase in warning. It was steadfast to Tythian who delighted in all the things he might've wanted to do to me. Even Iris had stepped forward as a precautionary measure. Not that he would've broken our fight or cared for the victor, but because he had to screen Tracey and Patricia in protection. She might've been ready to agree to Tythian's terms, with her own added conditions, but times were still tense. We were not part of this Council, and just because she agreed to this alliance, it didn't mean she had any respect for us or the covens we represented. She was a desperate woman trying to keep her Council alive, and we were the group crazy enough to extend a hand.

"Come along, Chase," I ordered for him to hurry, all too keen to be rid of this place and those claws of Patricia's that dove too deeply into his skin. *Mine.* He was mine. And I was so close to being able to claim him as such all over again. But for now, I'd have to act with indifference. "Or stay. It might be a nice way to be rid of you."

Chase cocked a smile, tugging at his dress shirt from Patricia's prying hands. "Well, at least they treat me nicely here."

"Until they discover your 'attributes' are most disappointing," I chimed as I spun and walked toward the others.

"Still pissed off you haven't yet been able to find out yourself?" he mused.

Before I could wager another daring taunt, Patricia tugged him back by his arm. "We're not done here yet." I could smell her arousal from here. All hot and bothered by herself, all for my man which had me tempering a thirsty bloody rage. I suppressed the primitive urge to claim him in front of her.

"Patricia, they'll be making their leave," Tracey announced, bored of her sister.

"But I want him to stay!" Patricia stomped her foot. The rest of the party silenced as her emotions began to wave out into a tantrum. "You didn't give me what I wanted!" she shouted at Chase and pegged a glass of liquor at him. He dodged it easily, and it continued flying through the air, tumbling toward me. I caught it, narrowing my gaze on her, and crushed the glass in my hand. It shattered into hundreds of pieces and embedded itself into my hand and onto the floor.

The pain was a welcome relief, a small awakening from this tender game we'd been playing. But her response was truly the greatest and most rewarding gift.

"It's because of her, isn't it?!" she screamed wildly and lunged forward. Others mounted on her, the woman Tracey had been talking to earlier having the firmest grip. It didn't matter that it was me particularly or some other woman. Patricia was a spoilt brat who viewed all women as competition. It made it oh so sweet that her rage was hell-bent on me. "Get off me! How dare you!" she screamed as she tried to twist out of their clutches.

"Patricia, I gave them permission to tie you down if you went too far," Tracey announced bitterly. "I love you gravely, but you're a brat, and sometimes you must be punished for it. Perhaps I've let this behavior go on for too long," she solemnly said in thought. She waved her hand to the woman in charge of this floor with an unspoken order. She instructed the others to drag Patricia into a private room. I wondered what punishment Tracey deemed appropriate for Patricia, surprised there was such a thing as consequences for her doting little sister.

The wild screams and echoes of Patricia were delightful music to my ears as we followed Tracey up the spiral staircase and to the highest level where we'd feasted earlier. She waited patiently for the three of us to enter the room and instructed Iris to guard the entrance so no one would overhear.

"I agree to your terms if both covens agree to my conditions. Firstly, once the matter is dealt with, Oppollo disposed of, and the Council in new order, I will have no association with the covens and will deny any part in this. Second, I will be finding a new place to relocate, and if a coven already resides there, they are to be removed prior to my arrival."

"We aren't in conjunction with all covens," Chase countered.

"I don't care." Tracey narrowed her gaze on him. "Then you will find a way to deal with it."

"But you don't want anything to do with us afterward, so how would—"

Tythian pressed his hand to Chase's chest with a scowl before Tracey erupted. "We can agree to those terms."

"Oh, no, there's one more," Tracey announced smugly. "It is your plan to position numerous armies around select Councils you feel will fight alongside Oppollo and come to his aid. You want to use this

Council meeting as a distraction while they're away from their Council threshold and attack. You can understand how I might feel slightly wary that I too am in a vulnerable position while I'm away from my own court. So, in exchange, think of it as an insurance that you won't attack my people while I'm gone, I want *her* to be by my side." She pointed her finely manicured finger at me.

"Are you joking?" Tythian queried deadly serious. Tracey's lack of response was enough to deem she was deadly serious.

"You can't be serious," Chase chimed in. "You want us to give one of our most valuable warriors over and put her into the heart of the Council room and meeting? Across from Oppollo who has a target on her?"

"I didn't think you cared so deeply about the little miss," Tracey toyed.

"I don't," Chase adamantly said. "But her father sure as hell is going to have a lot to say about it. They'll know who she is," he exclaimed as if he thought she was half crazy and couldn't see the obvious herself.

"I can easily change her features. That's no problem at all."

"You won't be touching me," I chimed in, seething at the thought of those elongated fingers coming toward me. The power to manipulate me into a monster that she so dearly showcased in the depths of her private gallery.

"Cesar won't agree to that term," Tythian forwardly agreed. She shrugged her shoulder.

"It's leverage as simple as that. I won't go forward unless you have something to lose as much as I do if you choose to betray me."

"And who's to say you won't betray us?" I evoked with an eyebrow raise.

"No one, dear girl. That's why these games are so dangerous," she said, her voice velvety smooth. "If you want my intel as to who will back Oppollo, the locations of all the Councils, and the Council meeting location, you really have no choice. Go to your master, Tythian," she seemed to delight in the command as if he were some dog. "And inform him of my conditions. Unless I have leverage, I won't act on my own. These are my terms."

"You don't want to make an enemy of us, Tracey," Tythian gritted through his teeth.

Her eyes hardened on him in a deathly gaze. "Oh, but, Tythian, we naturally already are. Less you forget that I am of the Council order and you are a part of a coven. I could have your very group squashed within weeks if I let it leak of what you've approached me about. Do not think you are higher in might, simply because I find value in your offer. But do come again for other reasons." She rolled her gaze over his body seductively. "For that I might make an exception."

"Now go," she shooed us. "I'm done with this conversation, return to me within two days and let me know of your decision. We are either allies or thereafter, the Council will come for you. Don't be late. Iris." She looked around idly as if daring one of us to target her exposed neck. She was taunting us. "Iris, be a darl and lead our guests out. From what I've heard, the blizzard is looking exceptionally rough today."

Just as we had been guided into Tracey's Council, we'd been led out in the very same way. Iris left no lingering impression. He was stoic and said nothing as he directed us back into the harsh elements of a raging blizzard. After a few minutes of walking and out of eyesight range, Tythian teleported us back to the institute.

"I can't believe she actually has the nerve for such a request," Tythian escalated outside the gates of the institute. "The sheer audacity as we offer an extended hand. Then again, I don't know why I'm saying this to you. For all I know, you could've planned this with her."

"Pardon? Coming from he who was fucking her in private conversation. Or were your lips not wet enough to actually speak?" I spat back, taking a step back from him, disgusted that I had to touch him so he could teleport us back.

"You might want to keep your woman on a leash, Chase, she—"

Chase moved so fast that it caught both Tythian and me off guard. He bunched Tythian's shirt at the front of his chest. It was oddly satisfying to see, considering how often Tythian outmatched Chase in the sense of age and experience. It was from the element of surprise that Chase was grappling him against the pillars that constructed the fence.

"You don't speak about her like that *ever*. I don't know what's gotten into you lately, but you need to back *off*," he growled a little unhinged. That's when I realized he still hadn't switched. That small button within him that helped him guide his emotions into a minuscule corner was still off. Even I didn't know what he'd be capable of right now.

"Chase," I warned him from behind. Admittedly, with his emotions sheltered, mine too were minuscule, and I preferred it. But watching him like this wasn't the reason why I fell in love with him. Though I had my indifferences with Tythian, I didn't want to be the reason why Chase was divided into choosing any kind of side. Chase and Tythian continued to square one another off. *Chase,* I tried more gently and placed my hand on his shoulder.

Tythian and Chase were friends. But I could see it wearing thin, eroding like all structure we'd once been bound by within our respective guilds and roles. Chase looked over his shoulder at my hand that was clasped on it. He seemed to soften slightly. No matter how small his emotional connection, he knew what it signified. We were no longer at Tracey's Council, we could touch and be how we were always meant to be around one another.

He dropped Tythian's shirt and stepped back, eyeing him warily. Tythian brushed off his shirt, disgusted as he looked between the two of us. He stormed back toward the institute, no doubt on his way to offer Cesar Tracey's conditions.

"Well, it's good to see everyone ended up back here in one piece," Balzar dryly joked from behind. We turned to face him. He was carrying a mounted stack of firewood on one shoulder and two dead birds, hanging from their feet in the other hand. "How'd it go?"

"I'm sure you'll hear all about it in no time," I said, eyeing off the birds. Balzar was one of the four brothers who were undoubtedly a part of their scheming. He would stand at the table as they discussed what *I* was to do and what part of leverage I was to play. The thought infuriated me. I was as much a prisoner here as I was within the Hunter Guild. But at least here, it could house the few I wanted to keep safe. "It's unlike you to bring back ... remains?" I gestured to the birds.

"They're for your little runts." He gestured over to the small patch of grass around Chase's and my wing. "Your wolf woman has been training them for hours every day until their little legs give way. It would appear I'm one of the few who remembered they need to eat."

Just as he had said, Titan and Chris were panting harshly in their human form. And then with hesitation as if they were about to regurgitate, they painfully shifted into their wolf form silently instructed by Fire who remained in hers. I checked the obvious safeguards and posts, securing their safety. I trusted Fire's skillset alone to defend them considering she'd fought by my side countless times. But it was habitual to make sure the area was secure. Above, looking down from the alcove of our wing, was my mother. Her huntress eyes glowed down as she watched them with arms crossed over her chest.

I could sense Julia still in the wing of our tower. Adjacent from the wolves practicing was Lincon who sat upon a rock, watching them with a magical gleam in his eyes. Kora and Kasey acted indifferently by his side.

I could sense Darcy close by, which meant Jerimiah was guarding Dillian and Tori in their cells. I called it 'protecting,' but I felt like I was imprisoning them instead.

"Who else knows about Fire?" I asked Balzar. Not many knew about her ability to turn into a woman. And she had no intention of turning into her human form often. Her wolf form was a mask she wanted to continue wearing in the house of vampires. Not that I could blame her. She wanted to be seen as the monster she was, not allowing anyone a moment of relapse to misjudge her strength and cockily try something.

"I only know because Tythian mentioned it. But it's staying low. For the most part, everyone's trying to ignore them. Cesar's not impressed by it, but your mother's been quite firm on the old bastard." He lightly laughed to himself, surprising me.

"Reminds you of 'like mother like daughter,' doesn't it?" Chase joked. I smacked him in the shoulder playfully. It felt good to be able to reach out and do as I pleased now. He hadn't yet opened his valve of emotions but simply being able to touch him brought me much relief.

"I can still hear your thoughts, you know," he grumbled as he leaned into my ear. The tone of his voice was like the gentlest of caresses, raking down my body. "I'm going to check up on the conversation being had with Cesar and make sure nothing's miscommunicated. Perhaps you should check up on the others." He pressed a fast kiss to my cheek and darted toward the entry. My hand lingered in the air, outstretched from how fast he'd left, and avoided my touch. He was running away from me. *Was he still upset about the dagger in my chest?*

"How long were we gone?" I asked Balzar as I took stride beside him. I didn't want to engage with Titan, and I made sure to ignore them. I could feel Fire's tug on our unknown line, ensuring she saw me. It felt more or less a 'welcome back,' and I see you gesture.

He looked between me and the others but said nothing about my ignorance. Lincon yelled out and waved from a distance, and I knew Balzar could understand why I purposefully ignored *him*.

"Four days, we honestly thought you'd be longer. Everyone's been on edge since the three of you left."

Four days? I paused at the entrance of the institute. It hadn't felt like that at all, but then again, time appeared to have frozen within Tracey's Council. Had this to do with the reasons why they were so outdated?

I pushed the wooden doors open. When I did, a silence enveloped the room, and everyone's prickly gazes were on me. I wavered over them, looking down my nose at them until I understood why. I briefed a glance at my over-the-top attire and avoided shaking my head. I'd have to change immediately.

"He's been asking for you, you know?" Balzar commented, and that stifled my first step. I was too scared to ask who *he* was, even though I already knew because I could sense him, like a fine pin in a haystack. I was so acutely aware of his presence the moment I stepped inside.

"So, he's finally awoken." I followed the scent of my familiar up the stairs, ignoring the mixed greetings and whispers as I strode through the room.

Chase's scent was intoxicating to me as I followed it, enjoying the taste, imagining him on my tongue. But my wild imagination was short-lived as I focused on *who* I had to address. Instead of turning into Cesar's quarters, I continued on. I squared my shoulders and prepared for what I was soon to witness. I'd failed them. I'd failed *him*. And now he could tell me how much he hated me and curse me for my selfish actions of keeping him here. And somehow, right now that seemed more painful than losing him altogether. I placed my foot on the first step following the staircase into darkness—into the cellar where only vampires lingered.

CHAPTER 10

I SCANNED OVER the minds of Tori and Dillian who were varying in response. Tori seemed coy and scared. Dillian… I couldn't gather much which only led to greater concern.

"Good to see you back in one piece." Jerimiah curtly nodded at my arrival. His long black hair was pointedly styled into a long ponytail like it always was. The thing with turning into a vampire was you never truly changed. Ever. Unless you had a gift like Tracey's. Much like Dillian and Tori, they were frozen in time.

"You're one of a few to think so," I darkly joked. He didn't find it humorous. Nor did I. He stepped aside, no longer blocking the entrance. Chase and I had much to thank Jerimiah for and his group of twenty. Between them, they were keeping peace within the institute as they guarded the line that divided the two covens. And I'd found fondness toward him and Darcy, trusting them with something as important as looking after the others while I was gone.

"Esmore?" Tori croaked. His voice sounded too parched for what should be a velvety smooth youthful tone. I said nothing, but stepped closer. Only one flickering flame was ignited in the cellar. The moldy smell seemed more offensive now than the cool, harsh snowstorm I'd just walked out from. It was damp and rotten in here—an injustice to what my friends deserved.

Shadows flickered over his pale face as he leaned toward the door. He'd learned to retract his fangs already, which I was impressed by. I wasn't sure if that was considerably quick since I'd never been around a newborn vampire before, but Tori oddly seemed like himself—all but the dull brown eyes that I'd been so accustomed to being a fluorescent tone instead. His shaggy blond hair was in upheaval, and he was dirty from sitting in the filth of this room for too many days.

A second movement caught my eye. No words were spoken, and I was too scared to look his way. But he deserved to be honored with that at least, despite my fear of how he would look at me in return.

Dillian sat at the back of his cell, his head dipped slightly forward, with black hair dangling in front of his dull pink eyes. He had one hand propped up on his knee as he watched me with a vacancy in his gaze as if instead of using his gift to see long-distance, he was retracting it, so he didn't have to see anything at all.

"When do we get out of here?" Tori asked with disdain in his voice. "It's revolting, and I can smell everything. I'm sensitive to everything," he said, rubbing himself in an insecure manner. Where Tori seemed to revert into some innocent version of himself … Dillian was the opposite. He seemed cold and impassionate.

"We're keeping you in here for your own safety," I said in a small voice, though I knew what Tori meant, he felt like a prisoner. They *looked* like prisoners. I tried not to drag myself back into this small room with them like during that time Chase had been in the end cell beside them, and I'd spiraled into madness. This room brought back unnerving memories. Something inside me had broken, and as Dillian and I stared at one another, neither of us willing to remove our prominent gaze, I realized I was far from the only one who'd been broken.

"A little late for that, wouldn't you say, *Esmore?*" The way Dillian said my name rolled my spine straighter. Tori seemed to stifle and sink into the background, silently. It was so unlike his usual way. So mousey and quiet compared to the robust teenager he'd once been. And Dillian …

"I would agree," I said quietly. I had been too late. I'd let this happen to them, and I didn't even have a lead to avenge them. I had taken away their right for an honorable hunter's death. My selfishness drove us into this dark room that was being eaten alive by the hatred that dripped off Dillian's every word.

"You should've put a dagger in our hearts," Dillian added dryly, watching me with those impassive eyes.

"I know," I replied. I knew that. But I couldn't let them go. Julia couldn't let *him* go. But the decision had fallen in my lap, and here we were.

"At least Teary had an honorable death. Well, presumably since she's not here with us. But who could be the wiser, I mean it's not like we've been told anything." His voice sounded foreign. So, abash and vengeful to his usual bright and lively self.

"At least Julia's alive," Tori squeaked.

Dillian snapped. "Don't speak of Julia." He banged his hand against the cage to rattle Tori, who flinched.

"We didn't want to let either of you go." I drew his attention back toward me. I was surprised by the way he so coldly spoke Julia's name. I wasn't sure if it was for self-preservation of what they once had and in protecting her, or if he'd truly lost his love and attachment for her.

"Well, congratulations, now you're stuck with us *forever* unless we can stake ourselves first."

Tori grimaced. I imagined the same thing had gone through his mind. But from what I'd witnessed and even experienced myself, one thing you didn't often see is self-mutilation or vampires trying to end their own life. They wanted to survive, it was in their mechanics. Dillian and Tori were still freshly turned, adapting to all the new senses and profanity of this new world. They would be strung out and on edge for years to come.

"I'll come back some other time," I said. If Chase had dipped into his emotions once again, I would've coddled myself against the wall, imprinting on every part of them that had now changed, guilt riding me for every horror I'd now enforced upon them.

Dillian scoffed. "Rather cowardly of a Token Huntress. Getting a little hard to hear the truth, isn't it?" he asked, looking from under his thick eyelashes with a predatory gaze. It was so unlike Dillian. The vampire had eaten away at my good friend, and I hoped, I prayed he was somewhere inside.

"There's nothing I can say right now to comfort you," I dryly replied.

"Comfort us?!" Dillian flashed into action smashing against the cell and charging at me. He slapped his arms against the railings. "Look at us!" Jerimiah took a tentative step forward as if to protect me. The silver of the bars sizzled Dillian's hands, but he showed little discomfort. "Look at what we've become!" Dillian's eyes sparkled with rage in a way I'd never seen him before. It was like looking at a completely different person. But he was entirely coherent. "You were our *Token,*" his voice sounded like a beckoning whine. "You were supposed to prevent this from happening. This might've been your chosen path, but we never wanted this for ourselves. You promised us *safety.* And like the fools we were we believed you. The *only* saving grace was that Julia wasn't infected with *your* hideous disease as well."

A cold brush of numbness washed over me. Dillian was in there. Amongst the hatred and self-loathing, I could manage out his words through all the suffering and rage. I heard him clearly, his every word precise in the way he knew how it'd hurt me. Or formidably in the way he thought it would not. I didn't show emotion in front of the others. This was my cameo, even while I was with Chase.

Dillian was right about one thing, well about all of it actually. But it was a shining beacon, in his eyes and mine, that Julia hadn't been turned too which only made the attack more precarious. I hadn't yet figured out the attacker's intent. Perhaps Julia was a mistake. Maybe they hadn't gotten to her in time before we'd appeared.

His words echoed. *'Your hideous disease.'* He blamed me for this cruelness, and I shouldered that. I felt it in every part of my being. Because Dillian was my best friend, and I failed him. I never wanted this for myself, but I certainly didn't want this cruel unyielding thirst and self-hatred to weigh on him as well. And yet here we were, lumped in a row of cells. I once thought I was righteous. I considered I could take on any enemy and even the world. I never realized the greatest enemy I was facing was myself.

I threw an apologetic look in Tori's direction. And I'd dragged Tori into it as well. "I'll come back and check up on you again shortly," I said, pardoning myself from the room. Dillian was right. I was a coward and could no longer face what I'd done. I needed to step out if only for a moment, to jumble coherent thoughts and a plan together. I'd done this to them. And now what?

Jerimiah tried to catch me on the way out. "Esmore, please realize heightened emotions and blame are all natural in the first stage of turning. He doesn't really mean—" I placed my hand on his shoulder to silence him. It felt bizarre to find a small piece of strength from his being here. He who was a vampire that I'd only met months ago, and yet I felt comforted to have guard my former hunters' lives. The remains of my team were in tatters. And so was I.

"Thank you." Every step felt like an elevation from a hideous version of myself as if I was trying to hide from its reality. But I couldn't help but feel the chains that dragged me back into that room. No matter how this would turn out. A small part of me would always be weighted and dragged back into that room.

I wasn't surprised that Chase waited atop the stairs. His gray eyes twinkled with empathy as I silently begged him not to open his emotions now. *Not now,* I thought. But it was too late.

Like a barrage of lapping waves coming down the link, I was overwhelmed by the floodgate that had been opened. He opened his arms wide as I stepped into them and burst into tears. An amounted strain I couldn't understand filled me, drowning me with hysteria. He gently picked me up and walked me into the bathing chambers. He closed the door shut and allowed us both to slide down the door as he rested me on his lap.

Chase soothed over my hair, nestling my neck into him as I sobbed and grieved for all that I'd done and lost. Dillian's words repeated in my mind, and my inability to change anything or help them felt like a vice. How could I help them when I couldn't even help myself?

We'll get through this, Chase caressed my mind like it was more of an atomic bomb than his own. And despite the concern for his mind imploding and turning him into saber, he was steady as a rock—anchoring me to this world. I wrapped myself in his warmth, saddened by the neglect I'd felt over the past four days. I'd missed him, but most of all I'd missed my counterpart enveloping me with rational sense.

I didn't fear Chase turning saber because of the emotions that flood gated me. Because it wasn't like the other times, where I had a fighting spirit and aggravated him. Chase held me tighter as amongst sobs and thoughts, I tried to think of his welfare. How cruel it was that our emotional balance was tangible to hurt one another in such a way.

Chase wasn't going to turn because I wasn't angry, I was just tremendously sad.

And selfishly, I thought how I'd rather that anger and rage guide me into my next action. Because here I just felt so utterly numb and powerless.

CHAPTER II

T HE EMOTIONAL EXORCISM left me depleted. Though I knew the moment I stepped back out into the hall where others could see me, I would have to harden my exterior into the cold Token that I was. So adjacent to what I truly felt inside.

Chase was there for me in more ways than anyone possibly could be. But even he could say very little. My emotional barrage was much a reminder to him of years misguided and seeing the loss and turn of loved ones. He'd lived hundreds of years longer than I and had seen so much more. And yet, somehow, even after all that time, it appeared that the emotions still came up raw for him. If time hadn't fixed it for Chase, then what would for me?

Weakly, I ventured to my wing, leaving Chase to converse with his coven. I didn't have the will to put up a front right now. My instability would only lead to a rupture of some kind, and I'd decided to take myself out of that situation, especially so it didn't put a strain on Chase.

There were fewer murmurs behind my back when I walked with Chase, no one so daring as to disrespect his familiar in front of him. Some of their responses to me had changed, respecting me for confronting Oppollo's assassins, and ensuring they didn't come closer to our coven.

But I was equally despised for being the reason Chase spiraled into madness in the first place.

The moment I felt Lincon's presence blocking my entry to the staircase, I took a deep breath, counting to ten as my father had taught.

"Yes, Lincon?" I said, rounding the corner.

He was leaning against the wall, overlooking a dead flower that he'd dragged from god knows where. He studied it as if it were the most beautiful thing he'd ever seen, and inhaled a sharp breath with a dashing smile.

"It came to my attention that you checked on the little twerps before me. I found it bizarre, considering I'm your utmost favorite."

Six. Seven. Eight. "I don't have time for your little thrills and games today, Lincon." I tried to push past him, but he stood in my way with a wobbling bottom lip.

"But don't you want an updated report on how I managed the fort while you were gone?" His eyebrows twisted with a saddened expression. Nine. Ten. I stared at him, abhorred by his sincerity. Had it been anyone else I'd take their report seriously, but it was Lincon.

One. Two. Three. I began counting again. He didn't move. I sighed. "What is it, Lincon?"

He beamed with enthusiasm. "Nobody reciprocated my taunts, which was very infuriating, and Cesar kept a close eye on me personally which was flattering, but also frustrating because he wouldn't let me engage with anyone."

"Perhaps because of your taunts and attempt to pick a fight with anyone who so much as looks your way?" I suggested sarcastically.

"Do you think he was on to me?" He quipped and began stroking his beard thoughtfully.

I barged past him and sluggishly stepped up the stairs.

"How did it go with Tracey's Council?" He asked, chasing me up the stairs. "She's been begrudging Oppollo for years, surely it wasn't that hard to convince her of any foul play." I stopped atop the stairs and looked down on him. I was always on guard with Lincon. His age and knowledge surpassed all my expectations, which is what made him so dangerous. Lincon, for whatever his worth, was conscious of who and whys. Had he been a sane man, I might've been better able to incorporate him into my group. But he was as unpredictable as he was crazy.

"You know Tracey personally?" I asked speculatively.

A cheesy grin spread on his face. "My dear, I know everyone who has ever had a hand in creating the world as it is. Tracey is a mere blip on the radar. Though a beautiful one. Is she still doing all that stuff to her face? She never practiced on me, I was so disappointed. Oh, how is darling Patricia? Always an irritable one that one. If you ask me, I dare say that family is a little bit nutty," he said in a hushed tone as if it were a secret. "Oh, did you accidentally kill one or four of them?" Four. Five. Six. The only one nutty was him. Lincon wasn't healthy for my vampire side. He indulged in the ruthlessness to kill and savor the torture. And more frequently than not lately, I'd found myself compelled to the same notion.

"Where are the twins?" I asked, not at all wanting to engage in his idle chat. Any form of bonding to Lincon was unwelcomed attention.

His eyebrows furrowed, discouraged that I'd blown him off. But he answered nonetheless. "Oh, you know, about. Don't worry, they're never too far from where I can reach them. They're my new little toys so I keep them hidden and out of sight from others who might want to plaaaay," he purred.

My grip tightened, my fingers digging into the palms of my hands. "Lincon, if anything happens to them—"

"Oh, of course not. Of course not. Though, if I'm being honest, that Kora certainly needs a check-in. She's going a bit crackerjack, if you know what I'm saying," he said as he circled his finger around his head, insinuating she was crazy. I sighed, appalled at the state of my former hunter team, and how I'd manage to let this vampire create some kind of bond with them.

I hesitated to say anything more. If I sparked any interest toward him it would create an inferno of events. Kora and Kasey made it clear they wanted very little to do with me as well. Whatever games he was up to, they'd insinuated they were fine on their own.

I ignored all other advances he made. He sighed and vanished, and I took a moment to look over the edge of the balcony, hiding in the shadows as I watched Fire tirelessly train Titan and Chris. I watched on with heightened interest by the way they interacted. Even though Fire never shifted from her wolf form, the children understood her command. She forced them to do various sets. From shifting back and forth to challenging one another both as human and wolf.

Not much to my surprise, Titan had the upper hand. She was her father's daughter after all. I wondered if over the years it would change when Chris physically became stronger, or if she'd be a natural, understanding how to use her body stealthily. Their movements were clumsy at the best of times, but few of their strikes landed with fierce precision. And it certainly wasn't from lack of concentration. They'd only trained for a few months within the Human Compound. It could only do so much to prepare them for the reality of now.

"I used to watch you in the same way when you were younger and trained, though similarly, I hid in the shadows so you'd never know I was overlooking your independence," my mother said behind me, leaning against the doorframe. I only wanted to sink further into the shadows. "It's good to see you've returned safely."

I dragged my eyes away from Titan and Chris and set them on my mother. She was magnificent in this lighting, beautiful in her Amazonian ways. I was now almost humiliated that I might not ever become what my mother was. A complexion I'd never have, an insecurity I'd never delved into. But as I slowly became undone, I realized that she remained stable and pragmatic throughout all of it—something I'd considered myself too, until recently.

"Yes, well, it will be up to Cesar and Chase as to whether the meeting was in vain or if they're willing to oblige to her terms," I embellished. I was too tired to explain what those terms were and how they centered primarily around me being used as leverage. I hadn't yet made my mind up as to how I felt about it.

"As expected," my mother grimaced, crossing her arms. "Louise reached out while you were gone. She wants to meet with us again."

"I only just got back," I grumbled. My mother and I both froze at that singular statement. As a hunter, never did we have the option to laze about nor complain. *I* had never complained.

"I know it's been a lot the last few months …" my mother said gently, the tone foreign, creating an uneasiness between us.

"Pretend I said nothing," I said, walking into the room. "What did she say it was about?" I froze when Julia looked up at me, tending to a small section of plants.

"Esmore," she said quietly to herself and began wiping at her sooted pants. Lavish fruits and vegetables grew from the small garden she was tending to. "I owe you an apology."

I raised my hand to her. "There's nothing to apologize for."

"I wanted him turned too. It wasn't fair that I blamed you because of my own grief and—"

"It's really not necessary. I will live with my decision as much as you will. I always had the right to take that away from you. I *did* allow this to happen. So please. Don't make it worse," I earnestly pleaded. I deserved her rage and the weight of her mourning. The man she'd fallen in love with was no longer here. Or from the brief moment I'd shared with him, he was certainly in a very dark and hindered place. And I worried, just like Chase, I'd fail to bring him back completely. Vampirism changed everyone in mysterious ways. The outcome was never in our hands. Only a cruel fate could be the handler. Julia reluctantly nodded and buried her head back into her work with the plants.

"Have you seen him?" she asked reluctantly.

"I have." I turned to my mother, avoiding the discussion. "What did Louise want to discuss?" Whatever was on the other side of that conversation compelled me more than the one lingering in this room.

My mother was hesitant to hijack Julia's attention, but she was built for pragmatism over emotion. "She said it had to do with the wolves and Campture's whereabouts and current scheme."

"Campture?" Both Julia and I snapped to attention. A tension rolled in my stomach, shortly followed by an alarmed check-up from Chase. I was mentally teleported back to that basement and what Campture had allowed James to do to me in that room. What *they'd* done all in the hope to find information about my heart and gift. *I'm okay,* I lied to Chase, pulling myself back from that flashback and building a wall so Chase couldn't reciprocate my stress. I never wanted to pull him or me back into that night filled terror again.

"When do we leave?" I asked, now finding more incentive to go. If I could cross paths with them once more … if I could end this hunt and bounty on my head all because of what they'd started … if I could finish it at the place of where it all began … maybe then I'd find eternal peace.

"Cesar said he'd discuss the logistics with Tythian when he returned. He's reluctant to let us leave. During the time you were gone, one of Cesar's allied covens had been ambushed and taken out."

"The Council moved against another coven?" I asked, taking a seat on the recently made bed. A few rugs and dirty blankets had been thrown in the corner of the room where I imagined Fire rested. I wondered if

Titan and Chris slept with her as cubs or if they resided with Julia in human form on the bed.

"They have been the last few months, more so than usual. It would appear it's hastened with the lead up of the Council meeting coming to fruition," my mother shared, leaning against the doorframe.

"Do you think they know Cesar's rallying alliances to attack around the time of the Council meeting?" I'd hoped not. The best form of attack was with the element of surprise.

"We have belief they'd have knowledge of this. Depending on what level of magnitude their understanding of that is, is a completely different question."

Everyone was starting to play their hands. It was strange to have no major factor in the articulation of the plan. I was seemingly being told where to be and when. While Cesar and Chase focused on the main war, my mother and I were acquiring our own information and implementation in a way that we knew how. It was a shame that revolved around our association with the Hunter Guilds. "We still have time," is all I said to no one in particular.

We had time to strategize and gain the upper hand in this war. Hopefully, we would last out while the Council picked covens off one by one. I crossed my legs and perched my elbow to hold up my heavy head.

"Why don't you get some rest," my mother suggested. I needed rest. But I wanted answers more. And I could only rest with Chase.

"It's around that time," Julia said with warmth in her tone. She stood up, flicking bits of dirt off her pants. The corner she'd recently inhabited had a few stray leaves and dirt spillage.

"Time for what?" I asked, curious as to where Julia had a place to be in an institute like this.

"We've seen him every day," my mother spoke on her behalf before I could argue my discouragement. "I conceal her scent so they're not so compelled to … lose control," my mother said, trying to refrain from the ugly truth of what 'lose control' entailed. "Though admittedly, Tori seems to have an unexpected form of restraint." I'd noted the same thing.

"Dillian wasn't exactly brimming with excitement when I visited him before," I said sluggishly.

"He's never enthralled to see me either," Julia added with that backbone I'd noted in her before. "But even if he doesn't want me there,

I'll support him through this." My mother and I exchanged a glance. It wasn't something to be supported through. It wasn't a condition. It was a complete and utter change, and for all we knew, Dillian might never return as the person we'd known and grown to love. That cold and vacant form in the cellar was a shell, something sinister lurking now. I hoped he'd come back, but I was too fatigued to even raise my hopes.

"Good luck then," I suggested, having nothing more to say. If anything could bring him back, then surely it would be Julia. I was, at this point, nothing but fuel to his fire of resentment.

"Try to get some rest, Esmore," my mother added as they left. "You'll need your energy for when we visit Louise, and who knows what that might entail afterward."

"Indeed," I said lowly. The door clicked behind them, and it wasn't long until I felt the presence of Darcy standing station outside my door as guard.

Get some rest, Esmore, I can feel your fatigue from here, Chase's velvety voice echoed through our link, and he was sending waves of influencing fatigue over me.

I was apprehensive to sleep. If I did, I'd be bombarded by the shadow that would linger, or injection of Fier creeping into my sleep. But the call was beckoning, and within seconds, I had my head on the pillow.

I'll join you shortly, Chase cooed, being the last thing I remembered before I was swept into a bitter-sweet sleep.

Chapter 12

They were waiting for me. A phantom that always waited but never spoke. I circled the old wall of my Hunter Guild as if on any regular duty coming back from a mission. I was yet again alone, a metaphor that wasn't lost on me. The mist was thicker than usual today, rising to my thighs with an unrelenting cold chill to it.

I wondered if the presence that lingered and watched me from the treetops brought me to this place because it knew my mother had mentioned James and Campture for the first time in what felt like months, even years.

"Are you going to come out?" I probed the entity and stared off into the unsettling darkness and depths of the leafless forest. I could hear in the distance a bird making a deep hoot. The rest of the forest had become quiet with the anticipation of what was to come.

I looked down at my usual attire, leather boots, pants, and sleeveless shirt. I had my Barnett crossbow and sword strapped to me. Nothing felt out of place except for the reality that this entire dream was abnormal.

I looked up at the gate to the fortified Guild. It had since perished and burned to the ground. But right now, it was as if nothing had happened. I'd laid my eyes upon this entry so many times. A bizarre nostalgia crept under my skin. I could feel the lingering presence of many beyond the wall. It felt like dark, unseen hands were reaching out to grasp and touch me. I had the urge to slap them away had I been no wiser to this being a dream. There was very little I could do here. And yet, the entity often didn't do much at all other than spook me with graphic fears.

A twig snapped behind me, and I swung around, retracting my Barnett crossbow and mounting an arrow. I lowered it slightly, unsure of the guarded message the entity was trying to give me. Was he trying to madden me?

There in a dirty white long dress, stood Whitney. She looked pale, too cold, and disorientated as her gaze scattered about me and then eventually focused. She was unmoving as if she didn't know what to do.

"Esmore?" I turned to face the familiar voice.

"Sydney?" I said, startled by his sheer size that seemed to draw the forest into him like it had no existence at all. It was nothing but darkness behind him. Blood marred his neck from where I'd bitten him and ultimately ended his life.

"Esmore." Teary's thick accent broke my fixation on Sydney, and I spun to my right. There in front of the thick, dead forest was Teary. She had soot and fire marks all over her body as if her own wild flames had licked at her. Her neck was marred with blood in the same way she'd been killed.

"What—" A weight clamped down on my shoulders and back as those invisible hands began to drag me toward the Guild entrance. Was this my guilt, so evidently displayed in three forms of those I'd failed the most?

I tried to pull free of the groping hands, but they tugged back further, unarming me. Whispers began to rise behind the walls in an uneven chant from voices of hunters I'd once known, but couldn't place their face now. Had they all died at the Guild? Did so few survive after the attack and ambush?

"You did this," one of them whispered as they tugged at my hair.

"You should've saved us," another condoned. I felt the mighty weight and presence of the entity mask over me as I was pinned with my back to the wall of the gate. It felt like I was falling into a dark hole that was soon to take me under. A robed figure walked out from the forest, hardly receiving any notice from the others as he crept by Teary's side.

"They're not all dead," another voice whispered, startling me. *Who wasn't all dead?* I tried to reef an arm free so I could defend myself against the entity that was finally revealing itself.

Whitney's gasp drew my attention as she revealed bright tiny little fangs. A savage snarl vibrated through Sydney as he too showcased glistening fangs. A tear pricked my eyes as I circled the group that was imposing on me. Teary uncharacteristically smiled at me, her fangs a prick of pain. She had never been turned. She'd been completely drained. They were all … dead. All of them. Their ghosts here to haunt me.

The hooded entity slowly raised their head, but only enough to reveal a firm male jawline and large fangs that appeared with his wicked smile. *"It's always for fun and games,"* he said in a sensual voice that rattled my core. His voice came from nowhere and yet everywhere at once. An echo in this world he'd created.

"Who are you?" I seethed furiously. His smile only crept higher. With the click of his fingers, the three of them pounced at me, barring me as bait as I was pinned against the gates, with hands of the dead I couldn't see.

The moment my dream was interrupted, I knew it was because Chase had joined me, his weight pressing against me as I was caught in an in-between state of sleep and waking up. He was like a safety net for me, covering me in a way where that entity couldn't reach me. I dozed in and out as my mind lingered on the reasons why I had such dreams and what the entity gained from these encounters.

Chase, too, had admitted he felt its presence before, but it seemed Chase was a deterrent to him. Or it appeared that it was only strong enough to take on me alone while I rested. I plummeted at the thought of it lingering in New York when we met with the Head Hunter Guild. My mother and Lincon had warned me not to approach it. I wondered with sickening delight, to bring this to an end, as to whether it, no … *he* would be there when we met with Louise and the others again.

I could feel Chase's influence pulling me back under, dragging me into the depths of sleep. A proper sleep where I would not be attacked or fiddled with in an uncanny way. With Chase, I was safe and so easily fatigued in his embrace that had me tumbling into a true and rewarding stupor.

I woke to Chase embracing me from behind with his hand curled around my waist. Where I might've once wished to wake up to easy breathing whistling past my ear, I'd grown accustomed to Chase's sturdy and unflinching frame. There was no heartbeat to be heard, once I might've considered it an abomination, but now I followed the easy flutter of the link we shared between us as if it was a living pulse itself. He was safe and resting. Dead to the world, in a literal sense as we found comfort beside one another.

I knew this moment would be short-lived until the others would return, and from the casting of the sun in the small alcove window, we hadn't been asleep for long. I went to raise myself from the bed, but Chase's iron grip was firm around my waist. *Stay like this for a little longer,* he pleaded.

I nestled back into his shoulder. I thought he was sleeping. But much like me, I imagined that came at the cost of always having senses vulnerable with one eye open. He was weighed down heavily by guilt, not wanting to meet my gaze. This thing that was coming between us was the guilt he held for puncturing the knife into my heart.

Chase, I'm okay. And you know we had to do it, I reminded him. He wouldn't let me twist to face him.

I never want to know the feeling of hurting you again. I understood and pitied him for having to do such a thing. But as I reminded him, if I had to, I would have done the same. Knowing that he would live and it was better for us.

Chase, it had to be done. And it will only hurt us more if you pull away from me because of this. Please, I need you right now, more than ever. I entwined my fingers with his. *Please, I've missed you. Don't pull away from me now.*

He was fighting with himself. Unable to atone for what he considered his wrongdoing and corruption of his greatest values. I was his everything, and hurting me—that act itself had broken a small piece inside of him. But we didn't have time to let things divide us with the war looming so closely. We needed to be indifferent to the many things we'd hate ourselves for doing. We just needed to keep moving forward—together.

It killed me not being able to touch you for the past four days, I admitted. I craved him. His finger curled around my now loosened hair. I looked down on our attire that we still hadn't changed since returning from

Tracey's Council. Now awake and alert, it was a priority to wash away that experience and Patricia's grubby hands on my familiar.

I'm sorry I put you through that, he censored, pressing a cold kiss to my shoulder. Relief swept through me as he slowly released his guilt that was coming between us. I twisted in his grip so I could look at him. He'd unbound his hair from the tie he'd been wearing. I pushed back part of his fringe, tucking it behind his ear.

It served its purpose, I said gently. *But I will NEVER share you with another,* I growled possessively. *Especially with that little brat.*

Chase let out a full belly laugh, the sound fluttering through the room and making my toes curl slightly. He caught my hand and pressed a heated kiss to my open palm. "I only want you," he said with so much tenderness that the unsettlement and anxiety of the day melted away carelessly. With Chase in this moment, everything felt like it was safe and certain. As if a thought just occurred to him, he reached for his pocket. "Which means I can finally claim you again." He pulled out the blue gemmed necklace, the one matching his earring.

"Well, you've already claimed me in more than one way," I growled, placing my hands on his ass and squeezing. He chuckled, the vibration elating me with the same joyful and carefree endurance. He wrapped his hands around my neck and fastened the necklace.

I rubbed the blue gem with all the sentiment in the world. Such a small gesture, but this was where it had all begun for us. He'd claimed me before I'd even understood its power or force. "And I will continue to do so." He curled his hand around my throat in a possessive manner as he tilted my head back slightly. I hissed in anticipation for the kiss I'd been longing for. Not touching Chase or being a part of his euphoria was a starvation I never wanted to know again.

His kiss was slow and sensual, claiming and marking all the same. His gentleness turned into an eagerness, a savorable delicacy as his tongue claimed mine. I tugged him forward by the shirt, desperate to have him closer, consorting to have his scent smear me with total domination.

This dress had me thinking wicked thoughts, Chase said, grabbing under my thigh and pulling it up over his waist. My thick leather boot dangled on the other side of him as he ground into me and through the very sheer material of the dress. I could feel his arousal, better yet, I could smell and taste it all the same.

"Chase," I murmured his name, like the elixir it was on my lips. I could feel his length rubbing against me through the material, the friction igniting passion I could only feel for him.

A light tap on the door interrupted us. Chase continued grinding against me as a small unearthly growl crept from his throat for the intrusion. I continued to kiss him, excited all in the same, but I could sense Yolo on the other side of the door.

"Come back later," Chase yelled out to the door. The second tap that rattled the door forced us very slowly to our senses. Chase let out a depleted sigh, hot and bothered as he threw himself back into the bed with a dramatic sigh. "Two minutes is all I ask," he said childishly.

I pressed my fingers against his lips with a small smile. "Yea right, two minutes. You and me both." The link between us glowed. Chase filled me like no other, quickly erasing the shouldering thoughts I carried like weights.

Yolo stepped into the room with an abnormal steadiness to his usual bouncy step. "Bad time?" he asked with a cheeky grin. Though his childish charm remained, I'd noticed the change in him recently and felt it had something to do with his counterpart Jenn.

Chase eyed him seriously. "You know it is!" Though he returned the smile.

"Good to see you back. Cesar informed us of the disposition we're now in and the two days to decide. All exciting days still, I see."

"It would appear so," I replied. At no point had I been included in these conversations or even asked what part I wanted to play in this. I was at prime risk if I were to be in that position. Yet, if it were asked of me, I'd do it. It was simply unfavorable that I wasn't included in the conversations.

I swirled my finger as if to indicate to Yolo to look away. He was confused as to why until I collected a new pair of leather pants and shirt. The moment my fingers brushed against the bottom of my dress and lifted up, he was abashed and looked to the door. I could feel Chase's smile as he watched me very attentively dress. His gaze traced the edges of my body like it was the first time he'd ever had the chance to study it.

I might've been putting a little more effort into my change than usual. I felt free as a bird once I had the chance to change my attire into its usual battle-ready appearance. I reapplied my weapons. Always comforted to have them on me, unlike the days when I had to check my weapons in and out at the Guild.

"Cesar wanted to see you, Chase," Yolo said. "There's been another attack on a coven."

"Another one?" Chase perked up out of bed, snapping us out from our arousal. "The last one was only days ago."

"Yea, luckily they didn't overpower them like the last, but it's not great. Cesar's in communication with them now. They want to settle in here to relocate for the time being, but Cesar's not budging. He's worried it'll only draw attention to our location, but it's causing friction."

"I have no doubt." Chase sighed, flicking off the bed and readjusting himself so his erection wasn't so prominent. Yolo pretended not to see which only forced Chase to smirk. He'd never been shy.

"And I thought I'd let you know that the cubs and Fire are on their way," Yolo advised. The thought of confronting Titan and Chris made me uneasy. I wasn't yet ready to face them.

"I need to go," Chase said, pressing a kiss to my cheek.

"You two are so domesticated," Yolo said. I turned to prod at his taunt until I saw the vacant gaze in his expression and held my tongue. I realized he wasn't taunting us, he was thinking of another time ... of Jenn.

Yolo and I followed Chase out the door. Darcy was no longer stationed at the door, relieved the moment Chase had entered the room. But I felt him lingering close by, as Chase had stationed him as my personal guard. I felt the presence of Fire coming up the staircase which meant Titan and Chris were homebound.

"You need to face them, you realize that, don't you?" Yolo said precariously.

"Yes," I admitted. "But not today." I heaved myself over the balcony. The wind breezed past me. My feet jolted slightly as I landed smoothly and predatory-like and continued my walk casually.

"Fire isn't going to be very happy," Yolo called out after me. Of that I was certain. I had never considered myself a woman who ran away from confrontation or responsibility. But after my dream and lurking dejection after being haunted by Sydney's ghost or my own guilt and paranoia, I wasn't quite ready to face his daughter after my recent failings. The vision of dead wolves sprung to mind as I pushed it back into the depths of the vault I'd locked it into.

I'd seen many dead bodies. I'd killed so many with my bare hands. But they'd always been vampires and sabers … but everything had changed. Now I saw many things, and I did even worse. So no, I could not face the innocence of a child I'd sworn to protect, today.

But maybe after I'd found out more information on the wolves that Louise was able to provide, I'd be able to salvage myself somehow. Be able to face the little girl who I'd wished I could offer another path. Anything other than this.

CHAPTER 13

I CIRCLED BACK through the front entrance of the institute. The giant doors were already open. Instead of their usual central line to divide the covens, the gargoyles were sporadically placed. Though no vampires seemed to be crossing boundaries, they were leering at one another in a bored manner.

In a separate room, I could hear the smash of bottles and profanity. Catching my attention and resting beside the door was Clarissa, who watched Spungee play with the same rodent he'd acquired days ago. Now it stunk and had begun to rot. I looked away, vexed by the gruesome plaything he'd acquired as he gnawed on its ear.

"That dress was becoming on you," she said in her usual monotone. I peered down at her Lolita dress and style. I'd seen her in *only* that dress, and yet she somehow maintained its prestige with not one ounce of blood, dirt, or odor. Not that vampires had to deal with such things. The minority of what I now dealt with was tearing my shirts as wings sprouted from my back.

"It wasn't to my liking."

She said nothing but simply assessed her perfectly framed nails. "The coven is becoming weary of the news that other covens are being targeted. Do you think we should relocate?"

I wasn't certain of her motive and why she would ask me when others were listening in on our conversation. Chase was their leader, but I supposed it was a paramount of respect that I would know what his answer and inclination would be. Their lives depended on it.

"I don't know what Cesar and Chase have agreed to yet. But in my opinion, I think they'll suggest we stay for the time being. We haven't been here long. The likelihood of them finding our whereabouts so quickly is low."

"Yes, but you have had traitors," she said nonchalantly. Had it been anyone else I might've made an example of her and how daring she was to undermine our protection. But I'd grown to realize it was her bland personality that hadn't known pleasure or enjoyment for the majority of her existence. She was purely matter-of-fact. It was true, an assassin had broken in only a week ago. But that was because Linda had guided them here. And she had since been dealt with.

Since Cesar and my mother had stretched out their gift and concealment of our territory to deter anyone who might stumble across our scent or noise, the chances of them being able to enter our 'hidden' territory was lacking. But so had it been with the hunters when they were attacked.

I furrowed my eyebrows. Only someone who knew their specific location had been tipped off or stumbled randomly across their hut. A stark thought rooted in my mind. Only very few knew their location. My mind jumped to the few members who'd helped build the second hut for the wolves. I didn't have a specific list of which members those were. I looked in the direction of where they loitered. They watched me wearily as most often did now. I'd once led them into a glorified battlefield. Now they looked at me very differently. Sure, they'd follow me into battle, they had enough respect for my ability to fight. But past that ... well, everything had gone to shit for them the moment Cesar had dragged me into their coven.

"Linda has been dealt with," I said to Clarissa, wanting to hurry away and confirm my suspicions with Yolo as to who had directly come into contact with their location. Even then, they couldn't pinpoint the exact location because they were teleported in. Unless ... the person who'd done the damage was the only person who could teleport. *Tythian.* But he had been with us …

"But have they all been dealt with?" she asked in a low tone that only I could hear.

"What do you mean by that?" I asked with gravel in my tone. It was a warning. If she was purposefully messing with me or trying to insinuate drama, it would be her who'd take the fall.

Clarissa had suddenly noticed the various glances in our direction. "I'm simply saying," she said no longer bothering to lower her voice as others in the room listened in. "That I imagine there might be other traitors amongst us. A group of vampires this size, and an upcoming war, that's bound to tempt some with ulterior motives—in my experience anyway."

She was acutely aware of our onlookers. She was particularly the most observant I'd noticed from Chase's coven, but it didn't mean she had names. When I rolled my mind over hers, I could only gather remnants of superstition.

"Or you can pretend like I said nothing," Clarissa said, not at all appreciating the snarls and stares being thrown her way for the insinuation she'd boldly made. "After all, it's not like you're one to listen."

I restrained myself enough not to jump on her. There was no malice or mischief in her eye, just a hollowness of observation and merely existing.

"I'm sure Chase will inform you shortly of their decision," I said and spun on my toes again. With perfect timing, my mother and Julia were making their way down the narrow hallway to cross over the path to the other wing.

Vampires shriveled around me, too scared to catch a whiff of Julia as she meekly walked past. The temptation of flaunting a huntress about in a houseful of vampires was savage, but their instinct to attack and feast was countered by my mother's ability to conceal her scent.

I met them atop the staircase, still not willing to join them for the walk and confront the wolf pups who were in my room. Instead, I walked in the opposite direction, tracing the link between Chase and me. It wouldn't be long until my mother would join me, and we could debrief on seeing Louise and what information she had to provide. And then when I returned, I could talk to Yolo about what members knew of the location where the hunters and wolves had been.

For the first time in a long time, after obtaining a few moments of sleep, I felt that I could think clearly enough.

I could hear them arguing down the hall. Mostly Cesar screaming and shattering glass about the place in his fit of fury of being trumped by the Vampire Council. I braced myself with my hand on the door, not at all wanting to be a part of this discussion. Before I opened it, my mother was already back down and stalking my way.

I tapped on the door. "No!" Cesar barked back. My mother pushed me aside and opened the door. I peered over her shoulder at the daring look he glanced her way. Under what I imagined was her frightful glare, he threw his hands in the air defeated.

She entered, and I slipped in behind her. Chase was trying to refrain his smirk. My mother and Cesar's relationship still bothered me, I didn't linger around long enough to see how they interacted, but when I did, they were not so silently butting heads.

Tythian, Balzar, and Connor were in the room. I'd noted Yolo hadn't yet returned and was probably standing guard with the wolves, which I could imagine rubbed Cesar the wrong way. I stood across from Chase and briefed a glance at the map with numerous circles and colors. The longer I studied it, the more confused I became. Obviously, some pinned the location of those already targeted, and others perhaps the few Council's they might've known of.

Between Tythian and Chase, they had a few Council locations, but not all of them, and that's where Tracey's alliance was beneficial for their current plan.

"What is it, Trinity?" Cesar growled, and I could tell he was fighting against himself from imploding once again. She gently placed her hand on his forearm. The gesture was foreign to my eyes. My mother was as cold as Cesar, but there was a tenderness and comfort between them that I'd dare say might've been the closest thing they could cast as love. Perhaps behind closed doors, and unsuspecting of the peers in this room, they truly did nurture their relationship and lower their guards. Just like Chase and I often only did with one another.

"We must leave soon. To meet with hunters," she said delicately.

What's this about? Chase intruded on my mind. I quickly mind-dumped the discussion I'd had with my mother, and I could feel the tension straddle him. He eyed me from across the table, still suited in that ridiculous outfit from Tracey's Council. He wasn't at all comfortable with the idea of me risking another encounter with them, especially with the mention of James and Campture.

A predatory darkness crept over his gaze, and I found myself sending soothing thoughts his way. He was one of few who knew what had happened to me in that basement. And he wanted to kill them just as gruesomely as I did. *We're only meeting with them to find out what information they have about the wolves, and it serves us to know what Campture and James are doing considering they stuck a target on my back.*

The hunters can't be trusted, he warned. He was the first to warn me against them even when I still served my own Guild.

I know, but what choice do we have? Any piece of information or alliance was better than nothing during such perilous times.

"I never agreed to that," Cesar said in a low tone. His knuckles whitened as he fastened his grip on the edge of the table. I was certain he was about to flip it.

"Well, it's not for you to agree to. It depends on whether you would prefer us to travel by foot or teleportation," my mother said with no inclination of succumbing to his peer pressure.

Connor's icy blue gaze fastened to Tythian who said nothing but was clearly irritated. His usual calm and collected demeanor slowly melting under the scrutiny of this upcoming war. He'd become the safest and fastest means of transport, but it was wearily costing his patience. I assessed him from the side, skeptical that I was letting my personal grudge against him cloud my judgment. Would he betray us? Had he betrayed us? Was it him who'd hurt the others and attacked the hunters and wolves? I knew logically speaking he'd been with us. He was the one to teleport us into the chaos that remained.

What are you thinking about? Chase asked me cautiously. I'd closed off to him, hindering my own thoughts. Chase and Tythian were friends. As much as I seethed Tythian I couldn't accuse him without proof. Especially considering who he was and where he stood at this table.

Connor's gaze was now fastened on me as he took me in mutely. No one was so daring as to look at my mother directly as she so easily opposed their coven leader.

"We can't rely on their information," Cesar held his stance, but I could tell by the way his shoulders sagged he'd already forfeited to my mother.

"Because they're hunters? It's no different to the alliances you are stringing with Vampire Councils." I could hear the hostility in my mother's tone. She didn't trust the hunters any more than I did. But she had put her trust in Louise's words and worth.

"But we haven't decided if we're even agreeing to Tracey's terms. Is it wise to take a secondary risk with Esmore being so far away from the security of this coven?" Tythian argued.

Cesar looked up at him through his bushy eyebrows, sagging into his shoulders over the table.

"And is it up to you as to whether my daughter will be held as leverage? Or will she have a choice in the matter?" my mother quipped back. Tythian's throat jutted out slightly as he wearily looked over to Cesar who had a stark warning in his gaze. Speaking back to my mother snidely wouldn't be condoned.

"If we keep losing covens at this rate, it might be the only option we have," Cesar said, depleted. "If we pull back now on our agreement with her, she'll likely go directly to Oppollo, and if he knows Esmore's still alive, then he'll start seeking her out again."

"Doesn't exactly make for good reasoning as to why she should be held as bait in the very same room that he'll be orchestrating," Chase was quick to reply.

"Esmore?" Connor asked. I was startled that as the others bickered on my behalf, he had been the one watching me, curious as to what my answer and decision for myself might be. I couldn't let them in on my first feelings and desires. The thought of being amongst a roomful of the most powerful vampires should've terrified me, but it left an ecstasy-like jolt to my system. I could end them all there. So shallow were my thoughts, when in reality I knew I wouldn't harbor the strength to take them all on.

But this vampire side of me didn't face reason. Where some might've understood survival, placement, and self-preservation, I only dawdled at the idea of facing Oppollo once more. If I could end this now for everyone, then they would all be safe. I was deluded into thinking that maybe no one else would have to fight.

Even then, I was supposedly not there to act but simply stand as a bystander under their noses so no one knew. That was what Tracey had said. But she could betray us as much as anyone else. I realized then that Connor asked me, not out of pity for not being able to voice my own opinion or thoughtfulness to my safety. He knew I'd say yes as the ever-ready huntress prepared to always be in the midst of battle. If I said yes, we'd stop dancing around this argument. When I said yes it would put all of their minds at ease, so they didn't feel like they were forcing me. Because even if I said no, there still might've been a chance they'd make me.

The thought of Tracey's and my conversation came back. Was I simply a pawn to them? I circled my gaze around the room. My mothers' hand was still on Cesar's forearm. Did my mother and Cesar look at me as some prized piece on their board or did I actually hold that much value?

Tythian and Connor would want me to go, easing the transaction, but it was Cesar's precaution around my safety that would block the ease of that. And Chase. I looked at my darling lover, familiar, and husband. He shook his head once. No matter the cost or risk, he didn't want me to go. Selfishly and lovingly, he refused to let me be in the center of such danger without him by my side.

This is who we are, I said to him gently before I stood to attention in front of the room. "If it is best. Then I'll do it."

Chase turned his back and walked out the door. I watched on, perplexed. Did I walk after him or leave him be?

Chase ... I called out to him, startled by his response.

You can't keep making these decisions on your own. It's not just about you, he growled back through our line with a fierceness that was purely directed at me. For all his love and tenderness, it was the first time he'd ever been mad with *me.*

"Leave him be," my mother said from behind me as I stared at the door dumbfounded.

"We still have two days to decide. Hopefully, we can find a way around it," Cesar said, staring at the board once again. Tythian and Connor exchanged a glance, no doubt thinking the same as I did. But was there another way?

How was this selfish? I thought by doing this I was taking others out of harm's way? Chase wanted this alliance with Tracey. So how had he insinuated I was being selfish because of it?

I reached down our line to communicate with him, but he'd shut me out. I gawked at the door, suddenly feeling very alone and cold. Chase had never shut me out before. And for the first time, I tasted the bitterness of how I'd been treating him. Of the small denials I'd often block from him through our connection and the secrets I would hide.

It was a bitter coldness harsher than the billowing blaze outside Tracey's Council. Chase was indisputably angry with me.

Chapter 14

CHASE AVOIDED ME right until I was about to take my leave. He'd opened our line, bidding me farewell and that he loved me, no matter how infuriated he was with me at the time. I didn't have the strength to focus on him or the unraveling of his angst and why I'd upset him so much. I understood he wanted to protect me, but I could only be so cosseted. Though in his eyes, he probably saw me as the furthest thing from being coddled and deemed me reckless. But what choice did I have?

I'd deal with that conversation when I returned, for now, I had a new mission to focus on. One that fluttered an anxiety within me. Not because I would be meeting with Louise and her group of rebels again, but because the mention of Campture and James stirred untouched wounds that had been festering this whole time. I thought I was above it. I thought I'd pushed it into the Pandora's Box like everything else. But the possibility of encountering them again … of their names alone put me on edge.

Despite having already confronted Oppollo's assassins, Cesar instructed us to continue wearing the capes and masks. We hadn't done so at Tracey's Council because we didn't want to be misinterpreted and greeted as Oppollo's messengers. But now we were back to our old tactics, confusing other Councils that might've stumbled across our engagement. With wicked delight, I was curious about what rumor or motives would be made if another Council thought they saw Oppollo's hand-selected assassins meeting with a group of hunters.

Like last time, Cesar wouldn't allow us to go without an arsenal. And also like last time, Lincon snaked his way to the forefront. Except this time, he was adamant Kora and Kasey came along for a 'field trip.' I was hesitant to allow them to come. I had concerns that seeing a stable organization from the Hunter Guild might trigger them in some way. I hadn't been on a mission with them since … everything had gone down.

But even then, if I was willing to have Tythian, Lincon, and a league of vampires at my back, I could certainly have two hunters who I'd fought with through blood and loss for years, even if we did have our indifferences.

Kasey grumbled her complaint about the stuffy mask and being forced to wear—as she'd like to call it—a body bag. After she'd said it, it did strangely remind me of the many bodies we'd covered with the black cloth before setting them alight in the Hunter Guild's shrine.

Once again, Tythian and Balzar were instructed to heavily watch over my mother and me. In groups of two, Tythian teleported our handful of twelve atop a hill that looked down on the remains of New York City. Daylight had begun to drift to night, and I looked up at the half moon with a grimace. I'd once valued its beauty. I now felt perplexed by its symbolism and knowledge it counted down the days to when the others would be forced to shift into wolves against their will.

We watched on for a few moments, my mother leading the team as we searched through the thick fog for any signs of a setup or ambush. We'd decided to meet at the same bridge as last time. Its structure was still baffling to me much like all the cities. Despite the world going to ruins and the cities often sheltering sabers, New York was the exception. It was a time before mine, but these towering buildings and bridges would last forever even generations after my own to come. A lifetime and era that will live on forever, but only in its remains. A sad reminder to those who might've known what it was like to exist in such a time, but even then, it'd been three hundred years. If anyone was still alive to see it, it was because they'd been turned into a vampire. The very reason the war began.

"Someone's coming," Lincon gasped and bounced on his tiptoes excitedly. I edged a cutting gaze in his direction. I placed my hand on my face mask, ensuring it was still securely tight before following my mother down the slippery slope of the hill. We glided down with ease, dropping off silently into the night. The fog billowed around us. The others waited atop.

We came to a standstill, waiting for them to come into view so we could greet them mid-way. When they did, they evidently outnumbered me and my mother. But arrows were nestled into bows behind us, our group ready to attack. My mother and I approached alone, if only in good merit and feigning trusted comradery.

"It's good to see you again, Trinity, and that our form of communication is viable," Louise said in the way of introduction. I hadn't asked my mother in what way they were able to communicate with one another and so quickly. But I decided to let my mother hold her tricks and methods to herself. If it was an important detail, she would've disclosed it to me.

"It's rather stimulating when something goes to plan once in a while," my mother said with all the seriousness of a steel beam. And yet I feel as if that was her attempt at a joke. One that was received well by Louise who offered a polite smile. Beside Louise was Sabe. His dashing smile unnerved me like always. The other four flanked them, weapons loosely an arms width away.

Louise and Sabe looked into the distance, upon the hill with our small arsenal that was ready to attack at any moment.

Sabe squinted. "It's smaller than I remember from last time," he said coyly. His voice was as smooth and coaxing as the sweetest syrups I'd once been allowed to try. It was much like Fier in the same way, seemingly sweet but entrapping if you got tangled in his web.

"What news is so urgent?" my mother asked Louise, ignoring his charm. He only smiled wider and rested his gaze on me. I watched him coolly, letting my lack of words reach him with a bored expression. I wanted him to know *he was beneath me.* It was all a standard negotiation stance of intimidation even if we were coming under the pretense of being allies.

"Once you informed Michelle of these wolf shifting humans—"

"Werewolves," I interrupted her. "They're called werewolves."

My mother and Louise looked surprised by my interruption. But the long-winded name was vexing, and it had been Fire who'd insisted they be called that. And so, I wanted to honor her. She wanted a label for their kind, and so I would spread it.

"Werewolves?" Louise seemed to taste the word. "Michelle made it a priority to send word out to other Guilds and small teams in surrounding areas to check on some of the human government bases. As you said, few of them are involved with this scheme. Michelle wanted to lay low and see what they might do until one of them attacked a Guild's human camp. The hunters were able to overpower them, but there were still many casualties."

"For the hunters?" my mother clarified.

"For both the humans and the hunters. It's not as you described, when they bite vampires, it's deadly to them. Hunters are definitely an exception to this. But the wounds were enough … not all of the hunters survived. As fate would have it that was around the time of Campture's arrival and her wandering Guild."

My mother's stance was rigid. Campture had always been a forceful woman, one who so daringly wanted to move up in the ranks. Within our Guild, she was already at the top. Now with no place to call home, who knew what her wicked schemes or objective was. What made her even more poisonous was her ability to read minds. She could feed off anyone's thoughts or fears.

"What did she offer Michelle?" my mother asked presumptuously.

"In exchange for sanctuary for her people, she offered Michelle that her team go out personally and exterminate the closest compounds. She anticipates when word gets around amongst the human government, they might think twice about attacking their human camps."

"It's an all-out war," Sabe said, his voice not so swimmingly smooth. "It'll be the hunters preying on the human government when our attention should be focused on the Vampire Council's movement before their meeting. But if this plague continues to spread, then there won't be any humans to protect."

"You don't agree with Campture's judgment?" my mother said coldly. Intangible thoughts howled through my mind at the thought of what I considered to be an injustice to the werewolves. They had no choice in this matter. They were being played as pawns and considered as some plague. They *were* human. Just as much as Fire, Titan, and Chris were.

They didn't ask for this, and it went against my instincts to hunt them just because they were being controlled by the wrong hand.

It might've been biased, I'd hunted vampires all my life. But they had the intent to kill and conquer. These werewolves … they were survivors and fumbling in this new world like newborn babes. If they had the right leader and direction, then their power could be used for a better purpose.

That's when I noticed Louise's cool gaze on me. Like all the other times I'd met her, I was unnerved by that one eye and eyepatch that seemed to see through me. "I don't agree with Campture's intent." Louise looked back up toward the hilltop at our arsenal. "And again, there's little I can say so publicly because of your audience. But it would be problematic not only for us but *you* if she continues on this path."

"For me?" I asked speculatively.

"The way my foresight works is subjective. It can change at any moment when new elements are introduced. Time changes and so does one's path. If I were to interrupt certain sequences, then it'll change the outcome. It's something that weighs on my conscience, but in this case, if we don't intervene it will be much worse. This is a warning. They must be dealt with *now*. Not that it's much better to have a plague of wolves running about, but what it will create and the power Campture will receive from this is …"

"She wants to take Michelle's seat," Sabe interrupted abruptly.

"Sabe," she hissed.

"What?" He let out a hearty laugh that probably had most swooning for him. My mother couldn't have stiffened any more beside me. Nor could I. The unquenchable image of Campture ruling in the highest position for any hunter was disconcerting.

"And let me guess, her embarrassment after her Guild falling because of my daughter is not something she will ever let go?" my mother said solemnly.

"Not until death," she added.

"Yes …" Sabe eluded. "And it's also not good for any of us. We don't necessarily agree with how Michelle is running the Guilds, and for a long time have had concerns about the future of our kind. This would only interfere with those plans. For everyone involved."

There was a lot of pressure in this conversation, what they expected of us, even what the vampires saw me as. The threat Oppollo deemed me as. Everyone had a preconception of who I was and what I would do. And yet right now, I felt like a singular warrior standing beside her mother, seething and raging at the idea of my snaky Head Huntress trying to hurt me in another way. This was personal in every single way. Pockets of memory continued to foam to the surface, reminding me of what they'd done in that basement. Of a time I had been so weak and powerless and couldn't protect myself. It wasn't what they had done. It was that they were one of few that sinisterly overpowered me and ignited my first sense of shame.

"And you can't move a hand against them?" I asked. My voice was vacant. So far away as I drew my gaze toward the city beyond them. If what they were saying was true, it was highly probable Campture, James, and all the others who opposed us were sheltered in the city right now. They were so close. I could reach them. I could snuff the life out of them.

Sabe answered my question. "If we were to do anything, then it would raise speculation and be an act against Michelle's orders. He approved of this. Our hands are tied. However, if vampires were to intervene …"

"Then it would look like you had no part," I finished for him. I toyed with the idea of walking into the thick smog of the unknown and creep into the city. To sneak into their rooms while they slept and to slit their throats. The vampire part of me inside danced and paddled in the thought.

"Esmore," my mother jarred me awake. My vision had gone purple, and my fangs had slipped out. The imagery of my blade sweeping across their throats had consumed me.

"Apologies," I said with a sinister tone as I tried to draw myself back in. They might not be able to see the fangs beneath the mask, but my mother knew my fluorescent purple eyes were a telling sign of my vampire coming forth. "The thought of reuniting with our old Guild fills me with a wicked excitement."

My mother was watching me, and I could tell by her gaze, even through the mask, that she was concerned. Not that the untrained eye would notice any variance in her expression. But I'd grown up to understand her subtle changes.

"When do they plan on moving out?" my mother asked, daring to take her eyes from me.

"Tomorrow."

"Tomorrow?" I repeated. That gave us hardly any time to prepare. I looked over to my mother, feeling an odd sense of relief that I came back from Tracey's when we had. If I hadn't … would she have gone on her own? I assumed we would take her up on this offer. What else could we do? We wouldn't pull away from such an opportunity, would we? And we could protect these werewolves. But yet again, I knew my mother's main focus was on my safety.

"Heed my warning, Trinity," Louise said. "If this is not fixed and set in stone, this will affect all of us. The plague is no less an issue, but what Campture has planned is far worse."

I had no doubt. My mother looked back to the vampires who were on the hillside. She was silently still as she considered this. She had little time to converse with Cesar. She would be acting on her own. *We* would be acting on our own, and it would only create further friction on our relationships with our familiars. I thought of Chase and how he might react. Would he leave the room once again? Would he consider me selfish?

But this was the world we knew, and my mother trusted in Louise's word and gift. If this were to get out of control, the unknown seemed like it was about to catch up with us a lot sooner than the building of the new race and werewolves. My mother looked at me, presumably for my counsel. It was her decision. She was the Token in this instance, but I nodded my head. I would support her. I wanted this, not only for the wolves but for myself. The sickly sweet tension of meeting them on a battlefield aroused me in a way I hadn't known I'd be holding out.

It was vengeance. My sweet, sweet, so deserved, intoxicatingly beautiful vengeance.

"Where do we go?" my mother asked. And behind my mask, the corners of my mouth tilted up. Now I couldn't wait for dawn.

CHAPTER 15

"ABSOLUTELY NOT," CESAR quipped as soon as we returned. We didn't have much time at all to prepare. But enough hours in our day to set up a decent team and advantage.

My mother raised her hand to me to wait at the door while she followed Cesar into his room. "Stay here," she ordered. I might've argued had I not understood that we could be doing other things during this time than both of us bickering with him until he consented.

With little time to brace myself, I heard the scuttle of Fire's feet drag out into the main hall. She now braved entering the main halls of the coven, either cockily thinking she could fend all of them off or having way too much faith in the gargoyles. I doubted the latter.

Frustration rolled off her in waves, and I knew I couldn't avoid her any longer. I wanted to get this over with quickly. I walked toward the second room and opened the bathing chamber that was often empty. I held the door open for her, removing my stuffy fox mask. I stared at the room, assessing the remains of the scuttle that had broken out only a week before.

Fire's snow-white fur was a welcome sight as she sauntered into the room. I closed the door, and she shifted into her naked human form. Her white shoulder-length dreadlocks were always what grabbed my attention first. They were so striking against her beautiful dark skin.

"You ran away from your responsibility like a coward," she accused. She wasn't wrong so I simply stared at her. I knew this was about Titan and Chris.

"How goes their training?" I asked, picking a piece of dirt from my robe. I didn't want to let anything or anyone in right now. I wanted to keep this traction and narrow-minded focus on what was soon to come. My attention and mind were already focused on Campture and James.

"That's all you have to say?" Fire boggled.

"Fire, I'm really sorry, but I can't do this today," I said, bored. I had a team to rally.

"You're doing it again!" she said sharply, her blue gaze striking with a wild fierceness I could only associate with her wolf counterpart. I wanted to step out of the room, but I felt jerked back mentally and almost physically by the bizarre bond we shared.

"I'm not doing anything," I grumbled, confused by the strings that bound us together. It wasn't the same with Chase. I couldn't speak with her telepathically. Not when she was in her wolf form anyway.

"You act so self-righteously. That persona of, 'I'm going to throw myself into battle and pull away from everyone I care about.' You're doing it again! These children need your guidance." I crossed my arms over my chest.

"I'm the last thing those children need to be around," I clarified darkly.

"Oh, well, shall I get rid of them then, my majesty?" she sarcastically bided.

I snarled at her. And her response and snarl were nothing short of feral. "How daring you've become with your words," I condescended.

"At least I know how to use them," she replied, insinuating I wasn't opening up to her. And I wasn't, I wouldn't. We had fought many battles together, and we had almost died in one another's arms in the last. I respected her enough as a warrior to tell her the truth.

"You can do more for them than I can right now. There are things I have to deal with."

"What could be more important? You were so enthralled to make sure they were alive and safe, and now you throw them to the side like they mean nothing."

That wasn't the truth. But I couldn't tell her that association with me felt like more of a penalty than any other. People continued dying around me. Even worse, I'd failed them and that was shame I didn't want to face right now as I reared myself into the pit of wrath and vengeance.

"The hunters have a small team that will start hunting the werewolves. Tomorrow, they'll ambush the first Human Compound. A small one with very little defense. But after that, they'll move on to the next one and then the next."

My words hung in the air. Fire seemed to draw back into herself, quiet as she watched me considerately. She looked no older than forty, but her aura radiated with wisdom and parental guidance.

"And why do you care?" she asked pointedly. It seemed strange to me that I had caught an attachment toward her race, yet she had not. Then again, I didn't witness or experience her time kept in the labs and how they might've pitted them against one another. Instead of wanting to become their savior when she could fight, she'd decided to attach herself to me—neither hunter nor vampire. I suppose we were the same in some sense, we had both been nature's mutant. I didn't want to express such weakness as to why I wanted to help the werewolves because I wasn't entirely certain myself, besides the illusion that by helping them I was helping Titan.

"The team of hunters is from my old Guild. With as little detail as I can offer, let's just say I owe them a particular visit." The moment I considered Campture's and James' faces my demeanor changed.

"You want to kill them?" she asked outright.

"Yes," I admitted hollowly. How did I look from an outsider, going after the very same people who raised me? But hadn't they championed the favor?

"When do we leave?" she asked. "Yolo and Chase's guards will look after Julia and the children. But my place rightfully is by you. Why do you think I was so infuriated when you delegated me to babysitting duty?" The edge of my lips twitched in an almost smile. It boded well with me that I could depend on her. She challenged me in multiple ways but would still have my back indefinitely on the battlefield. I could truly depend on Fire unlike the other fleet of teams that I often waited to be stabbed in the back from. Even tomorrow, it could all be the same.

"Tomorrow."

"Then I better go hunting so I have a full belly for tomorrow," she chided and shifted back into her wolf form. The cracking of bones and tearing muscle echoed throughout the room for a split second. Her white fur was immaculately clean, all except the marring of the scar on her left leg. I opened the door for her, brushing my fingers through the top of her head out of comfort. She dipped into the notion. We were okay. And we were ready to face what would come tomorrow.

She pounded down the hallway and jumped over the stairs. I could hear her in the distance snapping and snarling at any vampires who might've been standing too close or gawking her way. I could soon after sense one of the gargoyles trail her from a distance as Chase had instructed so she was never left alone in case any of the coven members got any cocky ideas.

I could sense Chase following my movement. He was closeted with numerous members of his coven. The moment we'd returned he wanted to speak with me. But I was purposefully ignoring him, uncertain how to respond to our earlier indifference. And also, I wasn't at all excited about how he might react to what was to come.

An unsettling sensation rounded up my spine, and I looked toward the direction of the cages. I could sense Lincon, Kora, and Kasey. I bashfully paved my way down the hall to interfere. If Lincon and the girls were taunting Dillian and Tori …

Jerimiah was pressed close to the wall. Kora had stifled his mobility. He seemed almost relieved when he spotted me. Lincon was sifting through the winery in the same way that Chase had once done, while Kora and Kasey sat across the cages. Kora had her knees pressed to her chest. Neither of them had yet taken off their coats since we'd returned from our mission.

I studied everyone in the room. Tori was eagerly leaning against the bars. Dillian still nonchalant and disinterested in what might've been a conversation. It was bizarre to see four members of my former team; on either side of a fence, now completely different in form. Where the twins had been experimented on and looked partly saber, Dillian and Tori were freshly turned.

"How nice of our leader to join us," Kasey said, rolling her eyes.

"Oh, Esmore, I really do love the look of the wine range down here. Why didn't you tell me we had such a collection?" Lincon asked and held a bottle out as if he were studying its worn out and unreadable label.

"What are you guys doing?" I asked, perplexed by this meeting. None of them got along at the best of times even within the Hunter Guild when we were on the same team.

"Oh, you know, a lot has changed. They hadn't yet marveled at our new form," Kasey insinuated her saber-like fangs. Both of their lips were cracked from the dryness of always having a partially open mouth. Kora only had one fang now after she'd deranged and smashed the other out. Despite their ability to heal, for whatever reason, the fang hadn't. How she appeared was exactly how I imagined her mental state to be, and that was worrisome. "And, of course, we hadn't seen them since you allowed them to be turned."

My fists clenched at her sly accusation. I was to blame, but I certainly wouldn't stand for her creating further friction between us. I felt on edge and realized Jerimiah was still under the influence of Kora's gift.

"Release him," I growled at her. She shrugged. And Jerimiah's body sagged slightly behind me.

"I'm sorry, I—"

"Am weak!" Lincon finished for him with a taunting smile. "It's okay to be man enough to say it. Beaten by a little girl, a former huntress no less. No offense." He raised his hands to the audience in the room. Lincon forever playing the stirrer and clown, hoping someone would bite so he could latch down on them. Not that he ever needed an excuse.

I could feel Chase making his way toward me, checking up on me to ensure I was okay. The truth was, I was far from okay, still trying to grab hold of the anger and pride that would solidify my actions in the new day.

Within seconds, I could feel his hands around my arms, silently pressing my back against his chest as he towered over me like a silent guard. We hadn't yet spoken, but much like myself, I could feel the coolness radiate from him, much like the armor I now wore. He was cold and hard. And indisputably already knew about tomorrows' mission.

Kora's deathly gaze shifted from Lincon and then on to me. "We were just telling our team about Campture and James and how we get to reunite with them tomorrow." Her sharp gaze was relentless. "I suggested they come … for old time's sake. You know, working as a team and all."

"I don't think they're ready," I growled lowly, infuriated that they'd come down to only rile the two and feign a disposition of favoritism.

"And why is that for you to decide?" Dillian's tone was low and deep. Cutting even as it took me a few moments to figure out how I should reply. The others looked at me, Kora's gaze patronizing as always. Some things hadn't changed that much.

"Then perhaps you should come," Chase encouraged with bite to his tone. It was enough to make Kora and Kasey flinch. Kora's gaze dropped to the ground.

"Dillian and Tori, if that's what you want then you should come," Chase gestured. He squeezed my arms when he felt my desire to dispute it.

You cannot always keep them safe. If that's one thing we've learned, he said more coldly than usual. I twisted to look up at him. Though there was the softness he often looked at me with, there was also a sharpness that had me wanting to submit and straighten my spine all at once. *I'm coming with you.*

But your coven—

Can wait. And some will join. I'm still mad at you, and we will be having a discussion later. But this is one thing that I won't let slip. They hurt you, and they will pay for that. And if they wish to join then so let them. They all have a right in this room to pay their vengeance. You more than anyone, and me for not being there to protect you.

I wanted to hug him and kiss away the parts that he was allowing to be swallowed by guilt for a time that he couldn't protect me. And then with total clarity and shame, I realized I had been blaming myself in the same way for the wolves and my former team that now loitered in this very dark room.

How could I criticize him any differently? How was I so willing to forgive him and tell him it wasn't his fault when I was strikingly feeling the same? I was dishonoring us both. All of us, in fact by not letting them go. Their fates were no longer in my control, they never were. And painfully, I realized that this might be the remains of my team, but I'd have to start letting go.

"Jerimiah, give me the keys," I asked politely. He seemed uncertain but said nothing as he unhooked the keys from around his neck.

"If you wish to do this, you do this for yourself. But I can't tell you what will happen. The most I can offer you is a position in my arsenal."

"But that's where we've always wanted to be," Tori said loyally.

"Not always," Dillian murmured. With great reluctance, I poked the key into the hole and clicked it open, making sure to avoid the silver so I wouldn't burn. Dillian's door creaked open, and he watched me with suspense as the door edged inch by inch.

I left myself open, welcome to the idea if he wanted to launch himself at me. The cage wasn't large enough for him to stand upright completely. Wind blew around me, from the speed of which he shot out of the cage and now stood behind me. He twisted his wrists and stretched his legs. There was something sinister in the way he studied the room one last time as if something wicked had just been broken free from its seal.

He made no move against me, instead he ignored me. I buried away the hurt and slotted in the key to Tori's cage. Like Chase was doing for himself, I hardened, embracing the moment he flicked the switch and bottled his emotions. It was levitation for me, and a promising gesture so we could ensure, no matter what happened tomorrow, he wouldn't turn saber.

CHAPTER 16

T HE DAY WAS delightful in all that it promised—bloodshed, vengeance, power, and forging a different future. I felt robust for the first time in a long time. It might've had something to do with the arsenal at my back of both friends and family. The wind whipped a loose piece of my golden hair. I was holding Chase's hand as we stood strong atop the gully, hidden amongst trees in our hoods and masks. I felt like I'd stepped into my power once again, as I had as a Token Huntress, where I was in control of the ambush we were about to orchestrate. Instead of being pulled back and forth, we had the upper hand and element of surprise.

On my other side, and silently listening for incomers was Fire. I let my spare hand dangle in the tips of her snow-white fur as if offering energy from the gentle touch. Like a fierce wall, my allies were both beside and behind us. My mother was positioned behind me, flanking and leading Dillian and Tori. Tori was twitchy, overstimulated by the new world and day he was experiencing. He'd soon learn to be grateful for that hood that blocked out the sun, not that there was much shining down on us. A small splatter of rain had begun a rarity and promise for a thunderous battle. Dillian remained silent, his cool gaze shifting intently from my back and then to the position we anticipated the hunters to cross. Had it not been for my mother being positioned between us, I would've dared change my position, uncertain of his loyalty.

Chase's hand squeezed mine the moment any subtle change in my emotions crept into distracting me, he pulled me back to pinpoint focus. He was just as, if not more intent on what today meant. Everyone had their reasons for being here. But I understood his and mine more than anyone's.

Lincon giddily hopped from foot to foot with his arms wrapped around Kasey and Kora in what looked like a headlock. Neither looked impressed nor did they swipe his grimy hands away. My mother was using her gift to conceal our scent and position, though we still had to hide amongst the mist and trees. Besides my private group of allies, or what was once my old team, Cesar had enforced Tythian to teleport and join us alongside Balzar, who led the elite. With Shaz and Lydia's deaths, and another two when we fought off Oppollo's assassins only eight remained. He also offered another ten soldiers, matching the same number of handpicked vampires Chase had chosen from his coven. Ridiculous, I thought for a mere slaughter of the group we were to dispose of. But it was the only way Cesar was willing to permit my mother and me to go.

From the information we'd been given by Louise, Campture often ventured out on her missions with a team of no more than twenty. It was almost frightful to think she was now leading missions herself. How the shift of power had changed from her barking orders from her office, sneering down her nose at me, to now being on the field and ensuring every mission went by her jurisdiction.

The hunters of my Guild were powerful, but as I had learned, so were we. And so were the vampires who shouldered me in anticipation for how this day would play out. We'd been set in our groups to ensure no one strayed and we had one another's backs. I was reluctant to bring Tori and Dillian, this power of theirs was new, and it'd take them time to adapt. But I had no right to take away their choice any longer. And I remembered the first time and taste I had of letting my vampire self loose, descending on Tracey's Council and leading the elite twelve.

My fangs ejected and my eyes gazed purple, all in remembrance of the sticky blood I'd so much enjoyed that very day. They would be enthralled by it as well, Dillian and Tori. They'd understand why this beast was such a curse but also a hunger for power that might never be controlled.

We weren't far from the first Human Compound the hunters anticipated to attack. Dillian could make it out using his gift. It was out of reach for the rest of us, but would only take mere minutes to reach. A curious part of me wanted to inspect the site myself and how it differed from the one I'd infiltrated. I rustled my fingers through Fire's fur, thoughtful about the wolves' conditions. But for now, our focus was on the hunters.

Chase's hand tightened around mine with anticipation. *We are going to destroy them.*

His dark, sinister tone vibrated through me, encouraging my power and joy to dance in this darkness alongside him. His mask was similar to Balzar's design, with two filed horns on the forehead. As soon as he turned the switch and bottlenecked that emotion of his, we were free to unleash. I was free to breathe, and he was free to attack in any way he wished. I would see his power flex once again in the way that aroused me and pleased me to have claimed him as my familiar.

Yes, I agreed.

"Someone's coming," Dillian announced as he looked into the distance that was adjacent to the Human Compound. "They seem to be moving away from it though and loitering in some ruins."

"Wasn't the information Louise offered that they would cross paths with us here, in this gully?" Tythian asked my mother from behind.

"Yes." She sheathed her sword. "But fate can change at any time by the smallest of elements. Let's close in around them."

"Do you think they've already been to the Human Compound?" Balzar asked incredulously. But behind his gaze, I could see a kind of hopefulness, reminding me that he and Tythian had no softness for the wolves. Perhaps they'd hoped another group had been burned before we attacked our real enemies here.

"The compound hasn't been touched from what I can see," Dillian announced. He was reluctant to speak, but like old times, his informative matter on the task was firsthand. He was a soldier through and through. It was comforting to see some familiar part of him.

"Why don't we split into two groups?" Balzar suggested. "Circle them, one come in from the front, the other from behind. Block them in."

"That's not a bad idea," my mother honored consideration. "We will confront them from the front. You circle around the Human Compound and come from the back."

I watched the separate groups shift as Chase dropped my hand. I stood in place watching the two groups march in separate directions. Tythian and Balzar's silhouettes folded into the mist and vanished alongside their group.

"What is it?" Chase asked.

"Something doesn't feel right," I said skeptically. I couldn't place my finger on it, but something was off, and I'd learned to follow my instinct. I wanted to follow them and make sure they were okay. But they were more than capable of handling themselves. Then again, I had paranoia for anything that Tythian was involved with.

"No, it doesn't," Chase agreed. "But we can either follow them or continue with the others." My mother and the others had already descended the hill. Chase's coven members stayed behind with us, uncertain as to what was happening. My mother looked up at us from the gully and waved at me, hurrying me along.

"We need to go." I had to remind myself of what our mission was. And it might've been something small and unhinged that had me regressing from this plan.

It didn't take long for Chase and me to take the lead beside my mother at the front. Fire kept to our pace with no issues, the mist sweeping near her shoulders and swallowing her almost whole. Chase's coven members remained at the back. I didn't know any of them personally.

Dillian kept tabs on the hunters' slow movement, they'd now circled back toward the human camp. Had they become lost? Had something else intervened their path? Or an unnerving reality hit me, what if we'd been set up? We made sure to keep to the higher terrain that rolled with gullies and hills. The rain that splattered became harsher, beginning to take on a steady pour. In the near distance, thunder rumbled, it would only be a matter of minutes before it swept overheard. It wasn't the most convenient weather to fight in, but it was as much a disadvantage for them as it was us.

We found foliage and hid amongst it, my mother commanding us to stop. It was peculiar to follow my mother's lead after being a Token myself for so many years. It almost made me feel like an apprentice once again, following orders from Drue and ensuring I never stepped out of line. We came across old ruins. A distance apart from where the hunters were positioned, we crouched against broken walls amongst dead spiky shrubbery, peering through the temperamental weather. Rain pelted my hood as we watched on, hardly able to make out their form. We depended on Dillian for his report.

"They've stilled."

"And where is Balzar's group?" my mother asked. Dillian looked toward the Human Compound. I wondered if the mask was an obstruction to his sight.

"I can't see them yet." His eyes flashed back toward the hunters. "They're looking this way and have their weapons raised."

"There goes the element of surprise. Can you identify any of them?" my mother asked, unsheathing her sword once again.

"I can identify most of them," Dillian solemnly replied. A somber silence ran over us. They had once been allies. "Campture's leading the front." Dillian continued to rattle off names as I quickly identified their gifts and mind dumped them to Chase. Five of the hunters Dillian couldn't identify, insinuating they might've come from Michelle's Guild.

"And James?" I asked with as much indignation as possible.

Dillian's gaze didn't shift to me, but I could tell under the robe his body tensed. As if it was difficult to speak with me directly. "He's not here." Frustration consumed me. I wanted Campture dead, but I equally, if not more so, wanted to dispose of James who tried to subdue me for years in our relationship, and now spouted nonsense to try and 'fix me.' Knowing he was still out there, out of my grasp to take vengeance irked me in ways I couldn't comprehend. I wanted to watch him hurt, hear him scream, and make him bleed. I wanted to return the favor of all that he did to me, when he made me feel helpless and alone. To be denied that when I'd built my expectation of that being today's reward, left me pissed.

Chase's hand reached for mine amongst the mist and curled over it. He felt my pain and understood it. *We will find him,* he vowed.

"Tori … your father is here too."

"My father?" The words were small. His size and height were no different from the men and vampires behind him. But inside, he was still just a boy. An apprentice only recently pardoned to leave the walls.

"Tori, if you don't want to do this, you can stay behind," my mother said, surprising me with her gentle consideration.

"Well, you might want to decide quickly," Lincon pressed behind us, not offering Tori any time to think, "because hunters are behind us right now."

"Wha—" Out of nowhere the presence of ten hunters bloomed behind us. Arrows and gifts tinkered behind us and against Kasey's wall. Not all the vampires were spared her security. Three of Chase's coven members jumped to attack, giving us only enough time to rise to our feet and prepare for the attack. Whatever gift the hunters had been using it shadowed them completely from any of us feeling their presence.

"Split!" my mother commanded as I felt the rising of the hunters in the gully run toward us. Black muck and blood exploded against Kasey's wall as two of Chase's vampires were killed. Within a second, Kasey dropped her gift, allowing us to jump into action.

The sound of weapons and gifts colliding ambushed our senses all at once. Somewhere, an almost complete wall was busted through from collision. I felt the thrum of adrenalin pump through me, as it did the same for Chase. I could almost sense the sinister smile behind his mask. Chase and I exploded into action. My mother embarked on her personal grudge and had eyes for only one—Campture.

I curled my golden claws with delight, angling them with potent and striking intent. The first hunter's evasive gift was a challenge, but one I certainly enjoyed. Tiny shards pushed out of her skin, pinpricking like minor blades. She swept her hands out offensively, throwing small blades in my direction. I pushed Fire out of the way, all too familiar with this huntress's gift. A vampire behind me had been caught in the shrapnel, barely making it out alive.

Fire burst into action, seamlessly integrated into my style of fighting. She circled the woman as I met her head-on. Two large blades flicked out of her wrist as she held them like swords, swishing them past me as I dodged the first one that scraped down in front of my chest. I smiled. The problem with this huntress was despite all her vigor and gift, she had always been slower than me.

I kneed her in the stomach, dodging the second blade that swept across where my head once was. I uppercut her, the firm punch busting small holes in her face from where my knuckles were covered with my gold claws. Just in time, I caught an arrow that had been aimed for the back of my head and looked toward the archer who'd fired it at me. Lincon had already descended on them, his delicate fingers wrapping around their shoulders with delight as he pulled them into the shadows of the ruins. The man began to scream.

Fire pounced on the woman before she'd even hit the ground and bit down hard on her shoulder, dragging her along the dirt. With speed, I unsheathed my sword and sliced the woman's hands off before she could puncture her blades into Fire's stomach. The huntress screamed, still being dragged away. I whistled once, warning Fire, and its timing was immaculate as sharp blades protruded from her shoulders, where Fire might've once had a lockjaw around her. The handless huntress horrifically searched her bloody wounds, unable to focus on anything else.

She narrowed her gaze on me and charged, bouncing into a wall as Kora and Kasey crept up beside me.

"I never liked her much," Kasey admitted, holding her two knives.

"She'll bleed out," Kora added as if they were both transfixed by the woman being boxed, screaming and bleeding out from her wrists and shoulder wound. Their sinister tone fueled my grappling influence. Kasey protected her sisters back as a hunter approached them. I left them with the remains of this kill. Unlike last time I challenged the hunters, I found no remorse for what I was doing, letting the darkness of my vampire self be my leading force. *They abandoned me. They tried to sacrifice me.*

A gurgling cry sprouted from a hunter as Chase dangled him upside down from his ankle. His mask had been removed and not much to my surprise, magically somehow his robe had been removed as well. Another hunter approached him, one of which I knew used a gift of the mind. That was unfortunate for him because very few could break through Chase's barrier. With relentless force, Chase plunged his hand into the chest of the hunter he dangled and ripped out his heart. Before the body had even hit the ground he was already behind the opposing hunter, towering over them with a dire expression, one that promised death in his wicked stormy grey eyes. The same as the storm that pillowed around us, ensuring the aftermath of a graveyard.

With relentless force, Chase bit into his neck, viciously ripping it apart. The hunter screamed and cried as Chase savagely ended his life by snapping his neck. A warmth pitted in my lower stomach as I became aroused by his violence. His gaze lingered on me as if thinking the same thing. As if right in this moment, if we could, we'd rip at one another's clothes. Blood. War. Tension. It sparked between us.

I heard a familiar cry as the ground shifted beneath my feet. The same hunter who'd challenged me numerous times began to use his gift to change and swirl the ground beneath us. Tori was the first in his line of sight as the ground swept into sinking pits, his ankle already caught. The exception being this time was different, I wasn't as weak as I had been the last time they'd ambushed me.

I called upon the Descendant, my wings tearing through my back and sprouting like the powerful beacon they were. I hovered low to the ground, sweeping across to catch Tori's hand. I became stagnant as the pull of Tori's calves and feet were embedded in the ground. Trying to tear him out might very well tear his shoulders or feet first.

An arrow pierced the hunters' shoulder, flinging him back and breaking his concentration. Atop the hill, near the ruins, was Dillian. His second arrow missed as the hunter jumped back to avoid it hitting target.

The sand around Tori softened as I reefed him out, dirt flying about as I swept us into the air. I lowered to the ground, dropping him as he rolled into a stance, coming head-to-head with his father—fate was cruel sometimes.

Before his father could even graft or lock his gift on the stunned Tori, Dillian shot arrows dividing the two. Fire jumped at Tori, startling him back into action as she nudged him toward Dillian. Tori wasn't as experienced as us, on top of that it wasn't a battle he was yet ready for though I appreciated his efforts for diving into the battlefield. He hadn't yet loosened his fantasy on his old life, and confronting his father was only evidence of that.

I rocketed to the sky, the wind and rain pelting on my wings and now torn robe. I loosened it and dumped it, freed of its weight. It was pointless now, if anyone was watching they would've noticed my black wings and quickly discovered we weren't Oppollo's assassins. The fresh rain pelted my arms and washed away the blood on my hands as I looked into the distance. Tythian and Balzar hadn't yet found their way to us. From this distance, I couldn't see and was apprehensive to leave the others as they fought below me. My mother and Campture fought one on one, despite the age difference, Campture held her ground. I wanted to intervene and be a part of the kill. But this was my mother's claim. I had come here for James …

I swept down to Dillian's level. His tipped arrow was pointed at me as I swept down and landed beside him. I stared at him through my mask, my purple eyes glowing. Would he really shoot me? Slowly the arrow lowered.

"Can you tell me what you see near the Human Compound?" I asked above the roaring rain. Fire found her way back to my side. Tori was now behind Dillian, pivoting between two buildings as he threw daggers at approaching hunters. How many were here? How many had been concealed?

Dillian raised his head above the remains of the ruins. He stared out into the distance as I flanked him with sword raised. An arrow shot at him, when it did, I was certain to slice my sword across it with precise timing, so it splintered either side of him. Below us on the field was a nightmare. Blood and gore swept through as Chase maneuvered calculatingly between hunters and their gifts, having the upper hand because he knew who possessed what. His coven, however, in the back were struggling as the two sides equally held ground. I could hear Lincon's hysterical laughter bouncing through the ruins, followed by tormented screams as he delighted himself.

"There are flames," Dillian said, "in the human camp. It looks like chaos has erupted. I think they're in there."

"Were they ambushed?" I asked. *Balzar and the others have been ambushed,* I reported to Chase.

"No, they're in there, killing the people in the camp," Dillian corrected.

I froze. They were in there killing the werewolves. I was stunned, and then a bubbling sweep of outrage rose. They dare betray us? They used this battle as a decoy?

"Fire," I snapped. I sheathed my sword back over my shoulder and collected her under the stomach in my hands. She growled at the discomfort of it. "Well, if only you shifted, you might be lighter and easier to manhandle," I grumbled back.

"Esmore, shouldn't you wait for the others?" But I'd already blown the dust around him and took to the sky.

Where are you going? I could hear Chase growl down our line.

They betrayed us, was all I could get out before a shadowy figure appeared behind me and sliced between my shoulder blades. I'd only narrowly missed them hacking at my wing. My grip loosened on Fire as I was jarred and whistled into a spin to change my course. I tightened my firm grip on her, ensuring my bladed fingers didn't cut in. But as quickly as the figure had appeared out of thin air, they'd vanished. I scanned the stormy skies around me, my skin burning between my shoulder blades from where I'd been attacked. I could tell the cut was deep as it warmed my back with fresh blood. But I let it do nothing to deter my course. It only made me torpedo faster, perplexed as to whether my shadow would reappear.

I focused on Tythian. He was the only vampire I knew who could teleport, maybe he dropped from the sky just to slash at me. But when I focused and latched onto his mind, all too familiar with his presence, I felt him within the human camp. Someone or something else had attacked me.

Esmore, I don't like this! Chase growled, all his viciousness and lack of empathy graded me like a personal challenge, no more than the wild rage that encompassed me as I swept through the rain and wild storm to bear witness to below. Vampires, wolves, and humans fought against one another, instigated by the very vampires who were meant to be defending our backs. I pinpointed Balzar who was outside sloshing in the mud and advantageously avoiding the sharp teeth of wolves who attacked him. Tythian was somewhere inside so I ensured to focus all my wrath on Balzar.

We'd been betrayed. And Cesar had gone against his word to protect the wolves. Now he'd purposefully instigated this because they wouldn't dare make such a bold move of their own accord. I was furious. For all I had done for them, and all that they asked, Cesar had lied to my face and to my mother no less. Taking this as ample time for what? To prove a point? To divide interest as we fought a completely different battle?

I swept low to the ground, preparing to drop Fire into the mix. "Protect the wolves," I instructed her. I would stand my ground too. I would make a point. She leaped out of my grip, latching onto one of Cesar's soldiers' arms as he screamed from the deadly bite. Another wolf toppled on to him tearing at his face.

Balzar's stance and gaze shifted to mine, and he defensively raised his hands. "Esmore—" he began to warn over the pelting rain, but I was already upon him. My wings swept abruptly stopping me as I pelted toward him. He crossed his arms in front of him, preparing for the impact. I smashed into him, throwing him against the rocky edged wall that did little to keep anything in or out. The camp was dirty and small, with little technological advancements. Humans screamed as they relied on the wolves to protect them. It wasn't yet a full moon which meant these wolves had been trained to shift of their own doing.

Rubble broke around Balzar as he groaned and pulled himself out. A wolf angled and jumped at him. Before I could intervene, to either protect Balzar or the wolf, Balzar grappled the wolf's jaws, prying them open and tearing them apart with all the strength of an aged vampire. And that only furthered my resolve as the wolf slumped beside the wall, the grotesque reminder that I had disposed of a wolf in the same way to protect Yolo.

"Esmore, you have to believe me when I say this was an order," he yelled over the pelting rain as he removed himself from the wall, rolling his shoulder. His prized weapon, the sharp knuckles bound to his leather gloves flexed back and forth. I'd knocked his sword out of his hand when I threw him against the wall. He briefed a glance at it, considering if he'd make it in time.

"I thought we were friends?" I purred and tilted my head to the left, the eerie notion making him change his stance and tone. My fingers danced against my leather pants in the same way that he adjusted his gloves.

"Esmore, please, you know I'm bound to complete my orders." Despite his truth and the small yearning in the back of my mind to not do this, I was just as wildly disappointed. I'd become attached. And that was a problem. This alliance would only go on for so long, and we would always be on separate sides. They wanted to kill what was different. They came and attacked this small camp and slaughtered these werewolves who had no choice but to be what they were as the vampires were once turned. I was disgusted in myself for finding sympathy toward them. Perhaps it was my attachment to Fire and then Titan that had a lot to do with this. And one thing I absolutely couldn't stand … was betrayal. Because this time, it truly stung. If Cesar was trying to make a point to his darling daughter, then I would have to do the same to pappa bear himself.

"And I have to follow out my own," I chimed back. Balzar rolled his neck, reluctant for the collision that was about to implode. But just as I had, his face changed, and he concreted in what he was bound to. We all had our duty. I let my vampire utterly and truly take hold.

CHAPTER 17

T HE COLLISION QUIVERED with pure power—warrior to warrior, trained in different styles and eras. And yet we respected one another, even if to the death with hand-to-hand combat, well accessorized of course. My golden claws made way for a spectacle as they slashed so quickly, the remains of gold slicing through the air like an apparition. Every slice I intended, he deferred with his hand, blocking it.

When I'd spin and aim for his knees and torso, he was already blocking the movement. Back and forth we went, equally matched and on even ground as we sloshed in the muddy terrain. Rain pelted down, sliding off my wings as I ensured to keep them away from his reach. They moved nimbly as an extension of my body. Where they might've once distracted me, they were now just another limb.

The only complaint I might've had was the small winces I was holding in from the wound between my shoulder blades that was slowly stitching up. It was as if time around us stopped as it often did in the midst of battle. We were aware of everything that happened around us, and no one dared to intervene.

Not the wolves or the elite who fought alongside and skillfully swept through the recently trained wolves. They had no chance. This fight was unfair. Fire had jumped and mauled one of Cesar's men, a vampire I wasn't associated with. Once she pinned him to the ground another two wolves jumped, joining her and ripping the vampire from limb to limb as he screamed.

Balzar's fist aimed for my sternum, the sharp blade knuckles scraping past my leather top and splitting it as I dodged the hastened attack. I sliced my hand up, clamping down into a grip and jarring his shoulder to pop it out. My claws dug in sharp. His fist aimed for my stomach, using my grip as a distraction when he cared little about his loosely hanging arm. I released the grip on his arm and jumped back, but his fist hit its mark. I felt the cool ting of his bladed knuckles pierce into my stomach as it shoved me back. My feet glided amongst the mud until I came to a stop. I charmed a perverted smile and looked down at my pooling blood. Well, at least he wasn't taking it easy on me.

He offered me no time to recover, which again only ignited fiery pleasure for my vampire. As he jumped for me, I smashed a wave of panic into his mind. He fumbled momentarily. Balzar's greatest weakness was that he hadn't yet developed a gift. And I would not be ashamed to use mine. I charged forward, puncturing my claws into both his shoulders and slamming him into the wall.

I crunched my wings against his forearms preventing him from moving them. No matter how mighty he fought against them, my wings were far more powerful than his mere vampire strength alone. He tried to knee me, but I blocked him with my own and pressed my body and weight against his so he couldn't move.

I charmed a wicked smile beneath my mask enjoying overpowering him. I reefed one of my golden hands out, and a small grunt escaped him. I wanted to see his expression as he feared me and realized how much more powerful I was than him. I wanted him to scream and acknowledge that crossing me had been a mistake. I wanted to know if he'd beg for my forgiveness.

My delicate and bloody golden claw sliced through the silk strap of the mask, closest to his ear. I ensured my claw drove a little deeper slicing at the side of his face as well. I wrapped my claws at the edges of his horn mask and pulled it off. He had nowhere to go. He was my prey. My scrawny capture that so excited me.

"Will you beg?" I crooned in lustful pleasure. The tone was not of my own. It was the predator that lay dormant within me. He spat at my face and my smile stretched. The mask had saved me the insult. I plunged my hand left and deep into his chest, crushing bones. His face twisted as he tried to keep his expression neutral. I was so close to his heart, my hand squirming about in pleasure so close to killing him.

My focus was purely on him. "I told you, it was an order," he gritted out. I could sense Chase trying to interfere. He was calling out to me through the line, but I purposefully ignored him, so intently enjoying my time with my toy. It was just the two of us. I licked my lips, letting my fangs pinprick my tongue. The taste of my own blood was ravishing.

The rain pelted over us as I pushed my face into his, inhaling his scent. His blood was enticing. I dared run my nose toward his ear and nuzzle my lips toward the small streak of blood where I'd cut him. The wound had healed, but the blood remained. "You know," I whispered into his ear. "I had come to like you as well."

Fires' bark snapped me out of my daze as I retracted myself from Balzar. A dagger that was aimed between my shoulder blades now skirted for Balzar's chest. I smacked the dagger out of the way before it connected. I snapped on the being who dared interfere while I toyed with my prey.

When I looked up atop the ruined wall, my gaze pinned the last person I expected to find but had prayed I would see. James' bulky frame gawked back at me. He was crouched on the wall, looking down on me with pure disgust in his expression.

"What have they done to you," he sneered somehow knowing it was me behind the mask. Maybe he knew in the way that I fought, the stances that I took or the shape of my figure. We had, after all, grown up together.

"James," I seethed, and before rational thought could take hold I burst into action, soaring to collect him from his arrogant perch. Other hunters poured over the edge. I hadn't sensed them. Where had they come from? Now hunters, wolves, vampires, and humans fought against one another. Rumbling in chaos as natural enemies faced one another. Fire ran after me, but I ignored her. I was focused on only one thing, and that was vengeance on the man who had made me feel so utterly weak and taken something from me forcibly when I was at my most vulnerable. It would taste sweeter than any victory I'd ever had before.

Before I'd even reached him, his skin turned to the steel-like metallic that was impenetrable. Weapons would never work on him. I slammed a wave of panic into his mind. In the same way I had with Bazlar. It stunned him long enough for me to grab under his arms and collect him. His weight was surprisingly hefty as my wings struggled under the weighted beat. I gritted through the mask rising with strong, powerful beats, irritating the wound between my shoulder blades.

The momentum I had from stunning him began to wear off as he growled and seethed as he wriggled from my grip. An arrow shot at me from below. Another twenty hunters were gathering around the human camp. This wasn't at all what Louise had eluded—we'd been set up. But what was I to expect from the Hunter Guild?

I shot into the sky and the thunderous rain as lightning struck around us. I might not be able to penetrate his armor-like skin, but I wondered how he'd fair being dropped out of the sky, or furthermore if he attracted a lightning strike. The reality was we were both in danger if that happened and yet my wings continued to powerfully beat. He reached for his belt with the small bag of daggers, ready to thrust one up.

With an already healing stomach, I thought it'd be better to drop him now and see how he faired. I couldn't see below to the human camp anymore so surely this was high enough. And there was only one way to find out.

As my fingers scraped against his smooth skin, loosening my grip, a fell swoop of black wings knocked into me. I was thrown back and doubled over in the air. I caught myself, giving my wings one large beat to momentarily stop myself. I scanned the sky, now in the midst of dark clouds. A shadowy figure struck back and forth at James, catching him. Thunder from behind erupted the silhouette of wings, weapons, and two figures fighting one another.

I was stunned and irritated. Someone had taken my prey, literally swooped him out of my grip. Those wings ... an uneasy clench of my stomach. I rocketed forward to get close enough through the billowing rain to see firsthand who had intervened.

I grappled at the link between Chase and I that I'd so quickly denied earlier. But perhaps it wasn't interference, maybe a warning, or maybe something else altogether. I'd been too consumed. Too focused on what I could claim and torture.

James was dropped from the sky and the figure dove down, giving chase. Black wings, larger than my own, clamped behind the all too familiar muscles I'd learned to love. *Fuck*. Chase had called upon the Descendant. I didn't have time to think about how or why it triggered or even if he called upon its strength for himself. What I did know was the Descendant controlled him, much like my vampire self claimed me.

Suddenly, James was only a distraction and not the main prize. I dove hard to the ground chasing after them. I had to stop him in this state. I had no idea how it'd risk his sanity or if it was already too late. Once again, my selfish thoughts and actions snapped clearly as I followed the one thing I wanted to keep safe in this world.

Chase grabbed James' leg before he'd fallen completely. By the look in his eyes, I could tell Chase wasn't conscious. He was on default, a puppet to the raw power of the Descendant. I tried to find him on the other side of our link, but it seared me to get close. This was different from the other times I'd been closed off to him.

James slashed at Chase's bare chest, the blade cutting deep enough to make him bleed before healing instantly. Chase was clawing at him, rogue-like, trying to rip him from limb to limb and becoming frustrated. I charged toward them, building enough momentum as I spun and slammed into Chase's back. James' foot slipped out of his grip. Chase twisted on me snarling and grabbed my throat. His firm grip intent on popping my head off.

Reflexes and survival kicked in as I punctured my finely weaponized fingers into his chest, close enough to make him stumble and loosen his grip. Without hesitation, I retracted my sword and sliced at the edges of his wings.

He unnaturally screeched, baring his fangs at me as flight unbalanced and he flapped clumsily to the ground. I swooped in after him, now that the clouds had cleared and the ground was a sure thing. As I advanced on him to help his fall, he twisted around to fend me off. He grabbed a firm grip on my leather boot and reefed me to the ground. The shift and force of his strength threw off my own flight and torpedoed me down.

There was a loud bang to hit and rock the ground beneath me. Stars danced along my sight as I willed the effort to stay conscious. I'd landed on my front, my arms and legs barely able to protect me. But my wings hadn't taken much of the brunt. They flexed back and forth as I groaned and coughed into the mud. My body felt stunned and weak. I grimaced as I tried to push myself up. I grabbed at the mask, flinging it to the side. My hair and face were muddy, all of me was filthy as I looked out into the distance trying to find where he'd fallen. In the near distance, I could see the unwarranted flames of battle. But it was so far away I couldn't hear it as if it was an illusion, and right now it was only Chase and me.

I shook my head, trying to shake off the tingles all over my body. I slumped and put enough effort in to try and sit upright. I was sore all over, but the small movement beneath me curled my senses.

"Chase!" I screamed at him. He'd been beneath me the whole time. *Chase!* I yelled at him again. His wings and body were in bad shape. Blood oozed from the chest wound, and his wings were crumpled. I shook my head again, *what just happened? All of it, it didn't make any sense.*

"Over here!" I heard someone shout over the distant rain. It wasn't a voice I recognized. The wind caught a hint of the scent, and I growled at the hunters who'd traced us, none of which smelt like James. I looked left and then right, looking for my sword. We were in the open, nowhere to go or hide him.

I flexed my wings again. They certainly weren't ready for flight. I stood over the unconscious Chase, my knees and muscles crying in distorted pain. I gave him one more grimacing look and vowed to protect him before they could creep any closer.

I swelled my power within me, a mixture of all that I was and the control of all that I could unleash. But it was neither my huntress nor vampire who were prominent. It was me, in total control with no distorted version or influence in how this should end. Either they died or I did.

I flexed my muscles, my calves and knees aching as I sprung into action. I took a sharp left. I'd flutter through them one by one. I collected daggers from my garter. I knew my sight was keener than theirs and so I had no time for hesitation. I couldn't give them time to use their gifts or get any closer to Chase.

When the first figure came into sight, I threw the dagger, ignoring the cry and ache of my body. I made sure to aim for her throat so the minimal sound wouldn't alarm the next one. They were fortified in a line in an attempt to surround us. She plummeted to her knees, and I leaped over her, quickly briefing a glance down to see her shocked expression as she grabbed for the object that cut off her air supply.

I plunged a dagger toward my next victim's throat, but my aim had been off. So I threw a second one aiming for their head. The small shocked sound would've been enough to alert the others as I heard the sound of unsheathing blades. I curved around the sharp laser-like beam, a small stem of it slicing at my wing.

I growled as it sizzled and bit into my muscle, a few feathers going astray amongst the wind. I threw my two remaining daggers in the direction of the hunter who had such a gift. It would be enough to distract them as I dashed left again so I wouldn't give away my position and advanced on them. The man grunted as a dagger plowed into his thigh. His fist was around it by the time I'd found him, he raised his hand, but it was already too late. I wrapped my hands around his neck and flipped him over my side, twisting and breaking his neck.

Fire's howl in the near distance supported my endeavors. I was not alone. They would not get to Chase. A sword sliced at my chest, surprising me as I twisted and tried to find the position of my attacker. Nowhere and no one. Another blade jutted out from nowhere. This time it sliced my arm, and its tip pierced the lean core of my wing. I hissed as I followed the blade, gliding my nails along its length and groping for whatever was on the other end. My hand found solid muscle. The hunter tried to pull back, to remain in their camouflage, but I drove my sharp nails around their wrist, reefing them toward me. So, this had been the hunter who'd camouflaged them.

I plunged my hand deep into their core and twisted my hand, erupting their organs on the inside. Their gurgling scream broke free, and the camouflage dropped as their focus was now on their intestines soon to be on the ground. With little remorse, I grabbed on to as much as I could and pulled everything out. I looked down on the hunter as they screamed and wailed in the muddy dirt. I spited him. If it weren't for his camouflage trick, we would've felt the others sooner. And James wouldn't have been such a distracting surprise.

A hunter swung two long blades, swinging them about more for show purposes than anything else. I fisted my bloody hands. My sword would've been easier to use in this instance, but I would make do. I guarded my face and rocked back and forth on my feet.

Out of nowhere a large black wolf leaped out of the pouring rain. The hunter was caught off guard, slicing as the wolf yelped but still managed to wrap its mighty jaw around his face. A second one followed, reefing at his arm to tug away his grip on the second weapon.

A wall of wolves broke into the fight, taking on the hunters. Somehow, they knew to avoid me, and I was certain it was because of

Fire as her brazen icy blue eyes crept out of the hazy-hued rain. Her fur was soaked. She let out another howl, and I nodded my appreciation.

I doubled back, following the link between Chase and I, grappling at it as I felt him stir to consciousness. A glimmer of silver grabbed my attention, and I ignored the satisfaction that rolled through me—my sword—as I ran through the rain I collected and sheathed it.

Chase. He was dazed, but I could feel his alertness prick at my voice.

Where are we? he asked. And I could envision the moan. His body was slowly healing. When I'd returned, he was perched on his elbows looking around abashed. His wings had since vanished, and he was looking at me with disorientation. But it was him. I dropped to my knees bundling him. "Thank goodness," I said, relieved.

His switch had reverted, allowing all emotions to bust through like a dam and all I could think about was sending a prayer to whomever it was I had that he was okay and he was here. No saber or Descendant in sight.

"What happened? I remember coming for you, and then sensing James," his voice turned into a growl as he stiffened to stand back up. I pushed him down. "The rest was black. I just remember being so angry and wanting to kill him so badly for what he'd done to you."

I rested my forehead to his. "I know. I know." Was all I could say as I was gentle enough with my touch to make sure I didn't prick him with my claws.

What happened? he asked again, looking around him at the impact and implosion of the ground beneath him. At one point as we fought, he must've registered it was me. He still protected me. I wanted to save him from this terror. He'd hidden from the Descendant for so long, and it had sprung forth from his desire to protect me and seek vengeance on my enemies.

"You turned into the Descendant," I shakily said as he assessed my wounded stomach. It'd already begun healing. It wasn't as fast as a full-fledged vampire's, but it was faster than any wound I'd heal as a huntress. Right now, I was buzzing with adrenaline. "And you saved me." I left it at that. He didn't need to know the in between. But in the way his face contorted it was fair to say he already assumed what had happened.

"Here," he said, biting into his wrist and offering it to me. "It'll help you heal faster." It reminded me of the first time he'd saved and healed me. Except unlike that time, I wasn't resistant to dip my lips to his wrist.

If it weren't inappropriate, I would've offered myself the time to enjoy his taste.

"Well, well, well, what a party we've had over here." Lincon's voice crept over the rain. I could sense my mother and the others who'd fought in our first position, sweeping toward us. The wolves growled lowly and surrounded Chase and me protectively. Chase instinctually wrapped his arm around me, but I knew the threat wasn't toward us. They were guarding us.

Fire loosened a low growl, which seemed to order them to back off. I didn't understand how they communicated amongst one another, perhaps telepathically. Lincon's silhouette came out from the rain, and he clapped his hands as he peered down on the wolves. "Oh, goodie, a whole bunch of guard dogs now."

"Did you know about the wolves?!" I demanded of my mother looking over his shoulder. If she had known … if she'd betrayed me in such a way …

"I didn't." Her mask and robe were slick with blood.

"Cesar ordered—"

"I know," she said in a more sinister tone. "*And* we were ambushed."

From what I could gather and the figures that congregated around her, everyone had made it out safely—all except a few of Chase's men. In the distance, I could sense Balzar and Tythian coming toward us.

"Looks like we have a disconcerting chat to have with Pappa Bear, oh, and of course a betrayal of a familiar," Lincon exasperated to my mother. "What a plot twist that one is."

She snarled at him as if provoking fangs if she had any. Fire nudged her head between Chase and me, checking on us both. I rubbed my bloody hand through her fur. "Set them free," I ordered her. She turned to look at the wolves who waited for her command. They were of different sizes and colors. They would be hunted by Balzar, Tythian, and the elite now if they didn't escape.

Fire let out a howl, one that was painful and longing. The others howled with her, grieving the end of a battle. The wolves plotted around us before giving chase to the storm and fleeing the old life they once had, chained to the humans who'd confined them to this fate.

I assisted Chase to his feet. He flexed his muscles back and forth, ensuring to stand on his own two feet so he didn't look vulnerable. The remainder of his coven members curved around him, ready to lay down their lives for him.

"Did you kill her?" I asked my mother. There was no other woman other than Campture that could be more prominent in our pursuit tonight.

"It is done," my mother said. And that's when I noticed the sickly cut down the inside of her arm. She was hiding it with the robe, but her blood was dripping thick. If it had been any other huntress I'd be concerned about the mass of blood she was losing, but I knew even now she was rapidly healing with her ability. A wave of relief swept over me. Finally, that vermin was gone.

"And the rest?" my mother asked. I understood her underlying question. Had we finished James? James was many things, but unfortunately, he wasn't an idiot. The moment he realized they were overpowered, and their ambush didn't work, he retreated. We'd lost our chance. But looking at Chase, I'd rather be unsatisfied for vengeance and leave that slaughter for another day than lose Chase to another darkness where I couldn't reach him. I shook my head.

The figures began to disappear as they approached us. Tythian was teleporting them out. Balzar and Tythian were the only two who remained as they crept into our inner circle.

"Can I kill them?" Lincon asked politely. "Please."

Balzar couldn't look me in the eyes, instead he stared at my mother as if no one else existed and it was Tythian that spoke. "Despite our separate missions, it seems all ended well. And now we are homebound."

"And if we were to refuse to go with you," my mother elicited. I watched Tythian skeptically, recalling the person who'd attacked my back out of thin air. It couldn't have been Tythian. But who else could appear and vanish into thin air like that?

"It is under my order by Cesar that I bring you willingly or not," he said arrogantly. Despite his usual cockiness, he knew he was overpowered. "He sends his condolences. But said it had to be done."

"Had to be done?" I seethed. In my peripheral, Dillian raised his crossbow, my tone exciting a possible scuttle. It made no sense as to why Cesar would purposefully evoke a divide amongst us when we were so closely coming to heads with Oppollo. Why were the wolves worth the risk of our alliance?

I watched my mother. And what made it worse was he was her familiar. I could see the vexing rage in her gaze. Balzar still couldn't meet my eyes. After a long pause, my mother straightened a little more, her neck and shoulders pulled back proudly. Hell has no wrath like my mother's fury and the stupidity of pissing off a daughter who closely followed.

CHAPTER 18

WHEN WE ENTERED the main hall of the institute, my mother shoved away the numerous vampires who didn't get out of her way fast enough. I was second behind her, the rest of our arsenal following and crafting a clear deviation between Tythian and Balzar who trailed last.

"Stay out here in case it goes bad," I ordered Lincon. Vampires rustled around us and Clarissa stood to attention. Chase side glanced her, and she nodded hurriedly, instructing everyone to gather. This could be war within our own covens.

Lincon was delighted as he removed his mask, offering me enough of a promiscuous smile that elicited he hoped this conversation went poorly.

The vampires could feel the tension as they rallied on either side of the main hall. Balzar and the elite shuffled to the side, standing guard and ready to order their defense if they would have to.

My mother stormed the hallway and down to Cesar's room. Had the door not already been open I was certain she would've kicked it down.

"How dare you!" she snarled with a fury I'd only ever witnessed a few times. Connor jumped out of his seat, and I unsheathed my sword pointing it to him in warning. He could use his gift on me, this was simply a courtesy that neither of us actually did anything. For now, this was an argument between my mother and her familiar. And then I'd be next. Connors familiar, Deemori, sat still in her chair. Three sabers scurried to alertness as she uneasily snarled at the blade pointed at her familiar's throat. Fire opposed the sabers who fixated on us. Suddenly this room was too small. Chase eyed Tythian off in the back of the room.

This wasn't just one discussion or argument between two familiars, this affected us all. I scanned over mine and Chase's wing ensuring Julia, Titan, and Chris's safety. I could sense Yolo, Jerimiah, and Darcy guarding them.

"You wouldn't have allowed me to do it if I asked for permission, which is also something I don't need," Cesar replied, unperplexed. He too had closed himself off emotionally, fortifying a wall against us. My mother swept in for a high kick, aiming for his stomach, surprising me with her brute as opposed to using words. He'd hurt her deeply.

He caught it with little hesitation, looking over the leathered leg admiringly. She unsheathed her small knife and struck at him. He jumped back, pushing Tythian to the side. And that's when his maddened expression reared its ugly head. Though he seemed more perplexed that she'd strike him rather than angry.

The rest of the room moved uncomfortably, uncertain if we were to intervene or if an all-out fight was about to ignite.

"I'd promised a coven nearby. The wolves had become a problem for them, and I told you I didn't want you going there to fight, hunters or not!"

"You don't orchestrate what I do and don't do. And you *certainly* don't craft your own plans within my own. You could've had us killed!"

"I know too well you can look after yourself, Trinity." He rolled his eyes, and the disrespect only revered my mother further. Cesar was so often serious and intense, and now he was trying to calmly dismiss the situation. He was still trying to manage his control of what he considered to be the superior leader here.

"And your daughter! What of her?! You risked all of our lives!" she snapped, throwing the knife now. It narrowly missed him as he ducked out of its way. Irritation pricked at him.

"I know too well what my daughter is capable of! And maybe she wouldn't be so helpless if you'd let us embellish her heart once again!" he snapped.

I was stunned. They'd spoken of my heart very little and the gift that was deigned my own. Now, this was turning into a lovers quarrel over their child when this hadn't at all been the reason we'd come into this room. Was Cesar trying to spin it into an underlining issue and argument they'd had numerous times already?

"Don't you dare try to change the topic! You betrayed me, Cesar!" Her tone wobbled, and had it not been for my familiarity with all the expressions my mother offered, I might've not heard the hurt.

Cesar too, was aware of the change, and his eyes softened. He looked uncomfortably around the room as he fought with himself as to whether to shield himself as the arrogant leader he was or to show some vulnerability toward my mother.

"I had no other choice," he said in a gentle tone. My mother's shoulders tensed. I'd never seen her shake from rage and pain in such a way. Was she not saying anything because she was about to cry?

"You killed them," I said on my mother's behalf to shield her from speaking and sharing her wobbly tone. The tip of my sword remained pointed at Connor, ensuring everyone stayed exactly where they were. While my mother might've been letting love and pain override her judgment, I was ready to flex my rage into words. "After we'd agreed to not make a move against the wolves, you slaughtered a whole camp."

"Well not all, if you hadn't come to their rescue," Tythian undermined me.

Tythian winced, and I could sense Chase had slammed him an emotional mental blow. Tythian showed his fangs, ready to leap over the table. It had been one of the few times Chase had ever physically opposed him.

"Stop!" Cesar ordered Tythian before he could react. "It wasn't intended to start a fight amongst our own. I knew you'd be mad," he said firstly to my mother and then me. "But I've told you, my daughter, my everything, these wolves are no good."

"Don't call me that," I seethed. "What right do you have? You are not a man who keeps to his word. Ever since following you we've only had hardship after hardship." Although I knew it had protected us in certain ways, I wasn't willing to admit it.

"Well, let me correct you, darling *daughter*. I'm not a man but a vampire, and you've caused your own havoc including these ridiculous pets you now house in my home!"

"Our home," Chase corrected with a firmness that challenged Cesar. "This is our treaty, mutual solace, and you broke that vow."

"And what will you do, little vampire? Oppose us? Challenge me? All because of some mangy mutts!"

So seriously Chase replied, "If she would ask it of me, then yes because that's what familiars do—they communicate and fight for one another. Not betray them, especially amidst a battle."

Cesar scoffed. "When you grow up and live a hundred more years tell me how easily everything is in black and white. I've told you once, and I'll say it only once more, it was not an easy decision. And I still care for you both deeply and would never jeopardize a mission if I seriously thought you were in danger."

I scoffed. How many times had he put me in danger?

"The coven I did this as a favor too, had taken over and resides in an old human military compound. The numbers and weapons are something we need when we oppose Oppollo. And I could secure that alliance with this act," Cesar ordained. "I knew you wouldn't agree," he said more pointedly to me. "But while you are focusing on your contribution as to what might help us, I've been focused on the main war this whole time. However young you might be, Chase, and taking personal attachments aside, surely you can see how necessary this was. My methods might've been unorthodox, but I found an opportunity and took it. Had it not been tonight, I would've done it the next. But either way those wolves would die. The only reason I set it up on the same night was so if you truly needed back up, my men were there. I never left you unguarded. And I know you far too well to deny that both of you can look after yourselves."

Everyone mulled over his words. "Your methods were wrong. Even if this is war, Cesar, you should've never used us in that way. And if you're ever so brazen as to not disclose something like that with *me* again, I'll annihilate your entire coven before your very eyes," Chase warned.

"You dare—"

"Enough, Cesar!" My mother snapped at him. "You betrayed us." The edges of her eyes were crinkled and wet; the expression snapped both Cesar and me into silence. For all my mother's strength and hardness from being a well-trained warrior, a betrayal from her familiar was the largest of sins. This was what had pushed her over the edge. "You failed us both, whether it was right or wrong. She could've been killed."

She shoved past us and left the room.

"Trinity, wait!" Cesar pushed out of the room behind her. Suddenly they weren't leaders, vampire, hunter, or anything else. It was the most human I'd seen Cesar as he followed my mother begging for her forgiveness, ignoring all those who watched on.

The room was a silent ambiance as everyone continued to watch one another with the residue of tense friction. Should we attack one another or not? Were we still friend or foe?

"You might not agree with his methods, but you know he's right. We needed that alliance. And the wolves are an abomination," Tythian said to Chase. He was still wearing his robe, but the mask had long been taken off. His hair was slick from the pouring rain we'd teleported out from. Fire growled at the remark, and he looked down on her with distaste.

My grip tightened on the sword, and I looked back to Chase, waiting for him to argue. But he didn't. I felt my stomach drop. Because he agreed.

CHAPTER 19

THE MAIN ROOM had erupted into chaos. The gargoyles were fending off the main instigators who were shouting and threatening one another. But no one had yet been so daring as to raise an assault, not without the order from their coven leader. They'd seen what happened to those who disobeyed, but it certainly didn't dispel the friction of what weeks had been curating.

Lincon was the worst of them all, tantalizing both covens as if he were the exception to any of the rules. If they'd attacked I knew he'd feign self-defense. This was how he worked best, how he most enjoyed playing with his prey, and no one was exempt from his games. And I'd encouraged that authority when I permitted him in charge before I stormed the stairs.

The twins were sitting on the second step. Kasey was casually cleaning her knife, rubbing the red hunter blood on the filthy cloth. It created a stir amongst the vampires and those who dared to take a step forward to even have a whiff of its potency, were stopped dead in their tracks. She fixed her gaze on them, using her power singularly to make them immobile.

Kora, on the other hand, was fixated on the cloth, staring at the blood. I'd realized for a long time now, Kasey was converting and stepping into the threshold and understanding of what she had become; Kora wasn't managing at all. Her single fang and distressed gaze made her look easily ten years older. The elements of the experiment had been harsh, and she'd never quite bounced back. Not like her sister had. Not under the guidance of Lincon.

I wondered if she was staring at that blood-soaked cloth as if it were the last of their salvation. They'd turned on their own. They'd killed hunters today. And now they were surrounded by a roomful of vampires once again. Alienated and caught in a place of in-between. It haunted us alike.

Tori and Dillian still wore their masks and robes, standing amongst the gargoyles with no place to go, like Kora and Kasey, they were a part of no coven or treaty. The snarls and commotion were causing them to stress. I could sense it in the way that Tori shuffled uneasily from side to side. Dillian remained still, his hand on his bow and arrow if he'd require to use it.

I could sense that my mother and Cesar had left the building. Chase jumped over the railing, meeting with Clarissa who followed his instructions precisely. Much to the loathing of the vampires in his coven, he was forcing them to stand down and return to their part of the wing. One vampire had become so brazen in complaint that Chase grabbed him by his throat and ripped one painful bite out of his neck. He spat the chunk of flesh across the room as his coven startled around him. Blood smeared his face, and I took one step down in preparation for if they'd turn on him.

But it did as he intended. His members winced at the vampire who gripped at his black oozing neck and shunned him. A few offered remaining glares but left the room as they'd been warned and piled into the next. Spungee's neck awkwardly clicked out as he walked over to the chunk of skin.

"No Spungee!" Clarissa hissed and slapped it out of his hand, yanking him toward the door. She alienated everyone with a gaze who seemed to linger in the main hall for too long as if considering challenging the coven across the room single-handedly was a good idea.

Go, Chase suggested. *I'm going to explain what happened and calm everyone down.*

My hand was ruffling through Fire's fur in a soothing manner. I felt like even now, we were still on different sides. He had a coven to run, and I had … I looked down at the disheveled remains of my former team. Fire nudged her head into my palm, drawing my attention. We couldn't telepathically communicate, but she was susceptible to my moods.

"Come here," Chase called to Dillian and Tori. They hesitated. "Anyone touches these two, and I'll kill them. They're under our protection." Clarissa stared at them with distaste. Her eyes all but said, 'well I see they've become our problem now.' My top lift curled, baring a singular fang at her. Clarissa always tested my patients.

Tori looked up the stairwell and to me for reassurances, and I nodded. They knew Chase was my familiar, but I doubt they had little trust in anything right now.

Balzar's supremacy was being tested as the others pushed back. But the tension changed when Tythian, Connor, and Deemori appeared, walking along the corridor. Tythian held his head high as if this was his personal coven and how it irritated him to see it in such an unruly sight. He whispered to Connor. Within seconds the first line of vampires dropped to the ground, screaming as they clutched at their heads. Balzar spun on them, scowling at the severe punishment.

"This is what happens when some act of their own accord," Tythian said to me as he continued to step down the staircase. Lincon perked his eyebrows, almost pleading for my permission to take Tythian down on my behalf. I was tempted to agree had it not been for my familiar trying to keep the peace.

I reined control, counting to ten as my father raised me to do. "Come on," I said to Fire, turning my back on them as they descended. I could feel Balzar and Deemori's gaze on me. The alliance might've still been intact, but the shackles that bound any form of trust had been broken. I drifted through the dark hall and up to our side of the wing. Today, I'd watched many of the werewolves killed simply because of what they were, but there was liberation in being able to set the remaining survivors free. So at least they had fair odds of defending themselves instead of chained in a camp being abused.

I pulled my shoulders back, unnerved by the whole situation. It only pushed me further into stepping into my responsibility. Fire had lectured me about the pups, and she'd been right—painfully so. I either had to let them go or figure out how I could truly protect them because as it stood,

I realized that this place would be no longer safe for them. The reality was, it never had been.

As I entered the top level, Darcy shifted from his gargoyle form. Jerimiah remained in his cemented glory. "Something must have gone really bad?"

I shook off the sheath of my sword, coming down from the high of the battle. "Cesar betrayed us and set his eyes upon slaughtering a whole camp of werewolves."

Darcy grimaced and looked back at Jeremiah's form which still didn't change. If he had an opinion, he was keeping it to himself. I respected them both enough that they didn't pretend to be saddened by it. They, too, wanted the werewolves extinguished. I was one of few who wanted to protect them. Had I gone mad? Should I be listening to the voice of reason which stood with the minority? But those were mostly vampires, and of course they would defy anything that could oppress their power. I looked up at the almost full moon. Only a few days and we'd have to chain Fire, Titan, and Chris up so they wouldn't attack anyone uncontrollably.

"And how does Chase fair?" Darcy asked.

I considered his question seriously. For now, he was okay, fatigued but not that he'd show it. I swept my mind over his trying to get a gauge on how he felt about what happened, but he was too transfixed on reining in his coven. We'd escaped the tragedy of what might've transpired, and we'd been blessed that very few had seen what actually happened.

It was Tythian and his mother who'd found him last time he'd lost control to the Descendant, months later. Our balance was unhinged. We were constantly yo-yo-ing back and forth in this state.

"His usual self," I replied coolly. I needed to figure out a makeshift plan, another way to reach or save him if I wasn't available or worse if I was the cause of his spiral. "Tell me, would you ever follow one of my orders if it didn't necessarily go along with Chase's?"

Darcy seemed uncomfortable by the question. And that was enough to arouse Jerimiah out of his solidified slumber. "You know Chase is our coven leader. And though we like you, genuinely we do," he flashed an uncharacteristic smile trying to be gentleman-like, "we cannot go against his orders to flatter your own."

"What if it was a request to help him? With his instability … you've seen him." They'd guarded him in the cells when he last turned into his saber-like form. "What if it was a request to protect him?"

Jerimiah hesitated to reply. He studied me seriously as if this might be some trick and I'd report back to Chase. Yes, as a part of his coven they had to follow his orders, but it was also in their belief to protect him unless challenging him for his position. From what I'd seen, Jerimiah, Darcy, and their group had no interest in leading any group other than their own and what would allow them to slumber in their gargoyle form. If anything, this had been the most active they'd been in a long time, and I wondered if they enjoyed or despised it.

Darcy's eyebrows furrowed when he asked, "What did you have in mind?"

"I don't know yet." I shrugged a shoulder as I continued to think about it. "But I'm worried that right now our combined instability isn't good for him."

Neither denied this. They'd seen it for themselves. "So, I want to try and figure out how I can protect him. Even if that leaves me vulnerable." They both went to oppose. It would go against Chase's order to keep me safe. I raised my hand. "I haven't got anything right now. But I just wanted to ask if I could depend on you both when the time came. That's all. I want Chase to live through all of this, no matter what."

Not that I could trust many, especially after Cesar's betrayal, but Darcy and Jerimiah felt like they'd come from a different time. They were, besides Yolo and once Balzar, vampires I'd come to learn to depend on.

"Anyway, I'm here to check on the others." I rested my hand against the door before opening it. They watched Fire warily as she strutted past. And though Fire appreciated that, it only ignited the line further between us. I took a hard swallow, preparing myself for the odd words soon to come. "Thank you for everything you've done up until this point."

Their gaze only risked flicking up for a second before striking back down to Fire. "It's our honor, Esmore," Darcy said with a lingering sadness as if knowing our days were numbered. Something was changing, whether it was before our confrontation with the Council or beforehand. No matter what, I wanted to ensure Chase was safe. Even if that meant I was out of the picture.

I walked into the room, eyeing its contents. Scraps of paper and what looked to be small portions of paint had exploded the room into color.

Yolo was in Jenn's form, elegantly lying across the ground with one arm propping her head up. She peered over at us with a smile. It was as if this room was a completely separate entity entirely to the commotion of what was happening below.

"Ellie!" Titan screamed and jumped off the floor. Chris and Julia were still brushing strokes on the paper with their fingers. Titan formed a lock grip around my waist near knocking me off balance. When did she become so strong?

Fire shifted. "Why are you teaching the young warriors finger painting?!" she demanded of Jenn regally.

"Oh relax, they're still children," Jenn said, finding a piece of cloth to wipe her hands. She wavered a glance over our blood-stricken attire. I tried to pry Titan off me, feeling disgusted in myself by my current state. I'm sure her father, Sydney, had walked in numerous times in the same state, but it didn't disconcert that she was still a child. Chris seemed to be slightly more cautious as he continued focusing on his paints.

Fire glowered at Jenn as she began racketing off lists of responsibility. Had I not been so focused on Titan's little body strapped to me for comfort, I might've found the situation humorous as the two came to blows.

"You were avoiding us?" Titan demanded of me with as much will as her father once harbored. The resemblance was uncanny. When facing her, I couldn't find the words to explain to her yet again that I wasn't safe for her. That this attachment she'd formed with me could end badly just as it had for everyone else who surrounded me. But invariably, I'd imprinted on her in the same way, bound by duty and her father's blood on my hands. If I guided her along the right path, the path of survival, then would his ghost stop haunting me? Was I doing this for selfish reasons?

"My name isn't Ellie, Titan. You need to understand that I've been lying to you." I pried her fingers off me, still holding her hands as I crouched to meet her eye level. "I'm not the person you think I was." No. I was the person whose hands were slick with blood, and only my fingertips were clean from where I'd removed my golden claws and put them in their satchel. Amongst the Hunter Guild, we'd never put such fondness or encouragement toward a child. We'd certainly never crouch to their level as if they were an equal. Whether she felt it or not, she was in a dangerous position. For everyone who knew of her existence, they would try to kill her. Just because of what she was. It was all too relevant as if I were talking to a childlike form of myself. Had I known back then, what would I have done? Would I have trained any differently or hidden in the shadows in the hope no one would see me? Biding time that I would never trigger my vampire half? But then I would've never met Chase …

"But you found us, you protected me," she said with much deliberation. "It doesn't matter what your name is. Dad always told me it's not what people say, but what they do that matters."

I could envision the rigid Sydney bowing down to his little girl as I was now, spieling life lessons and adult terms. They had nowhere to go, and my partial attachment to the werewolf race was because of this six-year-old child with big brown doe eyes and midnight black hair. I could almost visualize what she might look like as a woman one day—a warrior. If only someone were there to help her develop her skill and grow, giving her a chance. I was perplexed to think that by protecting them, *I* was in the wrong?

"Do you understand what I am, Titan?" I asked the question delicately. I don't know why I shouldered so much on that question. The others were saying I should kill them. And for some reason, I cared for how she would respond.

She furrowed her eyebrows, confused. She'd seen me as I was. No guard against my form of what was a monster. Something that should give her nightmares, but I might've not compared to what she'd already seen. I ejected my fangs and wings to make a point. She tried to take a step back, but I held her in place. The others had fallen silent. Jenn took a step forward, but Fire placed a hand in front of her, knowing I meant no real harm to the child. I narrowed my purple gaze on her. She was frightened, as she should be. Chris, as small as he was, tried to run to her aid, it was Julia who pulled him back.

Titan's expression changed from sudden fear to a wild curiosity. Her brown eyes looked over my wings, struggling to take them all in because of how closely she stood. And then it stopped on me. My ugliness of fangs and huntress eyes I'd once been so proud of. Now I mirrored monstrosity. Her small hand reached and cupped my face. I sucked in an involuntary breath, disjointed by the small touch. Her hands were calloused in a way that I knew would make both Fire and Sydney proud.

"You're different," she said kindly with more fondness than I could've ever anticipated receiving. "Like us," she said, looking back at Chris and Fire. Jenn and Fire were still watching me intently. Fire seemed almost smug as she shifted back into her wolf form.

Chase noticed my distress and yanked on the line. *I'm okay*, I reported back quickly. I shot up straight, calling back the Descendant, the pain eliciting a tingle of pleasure I now associated with it. "I need to talk with you outside," I ordered Jenn. "Now."

I let go of Titan's hand, and smartly she decided not to follow. Jenn threw a glowering glare toward Fire as if it was her fault she'd been singled out.

As soon as we clicked the door shut, I spun on her. "Can you please shift back into Yolo right now?" I didn't want to talk to his dead familiar who he eerily impersonated perfectly. They were two completely different personalities altogether, and I was becoming confused, much in the way I wondered if Yolo was as the shifts and changings were becoming apparent. Did he even know who he was anymore? Was he starting to feel like an imposter in his normal form?

"Oh?" Jenn said, somewhat offended, but shifted back into the shirtless Yolo. His wooden cross and tattoos were stark against his tan skin, unlike the fair complexion of Jenn's. He stretched his arms wide and brushed his hands through his blond shoulder-length hair, caught off guard when it stopped prematurely because he was used to the length of Jenn's.

"Did you kill him?" Yolo sneered, suddenly snapping to his senses and the mission we'd just been on as if he'd been dazed until the remains of Jenn glistened off him. I knew who he meant. James. Yolo had been there and saved me from that place. He and Balzar alike. I felt somewhat guilty for wedging my bladed fingertips into his chest when I looked back on what he'd already done for me.

"He escaped," I gritted out, trying to focus on the conversation at hand. Another time would come where I could seek my vengeance on James. This world was far too small for me not to be able to hunt him. And I *would* find him. I couldn't be there to see the devastation on Campture's face and those around her when her reign came to an end, and it was certainly a discussion I'd soon be having with my mother. In whatever way it changed the future, I'm glad she was now dead.

"Did you know?" I said accusingly.

"Know about what?" he said, raising his hands defensively as I poked my finger to his chest.

"About the werewolves?"

"What about the werewolves?" he asked, and his tone animated into a harsh bruise, already knowing he'd been left out of something.

"Cesar ordered Balzar and Tythian to lead in slaughtering a Human Compound of werewolves while we dealt with the hunters."

Yolo rocked back on his heels, his eyebrows shooting up as he whistled. He placed his hands casually in his pockets as he shook his head. He then restlessly put his hand through his hair again. "They didn't tell me," he said quietly. It was more admission that he'd been left out of their grand scheme not so directly that he cared about the wolves. But I'd seen the care he harbored for them, or was that just the ones from the Human Compound who Jenn had associated herself with? I wanted to know if I was entirely alone in my way of thinking.

"Why are you here, Yolo? Why are you guarding them?"

"Because you needed someone to guard them while you were away," he replied immediately.

"No. This goes beyond that. Don't bullshit me anymore. The others want them gone." I made sure to lower my voice so the children couldn't hear my voice. Julia was a completely different issue. "Your coven leader and brothers want them *dead*. Why are you standing in the way of that?"

He shuffled uncomfortably, placing his hands back into his pockets. For the first time, he seemed speechless. If his coven opposed it then so should he. He would be forced to one way or another, but something bound him here, and it was more than idle curiosity.

He seemed unsettled and looked around, ensuring no one else was listening. Reluctantly, he tapped to his head, insinuating I speak with him telepathically. I didn't want to because I didn't like it. But, if he wasn't comfortable enough to say it where someone might overhear, and I demanded such an answer, I could offer him this much.

Yolo's mind blossomed open to me. I pushed past all the pain and hurt, tragedy, and fond memories, most of which were filled with Jenn. It was more predominant than usual. *It's personal but not,* he started nonchalantly, and I thought I'd have to pry it from him before he continued. *Sydney was one of Jenn's ancestors.* His gaze locked with mine as if expecting to be scrutinized. I was confused. How? She'd died before ever giving birth, hadn't she? As if reading my expression, he interrupted, waving his hands about. "Not her!" And then he remembered he was speaking telepathically. *Her sister. And that bloodline trails down to Sydney.*

I realized he was chasing ghosts. *Was your infiltration of that particular Human Compound premeditated because you knew he'd be in there?* I thought about Sydney's history. He had been the first born without iridescent eyes and was thrown into one of the camps, separated from his huntress mother. It was only because his father broke into and removed him from the human camp that he'd ended up leading in the human government, following his father's footsteps. It was why he had an edge over the others because despite not being a hunter himself, he still had hunter blood.

We had planned on infiltrating a human camp for some time, but yes, I'd ensured that one specifically. Yolo was sheepish as he opened up to me, I imagined in a way he'd never been able to anyone else at all. This whole time he'd been chasing the lingering remains of his familiar.

"So, then Titan—"

"Is the last," he coyly said. I wasn't one to point out how sickly and unhealthy his fixation and endearment was because if I were in his position, I wouldn't know how I'd live on without Chase. I was beginning to understand everyone's relationships with their familiars were different. And I couldn't judge his if I wasn't willing others to judge my own. "But if Cesar is against it and if he were to order it …" Yolo was perplexed. *Please, Esmore, don't let anything happen to them. I know it's a selfish request, but I don't have the power to oppose him.*

"I attacked Balzar for following his order," I said in the way of dismissal. I didn't need him to beg me to keep her safe. But it now made sense to me why he was forthcoming to spend so much time protecting them. Right now, I was the only one stepping between those two cubs and their demise. Even Yolo's hands were tied.

"You attacked him?! What the hell, Esmore, we're meant to be siblings! Play fighting yes, but not for reals!"

"It's your little family, not mine!" I snapped at him, and he seemed to freeze under my harsh tone. Cesar had made my mother cry. Physically brought tears to her eyes from how affected she'd been by his betrayal. We were nearing the end of our happy family scenario, not that it'd ever been such a thing.

"Esmore, I know you feel that way. But for what it's worth, I do like you and Chase. And I'm sorry if we ever have to cross paths in an unfavorable way. I'm sure Balzar feels the same way."

I grimaced. Yolo couldn't speak on behalf of Balzar. But I appreciated Yolo's words nonetheless. The cracks were beginning to show in this treaty. What did I expect from a houseful of vampires?

Despite all of the factors, I wanted to leave Yolo in some kind of peace of mind, in appreciation for all that he had done for me. "I can't promise, but I'll try to keep them safe."

I was no longer in a position to promise people their lives. I'd learned the hard way of how out of my control that was.

Chapter 20

I WAS SITTING on a wooden stool, hunched over and scrubbing my hands clean with the small bucket of water and cloth Darcy provided me. I would've opted for a bath had it not been for the disarray the coven was in. Chase was checking up on me often despite his task and stress of having to unnerve his coven.

My clothing had to be replaced yet again, not only because of the blood and filth, but also the numerous tears in my leather shirt, punctured stomach, and where my wings had sprouted from.

"Here, Esmore, I found this shirt for you," Titan said, offering me a leather fitted shirt she'd pulled out of my drawer of clothes. She dusted it off and placed it beside me. Julia had remained quiet the entire time. Yolo had since returned to his brothers, no doubt disgruntled that he'd been left out of their planning. A daunting thought, I wondered if he'd known he would've been forced to take part in it. I supposed he had no choice. We were all bound by rules and obligations in some way or another. Much as Balzar had been, and yet I was still furious with his betrayal.

My mother's presence was a welcoming warmth. Though the way she walked in said otherwise, I was glad to see she was self-composed once again, if not colder than usual, her expression unreadable.

"What do we do now?" I asked casually, scrubbing viciously at the blood that wouldn't wash off as if my hand were to permanently be stained.

"Come for a walk with me?" I looked around the room. "It won't be far." My mother insisted, reading my reluctance. I trusted Jerimiah and Darcy to stand guard, although the uneasiness in the institute was like a choking miasma. But I could tell she wouldn't' risk asking me for privacy unless it was important.

I dropped the cloth back into the ill-colored bucket. "Stay with them," I ordered Fire. She was already being used as a pillow by Chris, curled underneath him. For all of her talk about responsibility and being soft on them, she was certainly contradicting herself. She was bloody and matted as well, but the children still took to her. I'd have to clean her off next.

Looking down at my disheveled appearance, I opted to grab Chase's long leather jacket from the coat stand. I'm sure he wouldn't mind, and I wanted something to cover up my clothing that displayed I'd been severely wounded in the last battle. The jacket edged along my leather boots because of our height difference. It smelt like him and was like a giant embrace when I put it on. Instead of walking through the institute, we opted to jump over the railing of our wing. It jolted my knees and limbs uncomfortably.

I followed my mother to the outer edges of the institute, out of earshot of those in the coven. Even though we were on the edge of the forest, we were still able to look up and see the flickering candle lights inside the tower.

She still hadn't found time to clean herself, blood was sprayed all over her robe and up her arms. Where she'd been severely cut was now completely healed. We stood there in silence. I didn't know if she expected me to speak first, to pry about her relationship with Cesar or if I should wait for her to speak. So, we stood there staring at one another, neither looking away. It built an anxious tension between us.

"Your father—"

"Please don't call him that," I said begrudgingly. And already by her tone and beginning of that statement, I knew she'd forgiven him, or worse, she agreed with him. I could change anyone else's opinion no more than they could change mine. I felt alone in this decision, in wanting to protect the werewolves. Was I so wrong in doing so?

"Cesar betrayed us, but he further explained the situation. I don't agree with his methods, and it jeopardized us. But from a tactical standpoint, I can understand its necessity."

Necessity, what a cruel punch in enforcing that I was in the wrong for reacting in the way I did.

"You don't think we should protect the werewolves?" I asked her.

"I neither agree nor disagree. Though I do have concerns about your attachment to them," she solicited. "Cesar has broken trust between us. He's created tension between the covens. But we do need to comply going forward together."

I tsked at her, throwing my hands up in the air. It was a sure way of saying this sort of behavior might happen again. I understood the importance of this alliance, but surely he would suffer more than this. There was a consequence to this sort of treachery. I hated nothing more than lies, deceit, and betrayal. The very foundations of the world we lived in.

I could feel Cesar creeping toward us. "Cesar, I told you to wait," she chided. I stretched my unyielding gaze toward him, letting him know oh too well how I didn't approve of him speaking to me.

"I know, but we don't have time to wait," he implied with his arrogant, self-serving notion. Perhaps I'd hated it so much because I could identify that I'd once held the same quality as a Token. I was inflexible in my methods if it were to risk my team. I supposed that was what differentiated us, Cesar had no issue with sacrificing others for his gain. "I'm sorry for forcing your hand, but you need to understand, my daughter, this association you have with the wolves is *wrong*. They do not need our protection, and though I allow the novelty of this," he pointed to the tower, "I do this to please you. It cannot go past that. Our focus and mission *is* the Vampire Council, and that's only three weeks. I need to make sure you're focused and ready for that."

"Because I'm being used as the leverage in your schemes?" I sniped back.

"Only if you want to," he replied earnestly. I was surprised that he was genuinely giving me a choice, or perhaps he was faking it for my mother's gratification. I looked at her uneasily as if this might be a trick of sorts. It was difficult for me to suppress my anger toward him, especially after seeing the state he left my mother in. She was a warrior, one of the fiercest I knew. But she was standing here amicably right now. Was I acting out of accord by throwing around my weight?

"You need Tracey's Council." I jutted out my chin, proving that I didn't have a choice in the matter.

"We need many things," Cesar corrected. His roguish tone had softened slightly as if he was crawling through his words for approval once again. He'd known what he did would hurt my mother and me, and yet he still did it. But Cesar had been fermenting on his hatred and revenge against Oppollo for centuries. I supposed even we weren't to come between that. "But I need to send Tythian back with an answer within the hour. If you choose to agree, you'll have to go with Tracey to the Vampire Council, concealed and changed of course, so no one knows of your true identity. If you are to choose not … then we will have to find a new way to receive such information."

We only had a matter of weeks. It had only been getting worse these past months, and it wasn't going to relieve. Though Oppollo might've not been targeting me personally right now, it didn't change the fact that covens were being slaughtered one by one. And it would be only a matter of time until they'd find ours. And with consideration, I'd also promised Fier Oppollo's demise. And in return, he would retract Chase's disease.

"I really don't have a choice," I weakly argued. For once, I didn't want to be considered as special or valuable. I'd craved the recognition within the Hunter Guild, and now I despised it. I just wanted to fight alongside my familiar, not be in the center of a war that had been escalating for centuries. My vampire self coiled in delightful anticipation. And then there was that. The part of me that thrived on being in the middle of chaos if only to see how I'd fair against the strongest. It was stupidity and malice all the same.

Cesar curtly nodded, almost thankful and my mother grimaced, her lips forming into a thin line. "There's another thing." I'd never seen so much uncertainty shine through her expression. I looked between the two, suspenseful as to what she was about to say. What could make her feel so uncomfortable?

"I connected with Louise, and she swears they did not betray us, but someone had tipped them off." I looked between Cesar and my mother. Well, that wasn't a baffling surprise. Plenty of vampires within here would have the incentive to stray for their own gain. Louise herself had been foreboding about it every time we'd sought her out.

"But can we really trust what she says? Sure, we killed Campture." I had to let that sink in for a moment. It'd actually happened, it had finally been done. A wash of relief waved over me for the first time since coming back. Campture was dead. The aftermath of the fight and time to reflect finally caught up. She was finally gone, for all those years of her looking down her nose at me and sneering at my unnatural state without my huntress eyes. And for all that she did afterward branding me as a traitor and monster, spreading rumors to have me killed. *Campture was dead.*

"I trust Louise," my mother said, realizing I'd fallen short, thinking about the implications of what would now happen with Campture gone. What would happen to the remains of the Guild? Would Kelf, her second take charge or would someone else rise through the ranks? Was Kelf still even alive? Would they merge with Michelle's coven? What would happen to James? Where would he go?

From our peripheral, we watched Tythian walk out as if basking in the moonlight. He was still icky with the remains of blood and mud on his robe. He was watching us, and I realized he was silently asking for my answer. Cesar curtly nodded, and Tythian vanished to tell Tracey we agreed to her terms.

Tythian made me uneasy, more so than usual as of late. And every time we'd visited Louise, she forewarned us someone who we were with was untrustworthy, and he had always been there.

"I don't trust Tythian," I said openly. It wasn't tactful of me to say, but I was driving off my instinct. By now, we had so much bad blood between us that it was highly possible I was just bitter toward him and accusing him blindly. But something in my gut didn't feel right when I looked at him.

"I'm aware that you and Tythian have your differences. But I would trust no one more in my coven than Tythian. He was my first and has been with me for centuries since. I trust him with my life," Cesar said dismissively. "Yes, he's been aloof lately, and I've noticed that as well, but to his credit, he still hasn't had time to mourn the grievance of losing his familiar."

My mother and Cesar looked at one another longingly, and I was almost ashamed that Cesar would box me in like that. What happened to Whitney was tragic, and it'd happened because she was protecting Chase and me. Of course I felt pity for him, but it didn't take away the edge of my distrust.

"We need to look into it. If you have further proof, Esmore, bring it to our attention," my mother concurred. I suspected she too had her doubts, but that skepticism could be stretched equally over anyone within this institute. "Cesar and I want to offer you a proposition." Again, she looked uneasy.

"Which is?"

"What if we offered you the location of your heart?"

Time swirled to a complete stop around us. *My heart?*

CHAPTER 21

I DANGLED MY leg over the cliff edge, staring at the nearly full moon. My mother had traded spots with Fire so I could take a walk and think over their offer. I idly brushed my hand through Fire's fur as she rested contently beside me. Chase's leather jacket flared around me as I leaned back and rested my weight on my wrists.

My heart? Did I want to be reunited with my heart? With my gift? The core of what I was as a huntress? Their words and offer were seemingly foreign as I slowly tried to translate what this could mean for me and how it could change everything.

My mother would lead me and a small team to the resting place of my heart if I desired. If before this upcoming battle, I wanted my heart, it could be mine. For various reasons they were for and against. It took away my immortality, theoretically speaking. If Oppollo were to grab for my chest again, I would squirm, and my heart would falter. I *would* die.

But if I were to accept, I could also gain my power and gift which had been taken from me. I could experiment with that of what I was born with and judge for myself how potent its strength was. If I could bend it to my will, who knows the degree of advantage we'd have. And selfishly, I might feel whole once again.

I sighed pathetically at the perfect red apple Julia had offered me on the way out. I'd already taken two bites, but its nutrition wasn't hitting the spot. After such a fierce fight my body only thrummed for one thing. Had it not been for Fire resting comfortably beside me I might've considered going hunting.

Chase's presence surrounded me as if the trees themselves were bending to his will and the sheer power that radiated from him. I couldn't tell if it was because he'd triggered the Descendant or if it was the tingle of war and misfortune that surrounded us, but he was glowering with sheer testosterone and glory. I twisted only slightly to watch him walk out of the shadows and gleam in the moonlight.

"I'd like to say my jacket looks better on you … but …" He shrugged his shoulder cockily as he strutted out, bare-chested and his body that I loved so much on full display. I tried to return the coy smile but fell short. My mind was a jumble. He carried with him a canister and two wine glasses. I stared at them and then his smug expression.

"I thought we could have a romantic evening," he said, sitting beside me and resting the items between us. He leaned over and pressed a kiss to my shoulder. I wasn't sure if it was me he was kissing or his jacket. He reached out his hand and began scratching behind Fire's ear. Although he didn't agree with protecting their species, he'd become accustomed to Fire. Watching him, it forced me to think back to the conversation with Jerimiah and Darcy. If I were to regain my heart, it would only further risk Chase. If I couldn't control my gift then what would happen to us? What would happen to him?

Even if it didn't affect him directly, I would transmit my gift to him the moment we were intimate. Then what if he lost all control? Where would that leave us? Was the risk worth it?

He flicked me between my eyebrows. "What are you so worried about?" I looked away, ashamed that I'd closed up on him again, giving him no insight into my most inner thoughts. I wanted to think this over selfishly first before I brought it up with him.

He was patient and began to pour thick red blood into the wine glasses, the blood was still warm and my mouth moistened at the smell. *Fresh human blood.* "Tythian brought back a few humans, I slit her wrist and took a bit for us before Dillian and Tori ripped into her." Immediately he seemed apologetic for the way he spoke. "Esmore, I didn't mean to make it sound so …"

"It's okay," I said still eyeing off the glass he offered me. I was trying to rein control as I stifled the thirst of my vampire. Would I still thirst for it in the same way that I did now if I had my heart?

"Today was a lot," he said attentively. The words that were unsaid were our bodies need blood to restore. I swooped the glass from his hand throwing it back like I'd never tasted something so sweet and divine. My eyelids burst open with a new admiration for the nearly full moon as I savored its taste that lingered on my lips. He chuckled and poured me another glass, reserving his own.

"Your eyes are so beautiful, I don't think I'll ever get used to their magnetic pull," he charmed. I was perplexed. If he loved my huntress eyes so much would he also accept all of me, literally, including my heart? It felt like such an estranged notion. How would the shift of power change? Would I be unbalanced once again after I'd learned how to adapt without it this past year?

I'd lacked emotion since the day my mother removed it from my chest unless I was with Chase. Would I once again be overwhelmed by it or would it be the same emotional rollercoaster, except naturally? Would it only strengthen my resolve to push down the vampire part of me that so often sprung to the surface? So many questions rolled around in my head.

"Hey," he said, gently hooking his finger under my chin and raising my face to his. "Talk to me. Is it about what happened today? It's a mess in there, but it'll be okay. Once this is all over, we can cut ties with them. We'll find our own place to go."

I couldn't even imagine what that would look like, but he believed in it so deeply. I wanted to believe in it as well. I placed my wine glass to the side. Fire stood up and stretched with a big yawn.

She sniffed the air and traced the small commotion of wild animals fighting in the distance. She sauntered into the woods, her ears pinned back slightly as she listened and prepared her hunt.

Her absence felt like it offered me some breathing space and a tender loneliness all at once. "Cesar and my mother offered to give me my heart's resting place."

I studied him intently as he took a shallow sip of his blood. I was hinging on his next words. Even I couldn't articulate how I'd felt about it. What would he think about it? I was pointing out the reminder that I wasn't complete and that I had never been able to give him all of me. But he'd been happy with all that I had to offer up until now.

"This is good, isn't it? Isn't this what you wanted?" he asked gently, cupping his hand under my jaw. I eased into his touch, closing my eyes and embracing his scent. If I could, I'd rest like this forever—that's what I wanted, and for the rest of the world to slip away.

"I don't know what will happen," I said eerily. "What if I change? What if I can't control it? I don't know if it'll kill me straight away or what if it begins to eat away at everyone around me, as my mother described and in the way it hurt her? *What if it hurts you?*"

"Sshhh," he said and swept me into his arms. He nestled my face into the nook of his neck. The lingering smell of his blood beneath excited and tamed me all at once. Familiar. "Don't work yourself up about this. We'll get through this step by step."

"There are so many variables, so many things could go wrong," I mumbled against his neck. He patted through my filthy hair, deciding to unknot it and rake his fingers through it to try and clean it as best as he could.

"But so many things could go right. Let me guess, they're suggesting this prior to when we go to the Council meeting?"

I nodded, and he sighed. He gently kissed my cheek and suggested I turn around with my back facing him. Delicately, he began to braid my hair. I stared out into the distance at a cliff adjacent to us. There was something soothing about being so close to the edge, and I wasn't sure if that was because I knew I had the ability to fly or simply because of the view. Another thing that was being left unsaid was the Descendant and what it meant for his instability.

"And do you think they're raising this offer selfishly or because they think it's what's best for you?" he asked carefully. Chase had been very open about his impression of Cesar, but he was still respectful of my mother and the delicacy of our relationship. But even then, they both strained their mechanics and instinct to be nurturing toward one another. They'd learned to tolerate one another.

"I think both. But they've left the decision to me. Much like I took away Dillian and Tori's right, I think maybe my mother has a guilty conscience of removing it from me. I can understand why she did it." Comparing it to what I'd done to Dillian and Tori was the first step in allowing me to forgive her for what she'd done. I'd been so begrudging against her for it. But I'd acted no differently in integrity when I wanted to keep Dillian and Tori alive. Chase remained silent as he delicately plaited my hair, the motion soothing as I wanted nothing more than to lean back into him. "I want to be whole again. I want to know what my born-given gift feels like. Its power could assist us in challenging Oppollo or it could tear *us* apart."

His hands stopped momentarily as he deciphered all that entailed. I might not be able to control it. It might affect his disease-stricken mind and prevent us from being intimate ever again in case he couldn't handle the gift itself. I didn't even know if *I* could control it.

He'd finished my braid and promptly pressed me back against his chest. I looked up so I could catch a glimpse of him. He kissed my forehead gently. "It was the risk I took with the Descendant and being intimate with you. And that's turned out pretty well if I do say so myself."

"But this is different, Chase, you know it. What if something similar to what happened today happens on a larger scale?"

He tried to conceal his agonized expression. What happened today didn't only scare me, but it unnerved him as well. Our own imbalance was only hurting one another. I was rightly capable of losing myself, and he risked turning into a saber.

"It won't come to that," he said quietly. His usual gusto and certainty were no longer in his tone. The Descendant coming to the surface only meant one thing for him, that all the boundaries he'd built, every single chain, was undone.

"Chase," I said, twisting in his lap and propping up on my knees so I could face him. His gray eyes watched me as his rough thumb caught hold of my blue gemmed necklace with consideration. Might've we been left alone, perhaps we could've figured this out and lived out our days. But with everything that surrounded us from the moment our paths collided, we were bound to this tragedy, and I didn't know how to dig us out. "What if my heart and gift could end this war quickly?"

He gave me a sad smile as if wanting to be hopeful alongside me. "But what if I lose you to it?" he said somberly. His pessimism caught me off guard. Chase only cared for my safety.

"But what if it was the answer?" I equally measured. Another small, lopsided smile. It wasn't only for its power, but it also encompassed the ideal of feeling *whole*.

"If this is what you want, I'm not against it, Esmore. I believe in you, always. And I'll be here for you if you make such a decision. I just want to ensure a seal-proof way that it won't hurt you."

I pressed his hand to my chest, where a pumping heart should've beat rhythmically. Instead, it was a phantom quiet flutter from my mother's gift. This desire for my heart had always felt so out of reach. And now it could finally be mine. "Nothing we've done up until this point has been a seal proof guarantee."

"I know, but I feel like I'm getting further and further away from you," he said, curling his fingers around my hand. *My love, you keep rushing into danger, and though I know you've always been a huntress, this is different. You're punishing yourself, and I'm worried you'll push it too far and I won't be there to stop it. I'm bound to you, just as much as you are me. I've already had too many close calls losing you when I've only just found you.*

He pressed his forehead to mine, and I couldn't find the effort or words to argue with him. He'd seen right through me, in all my recklessness. I didn't want him to suffer any more than he was, but I couldn't deny the allure of impulse. I closed my eyes as he did, savoring the moment. Maybe my heart would usher away the vampire's instinct and pride. Perhaps it would help me find balance even when I feared it was already too late. I was like poison to Chase.

I arched my lips to his, gently brushing them, savoring the motion and feel of his surprisingly soft lips. I loved him. But I didn't feel worthy of him. Not anymore. And I would do everything I could to heal him.

"Wherever you go, I go," Chase said, cupping my jaw and kissing me gently. His hand twisted around my fresh braid, tugging it back to incline my head more toward him. A small moan passed my lips, my body reacting to him in the way it always did. I only ever wanted to be in this state of ecstasy because of Chase. Not because I was tempted by power or caressed by the unearthly recklessness that one day might get me killed. And I feared that was what I was secretly chasing.

There was no other thrill like being with Chase. My thighs itched to be closer together, eagerly wanting to rub. If I were to find my heart, who knows when the next time I could have him in this way would be. Picking up on my desperation, he grazed his hands under my ass and lifted me onto his lap. I straddled my knees either side of him, his hard shaft predominantly pushing against his leather pants. I ground back and forth, a small elicit grunt coming from him as the friction between excited both of us.

He stood with me, my weight no issue as he continued to feverishly kiss me. I fumbled at our waists so I could unbutton the top of his pants.

He found one of my daggers that had dropped to the ground and sliced from the bottom of my shirt to the top, the tip of the blade jutting at my throat. It aroused me as the thought of danger mixed with pleasure. In a matter of seconds, we'd stripped one another, all except the jacket I still wore. *Keep it on,* he glowered exceptionally enthused to have me wear it.

He scanned over my stomach to make sure my wound had completely healed. I hooked his chin and attention back on me. *Eye on the prize,* I motioned as I glided my hand back and forth over his length. His muscles tensed under my firm grip as I angled my hand between us while he still stood, holding me. I was suspended in the air, the cool breeze only accentuating the tingles and goosebumps I already had, but for other reasons.

Every single stroke sparked a new imagination in all the ways and positions I could take him. Slowly, the tension began to recede from him as he let me selfishly have my way with him. I danced my fingers lightly along his collarbone and at the back of his shoulder blades, thinking about his beautiful black wings. They were beautiful. *He* was beautiful.

"Esmore," he growled sensually. His mouth was becoming parched as we kissed, and I squirmed my neck closer to him, understanding what he wanted most right now. I flicked my braid out of his way, my speed pumping him faster as he moaned into my next kiss.

"I want you to taste me, Chase," I said. His growl vibrated through me, and his fang nipped at my lip just by the tender thought. Without hesitation, he kissed along my collar bone, small, cold kisses trailing the tender dip in my neck as I arched into him. I froze my grip firmly around the base of his shaft as his fangs punctured into me. I moaned and squeezed harder as it twitched in my hand, even more excited by the blood. "Messy," I breathed. "I want it messy."

His fangs edged deeper and more savagely and I looked to the sky, my eyes wide from the satisfying pain. I moaned loudly now rubbing the tip of his cock against my clit and lips, riding him in a spirited way as he held me up. Blood oozed down my neck as the smell of myself fermented the air. The feel of his cool shaft brushing against my lips had me wildly riding and him harshly panting as he arched in to take more.

I clutched my other hand around his shoulder blade, not wanting to hold myself back any longer. The taste of him earlier to help me heal was a small treat, but now I wanted the whole thing. I drove my fangs into his neck, messily tearing into him, pleased with the spillage that rolled over his collarbone.

It was the warmth I so rarely knew or could feel promised to me in this delightful bundle. We held on to one another as lovers, gritting as we feasted into an intoxicating dizzy haze. With one hand he positioned his shaft at my edge, slowly letting me fall naturally on top of him. I moaned at the illicit drug that was feeding me life and the fulfilling pressure of his girth that was riding me into a high.

He dragged his fangs deeper and tore a little at my flesh. My whole body went rigid, ready to explode as he marked me.

"Chase," I whimpered, licking at the blood that covered his neck as if it was his shaft I was delicately tasting. His wound had already healed. At the callout of his name, he found my lips again. His tongue pushed deeper, competing against mine with a desperate force. We both felt like we were losing one another, and by physically being here in the now, together, desperately clinging to one another—we'd be okay.

He rested me on my back, the leather of his jacket acting as enough cushioning from the gravelly terrain. I kept my knees wrapped around his back, unmoving from the deep angle he positioned me in and his shoulder-length hair was stuck to the side of his neck and face from all the blood. The moonshine caressed around his skin like the beautiful god he was. And in the way he stared at me longingly, I could tell he was looking at me in the same.

His hips pounded into me deeper, and I moaned at the fulfilling length of him. I grazed my nails down the sides of his stomach, tracing the indentation of his abs. Every part of him was mine. Lover. Husband. Familiar. Making love to him under the moonlight engrossed me into the night, letting all other cares wash off me as I only focused on now.

I lay with my head on top of his chest and with one leg stretched over his abdomen, lazily enjoining the silence of the night. I circled a print into his chest, considering what it might be like for him when I one day had my own heart.

"If your heart is truly what you want, then we'll find it together," he said, brushing his finger gently over my neck. I kissed his chest lovingly. When I scanned my mind over his, he meant it in earnest. The doubt he'd shared earlier was of mutual concern. Neither of us knew what would happen. But now that I had the option to find it, I couldn't look the other away.

"I don't want you near me when my mother inserts it. If I can't control my gift, then I don't know what will happen. And I don't want to hurt you."

"We're in this together remember. Your fate is mine, and I might be the only one who can help call you back from it." He kissed the top of my head. I propped myself up to look at him, those gentle gray eyes staring back at me. I doubted anyone saw Chase in this way.

"You have to stay for your coven," I weakly argued. The truth was I wasn't sure what was to come. And though I could handle it on my own, I'd become accustomed to having Chase there as support, as my equal in every battle to face. The dependency struck fear into my very core, but I couldn't escape it nor did I ever want to.

"I made claim to my coven only so I could build an army to protect you. Clarissa and the gargoyles can cover me. Where you go, I'll go."

I was suddenly self-conscious. Was this selfish to do? I could be whole and complete, but a greater fear hung on the other side of that. What if nothing changed at all? What if this was wasted time in a period where we should be preparing for the weeks to come?

"At my mother's suggestion, we take a small team so we can locate it quicker."

"That doesn't sound ideal, she didn't just hide it in a little crook that we could easily reach?"

A small smile swept over my lips thinking of my mother hiding it in such a ludicrous and obvious place. "Have you met my mother?" I asked rhetorically. If she went to all that effort to conceal and hide my heart, she certainly would ensure no one would find it.

"Unfortunately, yes," he teased with a chuckle. "And she's just as terrifying as her daughter, if not even more."

CHAPTER 22

CESAR AND MY mother gave us one night to gather the right team for the mission. It also solicited us to stay with Fire and the cubs. Tonight was a full moon, and they'd be subject to turning against their will once again.

"And I get to come right?" Lincon perked. He was perched on the alcove of our wing, swinging his legs back and forth childishly. I'd spent the morning watching Titan and Chris as Fire trained them for another morning parlay. I was watching them as they danced about in both human and wolf form, tiredly spending their energy before the horrific night.

I hadn't told Lincon exactly what I was leaving for, only that I was taking a small team. At my mother's suggestion, we took Lincon and the twins, even when she herself didn't trust him. She said their gifts would help our task. Apparently, there would be enemies, the likes of which I hadn't seen before. Creatures that had mutated much like the rodents in the woodlands near the Human Compound.

Keeping it to a smaller team was necessary, the fewer people who knew the reasons for our leaving the better. Cesar hadn't even disclosed it to the brothers. Even that was too much of a risk to him. I'd told

Lincon we were going to connect with another Hunter Guild at my mother's suggestion.

"Esmore, it's very easy, you just say," he opened and closed his hand as if it were a puppet, "yes, Lincon, I'd be honored for you to come. How could I not have you by my side in all your manliness?" he squeaked in a girlish voice. I gave him an effective look that would've worked on most.

"You *and* the twins," I corrected. "And think of this as a reward for your loyalty." I'd learned with Lincon that he worked on a reward and praise system, surprisingly considering how unkempt he was. But, if I made him feel important then he was more likely to follow me earnestly. I still waited for the moment and day that he'd turn on me. And even now, I wasn't agreeable to my mother's verdict of finding them necessary. I intertwined my fingers and dangled them over the edge, slouching over so I could watch Titan try to maneuver and disarm Fire. Chris wasn't far behind her, but Titan had a knack and ferociousness that suited her. She was fast, and I wondered if that had more to do with her lineage of hunters or if it was the wolf's bite that prompted her to excel.

I could feel Yolo prancing up the stairs, his light-footed bounce always an unnatural beat considering vampires hardly made noise.

"You're dismissed," I said to Lincon. He frowned and watched Yolo as he pranced up the stairs. Lincon sighed to himself melodramatically, and free fell backward. I watched as he circled and landed delicately on his feet. He quickly scampered off toward where Kora and Kasey waited for him beside the front gates.

Jerimiah and Darcy were in their gargoyle form behind me. Julia still remained inside. It was difficult to let her out. Not only did she disrupt the other vampires because of her scent, but it disturbed Dillian who purposefully was ignoring her. Even with the suggestion of my mother concealing her scent and protecting her if he were to react, the liveliness had vanished out of him. I'd thought if any kind of love were to push through *anything,* it was theirs. But not everything went to plan or worked under the assumption.

"Are they training again?" He asked and slouched over the edge, the same as I did. We stood there silently watching over them. "They're fast little buggers, aren't they?" he rhetorically asked.

Both of our spines straightened as a group of six vampires walked on the outer edges of the institute. They were laughing amongst themselves before going on to hunt. Cesar had recently widened the hunting territory, with the intention to diffuse the angst and thirst amongst the covens. Tythian could only teleport so many humans in at a time, and even then they were allocated accordingly between Cesar and Chase and trickled down by their command.

Their laughter came to an abrupt stop as they leered over at the wolves. They were members of Chase's coven. One rested his hands in his pockets nonchalant, but his intense gaze was anything but. The woman behind him whispered into his ear and pushed him along. They all looked up in our direction, feverish to get out of sight.

It unnerved me that even with Cesar and Chase's law blanketing the three wolves into their protection, some still contemplated acting of their own accord, even when it would ultimately cost them their own lives.

"Cesar mentioned you were going out on another mission to meet some hunters?" he queried. Though he seemed suspicious he didn't lead on. "I was also advised Chase would be going with you?"

I continued watching the little ones and the vampires who came back and forth casually. On the other side of the institute, some trained amongst themselves, and I could sense Balzar had much to do with that. "He will be," I carefully said, not sure where he was going with this. From what I'd seen, Chase and Yolo got along. Out of all the brothers, they probably seemed closest in age and personality with their goofy tendencies. But as I was learning, I couldn't depend on that relationship to mean much. At any time, any of us could turn on one another. It was our nature—duty and self-preservation before emotional attachment. I looked at his wooden cross, curious in the way that it always contradicted who and what he was. A religion that believed in purity, even when he was the stature of the darkest kind.

Yolo pulled a small bag from his pocket. It was a leather square pouch and hard on the outside. He offered it to me. "Balzar told me what happened to Chase during the fight with the hunters." I pinned a threatening glare at him. If he'd seen, then who else knew? Yolo raised his hands in the air defensively. "Balzar and Tythian reported it to Cesar, and that's as far as word has spread."

It was pointless to threaten him over it. If that was as far as rumor spread, then we were lucky. But it meant Cesar would watch him more closely now.

"Esmore, I don't want to talk out of turn, but …"

"Then don't," I suggested. His woody brown eyes seemed saddened by my response as if our friendship had come further than that. And I pitied him that he looked at me in such a way. I kept my hard exposure up but gave in only slightly. "But it's never stopped you before now, has it?"

A twinkle came to his eyes. "Remember when we returned to the Human Compound, and I stole some of the syringes that sedated the vampires? There are two in this bag. I've kept the others. If it gets really bad with Chase, and if he's shifting too quickly into a saber or even the Descendant takes hold—this should mute his power and sedate him into a stupor."

The thought of having to use such a foul trick on Chase dragged down any remaining merits, but the reality was, watching him as the Descendant, no matter how beautiful, was an ugly reality. The same as when he bordered on turning into a saber. The triggers were becoming more regular, and I was partially to blame. I curled my hand around the hard square case. "They are ready to go. All you need to do is pull them out." He looked over his shoulder at the gargoyles, half expecting them to object or defy his cheap trick in some way. But they didn't. This wasn't to hurt their coven leader. This was to protect him from himself.

"How long does the sedation last?" I asked, feeling colder and sinking into a non-returnable place. Would Chase consider this as betraying his trust? But this was only as a backup. It didn't mean I was going to use it. This was only if I had no other option.

"Its potency depends on the vampire. Some as little as three hours until they start pushing through its effects, others it will stifle for eight."

I rested the small box on the edge of the alcove in contemplation. I pocketed my other hand into my back pocket, rolling my finger over the lock of Chase's hair when we'd sworn our vows and wedded. I would tell him about the sedations, maybe it would even ease his mind that we now had options.

I wondered why Yolo hadn't offered the sedations to me after I'd lost control when Dillian and the werewolves' camp had been attacked. I'd triggered the saber-like disease in Chase's mind then as well. But I couldn't hold it against Yolo, he wasn't thinking clearly either, just as shocked by the turn of events.

"Any recollection or idea of who ambushed you?" I asked. It was another thing I'd have to figure out, so I could seek revenge on them, and perhaps even Dillian and Tori wanted that claim as well. I wanted to be able to hand them at least that much.

Yolo sighed as if he'd tried to recollect that day over and over again. He watched Titan and Chris with a saddened expression, one that resembled the gentleness of Jenn. Everyone was dealing with their own demons, and his existent crisis was that of his own, but I wondered how many others had picked up that the two were starting to merge into one. Surely the brothers and Cesar had noticed as well.

"It's like they appeared out of thin air. When I noticed whoever's presence it was that crept up on us, it was too late. I was the first to be taken out. I didn't even have time to turn around. The next thing I knew I woke up in the institute with Dillian and Tori twitching and turning on the ground."

The reminder set me back into a feverish state, one that Chase was quick to dampen through our bonded link. I accepted his caress, my body defusing the tense restrictions that were clawing at me as I envisioned their dead figures on the floor once again.

"I only know one person who can teleport …" I pointedly suggested. He studied my side profile. It was dangerous grounds suggesting Tythian, but Yolo was clever, surely despite their loyalty he'd considered the same thing.

"I know what you're suggesting," he said somewhat defensively of his brother. "But the reality is he was with Cesar the whole time and then teleported you in. It's highly probable this gift is not unique only to him."

"Someone attacked me in the same fashion when I was alone during our battle with the Hunter Guild."

"You didn't report that to Cesar?" he questioned.

"No, I have a feeling it's more of a personal grudge because as soon as they missed their mark they vanished. Just like when we'd encroached on their attack against the wolves, Dillian, and the others." I still couldn't make sense of it. Whether the presence of who was invading my dreams was the same, they'd also been lingering in New York. I had the distinct feeling they were separate, but having two evasive presences targeting me from the shadows was only another additive to the many others who were hunting me.

"Could you get a feel of their mind? Who they might be?" he asked curiously.

"No." I twisted my back to the wolves, resting my elbows and splaying my leather-clad legs. They still felt slightly limp from the many hours I'd spent with Chase, though that was more figuratively than physically. I'd never felt more alive or energized after drinking so much of his blood. Not that I would announce this craziness to others, but it was an idle thought. "I wondered if maybe for a time it was Whitney, Tythians' familiar." Only Chase and I had ever met her. "She's appeared before me from time to time, but so has Sydney, and I know he's dead. In the same way that I saw Whitney die. I thought it'd be easy to conclude that it was her, especially with such a gift … but I know that's not probable, and maybe I'm just seeing ghosts."

Yolo watched me carefully before crumpling further into his shoulders. He let his blond hair cascade around his face, so he was hiding from me. "I know what that's like. For years, I saw Jenn everywhere after I killed her." The difference was Yolo had never recovered from that trauma and distorted his gift into such a way where he could *be* her. Chasing shadows and a ghost had become his purpose for living. "But it's probable someone else has such a gift. And a heads up, I wouldn't mention her to Tythian, it might arouse his wrath."

A burst of wicked laughter fluttered from me, unnerving him. As if Tythian hadn't made his disdain for me evidently clear already. But I wouldn't be so cruel as to rub salt in his wound. My guilt for Whitney's death far outweighed my cruel desire to hurt him. "I think I'll keep the fact that I'm seeing ghosts to myself, Yolo. Do you not think my profile is not unhinged enough already?"

"I think it's plenty unhinged, Esmore. You do know that I worry about you and what effects it's having on Chase," he said earnestly. This time I did look at him. He was one of few who'd say it so openly. "You are one another's greatest weakness right now. And as you figure out who you are and where you stand in this way, or simply stand for yourself, that disease in his mind is feasting off your primal urges. It's toxic."

"That's rich coming from the vampire who killed his own familiar," I said, taking a swing where I knew it'd hurt him the most. We might've formed some kind of relationship, but I didn't regret silencing him on this topic. I didn't want to hear it from an outsider's view how much damage I was causing. I already knew how bad I was for Chase.

"And you might not be so far from killing your own," he added just as spitefully. A snarl ripped through me in warning. If he were to say anything else who knows how I might react.

He kicked off the wall and sauntered down the stairs. I looked back at the little black leather box he'd given me and hated it all the more. He gave this to me because he thought I couldn't control myself any more than I thought I could. No matter how much I'd been trying to look composed, I'd been seen right through.

I looked over my shoulder, where Tori edged toward Fire and the cubs. He was wearing one of the robes, blocking out as much of the sun from irritating his skin, despite it being an overcast day. Resting against the edge of the fencing was Dillian, with arms crossed as he watched them with consideration. Then his dull, dead eyes looked up to watch me.

It was strange to see Tori train with them as if his change meant nothing. Conscious that one simple bite from the cubs could kill him, and yet there was no fear, maybe because he'd trained with them before all of this. Had it not been for the werewolves having such a repulsive scent, I doubted he'd be able to act around them in such a civilized manner. Dillian, however, kept his gaze on me. And I wondered if it had something to do with the huntress who was only a few meters at my back, hidden behind a door where she was guarded.

I couldn't figure out why Dillian was so forceful to join us on the battlefield instead of remaining where he could protect Julia. But from here, I could tell he was holding back much restraint not to storm these stairs. And it had nothing to do with wanting to see his lover. It was all to do with the intoxicating scent of her blood. And for him, being the woman he'd made love to and spent so much time with, it'd be like coming off an illicit drug with withdrawals.

I stepped away from the alcove, having promised Chase I'd join him for half the day training with his coven. We only had three weeks until the Vampire Council meeting. And our side mission prior to that could go extremely wrong. Or it could make all the difference.

CHAPTER 23

THAT NIGHT I'D remained with Fire, Titan, and Chris in the cellars and watched the painful torture as they tried to viciously break out of their cages and attack. I sat midway on the staircase, making sure I was out of their vision, and asked my mother to conceal my scent, but I highly doubted it made a difference. I just wanted to make sure they didn't permanently hurt themselves in any way. But the disturbing snarls and howls that encouraged one another only sounded like internal screams. Because I could see the humans beneath the wolf mask. I knew of their pain and scared little cries as their self-control was eaten alive internally by the beasts that lay dormant within.

When dawn broke and the wolves returned into their tired sleeping human forms, Yolo and I collected Titan and Chris and took them back to our wing. Fire was weak but walked of her own accord, and she gave nothing away as we walked across the main hallway where on looking vampires stirred. I hadn't realized last time how exhausted it made them. And having held the dead weighted Titan who trusted me to take her from the filth of the cage to the security of our wing was example of that.

As much as Fire prompted to join me for our new mission, I had to leave her behind. At this point, she'd only be a liability. Had we more days and she rested then it would've been probable, but for now I much preferred her acting as internal security while we were gone. Jerimiah and Darcy promised their lives to protect them. And Yolo would stay in the room unless otherwise called forth by Cesar or the brothers. My mother had forced Cesar to guarantee their security as well. After his last deceit, he'd submitted willingly. Not because he'd changed his mind about the werewolves' existence, but because he'd vowed to make an exception for me.

Once again, we were forced to wear our hooded robes and mask. Chase and I had both adopted a new one since our last ones had been left behind in the battle against the hunters. Mine was seemingly an exact replica, and I was certain Tythian was allocating the wolf masks to me purposely. Chase, however, was saddened when he didn't get to exploit his Spiderman mask once again. He was given, instead, one similar to the one Balzar wore once again, with red horns and an agape red mouth.

My mother suggested the robe would also assist not only for identification if any Council were to see us, but also because it'd help with screening the sun. Apparently where we were going was hot and sunny.

Chase and I geared ourselves in the wing, consciously being quiet so we wouldn't stir Titan and Chris who slept in the bed. Fire rested on the end, her heavy breathing a fine example of how exhausted she was from the night before. Julia was awake, seated in the nearby chair, but paid us no attention. Instead, she stared out the window longingly.

Chase caught me watching Titan and Chris and gave me a speculative look. *Are children something you ever wanted?* he asked me carefully. I snapped my head toward him, surprised by the question.

What? No. It had always been a repulsive thought in the way that James had always tried to force me to be his child-bearer and wife. Chase adjusted the robe over his bare chest opting to leave his jacket behind once again. *I mean …* But Chase wasn't James. The thought of even comparing them disgusted me to the point of wanting to vomit. Chase would never force me into such a situation. I couldn't ever imagine a time where we wouldn't be fighting for our lives. How was anyone able to raise a child in this world? *Did you?*

His temperament changed into a kind of longing, and I realized gut-wrenchingly, it was. *Vampires cannot have children, Esmore.*

Cesar did, I said all too quickly and surprised myself by the sudden desperation. Not because I wanted children myself, the thought had never earnestly crossed my mind. But I hadn't thought such a trivial thing was something Chase longed for himself. It wasn't that far a stretch from him wanting us to be husband and wife, in a tradition from the time he'd been turned.

Are you saying if you could, you would have children with me, my love? I was frozen on the spot. Speechless. My mind went blank. Here we were about to go on some voyage to find my heart so I could be a complete functioning being, but this was what stunned me, the topic of having babies? From my lack of response, Chase dismissed the conversation as he strutted over to me. *Cesar and your mother were an exception because of her gift. And I'm so glad an exception had been made,* he said lovingly. He held out my Barnett crossbow. Now he turned to watch the children quietly sleep. I was hesitant to leave them behind and leave this conversation as it was, but Chase was ready to leave, silent on the matter.

We met the others on the lawn at the front of the institute. My mother, Lincon, Kora, and Kasey waited patiently, fully robed and masked. Tythian adjusted the cuff of his dress shirt. He was to teleport us to a generic place, one of which he'd seen before and could take us to. My mother said it would take us two days on foot to reach the place, so we'd anticipated with Tythian we'd meet him in the same spot in five days' time.

What I wasn't expecting to find were Dillian and Tori amongst our group. "What are they doing here?" I asked objectively.

My mother was quick to intervene. "They came to me asking that I bring them along, and I have nothing against them joining us." I wanted to argue with her, with them. But pure irritation and hurt rose, they didn't even come to ask me, they went to my mother instead? Chase's fingers curled around mine.

Kasey shrugged her shoulder. "I mean, they have the same right as much as we do to come, don't they? We're all in this little fucked up happy family play together."

Lincon crooned with laughter, all too pleased with the spitefulness that crept out of her. Kora shifted uncomfortably as Lincon encouraged and favored her sister. So evidently, it'd been Kasey who'd tipped them off.

What I couldn't make sense of was why Dillian was actively trying to relocate from Julia. Yes, I expected him to put distance between them, but not to the extent of where he might not be able to protect her. Or maybe he didn't have the urge to protect her any longer?

"You said we could choose for ourselves, Esmore?" Tori questioned innocently. Dillian didn't so much as look my way, but he did brief a glance at Chase's and my intertwined hands, and I felt the roll of jealousy creep over him. I unfurled my hands from Chase's almost ashamed that it might've seemed like I was rubbing it in his face.

"You can," I replied to Tori. I'd promised them I could no longer protect them, that objective had long sailed, but the shell and remains of Dillian still tortured me. And I buried it deep so Chase wouldn't pick up on it. Seeing him in this way only made me question if I'd done the right thing? But had I not …

"Are we ready?" my mother asked, shuffling a small backpack over her shoulders. Tori and Dillian wore the same. It reminded me of when we would go out on missions within the Guild. "We only needed a few supplies besides our weapons—mostly water for me. Unlike all of you who have the potency of vampirism, I still need water and food to survive." It wasn't a mocking joke, but it edged a silence over us. If it hadn't been for my mother's ability to conceal her scent and allure, Dillian and Tori wouldn't have been able to control themselves around her.

"Goodie," Kasey remarked sassily under her mask. I gritted my teeth. She'd always been like that within our Guild, and I felt more infuriated that she was disrespecting my mother's lead in such a way. My mother was unperplexed and nodded to Tythian. He appeared irritated to yet again follow Cesar's order to be used in such a way. But, obediently he did so, grabbing us in twos.

Chase and I were the last two. I linked my elbow around Chase's arm, ensuring for whatever reason we weren't separated, and delicately pressed my hand to Tythian's extended arm. My mere touch acted as a burning sere in the way he revolted against it. Had Cesar been here, I wondered if he'd so openly show his despise. And mutually so.

A blinding light transcended upon us as Tythian teleported, and an unusual heat bore down on us. Kora was vomiting into the side of the cracked and long-winding road. I contained the nauseating swirl of my stomach, having become accustomed to the teleportation. I peeled my eyes open, the first thing I saw was a whole lot of nothing. A desert with rough bushes that looked as if it went on forever. On either side of the cracked and ruined road was desert land. Tori pulled down his hood even further, the sun clearly irritating him already as he tried to hide further away from it. My skin prickled with itchiness it often felt directly under the sun. I would fare far better than the others because I was still half huntress and I could only imagine their discomfort.

"Wow, Route 66, doesn't this feel nostalgic?" Chase said to Tythian who looked at a worn-down sign that was hardly readable. Tythian looked at him bored and teleported out. "Shit, now I am feeling old."

"I think I wandered out here for a few years once for fun," Lincon considered. He'd raised his fingers to the chin of his mask as if to stroke his goatee. "Such savagery out here. Nothing delectable to feast on and those dang bugs. My goodness, really Trinity, this is the excursion? I can't imagine any Hunter Guild surviving out here."

My mother adjusted her backpack, ignoring Lincon much in the way we all often did, especially when he spoke to her so informally as if they were lifelong friends.

"Be on your guard," my mother warned. "The further we walk into the desert, the worse the creatures become."

"Creatures?" Tori asked inquisitively, scratching at his arm. Watching him already so irritated was like a silent torture. They'd hardly any time to adjust to this new life. I suppose I had been no different, nor the twins. But still, if I could've helped their transition, if only slightly but time did not permit such a luxury.

My mother nodded. "The last time I was here, with a lesser party than this"—meaning Cesar and herself—"we were challenged numerous times by the creatures that dwell here. Perhaps in the time before the war, they were known as arachnids and serpents. But like few of the creatures that were affected by the mutation, they too changed."

"Like the rodents?" I asked, thinking back to my time spent in the Human Compound and the oversized rodents that would often attack the walls and pick off the members to feast on. We had been protected by such monsters in our Hunter Guild, mostly because of educated positioning. The only thing that truly opposed us was the possibility of sabers passing by.

Lincon interrupted, "Basically, things with very hard bodies, fangs, and sharp stingers. A poison that'll leave you frozen for hours, and that's depending on if they don't try to eat away at your body before you start to come to your senses."

"You got eaten by one?" Chase said gruesomely.

Lincon shrugged. "I was curious and let one gnaw at one of my legs. When he got a little too close to my heart was when I cut the entertainment short. The poison though was a buzz, I really had such a horrific and inspiring hallucinate trip."

I could sense the considerate smile on his lips while he thought about his pastime. "Well, let's ensure no one here has intentions of submerging in some weird hallucination. It'll only slow us down," I chastised, more pointedly to Lincon, but it was a warning for everyone.

My mother searched into the distance, her head angling weirdly as she studied either side of the road. It all looked the same to me. Then she perked up, and I wondered if she was tracing the unique glamor of her gift. If that was the only link we had to find my heart in such a barren and visually inseparable location, I certainly had my concerns. "This way," my mother said and looked at Kora who wiped her mouth with her sleeve and placed the mask back over her face. "Are we ready to run?"

"Oh, goodie, shall we have a race?" Lincon asked excitedly.

"Everyone remain together," my mother instructed. "We can't risk anyone getting lost. If you do, you might never be able to find your way back."

Lincon tsked. "Esmore, your mother is more of a buzzkill than you," he whined. I shook my head, still deplored my mother intentionally requested he join our group. I held my hand out to my mother, suggesting she lead the way. We didn't have time to waste.

Chapter 24

"This heat is fucking killing me!" Tori complained, thrashing about his robe uncomfortably. I was irritated by the sun, and I could only imagine how it affected the others. It was the first time after hours of running that we'd finally stopped. We were limited by my mother, who although extraordinarily fast and maintained stamina, was still slightly slower than the rest of us. Shortly followed by Kora and Kasey.

Kora sat down on the golden sand, evidently exasperated. I wasn't sure if it was because of the extent of their mutation, perhaps they hadn't changed all that much from the hunter's abilities besides physical form. Or worse she was malnourished. Either was possible, and this wasn't the first time weariness hung over Kora's future. My mother took out a large bottle and portioned out the water. She offered it to the others. Kora and Kasey were the only two to accept. I took two small swallows myself, momentarily taking the mask off and tightly securing it back on. In this kind of terrain, we had to stretch out our resources in case we were stuck out here. I hadn't seen any form of water pool nor could I feel an ounce of moisture coming from any direction. It was just as unsustainable as my mother and Lincon had suggested.

"Let's keep moving," my mother ordered, shuffling the water into her backpack. Chase and Dillian were looking into the distance, their attention caught on something I couldn't see myself.

"What is it?" I asked, depending on their far keener sight.

"It's nothing for now," Chase grumbled. "It's either a whirlwind or something else. We should keep moving."

"We'll keep running until nightfall, and then we'll take another break," my mother ordained. Tori looked at me expectantly as if I were to interject that she was giving the orders. It was still an oddity having my mother lead as Token.

"Oh, Trinity, I really hope you know where we're going," Lincon crooned. "To think of all the fun I could be having elsewhere instead of choking back dust pockets."

Everyone shuffled around him, once again ignoring his theatrics and shifting into a run.

The chill in temperature was nothing compared to the snow and frozen ice of Tracey's Council, but a significant contradiction to what we'd been forging through during the day. My mother sat by herself, committed to staring at her water bottle instead of periodically drinking it. We were all feeling the day's run, and irritation passed through the group like a physical entity. From the moon cycle, at least I knew we were on the same continent. It blazed down brightly, no fog, mist, or cloud to distract from its invasive glow. We'd since taken off our masks and pushed back our hoods. If anyone followed us this deep into the midst of nowhere, they were certainly a fool, and we would've sensed them.

Lincon was dancing around Kora and Kasey, stomping and singing as if he were drunk on the drugs he'd often been fed in the Human Compound. I rested my hand on the hard case that I'd strapped to my hip, ensuring he hadn't slipped them for himself.

"Do you want to talk about it?" Chase asked, pointedly nodding to the hard case. I was reluctant to be honest with him, scared of how he might react. Tormented that he might shun me for holding on to such an object.

But I opened up to him, allowing him to see the majority of the conversation Yolo and I had, all except the part where he mentioned how toxic I was to Chase. To let him in on that intimate discussion was too raw on my greatest insecurity. I wanted Chase to be able to depend on me, and it was Chase himself who tried to ease my worries after I'd advised him the same concerns.

"Ah," Chase said thoughtfully. "I see. I can't say I'm a fan of the idea considering I don't know what it is. But, if I do lose control and it's the only way, then I permit it," he said gently and pressed his forehead to mine. I released the tension in my shoulders I hadn't known I was holding on to. I didn't want him thinking I was turning on him. Only that it was a last-minute precaution. I didn't want to use a man-made contraption against him, but if it was our last hope …

Dillian was ahead of everyone, perched on a higher surface, looking out into the nothingness as a lookout. It took me back to all the missions we'd been on together before this. "Excuse me," I said, tapping Chase on the leg.

I slid multiple times up the sandy terrain but eventually reached Dillian who didn't so much as look at me. "Do you see anything out there?" I asked.

He continued to search. From what I could see there was nothing, but his keen sight far out saw my own. "No."

I curtly nodded, irritated that I wasn't able to have a normal conversation with him. I had done this. I understood that but having no inclination as to how he felt or what was running through his mind was pure torture. At least I could read Tori. But Dillian had seemed to sink into a black hole out of my reach. "Why did you push to come here?"

"What?" he asked. "It wasn't a favor to you if that's what you're asking." The quick reply was a strike to my patience.

"I never assumed that," I gritted out, trying to remain calm. This wasn't the Dillian I'd known since childhood and grew up with. This wasn't my best friend. And I wanted to break apart any and all walls to see if there was a glimmer of the old Dillian in there. I wondered if this was how he now saw me in return? Had I equally changed just as much?

"What do you think of me?" I asked him. He looked at me nearly shocked. There was an expression I couldn't quite understand. I don't know if it was hurt or pining, but it was covered by that malicious expression that was soon to strap another scowl on his face.

"Quite honestly, Esmore, I don't think much of you at all. And maybe that's what your problem is. That I'm not fawning over you like everyone else because they think you're something special. You feel guilty because of what you did to us. And you should. Our blood is on your hands.

But you can no more control the situation than what you can of my opinion of you. I came here because I didn't want to be in a houseful of vampires. They are no more my kindred than you are still mine." His words wounded me savagely. "Because of you, I have no right to be near or caress the woman I once loved. I know I loved her, but I can't *feel* that. All I can smell is her scent, even from across the institute, and I know given the chance I would bleed her dry trying to quench this evil leeching thing inside of me. And I wouldn't feel remorse for it. But I *know* it's wrong. So no, Esmore, I don't care about you or what you think of me and how you are going to salvage your hurt little feelings about how you screwed us over and left us for dead. Actually, death would've been better. But you didn't even let us have that."

A breeze swept past me as Chase's hand gripped around Dillian's throat. His expression was devoid of any emotion as his gray eyes turned into that wild storm they transfused into when he was ready to go into battle. "You do not speak to her like that, ever." His voice was haunting.

"Chase," I reprimanded him, tugging back his hand. For all of Dillian's indifference and harsh words, he seemed to care what happened to himself as he clawed at Chase's hand that suspended him in the air. He was inferior by power and age. He instinctively bore his fangs at Chase, encouraging him only to hold firmer and display his larger ones. "Chase, please!" I growled, my own eyes hazing purple and baring my fangs at his back. Dillian had every right to his thoughts, and I deserved every lashing.

"You don't know what she went through to try her best. From the very start, she has always cared about your safety. *You* were too weak to protect yourself. *You* were too weak to protect *Julia* from such a hateful fate. Now you've dug your own grave, lie in it." He dropped Dillian. His feet buckled beneath him as he stayed close to the ground, submissive.

Chase stormed in the other direction towards my mother. "Chase!" I snarled behind him. He'd blocked his mind off to me once again, so I couldn't read his thoughts. My mother warily watched from a distance, now standing in case she had to intervene.

Tori was standing idly by as if he were to intervene, and have done what? But I was satisfied at least someone was on Dillian's side. It only hurt me further when Tori's loyalty was equally shared with me because I didn't deserve it.

I stormed past Tori to follow Chase, but he grabbed my elbow. I looked down on the touch, warning him with an effective look to let go. But surprisingly, he held on with strength he hadn't had before, though he did loosen it as if not aware of his own power. "Dillian didn't mean it like that." I tried not to scoff at the misinterpretation. "He's hurting, that's all. It's hard for us, this thing is new." He shrugged. They called it a *thing* and *leech*. Not yet titling what it truly was, of what *they* truly were— vampire. "Coming on these missions feels like normality, like the old days, as best as they can. We need something to hold onto."

I shook him off, all too accustomed to that feeling and aware of my rising anger and beast. But there would be no normality or something they could hang onto. As they were soon to learn, this world had changed in ways they will never comprehend. And nor could I deny that Dillian was wrong. His thirst for Julia might never go away. His ability to feel may never come back. Everyone changed differently, and although I prayed to whoever might hear me or be a higher power in this world that he did return the way that I knew him, it was an awfully big ask from a creature who didn't deserve such redemption.

An eerie silence rolled over our camp, and suddenly everyone was quietly conscious of the shift in the air. The ground beneath us pulsed with little scuttling shifts, the sand edged inch by inch closer to us as if creating a sinkhole.

"Oh, no," I heard Lincon click his tongue, "looks like we're not the only hungry beasties out here."

I unfurled my sword, something telling me my bow and arrows would do nothing against whatever was coming, especially against the magnitude of the ripples. I could hear a scuttering noise and Tori and I naturally turned back to back, leaning on one another, ready for whatever angle the creature might come. Chase and my mother did something similar. Kora and Kasey were with Lincon as he smiled from ear to ear watching everyone's reactions. He was excited to see the show.

A deep hissing noise pierced our sensitive ears as a cloud of sand burst from the ground. A crusty exterior-like creature emerged with exceptionally large prongs at its front and a large, spiked tail that thrust into the spot Tori and I once stood. In unison, we jumped out of the way. Where we once stood sand billowed into the air. We repositioned ourselves near Dillian, grouping into three, swords armed.

If my education served me correctly this was called a scorpion, but at a larger magnitude than what I'd seen sketches of. It was towering over us, its tail reaching the height of a second-story building. "On your left," Lincon chimed to my mother. Another one appeared, erupting from the sand as it snapped its operative claws at her.

Chase pushed my mother out of the way, gliding his sword along its front skeletal-like arm. His sword scraped along it, hardly causing damage. Shit, their thick exterior would be hard to penetrate.

A third appeared closest to Kora, Kasey, and Lincon. It drove its stinger toward them but connected harshly against Kasey's projected wall. Kasey squirmed her hand angularly, focusing on the sheer size of the scorpion but it froze, losing all mobility.

Dillian, Tori, and I were forced to split once again. The scorpion targeted us with its stinger. I waved my hand in a gesture that suggested to circle it. "Aim for the legs and eyes," I shouted over the hisses of the creature. We might not be able to slice down its exterior, but its legs were the smallest part of it, surely we could hack through that. Maybe not all eight, but enough to throw it off balance. And maybe if its eyes were penetrable too, it'd retreat or give us the upper hand.

Dillian aimed his bow and arrows, aiming them as Tori and I distracted the creature. It continued to try to clamp its mighty claws around us. Dodging them, Tori and I rounded its front first with complete synchronicity hacking straight through the back two legs. The creature dove forward, hissing at the imbalance. Dillian shot two arrows, seconds apart. The first one bounced off its hard exterior shell. The second hit target puncturing into its eye. The creature waved back and forth, its hiss adamant as it tried to rear back and find new balance. Tori and I took advantage, hacking at the next pair of legs. Blue blood splattered across our robes in a thick heap.

The legs were a challenge to cut through, but it was possible. My vampire delighted in the savagery of my force. The scorpion tumbled, its back hitting the ground as it tried to drive its stinger back and forth unable to reach us.

It scuttled forward, digging into the gravel as its belly trailed behind it. It immersed into the ground within seconds. We geared to help Chase and my mother, halting. There was no need. The creature was on its back, blue oozing from several wounds under its belly where I imagined Chase had prodded until he found its heart.

A gnarly hiss seeped out of Lincon's prey as he chuckled to himself, watching the thing immobile and in pain. Whatever he was doing to it, it was torture. I couldn't sense the one who'd attacked Dillian, Tori, and me any longer. Obviously, the damage had been enough of a deterrent to make it flee.

"Lincon, everyone else is done. Don't play with your prey," Kasey nonchalantly said and ordered Kora to drop her gift. The creature now mobile to do as it pleased, it thrashed back and forth.

"Oh, no, look at all the fire." Lincon cackled to the tormented creature. "Where will you go?" He laughed. Chase was under the large scorpion within seconds, his sword and strength plunging the blade as deep as the hilt into the underbelly. The creature stopped squirming. When he pulled it out, blue blood sprayed on him.

Lincon's dark gaze shifted on Chase now that his personal fun had ended.

"Lincon," I warned cautiously. That haunting look in his eyes lightened as he looked at me and the playful dance of mischief crept back.

"Oh, I was only having a little bit of fun. Didn't everyone else have fun?" he asked everyone exasperatedly. They ignored him.

"That's gross," Tori commented on the thick blue blood that coated him. "I'll shoot the arrows next time."

Dillian scoffed. "As if you're as good a shot." It wasn't said vindictively, dry perhaps, but when pointed in the direction of Tori, it might've even been an attempt of humor.

"I don't think they'll bother us for some time," my mother commented, taking a seat once again beside the hideous creature that was belly up.

"Wow, and I thought vampires were the worst thing, these things are just hideous!" Tori spat. Though we all agreed, I watched Lincon and Chase stare off, the intimidation of power pressing between them in a silent challenge.

"Chase," I called out to him. I didn't want the two fighting. Lincon was the last person I wanted to make an enemy of. My gaze drifted over to Kora who stared at the dead creature at her feet. She hadn't even the effort to stand up during the process. There was almost a longing in her gaze that I couldn't quite understand, but it rattled me. Was she sad for the creature, or had she wished it was her?

CHAPTER 25

THE HEAT WAS just as potent as the previous day, and Tori tried to keep as many of his groans of frustration and remarks to himself. We'd only had a few hours rest that night, and the scorpions never returned. Now we were looking up at what looked like a rocky cave that was too large to go around, so instead, we'd have to go through.

"Be on your guard in here," my mother insisted. "The last time we came through here, I used my ability to conceal our scents, but if the creatures spot us, then we might be in for some grief. We avoided them last time. But with a group this large, it might be inevitable."

We all looked back at the foreboding dark rock cave ominously.

"This seems like a hurdle of trials just to get to some Hunter Guild," Lincon remarked, almost knowingly that we were up to mischief. "Not that I'm complaining of course. I enjoy nothing more than to show off my assets to Esmore. Show her how big, strong, and dependable I am."

Chase snarled at his provocation. I linked my elbow around Chase, pulling him back. *Don't let him get to you. You know he does it on purpose.*

I don't trust him, he adamantly added.

Neither do I. But Lincon *had* proved his worth numerous times.

"Stay close and remain quiet," my mother encouraged. Something sinister pooled from the dull orange walls of the cave that blurred into darkness. Whatever was in there was waiting like a menacing pull.

I could feel my mother's gift expand around us, but I wondered how much concentration it cost. Like when Cesar and my mother concealed places and numerous people, was it a consistent focus or an afterthought?

My mother stepped in first, leading us into the narrow entrance of the cave. Small spills of light escaped the epically high ceiling. The rough-textured surface of the ground scaled the walls unevenly, dipping into crevasses large enough to fit bodies.

After a few minutes of being wedged into a single line, following my mother's lead, she guided us into an open space. It was completely dark, the entrance light far behind us now. The rocky walls seemed to layer in texture around us as if we were in some giant bowl.

The extremity of how Cesar and my mother hid my heart was dawning on me as she followed that light tug toward it. I had despised her for it and the belief that she'd abandoned me. But even so, she'd gone through all of this, with only Cesar to ensure its safety. Though I still felt violated from the ordeal, an amount of respect followed for her intense dedication.

My mother warily stopped and listened. A small rock dropped, skirting from the ceiling and down the wall. Its noise was audible as an echoing water drop.

She waited for something to happen. But nothing did. Through the darkness, I could only just manage to see, but I wasn't sure how everyone else's sight fared. And I wasn't willing to ask in case it stirred something unnecessarily. Instead of walking centrally through the room and onto the other side, she skirted us along the wall. Every few steps, she would stop and listen out. When we reached the other side, she dipped into another small crack, and we continued on in a singular line.

Chase came between my mother and me, with Dillian and Tori to my back and the twins and Lincon taking the tail end. I looked over my shoulder in an attempt to see if I could see down the line, but Dillian's bulkier shoulders filled the space of the narrow walls snugly. He looked dead in the eyes as he watched me.

We still hadn't the urge to put our masks back on until we ventured into a day's run back. There was no point. If anyone followed us this far out we would've felt them tracking us. But now I could see his every expression and lack thereof.

My mother stepped out into another circular room, this time the canals in the ceiling were more evident and eerie. The room was coated in white, sticky web. From the ceiling, two webbed sack-like things dangled. For each person that came out, the person before them pointed to the floor, ensuring they didn't accidentally step onto the web. Whatever that was, it wasn't good.

My mother slowly and articulately weaved around the webs, jumping from rock to rock throughout the room. Chase and I followed her steps onto small sandy rocks, finding balance in every hop. Chase continued to look over his shoulder, ensuring I was perching myself correctly. And I did the same, particularly with Tori who was the youngest. Both he and Dillian would still be adjusting to their new heightened senses, and overstepping was a very probable thing. But he balanced nimbly.

My mother was on the other side of the cave, searching through the next dark and tight crack we could slip into. Chase covered her back, watching me intensely. At first, I thought it was because he was concerned that I might need his help to navigate the stepping-stones. This was child's play. But when I hovered my mind over his, I realized he found my focused expression sexy. I hid the smile that beckoned, all too familiar with his inappropriate timing of sexual desire.

We froze as another rock skidded down the back of the room, closest to Lincon. With our attention on him, he posed with a charming smile as if he'd been the reason we'd turned. It was nothing. I turned back toward my mother. She, too, had been too focused on the sudden noise, leaving her wide open for the oversized black furry spider that crawled out of the hole above her head.

"Mom!" I shouted as I reefed my Barnett crossbow and hoisted an arrow, shooting at the oversized spider. It seemed to purr, vibrations rattling around it as it scuttled with such speed to snag her.

My arrow punctured its back but didn't deter it from seizing my mother. My mother pulled out her sword slicing across its face to deter it. One of its fangs scraped past her, leaving a residue of thick saliva. Chase collected her so the spider couldn't attack again and placed her against a small patch that wasn't inundated with webs. She dropped to her knees panting and clutched at her shoulder. I realized it wasn't saliva but venom.

The spider's vibrating noises created an avalanche of movement across the cave, summoning others to its aid. I wanted to run to her, but I trusted Chase, and the commotion that vibrated through the cave was unnerving. I could feel my mother's gift of concealment dropped as she focused on her infected wound that made a small, sizzling noise.

As soon as the veil dropped, with precise timing, great big eyes and furry black bodies scurried out of the holes above us, and spiders rained down. I switched to my sword, slamming waves of disorientation into those who dropped directly above me. They froze mid-air, startled by the metal hit, and instead of landing on me, landed on the safety of their thick webs. I jumped on the first one while it was still disoriented and pierced my sword into its head. It squirmed, that deafening vibrating noise ringing out as a howl of pain as it shriveled beneath me. When its legs finally concaved beneath its heavy body, I yanked out my sword, blue blood spraying at me. Its corpse sagged into the web.

A dagger whistled beside me, slicing my arm on its way to puncture one of the spiders' eyes. Its legs crossed over one another, disorientated as it tried to fling off the blade embedded in one of its many eyes. Kasey had been the one to throw it. The spiders around her seemed to bow into submission as she used her gift on them. Kora, however, was placid, tranquil even as she watched the fight erupt around her. I realized she was assisting Kasey in using her gift, like the old times, but if only to create a hard wall around herself. A spider lunged back and forth trying to rip its fangs into her, but all she did was watch the spectacle unfold. She might've been intensifying Kasey's barrier, but her own power of immobility was practically useless as she spaced out.

My mother focused on her wound, working her gifts healing properties as Chase protected her. Sporadically, and from the twitch of the poison, her arm spasmed up. A large wave of crystallized ice projected across half the wall. *Shit*. Her arm was strapped in by the beautiful crystal. Cesar had displayed how their gift worked once before. It took everything it encompassed, never detaching or melting away, and now it had her arm all the way up to the shoulder.

Spiders backed away from the now slippery surface, towering over one another to get to her. She scrambled, trying to jerk her arm free but to no avail. "Cut it off!" she yelled at Chase. "You have to!" He was reluctant, and before I could scream for him to stop, he dropped his sword over her shoulder, slicing the arm cleanly off.

My mother howled out a wild scream, fighting back tears as she sagged to the ground, no longer hinged to the wall. I slashed through spiders, dodging them as I hacked at sensitive spots that were likely to deter or kill them. I had to get to my mother. I was furious at Chase for being so logical and being able to place his emotions elsewhere while he severed my mother's arm. *Would I have been able to do the same thing?*

The room filled with the intoxicating wave of fresh blood and I pushed my vampire urges down, willing it only to let me use its power, exchanging nothing else for its service. I focused on the next spider that almost tripped me from landing on the next rock. I skirted my sword into the side of its belly, dangling by my hilt so I wouldn't drop into the mass of the web below. I flicked myself over, taking my sword with me as I dragged it along its back and severed its head. It concaved toward the web, flattening. More spiders piled atop one another as we slaughtered through them. But they kept coming, their numbers only mounting.

Problem, was all Chase could grit out into my mind as he focused intently on his attackers. My stomach sank as I realized Tori and Dillian simultaneously lunged for my mother. Now that she wasn't focusing on concealing her scent, the blood was too arousing to not turn them into their most primal nature, especially when only recently turned.

Lincon threw a blade into the back of Tori's knee, making him stumble and fall backward into the web. He'd also thrown a dagger at Dillian who mindlessly dodged it.

"Don't kill them!" I yelled at Chase, fear gripping me. "Kora, fucking do something!" I blasted a wave of adrenaline through her. She was bleak but then flared into action, not of her own accord but because of my improv. But she focused her gift onto both Tori and Dillian, ensnaring them in her invisible trap of immobility. It gave Kasey enough time to refocus her gift onto the two, erecting an invisible wall around them. Spiders bounced back from the newly erected wall. Kora dropped her gift and focused on immobilizing the others. The problem was it pitted the two newborn vampires against one another. And Tori was lying on his back stuck in web. "Let me in!" I commanded Kasey. Tori couldn't defend himself, and Dillian was too much in a frenzy to realize his now pray was his comrade. A small scrap of ground was all we had, the rest being encompassed by sticky web.

She did, the bubble now encasing all three of us. The rest of the spiders had to be dealt with now, they were outnumbering us. I looked at Lincon, briefing him the quickest of glances before Dillian made his move. "Lincon, show me what you can do," I prompted him, and the smile that radiated from him was foul. His face seemed eerily sinister as something else crept to the surface. One second he was there and the next he was not. His speed and strength began to slice through the spiders with wicked delight. This entire time he hadn't so much as tried, until in a way to impress me.

I rolled to the side, avoiding Dillian's grazing and untrimmed nails. His hand slammed against the circular imprisonment of Kasey's gift. He wasn't conscious, his eyes held a maddening craze that swallowed any rational thought. I didn't know how to bring him back from this. Much like the same issue I had with Chase. Though this wasn't under the prick of thorny bushes and an improbable mind, this was simple instinct, and the only way to subdue him was to overpower him into submission. I hoped.

I sheathed my blade. He wasn't in his right state of mind to use any of his weapons. Tori was wrestling with the sticky web, only getting himself further tangled up as he stared up at the ceiling and at the spiders that dropped by thick white threads. Tori came back to consciousness a lot sooner than I would've thought possible. He was watching the spiders glitter from the roofing as Lincon ransacked their home. His loud cackle spiraling the room and creeping up my spine.

Dillian lunged for me mechanically again, but it was too easy to dodge. He was just a beast at this point, charging in with no tact. I swiveled around him and extended sharp nails, hugely off target. I spun around him, pausing with my chest to his back, and gripped him from behind. With speed and force, I flipped him over my shoulder and drove him into the ground, hard. The loud snap of his neck crunched and his body went limp.

It was ruthless, and I pushed away my internal self-criticism that cruelly anguished over having done such a thing. *It had to be done.* He'd wake up in a matter of minutes. He probably wouldn't even remember it. I unsheathed my sword and balanced with one leg on a nearby small rock. I cut around the sticky web that Tori was stuck in. "What happened?" he asked, disorientated. "Did you just break Dillian's neck?" he asked now more alarmed. Dark bodies dropped from the ceiling piling on top of one another. Blue blood was spluttering against Kasey's shield.

By the time I'd finally cut Tori out and reefed him up, Dillian was already beginning to stir. He cramped his hand around his neck confused as he looked disorientated. "Did one get me?" he asked, and then sudden clarity crept into his eyes. He looked over at my mother abashed. Her bleeding was still prominent, and she'd taken on a pale hue. Chase was bandaging his robe around her, his control over his urges absolute as he helped her.

With quick reflexes, he would slash and stab at any spiders that made it past Lincon. I traced Lincon's movement, it was almost too fast for me to keep track of. He darted back and forth, jumping off their bodies nimbly like he weighed nothing. His speed and precise slashing with the two long knives were impeccable. Nothing stood in his way as his fangs glistened with such a wide smile, shinier than the venom that dripped from the spiders. He was the darkness that swallowed them whole, and they'd been stupid enough to chase him. He had a maddening craze in his eyes, not like the instinct that overruled Tori and Dillian only moments ago; this was certainly of the loosened power and weapon that Lincon was. He'd fully immersed himself into the tainted curiosity I'd licked at now and then. I shuddered in disgust. Could I turn into that uncontrollable creature one day?

He was older than Cesar and seemed to know far more than he should. He held a reputation as vampires within the institute whispered his name, and now watching him in all his delightful glory, I knew why they avoided and feared him. And I'd been the one stupid enough to have him at my back.

Dillian was uncomfortable as he avoided my mother's gaze. Kasey's gift dropped as she seemed startled by her sister's sudden urge to actually be useful instead of watching. The usual lazy gaze pinned her and Kora seemed to wriggle into herself, quaint once again.

Air swirled around me that my reflexes didn't even have time to move against. Chase was at my front, his sword had collided with one of the sharp knives that dripped blue blood on my shoulder. Lincon's blade was at my throat. Chase had made it just in time to challenge it.

Lincon chucked behind me as he withdrew his blade. I could feel the darkness pool from him, and Chase's own magnificent fight against it. "I just wanted to see if you were fast enough to actually protect your familiar. You know, whether you're worthy of her," he purred. It was yet again another layer and edge to Lincon's tone, something dark and elusive to his very core. "Didn't I make you proud?" His breath whisked against my ear, sending a chill throughout my body.

"Very," I gritted out. Dillian had his bow and arrow steadied at Lincon. Chase wasn't willing to step away from me until Lincon had edged enough distance.

"Oh, come on!" Lincon laughed cheerfully. "As if I was really going to do anything! I love Esmore. She brings me so much fun, and we're best of friends!"

A chunk of spider fell from one of the holes and sprung into the web. It smelt in here. My mother had focused on concealing her blood once again, aware of Dillian and Tori and how it imposed on them gravely.

"Trinity, I'm sorry," Dillian said quietly as he dared not step toward her. She raised her hand panting harshly as if his words would knock away her concentration.

"Let's go," Chase said, picking my mother up as she gritted through the movement. Her arm dangled out of the beauty of her crystalized gift. Had it only been the venom it would've taken her a matter of minutes to heal, but to have such a fatal wound as well …

"Mom," I edged closer to her, making sure to jump carefully between the rocks.

"I'll be fine, Esmore. I just need …" She panted harshly. Time, she needed time to rest and heal. I'd seen her reinstate limbs and organs on a regular. That's why she was nicknamed 'the corpse' back within our Guild. But I'd never seen *her* so severely injured.

"Shit," Chase said, biting into his wrist and feeding it to my mother. She seemed reluctant to accept it, half-spluttering it out. Even I felt estranged that my familiar was feeding my mother his blood. But it was the only way to quicken the process so she could heal herself.

"Let's go," I ordered, leading through the narrow crack. Chase had to awkwardly rearrange my mother on his chest as she bled out over him, a trail of blood following her. I didn't once catch a whiff of it. She remained focused and considerate on ensuring it didn't disturb Tori and Dillian despite their efforts of staying at the back and furthest from her.

We crept into another rocky room darker than the last. I could sense just as many spider webs. I scanned the room and listened out. Nothing stirred. For all the commotion we created in the last space, it was possible we'd drawn all the spiders that inhabited this nest. But I still cautiously danced over the rocks, ensuring no beady eyes crept out of the holes.

We hurried through the sections, undisturbed. When we reached the other side, Chase carefully placed my mother down into the new ray of sun. She leaned against the rocky cave, panting in exasperated pain. Tori and Dillian created distance from her acting as lookouts.

"Mom, what can I do?" I asked somewhat desperately. This had been the weakest I'd ever seen her. I'd never seen my mother hold such a pale, haunting, and pained expression. She hissed as the venom dribbled out of her wounded shoulder and her skin began to stitch itself. My concern was the still bleeding and amputated arm.

My mouth opened and closed over my fangs as if tempted from seeing the blood instead of smelling it. "Esmore," Chase said carefully and pushed me back. "Let me."

"I'll be okay," she said with a curt nod as her skin perspired. "Just give me a little time."

Chase removed his wet robe from her shoulder that he'd used to apply pressure. Blood was still coming out. I worried she wouldn't make it in time. That was too much blood, wasn't it? Why didn't she work on her amputated arm first?

I cursed that damn gift Cesar had given her. My gaze enviably sunk to Chase's back as he strapped the material around my mother's shoulder again, and eased her through the pain by feeding her more of his blood. By reinstating my heart, would I be suggesting Chase to a similar fate? By giving him something so ugly and uncontrollable in the way of a gift that shouldn't be handled?

"Just a small break," my mother repeated hollowly. Blood was smeared over her lips as she nodded to Chase in appreciation. I wondered if she'd ever tasted Cesar's blood before. Would Cesar for once be grateful to Chase for helping her?

"We'll wait for as long as you need," I said, holding my mother's hand. She squeezed it lightly. The moment sincerely desperate as I clutched on to her as if this might be the only way she couldn't escape into the afterlife. That if I held her like this, in a way I knew expressed fondness and love, that she would understand her time was not up, and she had to stay with me. I'd never seen my mother look so wounded or weak, and something inside of me slowly broke as I watched the strongest woman I knew crumble into a sweaty, insufferable mess.

CHAPTER 26

M Y MOTHER'S BREATHING stabilized within the hour, and magnificently, but slowly a new arm webbed from her shoulder, layering from bone, tissue, muscle, and skin. "I just need time to rest, and then we can move on," my mother said breathlessly. I'd taken her backpack and removed the water to feed it to her.

"Take as long as you need," I said to her. Throughout the hour her hand hadn't left mine. We weren't naturally maternal by any means, but I'd never felt such desperation or ever come close to truly thinking my mother was going to die in front of my very eyes. She was magnificent. The thought of something killing her seemed improbable. I didn't even believe it when they'd informed me within the Guild. My mother always seemed like nothing could break her. But now, I realized my mistake. She was just as vulnerable in this world as the next. And she'd already gone to all this effort once to conceal my heart. I felt guilty for the harsh temperament I pushed toward her. All of a sudden, I held a lot of regret and shame as I did when Tori and Dillian had been turned, and Teary and the wolves had been killed. And even more. A long line of deaths trailed me.

It rushed me all at once. No one was truly invincible in this world, and instead of fighting against them, I should be treasuring the moments because I didn't know when the last might be. Like the pockets of time I was stealing with Chase, I should've been attempting the same with the others instead of remaining regal and trying to control everything. But that was how I'd been trained, and the only way *I knew* how to survive and keep others alive.

This could've happened to any of us, Chase interjected, snapping me out of my spiraling thoughts. I was grateful to him and all that he'd done for her. He'd immediately protected her and secured their position.

I just never thought that she wasn't … invincible and felt childish having such a presumption. I'd always strived to be as powerful and ruthless as my mother, and now seeing such an incident, I realized she was still … breakable.

Lincon was growing bored. "Is she dead yet? Or is Trinity back to her old glowering self and we can move on?"

I snarled at him over my shoulder in warning. He chuckled in reproach, holding his belly as it irked him in a hilarious way. Kasey rolled her eyes and sighed at him. I followed her gaze toward her sister Kora, who was staring into the distance aloof, sitting amongst the sand. A part of me rose to the occasion wanting to shake some life into her. That glazed expression reminded me too much of when she started self-mutilating herself. I couldn't even begin to guess what she was thinking, and when I swept my mind over hers there was a longing for something. But I couldn't gauge what it might be.

"We can begin," my mother said. "This isn't ideal, but I won't be a burden."

"We can wait," Chase haughtily said. He protected her as cautiously, if not more so than me. My mother looked fragile. A reminder that unlike us, she wasn't immortal. Or perhaps Kora and Kasey weren't either. Only time could tell for them both. *If they lasted that long,* I regretted thinking with Kora in mind.

"We still have a day's run. We'll just have more breaks, and when we approach the area I'll fall into the rear, so I'm not a liability," she strategized. Not because she didn't want to lead, but she knew she'd act as a distraction if we were trying to protect her as well. "I know my limits," she added. Chase and I shared an uncertain look. Thus, the stubbornness and willpower of a huntress.

"Oh, goodie." Lincon began tugging on Kasey's robe. "We're *finally* going!"

Kasey whipped her robe from his teasing hands, and he laughed. I was more cautious of Lincon. Not because he had a blade to my throat, but because I'd seen the monstrosity he was truly capable of being. This was what he'd once described as fun and what he so actively chased. And having no boundary made him dangerous at every turn. Equally so, I couldn't turn him away either. I had to make use of him or he truly would turn on me. The odd attachment between the twins and him was still a mystery to anyone who watched them interact.

"I must confess, Trinity, I never thought I'd be fighting oversized bugs. I'm so used to my fangs and brute strength being enough. A bizarre adventure indeed," Chase light-heartedly said, and she actually appeased him with a twitch of a smile.

My mother only requested to stop once during the run, and despite the hard push into nightfall, her once pale skin was starting to come back to life with color. When we did sit for a few hours of rest, she tried to hide her relief. We kept a rotation on lookout for any more crawling creatures that might try to take advantage of our rest. But nothing came. Either by sheer luck or with the amount of grotesque blue smelling blood on us, they instinctually knew it was safer to avoid us.

It was now Kora, Kasey, and Lincon's shift on lookout. We were going two at a time, but with the dazed and distant glare in Kora's eyes, she wasn't of much use anyway. The cool temperature swept through the night, once again in contrast to the harsh heat during the day. Chase, who was shirtless, should've looked cold, but he wasn't, and his pale skin glistened under the moonlight. We'd made sure to still pack his bloody robe he'd use on my mother's arm just in case someone picked up its scent during our travels, no matter how unlikely. My mother used her gift of concealment on it to make sure the scent didn't compel the others.

Dillian and I had removed our robes and given them to my mother when a few cool shakes rattled her from the chilling air. Tori and Dillian hadn't said a word to my mother, and despite us sitting together now, neither spoke to her. They felt guilty for turning on her. But this was all in the game of mastering control as they would soon learn came with this power and immortality.

Lincon strutted over, his arms waving back and forth dramatically. "We're not really going to see some Hunter Guild are we?"

"You're meant to be on lookout," I gritted out.

"Pish," he said and waved his hand at me. "It'd be our lucky night if more things tried to kill us." He looked at my mother, and an exasperated expression of concern rolled over his face. "Oh no, Trinity, are you cold? Do you want my robe too?" he asked, extending out his coat that hardly mirrored the black fabric it once was, now coated in blue blood. How he could still stand to wear that was beyond me. It was as if he was fermenting in his kill.

"She doesn't need it," Chase gritted out. I pressed a calming wave over him immediately. Lincon so much being in the same space as him was irking him in a way I'd never seen Chase react. He was usually so carefree and goofy. Whereas, for the majority of this trip he'd been this way.

Are you okay? I asked him. Was it because of something else? Was it because of the purpose of this mission? Was he as concerned about the outcome as I was? Surely, he was, and it was putting him on edge. He leaned back on his elbows, casually lazing as if being the example of 'okay.'

I'm fine, Esmore, I just really don't trust him. He has a reputation, you know?

I know. He'll serve a means to an end, I promised. Eventually, he'd grow bored, especially after we'd finished with the war.

Chase was eyeing him warily. He didn't believe me.

"Yes, so why are we actually out in the middle of nowhere? Why has Mommy Dear brought us out here?" He asked inquisitively. Lincon wasn't silly, but he'd certainly bitten his tongue long enough before asking, probably scared he'd be kicked off this mission.

My mother briefed a glance my way. It had been her who'd suggested bringing the three of them. And they'd indefinitely assisted. But I wondered if there was a further knowing to Lincon's past. He and Cesar knew one another, and it was possible he'd divulged that information with my mother. She didn't trust Lincon, none of us ever would. But whether it was for his feverish onslaught or something else, I wasn't sure.

"A weapon," my mother said carefully.

"Oooh, exciting," Lincon said, pressing his hands on his knees and leaning in attentively. "So, we can slay Oppollo?" He took a seat beside Dillian, who begrudged him for doing so but didn't say anything.

"Yes," I said curtly.

Lincon threw his hands up in anguish. "You're all no fun at story time. I remember the times I would roast limbs over a fire in settings like this.

I'd never eat them of course, how disgusting, but I enjoyed the smell nonetheless while sharing stories with my friends. And they were just as lousy at story time, mind you, they were dead and chopped up," he cackled, slapping his knee. We stared at him grotesquely. "Oh, come on! It's just a joke!" He scanned our disgusted expressions. "Just a joke," he said again, wiping away at his eyes from the amusement. He wasn't at all joking.

I told you, he can't be trusted, Chase added once again. And yet oddly enough, I felt more suspicious around Tythian's motives comparatively. I didn't want to bring it up, the wound all too fresh, but I did want to help Dillian and Tori find their culprit. Now that we were away from the institute with few onlookers, it felt like a good time to ask about that night.

"Do you remember much from the night you were turned?" Chase asked on my behalf. Dillian's dull pink gaze struck him and then shifted to me. He still wasn't daring enough to look at my mother. Tori, however, fidgeted unnaturally considering vampires were often still and stoic.

"I have no recollection," Dillian said in a dark and vexing tone. "I was inside with the others. Teary was the only one outside with the wolves at the time. A shadow appeared out of nowhere and broke Yolo's neck. Before I could even reach for a weapon, well, you saw what happened."

"It happened so quickly," Tori added quietly. He was staring at the palm of his hand as if it might hold the answers. "When the cloaked creature was on Dillian, I grabbed a sword. But it was too fast. It latched onto me violently, I remember feeling so much pain, and my sword cluttered to the ground leaving me unarmed. I think Julia tried to help me, but my vision became hazy, and then I heard Teary scream from outside and thought maybe she'd save us ... but ... but then I heard the wolves start howling and screaming and Teary's cry was amongst it, and then I blacked out."

"Wait, so you heard them scream before your captor completely drained you?" I asked skeptically.

"I don't know what I heard," he said begrudgingly. "It was a lot. I was dying ... I don't know precisely what I heard."

There might've been two attackers? I speculated to Chase.

Possibly. Or it's as he said ... his recollection is distorted.

"You never got a look at the attacker's face?" I scrutinized.

"If we had, do you think we'd be sitting around here talking about it?" Dillian asked harshly. Chase snarled at his tone and Dillian offered him a deadpan expression. "Don't you think we recall that night every day as well? Wishing we knew who it was so we could hunt them down, and I suppose the why is almost irrelevant."

"Be grateful that you have another day so you can figure out who did it and that they'd spared Julia in the process," my mother added to the argument with the authority that always made us consider our next words carefully as children.

The mention of Julia bitterly twisted Dillian's expression. He left the group and strode away.

"I think he feels guilty because he doesn't feel like he protected her at all," Tori admitted.

"What makes you so sure?" I asked. This was now the second time he'd opted for an opinion on Dillian's behalf.

He shrugged his shoulder and poked at the sand, childlike. "Because Dillian's always been easy to read. Vampire or not. Broody or light, I think his motives are the same. He just lacks the ability now to control himself and articulate his words. It all just feels ..." he made a swirling gesture at his abdominal, "messed up."

"I felt the same when I was turned," Chase said in a way of comfort. He had only been a few years older than Tori when he'd been turned, but their circumstances were completely different. Tori's was forced upon him. Chase's was premeditated, and he'd had exposure to his mother's changes before he himself was turned.

"I dare say my turning was a little bit different," Lincon pondered. He cackled wildly. "Whenever that was, it was so long ago!"

"No one ever forgets," Chase quipped.

Lincon's expression turned grave, and the darkness that brought his true monster to the surface appeared as if he recalled his own turning and events. "If my camping story disturbed you, then you certainly won't be able to digest my birth." His voice was gravely stark, and he daringly looked at Chase as if he was trying to penetrate his soul.

Curiosity wanted me to prod more about Lincon's past, but instinct warned me against it. That, and any interest I showed in Lincon was another marker in my coffin. Asking questions might only get me killed.

CHAPTER 27

"WHERE THE FUCK are we?" Lincon asked boisterously as we searched the grand scale of rolling Rocky Mountains. Trees and shrubbery thrived, and a river stretched through the distance, so contradictory to the barren desert we'd been venturing through.

"The Grand Canyon?" Chase asked skeptically.

My mother agreed. "Cesar might've mentioned something like that. We need to follow the river until we find the waterfall. It's possible the object we're locating is being guarded."

"Possible?" I repeated. Which meant more than likely where her and Cesar had hidden my heart another barbaric creature protected it. If this two-day trip so far had taught me anything, it was to acknowledge the lengths my mother and Cesar sought to conceal it. I became anxious, the thought of now being so close to it. To being whole and complete and whatever that might look like.

"Yes, there are snakes in this area."

"And I'm assuming they're not the usual little ones we had back in the Guild from time to time?" Tori asked with a hint of sarcasm. My mother gave him an effective look that put him back into place.

"Hopefully, they're bigger than the spiders," Lincon hummed with enthusiasm.

My mother ignored him, continuing to lead the way. Tori saddled up beside Chase looking at him with disdain as he scratched at his robe. His face was almost entirely blanketed by the hood, blocking out the sun. "How are you not itchy?" he pestered. Chase was bare-chested in the sun, unusual considering I'd become so accustomed to seeing him in his long leather jacket.

"You get used to it, kid, trust me," he said, patting him on the shoulder. At first, the movement seemed to frighten Tori, and he flinched until he beamed with a sheepish smile from the friendly comradery. Dillian watched on with a cold expression, but when I waved my mind over his, I could differentiate that it was curiosity.

"Would you believe there was a time when vampires couldn't even let the sun touch them," Lincon said in a sing-song way. "My father used to tell me of such stories." He whistled.

"Your father?" I'd regretted it the moment I asked because his smug expression bloomed. Chase stepped in front of me, acting as a buffer from Lincon's sinister gaze.

"Are you curious about me, Esmore?" he asked with wicked delight.

"Hurry up!" my mother shouted, annoyed that she was already down the first rolling hill and we still lingered up top. Lincon caught my arm as we tried to walk past him. I unsheathed my sword and slashed at him, but he was already out of reach, jumping back with a haughty laugh. My reflexes and tolerance for his presumptuous hands had tired.

"You must already know, Esmore, if you ever want to know something, you only have to ask."

I shoved Chase back before he could do anything. I didn't want him anywhere near Lincon. *It's okay,* I said, soothing him as I felt the rise and stress of his mind. I eased and pressed him forward. We'd had too much sun and spent too many hours with unwanted company. I couldn't believe I actually looked forward to returning to the institute and this whirlwind of a mission being behind us. *If we made it back.*

We often heard noises and hid stealthily for coverage, expecting to be confronted by some giant, mutated creature, but nothing came. I had thought the rodents were an exception to how twisted this world had become. Not only was it in ruins after the war between humankind and vampires, but the mutated creatures that grew from those shadows were indulgent on how vile it had become. And the humans were *still* experimenting. What world did they ever hope to rebuild or return to? Even if they could be rid of vampires, there was still so much left in their wake that they alone were responsible for.

My mother drew us closer to a beautiful and glistening waterfall that connected with the riverbed. It seemed so out of place considering the heat and red dirt we'd been running through for days.

Water crashed delicately on the surface into the small pool that seemed like a hidden utopia in comparison to the last two days we'd had.

"It's inside," my mother said, nudging toward the back as she'd promised. "I've concealed our scents, but like the other creatures, if they hear or see us it'll be the same."

A few trees that surprisingly thrived around the water were a stark green compared to the red rolling barren land around us. I took my natural lead as the Token, scoping out the cave entrance that seemed exaggerated in size. There was an opening behind the waterfall that I couldn't quite make out what was behind it. The cave looked larger than the ones we'd inspected already. If there had been that many spiders in the last one, I could only presume what might be lingering in here and the size of it.

"Can you see anything from here?" I asked Dillian. He was peering into the waterfall and shook his head. Even he couldn't see past the water. I pulled my Barnett crossbow, sliding an arrow onto it. Everyone else followed my lead and unsheathed their weapons. "We'll circle the water pool first. Take position and follow my lead. If I can't see anything we'll proceed to go in." I ensured Chase and I were either side, closest to the entrance. Behind me were Tori and my mother. Dillian and Lincon were directly across from the waterfall, and Kora and Kasey flanked Chase's side.

We stealthily walked around the rocky edge that surprisingly grew little mold. The crashing water sounded refreshing after all the sticky blood, heat, and irritation we endured. Tori was edging my personal space to dive closer into the shade of the cave.

I halted everyone and stepped closer to the entry trying to peer around the water. I could sense something was beyond the water but couldn't focus or pinpoint its exact positioning. The entire area felt strange. I looked up into the dire sunny sky, squinting at the severity of the sun.

I can't see unless I go in, Chase informed.

I'm the same on my end.

Let me go in first, I don't mind getting wet for you, he purred. I'm certain he could see my deadpan expression from across the watering hole. His laughter rumbled through our link.

Tori's waving hand grabbed my attention. We were spread out about quarter mile each, equally distributed around the mass of the water. Once he had my attention he pointed to the center of the water. In the middle, bubbles began to pop to the surface, and it wasn't the same foamy-like creation from the waterfall.

Dillian and I pointed our crossbows at the water. I could sense a sliding movement that put me at unease. My fangs ejected and my sight turned a haze of purple. My vampire was alarmed and excited all at once by the impending threat.

I lost focus on the drawing attention in the water, and jumped back, shooting an arrow the opposite way. A large, white, scaly snake's head plowed into the ground where I'd once stood, the waterfall sprinkling over its neck. My arrow barely made it flinch as two of Dillian's snagged it in the nose and then eye. At that, it did writhe back and forth. The angular head was the size of the rodents I'd fought at the Human Compound. Its body was thick with white scales that blended into an odd pink flesh between each scale. It hissed at me, its large fangs half the size of my entirety. I was disgusted by such a creature, yet my vampire part, the reckless self, was eager to please.

The bubbles that once surfaced in the water had stopped, and Dillian lined up his arrow, raising it in aim as the second white snake slowly rose from the depths of its watering hole, its red eyes intent on Dillian.

"Now, I'm definitely glad I came along." Lincon whistled. Everyone exploded into action. Tori and I courted our snake further away, mostly to ensure my mother attacked it from a long range. It slithered toward us in no time at all. Chase had jumped into the water, jumping off the first snake and onto the back of the one that challenged us.

The snake dove for me once again, and I jumped out of its trajectory and what could've been the crunching snap of its mouth. It was unaffected and quickly followed me before I'd even landed on my feet.

As light as a feather, Chase jumped in front of the snake and scooped me into his arms. It was unnecessary because I could've managed getting out of its way on my own. But from the cocky smile he had, I could tell he enjoyed the brazen act of being my hero.

What would I do without you? I sarcastically droned.

Some would thank me with a kiss, he teased.

He delicately dropped me to my feet, and we immediately jumped on opposite sides of the snake.

It's a shame Yolo isn't here then, I joked, thinking of their male admiration for one another. Tori's long sword barely did damage down the side of the snake. I noticed with interest there was sensitivity when he sliced into its pink flesh between scales. That was its weakness. As if knowing it was in danger it tried to retreat, slithering back toward the waterhole where its companion wasn't able to put up much of a fight. It was immobile, Kora's attention was on it, freezing it into place.

I looked up just in time to watch Lincon delightfully jump onto its head and talk to it for a moment as if in casual chit chat. I growled internally not even wanting to know what jibber he was speaking before the snake's eyes widened into a frenzy as he tortured it.

"Stay out here!" I ordered Tori, conscious of my mother's condition. I knew she could look after herself, but she had a whole team around her, she shouldn't have to—and especially because she had me. Chase and I followed the snake into the waterfall blindly. The wave of water washed over me. I was soaked, and my leather under my robe began making irritable squishing noises.

The white tail of the snake led further into one of the numerous tunnels of the cave. Chase followed it, and I made sure to keep to his pace. I swept my mind around us, ensuring there weren't any more that might ambush us. Surprisingly, it was quiet. But I could sense one more which had already made its way to the front of the cave—three in total. I trusted in the others to easily take it down.

A bit slow, my love, Chase teased. The size of this cave seemed almost endless as we switched from tunnel to red tunnel, chasing the tail end of the mutated white snake. The space was darkening the further we left behind the entrance.

Chase was only a few steps ahead of me, but he was joyously outrunning me. Hmph. I called upon the Descendant biting on his challenge. Wings burst through my back, the painful stretch a welcoming pleasure. They snapped open, pushing the wet robe down my shoulder blades. I sprung and swept past him, making sure to spray enough water and wind at him that he might have to wipe a hand over his face. I could see his smile stretch as I passed him.

I was upon the snake within seconds. It didn't so much as stand a chance. I perched on its head as it reared back and forth in an attempt to shake me off. I found a small part of pink-like flesh between scales and punctured my blade down. The skin was so soft and vulnerable compared to the rest of its body. It hissed and threw its head back and forth still trying to fling me off. I slammed down on the hilt of my sword, driving it deeper until the snake finally went limp.

It suspended in the air only for a moment before gravity took hold and it crashed to the ground. I pulled back my sword and hovered in the air, watching it crash, and dust come up as it did so.

"Someone was feeling a bit show-offy," Chase said as he danced his fingers with delight theatrically. I returned his smile as I flicked the blood off my sword. I wiped it over my robe, trying to find a patch where it wasn't already covered in blue blood before sheathing it.

"You antagonized me," I replied simply. His smirk lightened the mood as he stared over the mass of my wings. He reached out and lightly skirted his fingers over them. A tingle spread up me at the calming stroke that felt unnaturally soothing. If he did this for a period of time, I imagined I might even fall asleep.

"Beautiful," he remarked. In the dark he shouldn't have been able to see much, but I knew he could see me perfectly. "Watching you fight is equally stunning." His smile stretched, all too cocky and aware of what he was doing to me. I could lose focus in a moment's heartbeat gazing into those eyes.

I swept my attention toward the entrance. I could sense the two snakes they'd battled were both already dead. They'd made quick work of them as I'd expected of my team. Only my mother entered the cave. I assumed she ordered them to stay as lookout while we searched for my heart together, not willing to risk their safety in the process. None of us knew how I might react once it was reinstated.

The gentle stroke of Chase's hand was calming as I considered how close we were to our goal. To *my* goal. Chase lifted his hand to my cheek and rubbed at it. "Though slightly messy." He smiled as he wiped away a splatter of blood that had smeared my face. I retracted my mighty wings, the pain crunching bone and muscle into my back once again. My robe dropped around me as I sensed my mother nearing.

"Me? Messy? I've seen you butcher things, Chase Bourne," I swaggered past him, letting my hip bump into him. He smiled past me, hot, flustered, and riled from the fight. He caught me by the back of the neck and twisted me to face him with lethal and endearing intensity blazing in his eyes. The fight had riled us both, adrenalin pumping. A tease and foreplay all the same. His lips crushed into mine, no longer concerned about the potential threat around us. From what we could sense, there was nothing but tunnels and darkness where we could frolic as we pleased.

I reached out for his waistband pulling his hips into mine. He steadied me over the edge of the tunnel, pushing me against the harsh edge of the rocky wall. He ground against me once, a small noise escaping me at the thought of all the wicked delight we could have. I was flustered from the battle, and that adrenalin rolled into the one thing I wanted now.

He wanted me, and I wanted him. *Desperately.* He raised one of my legs over his hip, giving me greater access to feel how much he wanted me. I could feel myself filling with liquid warmth, readying myself for him all from simple kisses stolen in the dark.

"Esmore?" my mother called out from a nearby tunnel. I thudded my head back against the wall, clarity coming back to me once again as to where we were. Chase nipped at my throat, grazing his fangs. I hissed erotically at the small tease and scrunched my hand into his hair as I jerked back his head in warning. He had a cocky grin, and a small chuckle followed.

"Focus," I growled, more irritated with myself than anything. But I enjoyed this. The hunt, the fight, the excitement of frolicking in the dark after a kill with him. I shouldn't, it wasn't sane, but I did. With the intensity of his gaze, I knew that he, too, was thinking the same. Out here it was different. For a moment we only had to think about the kill and no political movement or consequence. We could simply be whatever we wanted without everyone else and their opinion.

But unfortunately, reality was crashing in with a time limit. "Over here," I called out to her. When I let go of Chase's hair, he rested his head on my shoulder. He was bothered that we couldn't continue on.

He took a promiscuous sniff and gagged. "You smell." I slapped him on the shoulder, pushing him back, which ignited another chuckle.

"You're not doing too much better yourself." I rolled him off me, trying to calm my heated body. There was no cool breeze or anything of the sort in these windy tunnels. It was stuffy and dark and yet I somewhat enjoyed it. At least we weren't beneath the berating sun.

"Oh, good, you two didn't get too far into the tunnels," my mother said as she caught up. "I instructed the others to guard the entrance though I doubt we'll have any issues from here. I also didn't want anyone else to come with us while we searched for it."

"It's in here?" I asked quietly. I couldn't sense anything, which only saddened me to know that I did not even feel connected to what was mine. They had hidden it that well, but surely, I should have some inclination toward it.

"It is," my mother said reluctantly. "Come with me."

CHAPTER 28

I AVOIDED CHASE'S intense, smoldering glare. I don't know what had all of a sudden gotten into him, but he was looking at me with his best, '*I want you now, come fuck me,*' gaze. It was unnerving as I tried to focus on my mother's guidance throughout the tunnels. But I narrowly focused on the temptation of how delicious he would taste.

Are you okay? I asked. I couldn't sense anything was astray.

I'm fine. It just gets me heated when I see you fight, that's all. You're sexy, badass, and completely mine. It stirs my nature, he growled. It vibrated through me, piquing my entire body's interest. I had to calm myself before trying to think rationally again. When we'd become familiars or even before then, he'd never been so possessive to claim me. Only when it was mutual, but now … it seemed different like something felt off.

Perhaps he felt it necessary to reclaim me before we went ahead with this experiment in uniting me with my heart. Maybe, this was his way of deflecting. Instead of his usual goofy nature, he'd returned to a more primal urge. I was his. It made me want to capture him for a few hours so he could have that leisure and feel a sense of security walking into it.

My mother was guided by what I imagined to be the pull of her gift. To Chase and me, we were none the wiser as we followed her. After minutes passed by, and I wondered if she was getting us lost in tunnels that rolled in changes of structure, she halted in front of a wall. I wondered if they'd concealed the entrance as well, and it was much like how they'd hidden Cesar's coven before it'd become compromised.

She looked back at Chase with a considerate glance. "Maybe you should wait out here."

Chase grabbed my hand, his speed surprising me as I could feel the wave of uncertainty wash off him. "I go where she goes." I wanted to tell him that everything would be okay. That *we* would be okay, but instead, I found myself adding just as much pressure. Now that we were here, I didn't know what to expect.

But what if I hurt you? I weakly asked. I didn't want to put Chase at risk.

And what if I'm the only one who can help you or your mother? he said just as cautiously. And now I wondered if the gamble was even worth the risk. But the thought felt obnoxious considering this was my *heart* and we'd already made our way here. This was my sole source as a huntress, and I'd been denied it once. If it could increase our chances of coming out of this war unscathed, then didn't I owe it to at least try?

"He'll join us," I said to my mother. He wasn't going to leave my side, even if I wanted him to. The truth was, I was scared to go in it alone. My mother was reluctant before squeezing herself in what looked to be two thin walls. Another tunnel I suspected. I rubbed my thumb over Chase's hand, sending waves of reassurance into him. But I was rattled at how meekly they came across because my uncertainty wavered them.

Only the scuttle and drag of our bodies against the rocky edges could be heard. It was eerily silent, and I hovered my mind toward outside to check up on the others, more so in reassurance to remind myself that I wasn't on some alienated planet even though that's how these past few days had felt. Everything from the mutated creatures and the odd group I'd come here with. It was all for this moment, and now that we were here ... all my gusto and badass warrior was leeched out of me. Doubt had never been something I danced with, but as of late at every turn, it was becoming more prominent, the risks greater every time.

Finally, I broke free into a small space. It was like a hidden cave, pitch-black and only because I depended on my vampire site was the reason I could see anything at all. My mother, however, was struggling more than me, and although I noticed she walked straight ahead to a pile of mounted rocks against the wall, I was certain that was only because she followed the gravitation of her gift.

I slowly followed my mother, every step a weighted resistance. She felt around the rocks as if trying to locate a particular one. The wall looked as if it'd been stacked unnaturally and I wondered if my mother and Cesar were here a little less than one year ago, scrounging in the dark to hide the subtle beat of my heart. She began pulling rocks away. I dropped to my knees beside her, following her step, and digging them out one by one. I watched her focused expression more than where my hands were going as I grabbed one rock at a time.

Even my mother was hesitant. They gave me the option to come here, but did they truly think this was the right thing to do? I caught myself, irritated. I'd been complaining about the bindings and rules of this agreement between covens, and it had now forced me to doubt when I was given the freedom of choice.

My fingers grated against something wooden and smooth. I slowly jerked my hand back, peering into the depths of darkness and small hole we'd created amongst the rocks. Strangely, the rocks mounted on top didn't fall and close in the gap. I could see a dull gold symbol covered in dust—an emblem of some kind. By my mother's expression, the way she stepped back and tilted her hand toward the wooden box, she didn't have to say it out loud. My eyebrows flicked up. This was it? I looked back to Chase, uncertain as my fingers danced along and sized the edge of the wooden box.

It's okay, he encouraged though I could hear the suspended pause. This is what we came here for. This was the mission. And now that I was here ... now that my hands were on it ... I wasn't sure if this was all I'd hoped it would be. My vampire self grew irritated by the self-doubt and suspense, and an impatient push pumped my body with adrenalin.

With one hand, I took firm hold of the wooden box and pulled it out. I realized as it came into sight, in the pitch black that surrounded us that firstly it was a black wooden box. It was no bigger than both of my hands and was sealed shut with a gold emblem. The center of it was a small heart that webbed out into swirls and petals as if a flower blossomed around it. Cautiously, I flicked the emblem up, and the dust seemed to unnaturally gravitate off it.

It wasn't until the seal was broken that I could sense it. That I could hear and feel the beat of what lay within. Chase placed his hand on my shoulder. I hadn't even realized I'd sat on top of my feet, still on my knees but completely unguarded as I curved the box toward me. I tried to keep my mind at bay for the repercussions that might come from this.

I'm with you, he reminded me. *Always and forever.*

Yes, I felt as I'd said it breathlessly into his mind. As if that was all I could manage when I gathered strength from him. Had I never met Chase perhaps the honor of reclaiming my heart might've been more transactional with the lack of emotions. But this felt right, this being with care and worry as much as rage and despise. I had always been disconcerted about my emotions, willing them away. I'd even hated myself for all that had happened and to those who I couldn't protect. But now I was fortified with the resolve to create my own path, despite what others had told me because I had the strength with at least Chase behind me. But more importantly, I had my power and merit, even when darkness consumed me, and I much enjoyed it. This heart was as much a part of me as I was it. If I was worried it would be the last to be tainted and dragged into the depths of wickedness with me … then so be it.

I peeled open the lid slowly, revealing the purple velvet lining with a singular heart beating. I stared down at it, loathing that such a vital piece of me had been taken out and hidden in such a box. If my mother had never led me here, would I have ever found it? This was everything to a huntress, and because of it, I'd become some vile mess letting the vampire run rampage over me. This was my fate, but it drew to attention that maybe it was too late, and this purity wouldn't help me. But maybe I could still help the others.

It thrummed rhythmically as if casting a hypnotic spell over me—I couldn't look away. My mother's gift had animated it here and now what lay in my chest bare and empty held no comparison to it.

"Do you still want this, Esmore?" my mother asked warily. It looked no different from what I'd seen of other hearts, except that it was beating unnaturally outside of my body. I nodded gravely in response. Did I want this? What would *this* involve? But I took myself back to the night before my eighteenth birthday. The excitement that filled me from awakening and discovering what my gift might be. It almost kept me awake half the night had I not been reasonable with myself about the absurdity of being so excitable over anything.

I recollected the cruel disappointment of waking up with not only my purple vision gone, identifying me as a huntress, but the hollowness of no gift, if anything I felt less. And then the cruel message that my mother had been killed. This, my heart and gift, had been all I had to look forward to, to reign one day as a supreme Token Huntress. And I had achieved those things without it, but I'd also pined to know its feel and warmth. I nodded gravely. I may have abandoned my merit as a huntress, but I couldn't deny the whole and complete satisfaction having my gift would offer. I could control it, I decided affirmatively. I had no choice, and this would not be one I'd fail at. I couldn't afford to.

I glanced at Chase's hand that tightened on my shoulder. My mother spoke up, "Chase, I know you're here to support my daughter, but for you both, please take a few steps back. If you distract her, it could be disastrous." He went to object, but I encouraged him to follow her direction. I owned my power and strength. And this I could manage. Or so I hoped.

Reluctantly, his hand dropped as he stepped back. I shifted to watch him, his gray eyes barely noticeable in the dark. It seemed fitting for the predator he was, but in it, I found strength and support like I was sitting on the other side of my own darkness and imbalance that was about to be made right once again.

My mother's delicate hand reached into the box. I gripped the smooth edges of the black box watching as she pulled out my heart. I looked from it to Chase, my anchor to this world. *My familiar. My Husband.*

My wife, he echoed in return as his eyes were unblinking and intently focused on me. I didn't look away as my mother focused and pressed my heart to my chest, her delicate gift wrapping around the hollowness of my insides like vines strapping to other trees to keep its old and dead roots embedded. I could feel the pressure of my heart absorbing into me, my body wanting to push it back out and reject it.

A cold shudder waved over me as my mother's delicate fingers pressed against the leather of my chest, and painfully I gasped a loud, sharp breath. Pain erupted from the inside as my body flared into an unnatural rhythm to what it had known and been its existence for the last year. Rapid breaths drew in and out as if my body tried to memorize what a rhythmic breath was, and how my lungs had to function around it.

Warmth thread through me like ants biting through into fiery paths as my blood began to pump. A feverish shake broke out. Chase broke my focus, taking a step forward. The moment he did, I felt like I'd lost my anchor as everything snapped.

"Don't!" my mother said, shoving a hand up toward him, warning him not to step any closer.

"Mom." I could barely and shakily get the word out as I tried to reach for her. "Mom." My body was panicking. *I was panicking.*

"Just try to steady your breathing," she said as she pressed a hand on my back. Her touch erupted the Descendant as if to push her away in its own strange way to protect itself. My mother was forced to take a few steps back as my wings curled around me, and I shuddered into myself. My body was alive, elicited with unfamiliar sensory all around me. Power built from deep inside curling into every fiber as I took another shard-like breath from the dusty room.

My wings only further curled around me in vain to protect me from whatever it considered to be dangerous. I felt as if I was being eaten from the inside out.

Esmore, my love, I heard Chase's voice boom into my mind as if it was the only thing that anchored me to this world, past my wings that crippled in around me. I could feel my vampire self within wither in pain as it was pushed back by the flow of my blood that now naturally pulsed through. I'd never noticed how differently my body worked, how mechanical it had been up until now.

And out flowed the dire need of my gift to expel, to be released from its choking holds. "Esmore," my mother said cautiously, and I could hear her scamper back.

Esmore, something is secreting from you, you need to calm, Chase said passively. I could feel him creeping toward me. My body shook as I tried to focus on something. Anything. But my body was rolling in fits, hiding from the world that may be. It only wanted to sit in this bleakness, even if it had to destroy everything around it to maintain that wish.

I could feel Chase's fingers curl around one of my wings as he delicately but forcefully pushed it back. I looked up at him through scattered purple eyes. His gray eyes that came from the darkness were somewhat illuminated when he saw me. "Hey," he said in his most coxing and loving voice.

Bits of skin flaked off his face as he tried to push in further, and I realized it was exactly as my mother had warned. Whatever this gift was, it was eating away at him. He pushed his shoulder through so his upper half was inside my cocoon. If my wings truly didn't want him in, they could've forced him out, but with as much control as I had I let them soften around his maneuvering. Flakes of skin and muscle stripped off his chest. He pressed his forehead to mine, the skin-to-skin touch eliciting another reaction from my body that pulsed with a harsh, damaging strike.

Chase grunted in pain. I tried to rally all of it into a bundle, as I'd learned to do with my vampire to try and push it down, but I didn't know where this gift was supposed to go and how I was able to constrict its power.

"Leave," I said with a shaky, hindered voice. I felt a teardrop as I realized, scarily, that my mother had been right this whole time. I had no control over it. It's as if all my fears and worries balled into a confident agreement. Everyone I cared for would die around me. I was reckless, and the only way to feel anything was by throwing myself into battle, by pushing the bounds until I finally found my end. My torture that I deserved. This is what that was, this was my torture and fate.

We're in this together remember, he pushed through a hand to cup my jaw, his hand being torn into painful strips as he got closer. *But only if that's what you want.*

I looked up and searched into his pained gray eyes. If that's what I wanted? Of course that's what I wanted. As if above all other reasoning and choice, I would always choose Chase. I wanted him safe. I wanted him alive. In front of him, I felt naked and vulnerable.

But I could be with him. I chose to be with him. He'd always offered me a safe space. Stripped past my title as a Token and a reputable warrior, he saw me for me, no matter my failings, shortcomings, and monster that I'd become. He was the beacon of acceptance I could only receive because I knew I would never truly accept myself.

It felt like we'd changed roles, instead of him being bound in his mind, trapped by the thorny disease that dared to take over him and turn him into a saber, I was building power from within ready to implode. To what magnitude I didn't know and I didn't want to find out.

Together, I replied more so for my own sanity and anchoring than his. I could sense the power leeching out of me, like an aggressive depression falling over the surface of everything within the cave. I called it back as if it were shadows whispering back toward me. It was unwilling, desperately snaking to escape as if a blossoming flower of uncontrollable growth. If I'd stayed here like this, I wondered if I would continue to spread out and how far.

"Let me take it back out," my mother desperately agonized from behind Chase.

"No," he growled, snapping my attention back to his intense gray eyes. By now, half his face had been peeled back in strips. "My familiar can control this. Esmore, you can." I felt his gentle touch on the outskirts of my mind, trying to find a way to help me push it back in like I'd tried to find a way to pull him back out all those times.

He didn't let me look anywhere but at him, the anchor to my darkness. I demanded the power come back to me once, entitled to me. This time, instead of allowing my vampire to be subdued, I called forth its strength, hoping its potency might waver my new gift in some way. It escaped, tentatively, unsure as to how it should work around the toxicity of my body.

At first, I thought it might be feeding off the waves of power. But then I realized it was threading through it, like natural leverage. It was coaxing just as the vampire's nature was. To pull in and allure, to have its prey brought to it.

I could feel the mixture of myself fighting against one another and realized the gift I harbored that came from my huntress origins was so angry and vile toward everything, just as I had been. It fed off my emotions and how I saw vampires wanting to extinguish all their kind. A pulse fluctuated out at Chase, and this time a painful grunt dropped him to a knee, but he ensured his forehead was still on mine, those intense gray eyes never letting me escape. My conflict ran rampant with the ways of the Hunter Guild. I heard my mother gasp close by as if she were trying to reach for me but unable to make it through. My gift was sensitive to my emotions. With clarity, I allowed serenity to come over me, willing my body to find balance.

The lack of emotion and countering the connection with Chase had thrown me out of balance. But before I met him it wasn't a natural one. The coldness left behind after my mother removed my heart was only the ghost-like hollowness of all these things I'd been harboring.

I called my power in, no longer letting it escape or do damage of its own accord. I'd been born with this gift for a reason. And I would control it. My heart began a steady beat as my lungs functioned of their own natural accord. My power vacuumed into me, and the moment it did, Chase collapsed in between my wings as if the power had been pushing him back. I caught him, trying not to touch the tenderness of his flesh-eaten face.

"I'm sorry it took me so long," I mumbled into his neck as I softly patted my hand over his hair. His skin began to recoup, tightening over his cold body. Comparatively to me now, he was cold. I shifted a wing so I could see my mother. She'd also dropped to her knees, a few peels of skin taken but nothing to the extent of Chase.

He nestled his cheek against mine, his eyebrows furrowing as if he weren't entirely sure if we'd make it. "Nah, I had all day," he lightly joked though I could hear the fatigue in his voice. He slowly drooped into my chest. At first, I thought he was rubbing his face as if to be playful, but then I realized he was listening.

His face was pressed against my breasts, his hand coming around my waist as he comfortably positioned himself there, listening to my beating heart. His eyes were closed with a serene expression on his face.

I could listen to this all day, he tranquilly said. *How do you feel?*

I contemplated as I stroked back his black shoulder-length hair and watched his blue gemmed earring swing from side to side every time I touched it. I looked down at my own blue gemmed necklace that he'd given to me the day he claimed me as his within Fier's Council.

Whole, I cautiously admitted as if I wasn't worthy of such a sentiment. But the truth was, I'd never felt more invigorated or balanced. For the first time in a long time, I felt like I'd widened my eyes with total clarity instead of the misfortune surviving day by day. I was powerful, and I was enough. If not by my own expectations at least I might be enough to effectively put a weight on our side of this war. So then there could be a day where Chase could listen to my heart uninterrupted. This additional power buzzed through my veins like little bugs wanting to escape, and the only thing keeping it in was the thinness of my skin.

I felt warm, vulnerable, and powerful all at once. Now the hardship would entail learning how to use it, and only in a matter of weeks.

CHAPTER 29

T HIS TRIP HAD left my mother depleted. Despite the harsh darkness, I could still manage to see patches of skin that had stripped from her face and arms. "I'm sorry," I said out loud as I nursed Chase. He was tired too. All of us were, and we needed those few moments of respite.

"Don't apologize, Esmore, I'm just glad your familiar was here to help you control it. For that I'm grateful," she said as she slowly stood, and it was the first time she truly spoke fondly toward Chase, despite it going against her nature to like him. What a bizarre arrangement we'd both found ourselves in being the familiars to vampires. "We should check on the others and start making our way back. I'll give you a moment alone."

Before leaving, she extended a hand out to me so she could take the black wooden box with the goldenseal. I was hesitant to give it back to her. This only meant she wanted it, just in case she would once again have to use it. She shoved it into her backpack and disappeared into the thin tunnel.

"Your eyes are purple now even without your fangs ejected," Chase said quietly. I raised a hand disbelieving, but when my fingers scraped over the dryness of my gums, it was my human canines I felt. A flood of warmth swept through me. My huntress eyes were back as if the past year was a terrible nightmare.

And yet I found myself asking, "Does it disturb you?" I felt vulnerable to his rejection. This was different. *I* would be different.

"Everything about you disturbs me," he said honestly and raised his gaze to mine. "In a good way." His smile softened the blow as he teased me, like usual.

"Things could change. This means we can't—"

"I know. No sex until we figure out what it might do." He sighed. "I swear, the sacrifices we've made already and now I have to be deprived sexually as well." I blossomed a smile and kissed him gently trying not to arouse him if that ever were such a thing. For now, we couldn't risk coming together in such a way. If we were to, I'd share my gifts with him. And this new power and its guttural existence might be enough to tip him over the edge.

He reciprocated my love. The kiss deep and slow, pinpointing us to this moment. We could help each other. I failed being able to bring him back the last time from his condition, but I wouldn't allow it to happen again, no matter what methods I might use. A deep peace settled over me. Not a restful complacency, but an ignited spark that was ready to lead again. I'd been so thrown about and torn apart and rebuilt in a broken pieced way. And now—now I had this power and drive to use it to destroy all my enemies as long as I learned how to use it in time. No one would ever touch Chase again. No one would dare cross me or those who I'd vowed to protect.

I rested my forehead against Chase's for a moment longer with a shaky breath, an actual breath that filled my lungs and body. I felt anew. But that also detested my once immortality. If Oppollo or anyone else were to aim for my heart, I would die this time.

"Let's join the others." Chase lazily stood up, following me out. The others were still waiting patiently at the front. From the laughter that fluttered from outside, I figured not so patiently in Lincon's case. My mother's skin had healed, her gift enabling her to heal much faster than most hunters.

"Stop laughing!" Tori yelled back, unwisely biting back at Lincon's taunts.

"But you look disgusting and honestly smell. How did you survive this long as a hunter, dear child?"

We walked through the gushing water. The first things to grab my attention were the two snake remains that hung over opposite sides of the waterhole. One looked as if it had exploded, parts of it chunky and festering everywhere. And Tori was crouched by the watering hole not far from it, scrubbing his blood-soaked clothes, hair, and skin.

"Oh, Esmore, perfect timing. You missed it. The snake gobbled Tori, and he cut it up from the inside, but look at him. Look at …" Lincon's plastered smile slowly dropped, and a serious expression washed over him. Everyone's attention turned on me. They would no doubt hear it. Perhaps not Kora and Kasey, but the others as vampires would now hear the rhythmic beat of my heart. I wondered if Dillian and Tori would turn on me or if my half-vampire self was enough of a repellent to even newborns.

Lincon's pointed nail rose in my direction as if accusingly. "You have your heart. Ah, well, now doesn't this all make sense." He seemed mystified, but I had my suspicions that he'd already known what we were here for.

"So, what now? That was the 'ultimate weapon' we came here for?" Kasey accused. "Because you have your heart. So what, you have your gift now?"

Dillian stared at me distantly. As if it sickened him that the reason we'd ventured this far was because of me. He'd called me many things the past few weeks. But this I would not apologize for. If only I had it sooner, whatever this was, maybe it could've made the difference to protect them, and in that, I had deep regret. But I would not apologize for this, not when he'd asked my mother to come of his own accord.

"Your gift?" Tori said very quietly. He was peering at his reflection in the water thoughtfully, a saddened expression twisting. I regretted deeply that he'd never know his. And maybe that's what he considered now, and maybe even he despised me for it.

"It might give us an advantage at the Council meeting, yes," I said. Kasey could mock me all she liked, but I would use this to our advantage, and I would no longer step around peoples' feelings or expectations of what I should do.

"Well, let's see it then." Lincon propped his hand on his hip.

"She needs rest," Chase growled. "It's not some parlor trick for your entertainment."

"Oh, hogwash. Everything's for my entertainment!" Lincon encouraged me again.

"I need to learn how to control it. And besides, we need to start moving back to where Tythian will meet us in a few days." The thought of Tythian made my new power want to flutter out and marvel with ease to destroy everything around me. Chase must've felt the shift because I felt his influence wash over me as if he were massaging the tightness out of my muscles. My power stopped flexing and eased back into my body.

"Oh, my," was all Lincon said. I don't know what had escaped or what he might've sensed, but he watched me dubiously. "Then maybe we should start heading back."

Kasey was irritated by the anticlimax of the situation, but her gaze wandered mischievously over to Tori who was still washing his filthy hands. With a speed that she rarely used, she shoved him into the water with a delighted smile that stretched over her saber fangs.

"Are you kidding me?!" Tori snarled as he splashed about in the water. Soon he'd realize that splashing wasn't necessary for a vampire. His functions and ways as a human would soon die out.

Lincon cackled, holding his stomach. "Good one! Oh, and this is why you're my favorite twin!" he rewarded, trying to force her into a high five. She ignored him, snarling at his bouncing energy. Kora watched on between the two and started walking after them solemnly, her feet dragging. I couldn't read Dillian's expression with such a guarded stature. Tori heaved himself out of the water, giving chase.

"And this damn sun!" Tori yelled, irritated as he scratched at his soaking robe.

"That answers one of my unspoken questions," my mother said as we walked around the pool of water. "I'd wondered if they'd be inclined to attack you with your heart beating in your chest," my mother elaborated. "And whether you'd be at threat from vampires who had little control within the institute. But I suppose your vampire-half is enough to deter them. How do you feel?"

"Different," I admitted. My gift was acutely interlaced to my emotions which was foreboding considering the lack of control I'd been dealing with since obtaining these other gifts. But I felt solid and steady all the same.

"Sometimes different is good," my mother said, surprising me in her attempt to sound optimistic, which wasn't a trait either of us possessed.

On the second night and trek back through the sun-bleached terrain, we'd managed to avoid any confrontations with mutated creatures. I almost wished something would come along just to diffuse Lincon's jitters. My power and beating heart settled into me a lot more collectively now. Of a nighttime, I flexed the new gift of mine back and forth, feeling it wager outside of my body like some kind of unnatural force field, but it was taxing as most untrained gifts were. Though its effects on my body still surprised me, Lincon hadn't asked to see my gift at work again, which was unnerving in itself.

We'd once again opted to change lookout schedules. Chase and I were somewhat secluded, lying down on the sandy terrain. Personal hygiene had become a thing of the past for our group until we returned to the institute, but this was expected on most missions. We'd just never been on one within terrain such as this. I had my head on Chase's chest as we stared up at the star-filled sky. As dreadful as the days were with the bleak open sky, of a night time it made for a spectacle.

I was playing with his fingers as he rounded his other arm around me, his open palm pressed against my heart. Something was endearing about the way he was drawn to it. But I also understood he too had his concerns for my new vulnerability. And time would only tell if I would age naturally as a huntress or if my vampirism would still override. There was so much thrown into the unknown that we could only take it day by day.

"Give it one more try, and then we'll get some rest," Chase instructed. I was reluctant, I didn't like practicing this way, but he assured me it was fine. I danced my fingers lightly across his, trying to focus my newfound gift to swirl and play around with them.

It had no issue with escaping my body, but controlling its movements and fine-tuning it to my command were entirely different. It skittered around his fingers, peeling away bits of skin. "That's good. It's not as deep as last time," Chase said as if it were nothing but a tingle. We'd theorized that if I could limit its potency, then maybe it would help me learn to control it on a larger scale. So instead of being overcome by it, I could navigate it to my will.

My mind was numbing from the amount of focus as I tried to push it away from Chase's fingers not allowing it to hurt him further. I called it back in, finding it easier to call upon my vampire-half to elicit it back. It was like a beast trying to manage another beast, and I wasn't very keen on the progress. I had less than three weeks to figure out how to use this gift.

I took a hefty and exhausted sigh. Chase's hand was perfectly smooth once again. *I don't like using you as a guinea pig.*

Ah, but see, if I asked you to do that a year ago you would've happily. She really loves me, he joyfully boomed in my mind and squeezed me tightly. He left small kisses along my face, and a small smile drew out of me. *Get some rest. I'll wake you if anything happens.*

A Token should be the last to sleep in her group, I blatantly replied, though the thought of sleep certainly was appealing.

Maybe so. But a lot of Token's don't have hunky familiars to guard them while they sleep, he teased. *A few minutes is fine. And besides, we'll have to deal with Sir Shabby Tythian soon, you might want to get your rest before we go back.*

I let out another depleted sigh and watched the others from the corner of my eye. My mother was teaching Tori particular thrusts and holds. I imagined the new amount of energy he realized he had was going to good use. He would still have to rest, but nowhere near as much as what he'd been used to.

Dillian and Kora silently sat beside one another on lookout as Kasey chastised Lincon for being so irritating. *You know, as bizarre as fighting mutated creatures instead of enemy vampires has been … it's been nice to be away from it all.* I felt guilty for admitting it. I was a warrior. A leader. But it was nice to be pulled away from the toxicity of it all before everything erupted and we fought for our lives yet again. Mostly, I'd enjoyed the step away from responsibility with Chase. Where he wasn't being pulled away by his coven, and I wasn't being pulled away from my sent errands and expectations. But our time here was coming to a close. Titan and Chris remained. And I wondered what we would now do with Julia, of that I would have to have a conversation with Dillian.

Me too, Chase kissed my forehead. *Maybe one day, once this war has been appeased, we can find a quiet place like this again.*

"Lincon!" Kasey shrieked. Lincon had kicked up sand into her face. She was spitting and seething as she chased after him. Lincon laughed as he ran off into the wilderness, excited by the thrill of her finally biting back. It would be nice if one day, this could be our normal, but a part of me, deep inside, understood that wasn't a reality to come anytime soon if ever. I shouldered into Chase a little bit more. Something was coming, and it put my inner monster on edge.

CHAPTER 30

TYTHIAN WAS RELUCTANT to touch me. He said nothing, leaving Chase and me as the last to be collected from our adventure. With the delay in collecting us after the others, I wondered if we'd been left stranded. But alas, he appeared, not bothering to hold out his arm to either Chase or me, allowing us to attach to him as if we were some kind of parasites.

The dreary gray of the overcast night and institute was a welcome distraction from the irritable sun we'd been standing in by the 'Route 66' sign where Chase rambled on about a road trip he and his mother once went on, showing his true age. The mist swept around our ankles, a comforting envelopment of the environment I felt most accustomed to. My mother waited at the wooden doors that were already open for us. We would have to report to Cesar first.

I heard Lincon in the distance mumbling to the twins that they were bound for the nearby watering hole to bathe. Tori and Dillian reluctantly followed them. I was certain it was because Dillian didn't want to leave Tori on his own with the others. Dillian briefed a glance toward the tower where I sensed Julia fluttering about and using her gift. Had she been trained as a warrior, she might've had a better sense that he was so close to her.

"Come on," Tori said, tugging him out of his trance. It was hard for me to guess where Dillian's mind was with Julia. Was he trying to attempt to outrun the reality of this situation? Or maybe he was trying to pause time to find a way to control his urges.

"You best not keep Cesar waiting, a lot has happened while you've been gone," Tythian gritted out. He looked down on me like I was some kind of filth, his gaze transfixed to my breasts—no, my beating heart. Chase's intimidating growl was the only thing to pull him away. I felt as if I had to cover myself up from his prying eyes or even better, I could let it escape and do *minimal* damage as a warning.

I followed my mother toward the entrance. From the rooftops of our wing, I could see Darcy looking down on us. It didn't stop there. From the moment I stepped into the dire and dusty room, vampires crept from their dark hubs and watched me. Whispers and murmurs began. I found Clarissa's gaze most haunting as she leaned against the stairwell, running circles through Spungee's hair. 'She has a heart,' 'maybe the rumors are true,' 'it's not right,' 'disgusting.' Everyone had an opinion as to what to make of our side-track mission and what we'd so evidently returned with.

"The mission was a success," Clarissa verified with Chase as he paused to speak with her. I was astounded Chase had confided in her. But then again, she was his second in every sense, and Clarissa lacked in motivation to be a threat and take over the coven herself. I'd realized he'd come to trust her, perhaps in the same way that I'd come to trust Darcy and Jerimiah, which could be equally foolish considering the lack of time we'd spent together. But, I'd known others for my whole life who had been willing to betray me in a heartbeat.

"It would appear so. Any problems while I was away?" he asked.

"A few scuttles between the covens, but nothing that couldn't be broken up. Only five died from the outcome. And from the whispers, I hear another two covens were taken out this week."

Chase gawked at Tythian who hmphed Clarissa as if she were less than vermin. My mother waited atop the stairs, all her discomfort and tiredness from the trip hidden as she eyed the vampires singularly who looked at her or me peculiarly.

"Good job." Chase nodded gratefully. "I'll speak with Cesar and be back. We have a lot of work to do."

"Yes," she breathed and offered a slight curtsy. The vampires around him did the same in way of respect though they skeptically eyed me once Chase's back was turned.

I could sense Fire's eagerness to find me but willed her to stay. First, we'd see Cesar, and then I'd attend to the others. Three sabers were snoozing outside the door which meant Connor and Deemori were likely inside. When I opened it, I noted Balzar bleakly standing in the room as well. He looked relieved to see us, but my begrudging stare was quick to push him back from any elated feelings. I still hadn't entirely forgiven him. I comprehended why he'd done it, but it didn't lessen my blow of fury in any way. Yolo slapped a casual arm around him as if trying to soften my blow. It was the first time in a long time, all of the siblings were in the same room at once.

"You were wounded," Cesar alarmed as he crossed the room and embraced my mother. She seemed to sag in relief by his touch, the exchange touching me much to my surprise, and although I wasn't an advocate for Cesar, my mother did love him … in whatever way that looked for them.

"I'm fine. I just need some rest," she said before remembering the audience in the room and breaking their embrace. Cesar rolled his shoulders back in the same way my mother did, taking charge of the room.

"You were successful?" he clarified, another twinge of concern flashing between my mother and me. "Are you okay?"

The question surprised me, and I felt confined by everyone's attention. Connor's gaze was just as piercing as Tythian's had been when he stared at my chest. Not for who I was, but the power I may now wield. This was how they viewed me, simply as a weapon. And so, I assumed to take a heavy breath in the darkness, ordaining that this was my domain and I could bend it to my will. I would not succumb to their rules or intimidation any longer.

"Marvelous," I said dryly. "I need to train and learn how to control it. But I dare say no one will be able to touch me when I learn the magnitude of its power unless they want their limbs peeled away." I amplified my tone into the dark, sinister voice I sometimes enjoyed taking on. So those who were a threat to me in this room would think twice about crossing Chase and me.

Cesar looked to my mother, obviously searching for clarification as to how stable I was.

"Fabulous! Another unruly gift that could be leeched dry from the little princess and be taken into enemy hands if they drain her," Tythian said, abhorred.

"Chill out, Tythian!" Yolo exploded in his usual calm demeanor, kicking off the wall.

"I didn't realize you were so against us gaining more power," I irked.

"Only when it's with holders who can't manage it. But no, I don't agree with depending on your hand in this war. No matter how much people may disagree with me." He offered a forewarning glance at Balzar and Cesar. The way he traced up and down Yolo was as if he were just as disgusting as me. The room was divided. Connor was still staring at me in the haughty way that Tythian sometimes did. I didn't think he liked nor disliked me. He was programmatic and did as he was instructed.

"Why don't you be my first test dummy and we'll find out together how little control I have," I suggested with a smile that showed fangs.

"Because control has been your strong suit in the past?" he retorted. I could feel my power well from his provocation, just as he intended to prove his point. Chase clasped his hand in mine, cowering it behind his back as he blocked me from Tythian's sight. I realized painfully that my power began festering on his skin. I focused on reeling it back in so no one could see. My hand was shaking as I narrowed my focus on bringing it under control. I just needed time to learn to control it, that was all.

"I've been informed another two covens were attacked," Chase said, with no hint of fear or pain in his tone. Cesar's expression twisted into rage.

"Those who have aligned with us are being targeted. If we needed any longer than a few weeks before we spread out, I fear we'd all be wiped out before we could do any damage. One might've stumbled upon the coven by chance as they migrated toward their meeting place. Wolves partly took out the other. Not all of them were killed, but they did enough damage."

"The wolves?" I asked. Cesar detested my innocent question.

"On the full moon before you left, a group of them raided a coven and took out numbers. They haven't been able to track them back to a human government camp. Coincidence or not, I don't like the timing. Tracey's given us the Council meeting location." Cesar pulled out one map beneath the other sheets and slapped it on top, pointing to a centralized positioning. "Councils have started moving. And so have we."

"You started moving without crossing it by me?" Chase lifted an eyebrow.

"No offense, boy, but it was you who pushed to go with Esmore. You'll learn in the time of war that you have to separate feelings from duty."

"Don't lecture him," I snarled, making sure to maintain the power fluttering about in my insides, begging for me to let it escape in wisps again.

Cesar gave me a deadpan gaze. "I honestly never knew having a daughter would be so fickle," he said, looking at my mother, dismissing me. She said nothing, only offering him a glowering expression because he'd gone off-topic.

"But I had to start readying the others before they left their covens. Some are even risking exposure early just because they feel threatened in the area with the intel their scouts are offering. The Council's narrowing down."

"So, what will be expected of us?" I asked, looking at the colored thumbtacks on his map. I imagined it might've looked more regal within his coven before we had to abruptly leave. As a makeshift, he had flattened maps, and colored thumbtacks to tag positions and I imagined a master plan of which covens would infiltrate from where. I also noticed that four coven positions were surrounded in red thumbtacks, assumedly being our position on the day. Cesar had formerly been discussing after Tracey's information that any coven who seemed to particularly bask in Oppollo's reign would be targeted while their leader was gone. I shifted uncomfortably at the risk. They could be prepared. Tracey could be betraying us. But without her, we wouldn't have had any of this information either.

"*We*," Cesar dotted his chubby index finger in the center of the map, where the Council meeting was going to be held, "will be in the center, where you are, my daughter. As part of the conditions, you're to go in with Tracey. However, it will not be unguarded. Lincon will use his gift to change your appearance, and your mother and I will conceal your huntress scent and the sound of your beating heart. We will be close by, waiting for your signal from the inside as to when we can attack. With

Lincon's help, we can implant a few others in the room with you to ensure you're guarded. When they are most settled in their meeting, that's when we'll strike."

"You would choose to strike them when they're all bunched together?" I asked, confused. Would that not make their strength greater?

"Understand that locking down Oppollo has been a difficult feat for years, and also it'll be out of our control if new Councils are arriving at varying times. Tracey has elicited once we attack from the outside her and her members will fade into the background. She doesn't want to be made responsible for tipping her hat and intel."

Chase scoured over it with his finger under his chin. "Balzar, what do you think?"

"I think it's all a risk and we won't necessarily win. We're depending on the element of surprise which we might not have if Tracey betrays us, which is why the moment if she does, we kill her. It would be my counter plan. If Tracey chooses to betray us then the reason she wants Esmore so close is not for leverage and protection against us to keep to our word of protecting her but to hand her over." An obvious choice. "However, Connor, Lincon, and I will be in the room if that were to happen. Connor and Lincon can stun the members and guards for long enough where I can swoop in to help Esmore if she may need it. And Tythian will teleport us out and bring us to the front lines assuming no one is already hurt."

"Ideally," Tythian took over, not being able to help himself. "If Tracey sticks to her word, Esmore, you'll be able to accomplish the assassination of Oppollo quickly, and the rest of our covens will be forced to ambush amongst the fluster. Even then, I'll still prioritize bringing you to the outside so you don't lose your edge inside. If you're all identified just as quickly then you'll be targeted and by the twelve Council leaders no less. I doubt any of you will make it out."

Balzar looked grim at that outlook. Deemori brushed a knuckle toward Connor who stared at the map military-like. The small touch and flutter seemed to shake him out of his thoughts as he briefed a glance her way. I wondered if death was something Connor actually feared. Or if it was now because he'd found someone to live for.

"Deemori will deploy an avalanche of sabers in there to draw them out. This may take some time though depending on how far back they'll have to stay without being sensed. Thus, Trinity and Cesar's gift of concealment will blanket over us," Yolo said too chirpily.

"This is all depending on it being at night?" Chase questioned. By his lack of surprise, they might've already gone through a contingency plan similar, perhaps with a few adjustments.

"Yes, the night and the ability to bring sabers forth will give us an edge," Connor implied, speaking for the first time.

Chase seemed perplexed as he studied the map, seriously.

What is it? I asked, squeezing his hand.

I want to be inside with you, he glowered over the map. I softened. As much as I wanted that too, he and I both knew it wouldn't work with this plan because he had a coven to lead. He was responsible for leading all those vampires into this war.

You know you can't, I said sadly, wishing the same. But if we stuck to this plan, then I'd be out on the field in no time, depending on how my personal mission goes. We could fight side by side. But depending on Tythian in that measure was equally daunting. He was watching me like a predator does in the darkness of their lair. But even if he did choose to slip up once, I'd make sure to fight my way out. *It's okay, we'll make it out of this together.*

I pressed a lingering kiss to the back of his shoulder. *We* would make it out. All of us.

CHAPTER 31

T HE MOMENT MY foot hovered over the final stair to our wing, Darcy and Jerimiah shifted from their gargoyle form and rushed me. I only had a matter of seconds to flinch out of my stupor state and unsheathe my sword to block theirs.

My heart pounded with a pump of adrenalin, and my vampire sprung to the surface, gleeful for a fight. I pushed my sword against Darcy's with amicable strength, giving me enough time to block Jerimiah's attack. They were twinning their attacks. "What are you doing?" I sneered at him until it dawned on me that they were the guards and protectors of this tower. They were instructed to ensure nothing got in without our approval. With my heart beating in my chest, they probably thought *I* was an intruder.

Fire came out snapping, her nails scratching along the cemented floor. Darcy took a step back, and she feigned to bite Jerimiah's arm, forcing him to retreat. Because of the bond Fire and I shared she knew it was me, the *real* me. But for anyone else, they might've considered I was some shapeshifting intruder.

I raised a hand as the two of them dreaded trying to go through Fire to get to me. "I can explain. It's me." Instead of being offended or infuriated, I was elevated that I trusted them with this task.

"Prove it?" Darcy asked suspiciously, looking from Jerimiah to me.

"I know you can smell Chase on me, and the only variance is now I have a heartbeat. Granted, that's weird and a long story, but what we went out in search of. I can also tell you that, Darcy, you despise it when Chase brings out a bottle of wine." He winced at the thought. "And, Jerimiah, you're absolutely elated when I offer you a piggyback when I fly." His face grimaced even more than when he thought I was an enemy.

In a show of goodwill, I slowly began sheathing my blade, proving that I was no threat. I also felt secure to know that even if they did choose to attack, Fire was still between us, fur hackled on her back with lips peeled back from her yellow canines.

"But ..." Darcy stared at my chest, not in a crude gesture, but as if he was looking through to the beating heart beneath, a common reaction I was beginning to realize. It only made me understand how lacking I had been before. That how I was had been the norm for everyone.

"I know it's a long story, one I'm sure Chase will brief you on. But for now, I've hardly slept for a week, if you don't mind," I said, pointing to their swords. Darcy waited for Jerimiah's hand to drop first and proceeded to do the same. The moment they did, Fire restored herself in a friendly manner. She nudged her head against my hand in greeting.

"If you could all keep it down, the children *were* sleeping," Julia said begrudgingly as she peeked her head out the door. At waist height were two small, dirty faces poking out. Both Titan and Chris were elated to see me though their skeptical gaze over my current upheaval and filth was apparent.

"Um, well, it's good to see your safe return then," Darcy acknowledged as he shifted back toward the door. "Sorry about—"

"Don't apologize. You did the right thing. Thank you to you both."

"But still, attacking our leaders familiar isn't exactly forthcoming," Jerimiah said uncomfortably, perhaps considering the consequence.

"What do you mean? I thought we were simply sparring." I shrugged a shoulder as I walked past. Darcy seemed to take an exaggerated sigh of relief. "Now come along, you two, you should be asleep at this time." I reflected on the strict discipline and few hours' sleep we as children within the Guild had. It was important for them to acquire the correct amount of sleep especially when training so hard. However, I had no idea if their requirement for sleep varied much because of their wolf gene.

"Esmore. you smell so bad!" Titan chuckled to Chris as she grabbed my hand and tugged me in.

"That's a rather bold statement coming from the two of you," I replied though I let her tug me in, conscious of making sure my power was tightly bound within.

"Is he okay?" Julia asked as she took a step back, giving me space to enter or simply evading my impudent filth. Her hard expression and exterior toward me had exhausted itself. "Your people are keeping him away from me," she tried to say diplomatically to not startle the children. I evened an intimidating stare at her. She went still just as I had intended.

"*My people* are doing no such thing," I tried to sound empathetic, but it came out menacing. Her shoulders dropped as that small will of strength left her. She was not only angry with me but herself as well. We'd both wanted this. Neither of us knew how Tori and Dillian would change, and Dillian's avoidance of her had much to do with his new cold demeanor and personal reasoning.

"Please help me have at least five minutes with him," she whispered, her gaze dropping to Titan and Chris who watched on. Fire nudged them toward the bed. "I feel like I'm going mad in here and I don't know what to do."

I'd make certain to talk to my mother and Dillian. We had to figure something out. We couldn't leave her here no more than we could bring her to the front lines with us in three weeks. "I'll do my best," was all that I could offer.

She hesitated, not at all satisfied with my response. But what did she expect from me? Last time I promised to keep them alive and find them safety, I'd failed. I wasn't in the business of making promises anymore. Fire shifted behind me, her naked form might've once startled the children, but I imagined every time they practiced shifting they'd become accustomed to nudity themselves.

Julia grimaced as Fire changed as if it infringed on our private conversation. "Run along to bed, pups," she instructed them. Titan tugged at my hand, childishly rebelling against the order. A lowly growl came from Fire's core that reminded me she was more wolf than woman. Chris tugged at Titan, thinking better of the consequence. At least he was reasonable and fore thinking.

"Come on," Julia encouraged in a more motherly, nurturing way. I had to hide my smile from Titan and her rebellious young ways. I could imagine the attitude she would've had after being so spoilt by Sydney.

I pulled my heavy and filthy robe off, feeling the weight of the mission fall off me alongside it. My hair was sticky and filthy from all sorts of substances. I didn't even bother hanging the robe and mask knowing they'd need to be washed first. I dropped them to the floor instead, too lazy to find the strength to wash them now.

"So, it was a success then?" Fire asked me as she carefully watched me sit on the wooden chair closest to the door. I contemplated her definition of success. We'd obtained our objective, but I wasn't certain it didn't have negative consequences.

"It was. But I need to train privately," I said hollowly, feeling the fatigue of the past weeks' mission mask over me. As an example, I willed my power to skitter toward the edge of the thick stick the children must've been using for practice. I focused on my gift only drifting from my fingertips and toward the wood. I honed it in, the fermenting aura curling from my fingertips adequately eating away at the top of it.

Fire's gaze shifted uncomfortably from the wood that was now half-eaten and my tired expression. My vampire complimented the gift, selfishly calling it back in. Power to power. Like to like. Willing it to be my tool instead of a combustible boom. The little control I had of it now would sharpen like any other blade I'd held. I just needed to practice with it and embrace it whole.

"It tires you?" Fire enquired.

"The entire mission tired me. But a few hours rest will restore what energy was lost." Even though I felt like I could sleep for days.

"Well, I would hope some exertion went for your efforts considering that smooth piece of wood took me many minutes to find. And now it's in shambles." She popped her hand on her hip. A small smile spread on my lips as I closed my eyes. In here, I felt as safe as I possibly could. With Fire, Darcy, and Jerimiah in the vicinity, I'd know if anyone dared to creep up while I slept.

"I'll find you an even bigger one tomorrow," I teased before my eyelids fell heavy and I drifted to sleep before the children had even settled in their bed.

Large shards of ice scaled as if I was back within Tracey's Council. The floor rattled beneath me as they escalated so smoothly that numerous reflections of myself mirrored my every step. I huffed in irritation looking down at my usual battle attire that was now a long flowing blue dress. The audible beat of my heart echoing unrealistically loud.

Between slits in the ice, I could feel a presence shift around me like a mist. I threw my hands up now agitated. I wanted rest, not hours full of a torturous dream by someone who wasn't willing to reveal themselves. "Are you actually going to announce yourself?" I asked no longer sucking into the saturation of their crafted world. If Chase hadn't confirmed he felt another presence when I slept as well then I might've thought it was simply my slowly unraveling sanity. My subconscious trying to filter through all my failures and tragedy.

My unnatural and eerie beauty reflected as if I'd grown up sheltered and in a land unbeknownst to ours. It was unnerving, a new kind of torture considering the games my shadowy friend had conjured in my dreams before.

I could hear a clock ticking in the background, adjacent and offbeat to the pump of my heart. As if the message was between a countdown and my newly acquired gift. Perhaps like a ticking time bomb. I could no sooner pull myself out of this dream unless Chase was to retrieve me.

I winced at the pain and intrusion of another who'd probably been waiting for me to rest without Chase for some time now. I fought against him, but like the last time, he raked his nails in, splitting my mind open so he could wander into the dream. The instigating presence to this dream fluttered into the unknown, now onlooking.

"Hello, my little golden bird," Fier purred in the way of introduction. I trailed his voice, and the click of his shoes clattered as he circled my mirrored cage. I could only see slithers of him sporadically. He flashed those white teeth in a charismatic and unfriendly smile. I willed to hide the sound of my beating heart but had no control in this place. "How interesting …"

He came to a stop so he could slither a glance through a crack in the mirror. I tried not to be distracted by the glowing reflection of myself. I purposefully looked into the darkness beyond, pushing away the compression of feeling like I was trapped in a cage. A reflection as to how I thought others viewed me—locked into their plans so they could exploit my power. But the chains bound me to this path in the way that I had to ensure Chase's sanity and life before my own. And unfortunately, one of those shackles led me straight back to Fier.

"How beautiful you are today," he sneered. "Only three weeks until the Vampire Council meeting and I haven't yet heard of Oppollo's fall. Come now, Esmore, please tell me your familiar's sanity is still enough incentive?"

I lashed out at the mirror, trying to kick it over. Instead, my boot hit hard ice, and a shake of pain vibrated through my leg. Fier chuckled at my embarrassing display. I looked above to see if I might be able to climb out, but the height of the ice was never-ending.

I had no choice but to reply, knowing that he could do the final damage and turn Chase into a saber with the click of his fingers.

"We're working on it," I gritted out, seething every moment I was forced to stay within his presence.

"Well, let's hope you have some traction by the time the Council meeting has set any new laws in stone. If I'm to be disappointed, I will turn him, and then my Council will personally hunt you, and the riff-raff remains of your kind. I will take pleasure in hunting you," he threatened. Before I could reply he vanished, inexplicably escaping in the same way that he entered.

The dream didn't fall away, instead I was forced to stare at my reflection and all the ugly angles, listening to the ticking time acutely understanding that the pressure was real. And I had three weeks to be rid of Oppollo or else Fier would stay true to his threat, unless I could figure out a way to ensure Chase's safety even if I were to fail or die trying.

CHAPTER 32

"Again!" Balzar instructed. His hands were limply dangling over the smooth thick stick he'd collected from the woods. He had it over his shoulders so he could stretch his back muscles, enjoying taking this authoritative position.

I'd become tired of training with him already, and it was only the second day. I focused on the log piece only a few feet away and conjured my power to bend to my will. I'd come to depend on my vampire-half to help me control it, my fangs nicking at my bottom lip a few times from the amount of focus I'd inevitably strained.

My power crept out in wisps, initially wanting to flare out naturally of its own accord, but I channeled it like a blade, instructing it to dance along the path to the log and avoid touching anything else. I'd already deadened the grass about us on the first day as my power ate away our surroundings when I'd lost control. That's why Connor was here too. I looked out my peripheral at him. In case I lost control, and he had to compromise me.

"Focus!" Balzar chastised as my power skittered away to see if anything living was on the ground once I'd loosened my focus momentarily. It rose to the occasion and festered on the wood, eating at it in mere seconds. It ashed into nothing, the remains of it floating in the wind. "Good."

I called my power, fishing it back harshly like a hook being dragged and reluctantly returning to its master. Its cool euphoric sensation rained through me as I absorbed it again.

"Next one," Balzar said, flipping a boulder in his hand as if it weighed nothing. I sighed, my muscles surprisingly sore. I ached yesterday for hours, just as mentally tired from the exertion. That night Chase stayed with me, so any unwelcome guests or dreams didn't bombard me.

Cesar had instructed Balzar to train me personally and I'd naturally objected. Chase couldn't attend because he had to prepare and train with his coven, and I'd been surprised that Cesar left Balzar out of the mainstream training and preparations for his own. But he'd insisted which offered us a reluctant form of bonding. We still hadn't spoken about the werewolves that night, and Yolo had been ushering me to 'keep the peace' and 'it wasn't his fault.'

Connor stood silently against a tree. He'd only had to intervene once yesterday when my gift continued to crawl out of my control. The moment Connor's talon-like gift scraped along my mind I'd dropped to the ground, and my gift suctioned back in. I hadn't made the same mistake twice.

"I throw, and you eat at it before it hits the ground," Balzar instructed. I was becoming impatient with how slow it was taking me to hone my craft. Patience might've been a virtue for some, but time wasn't a leisure I had. As my key motivator, I readied myself with a new gusto to control this gift. I nodded and raised my hands letting my gift skim the edges of my skin. It wasn't like my enemies would be positioned in one spot like the log. I had to be fast and striking.

I could sense my mother walking toward us, but I let it do nothing to deter my focus. My vampire readied itself prepared to push my gift for a striking blow. Balzar threw the boulder—high. He was giving me time. I focused on its movement and struck out my power. Instead of its usual slow crawling speed, it pattered about before, it struck hard, and the boulder mystified into ash with a great implosion. The ash skittered to the wind.

Excited by the thrill, it wanted to keep going, my vampire encouraging it to strike again at anything. I called it back, dragging it through the wind as if every inch held an enormous weight.

"Trinity," Balzar acknowledged. He evidently wasn't appreciative of the intrusion. Connor remained silent but attentive to the conversation unfolding. I wondered if they both thought their time could be better managed elsewhere. Even I agreed with that. However, Connor's being here felt like a safeguard until I acquired complete control.

"How's the training going?" my mother inquired. Balzar looked pointedly for me to answer. It'd been slow to say the least.

"Slower than I'd like, but we're making progress. It is … more challenging than I thought it might be to control my gift," I admitted begrudgingly, looking toward my mother for advice. Every hunter was different, they all had to adapt and learn their own skills. Sometimes they were assisted by fellow hunters, and there were guides on more common gifts. Mine, however, was uniquely fickle.

"Mine took years to master." It wasn't the encouragement I was hoping for. "But I do have word from the hunters."

Ah, I directed her to a more private location where the others couldn't overhear. No other vampires were permitted in this area to hunt for the next week, my training prioritized but expressively unstable. Anyone could be caught in the crossfire. After our return, my mother suggested reaching out to Louise to ask if she knew of any rebel hunter groups who might consider taking in Julia. We'd then argued when I asked why it couldn't have been arranged sooner. But as I'd watched it transpire, this mutual understanding between Louise and her group was only in recent events.

I hadn't yet told Dillian, unsure whether it would put him at ease or infuriate him. If only we could've actioned this sooner, then maybe Dillian and Tori could've gone too, even Teary. But I also didn't want to offer him false hope in case such a treaty wasn't possible. I hadn't even heard of rebel hunters until recently. And lastly, I wasn't sure if Dillian would be willing to give Julia up. Though he avoided her, we hadn't spoken about the situation since we returned from our mission.

While Tori found purpose and trained with Fire and the pups, Dillian swept through the rooms like a phantom. Sometimes he was with Lincon and the twins; other times within the institute, daring others to cross paths with him even though he'd been imprinted with safety from both coven leaders. His attention was always on our tower, where Julia was safely kept inside.

Once my mother and I were far enough away from the others, she offered a grim expression. My heart stopped. "Louise can make the arrangements, but it'll have to be in four nights. That's when their messengers next cross information on their monthly exchanges. If we leave it to the next one, it'll be too late."

I agreed, we had to get her out *now*. But I shuffled uncomfortably by the thought. Would she be safe? Well, I supposed she would be safer than here. It only saddened me that the hunters were adamantly against the werewolves as a species as well. If they hadn't been, I would've considered Titan and Chris. I still boggled over what to do with them, especially as the weeks began to dwindle down to nothing. I needed Fire by my side but couldn't trust anyone else with their safety.

"What will Dillian say about this?" my mother asked. I crossed my arms over my chest, tense from the amount of training but also the conversation to be had.

"I don't know, I haven't spoken to him much," I admitted, and my mother offered me a sharp pout. "What?" I said defensively.

"Esmore, he's your best friend." I considered how inapplicable that term might be as of now. He despised me. No more than I did myself for what I'd done. "You need to talk to him about it."

"Maybe it'll sound better coming from you," I suggested. She scowled at me.

"Fine. But I don't know if this was the solution he was after. And I don't know if she'll truly be safe with them," I admitted. After the anticipated ambush from Campture's Guild, they'd evidently been tipped off. But Louise vowed that wasn't her groups' doing and my mother believed her. It was yet again another disturbing matter that information was leaking out from our institute.

"Right now, nowhere is safe for anyone, Esmore. That's the reality of this time and age. I'll speak with Julia and see how she feels about it, though I doubt she'll want to leave Dillian's side."

"I don't think he wants her here," I admitted harshly from our previous conversation.

"I know, but that's a discussion for them to have," she said with little empathy. "And then we have to figure out what to do with the pups."

I considered my mother for a moment. She was putting so much out on the line to help me, and the scarcity of seeing her vulnerable on my last mission moved me. I awkwardly stepped toward her, and she watched me just as warily as if my new gift were about to implode on her.

I wrapped my arms around her in an awkward embrace. At first, she went rigid. I wasn't at all surprised, but eventually she softened and patted a hand on my back, awkwardly embracing me the same. "Thank you for everything you've done for me. I couldn't have had a better mother for a huntress to guide me on my path."

"Hmmm," she considered soundly. "I know maternal isn't something we do easily amongst our kind, however everything I've done has been to ensure your survival."

"I know," I was able to finally admit. I'd followed in her steps in hoping to protect everyone, but having her, Chase, and Fire truly have my back no matter what warfare stood ahead of us, reminded me of why I risked it all in the first place. Of why I'd done the same thing for my team and sacrificed myself too often to fight for them. It was indulgent to know that others did the same for me. That I added value to them in such a light. I cleared an odd lump that formed in my throat and stepped back, suddenly finding interest in a piece of ash that was on my leather shirt. I brushed it off.

"I'll speak with Julia and make the arrangements. Make sure you speak with Dillian. He doesn't have long to come to peace with what's about to happen." My mother tapped me lightly on the shoulder before heading back toward the institute. I admired the sheathed sword on her back as she farewelled the brothers and left.

Dillian could opt to break them out and run away together, but he was too practical for that, and he wouldn't have been avoiding her leading up until this point if he'd intended to do so. I despised being the messenger to tell him that he had to finally let go if that was what he chose to do. But I couldn't see any other way.

"Esmore! No one suggested a break. What year do you think you're living in?!" Balzar's voice boomed amongst the treetops. Another boulder flew toward me. He must've shot put it from where he'd been standing. I raised my hand, demanding the quick reflex of my gift like a whip. It shot out, bursting the boulder to ash and springing back into my body just as quickly offering me a buzzing jolt.

"Huh," I said considerately, flexing my fingers back and forth. As much as focus was required, perhaps treating it more like an invisible whip might offer a more lasting result. It gave me a spark of hope for the first time since coming head-to-head with Oppollo. But I hadn't yet used it on living things and more specifically on the undead.

CHAPTER 33

BALZAR, CONNOR, AND I trained into the early evening with the additive of weapons. Balzar and I were equally matched, warily dancing around one another in case the fight became too heated and reminiscent of when I'd threatened his life. Connor observed on the sidelines, waiting sporadically for moments until he would throw an object into the air. I was forced to simultaneously fend off Balzar and destroy the item before it hit the ground.

Balzar and I danced, striking at one another with deadly blows. Neither of us held back. "Stop," Connor said in his low voice as his attention gravitated toward the woodland. We did so, listening out for the same thing that he was trying to hone in on. A small breeze swept up the fog at our feet. "Somethings passing through."

The creature avoided our senses, restricting itself close to the border so we couldn't articulate what or who it was, but it was coming from the direction of the institute.

Is everything okay? I asked Chase. I could sense that he was in a fluster.

Two werewolves attacked a group of four on the edge of our territory. Only two made it back alive. Maybe you three should return for the night until the borders are secure once again. I could hear the stress in Chase's voice. It was taxing for him, and I felt guilty for not being able to fully sympathize with the vampires who'd been attacked.

"Werewolf," I informed the others as another growing presence impended on us. Two sets of feet galloped toward us. I could sense Fire chasing the second wolf that'd broken past our security. But how? They should've been deterred from Cesar's gift of concealment. Or maybe their sense of smell surpassed anything we'd encountered before.

An enormous black wolf rampaged through the trees snarling with fangs bared. Fire trailed him closely, snapping at his ankle as she chased him out of our territory. I swiveled my sword around my fingers. I didn't want to kill the majestic creature, but if it were to turn on Fire I wouldn't hesitate.

The wolf leaped for Connor who looked down at it filthily with as much hatred as he held for the humans. The wolf dropped, screeching in pain and glided along the dirt after losing his footing across the gravel. The intensity of Connor's gift and harsh punishment didn't offer the creature much time to escape. It whined and gasped its last shuddering breath before bleeding out from its eyes and ears. Its thrashing legs came to a stop.

Connor's gaze locked onto Fire with the same amount of disdain. I flicked my power out to the nearby tree beside him, blasting it into pieces. It was a warning shot and a few scathing pieces of skin peeled off his nose. His blue eyes redirected to me in challenge. I barred my fangs in the same light, reeling back my gift so it didn't lose control and eat away everything it could taint.

Fire skidded into the center of our opening, sniffing in the direction the other werewolf had gone. The sound of crunching bone and muscle tearing manifested Fire into her human form as she shifted. "I can smell her on these wolves," she blurted out, nonchalant about her back turned to Connor and Balzar who seemed mystified by her shift. She didn't often shift in front of others, much preferring her wolf skin. "The scientist I told you about, the one who created us. These wolves smell of her."

I gaped. "So the other wolf might be tracing back to their maker," I considered. "Take us to her."

"Esmore, we can't pursue without Cesar's approval," Balzar warned.

I sheathed my sword. I didn't have my Barnett crossbow with me but still had a few of my daggers strapped to the garter I always wore. Fire shifted back into her wolf form taking off, the dirt flicking up behind her and on the black wolf who still bled, wide-eyed. I shunned him, disgusted in the way he'd been tortured. These creatures were bound to fight someone else's fight, just as I had been. A sacrifice and a pawn all in the same.

"Stay behind and be a good boy," I goaded Balzar, and besides, I didn't necessarily want him there anyway. The last order Cesar had given him regarding werewolves was to slay them. I wasn't sure what I'd yet do, but if I could put a stop to the woman who was creating them, maybe I'd spare some of her future victims a torturous upbringing.

"Shit," he hissed as I took speed, chasing Fire as she tracked the remaining wolf. I could sense Balzar and Connor following me. A familiar group caught me off guard, especially so far out from the institute. Kora and Kasey were resting while Lincon feasted on a human. I had no idea where he might've found one, but he seemed equally surprised to see me as I dashed past them. From my peripheral, I could see him drop the wrist he'd been slurping from and curiously spring into action.

It took him no time to catch up to me. "Is something exciting happening?" he asked. Kora and Kasey were somewhat delayed, falling back even further than the brothers. I ignored him, focusing on Fire's trail. Lincon cackled to himself excited as we bound past our protected territory. As we passed, I noticed two of our spotters on the border had already been taken out, the remains of black mush where they must've once stood. That's why we weren't alerted sooner about our intruders.

A gunshot blasted in the distance as we raced between passing trees. The humans must've been hunting the escapee werewolves, exactly the same way I'd first come across Fire. She, too, had stumbled into our territory, and the human hunters followed her group from there. These two wolves were no different. But that meant one thing. The location of the science lab and Human Compound wasn't far from us.

Fire zigzagged through the woodlands, no longer giving chase to the wolf but having found a new path. She must've caught wind of where they'd come from. The wolf wasn't trying to return, it was trying to redirect and find a way to escape their radar completely. The wolf pivoted right as a group of eight humans came into view, chasing it down. Fire pivoted left, articulating our path to avoid the distraction. She swept us closer into the shadows and condensed trees.

But it didn't stop the back end of the group noticing us. One of the humans came into range and began panic shooting in our direction because he couldn't keep up with how fast we moved. He was so scared and had no idea what he was even opposing, he was simply shooting in the hope to fire at whatever his instincts were alarming him about. I couldn't care for dealing with such a lowly being. Lincon, however, circled back preying on the humans with wild laughter that reminded me much of the serial version I'd seen of him in the caves on our last mission.

Gunfire shot, and a howl echoed through the adjacent woodlands. I wasn't sure if that was the mourning for its friend who'd died in the escape or if they too had been shot and taken down by the humans already. Lincon flanked my back, splattered with red blood. He licked over his forearm with a wild buzz in his expression. Great, that's exactly what I needed, a jacked-up Lincon. But as I looked down my left side with Balzar and Connor following, I considered Lincon wasn't a bad counter to have in case the brothers became trigger happy with killing the wolves once again. I had no intentions of killing them. The scientist, however, I wanted answers from.

I growled, my fangs sliding through my gums. She would pay and answer for what she had done to these people. For what she'd done to Titan and Fire who were innocent bystanders in this war.

We covered a lot of ground tracking the scent, no wonder we hadn't come across it sooner, even when we had sent out scouts. In the stark distance of night, I narrowed my gaze on the wild flames in the distance. Woodland had been chopped down over the years leaving burned and dead stumps miles out from the complex. We maneuvered around the stumps ensuring not to trip.

Humans guarded the outside with guns, watching the flames eagerly rise and envelop the right side of the compound. A wolf scaled the wall from the inside, the moment it stood atop to jump four humans shot it down. My stomach curled. These *humans* who were so willing to experiment on their own kind to create monsters and then simply destroy them once they were done with the result. A strong presence oozed from inside the compound, and I couldn't decipher whether it was the number of werewolves that were trapped inside or something else.

"Oh no," I heard Lincon gape and slacken his pace. I'd never seen him back down *ever*. It was the same reaction he'd had when we were in New York, and I felt the same presence that tormented me in my dreams. But this felt different like it was someone else completely.

"Fall back!" I shouted at Fire, not wanting her so far ahead while the humans were taking aim at the wolves. She did so immediately, falling back behind me and letting me lead the point of our makeshift group. As we advanced on the compound, I was worried the powerful presence inside would slip away. "Kora and Kasey, circle and block off the back!" No matter how powerful this person, their gift should be enough to hold it up so I could question them. Before I could shout out any more orders, Connor pounded past me with a stride and speed I hadn't seen him adopt before.

"Shit, shit, shit," Balzar raced after him. Before I could even ask Lincon to be rid of the humans who guarded the wall, Connor crashed through them one by one, the only thing shining in the moonlight was his crazed blue eyes. Balzar chased after him, guarding his back with the few stray humans who might've made a lucky shot. I'd heard of Connor's hatred for the humans. I'd adhered to the warning of how he hated them so. But I'd never witnessed the quiet and controlled Connor turn into a savage. He didn't even raise a weapon, killing them horrifically one by one as he ripped them from limb to limb.

I shuddered away at the gruesome lack of tack. I'd been there, I'd done deplorable things. I was aware of his trauma from the time his family had been slaughtered. But I hadn't realized how powerful of a hold it grasped onto him even hundreds of years later.

The path was cleared for us as the two brothers paved their way through the human guards on the outskirts of the compound. Fires rounded everywhere as we dodged stray bullets. Kora and Kasey rounded the back end as Fire and I approached the wall. I focused my gift on the wall striking at it to create a hole.

My gift struck out at it, festering away the cement with an imploding boom. Another set of alarms rang out as ash spread toward us. My power loosened past my control, continuing to eat away at the wall far larger than I intended. I gritted my teeth, a pin drop of blood bubbling on my lip from biting down too hard, as I concentrated on calling it back. *A minor slip,* I argued with myself. I could sense Chase trying to reach out to me, but I blocked him out. I couldn't focus on so many things at once, not when I was only learning how to grasp this power. If I let my focus slip momentarily, this gift would flutter and escape me taking on a life of its own.

Despite his initial reluctance, Lincon followed me into the dark tunnel I'd created. Inside the walls had obviously been a corridor of some kind, but we passed it, breaking out into the open space of the compound. The right side of the establishment was up in flames still, quickly chewing away at the escalated towers where human soldiers continued to flood out from, panicked.

In the section we'd bounded in was what looked like fifty plus kennels, where wolves and humans alike scraped to desperately get out as the flames grew more vicious at the buildings behind them. The facility reeked of feces and decaying flesh. The humans were trying to escape the fire and leave behind the werewolves. The wolves began crying, howling desperately to escape. An explosion in the right-wing rattled the ground, and green smoke sifted into the air.

"You wouldn't believe how much work I had in there," a woman's voice rang out dryly. I hadn't even noticed her. I swept a dagger out of my garter, pegging it toward the edgy voice. I aimed for the predator lurking atop the adjacent wall. She caught the dagger that was aimed at her face, with two delicate fingers and shifted it back and forth with consideration. She was a still and silent vampire. I'd felt her ambiguous presence outside, but the moment I'd come in it was as if she'd vanished. I'd never seen anything like her. Another monster. Her blonde hair billowed against the wind, the only thing living in the vacancy of her eyes. Darkness had swallowed her eyes completely where no pupil could be seen, and a marring scar went down her neck. She wore a white lab coat that was smeared with putrid blood and substances my sensitive nose couldn't decipher. "I thought I told you I never wanted to see your face again, Lincon." She considered the dagger again as if to throw it at him, and was now ignoring me.

Lincon shifted uncomfortably and plastered a coy smile. He waved delicately as if being scolded. "Hello, Mother." *Mother?* "I, ahh, didn't know you'd be here. She brought me here!" He threw an accusing finger my way. But then he began to cackle madly, rubbing his face as if he found this hysterically hilarious. "I wish I could say I missed you, but I still seethe your hideous bitch ways."

"Hmph. I've always hated that maddening gleam you took on from your father. Is he dead yet?" she asked curiously, letting the dagger clutter to the floor. It was unnerving the way her dead eyes looked at him, with no pupils or iris.

"No, he's still somewhere in the bottom of the ocean where you left him," Lincon casually replied with a childish shrug.

"And yet he still manages to haunt me in my sleep even in the few hours I do find to rest," she growled, and this time I saw the size of her fangs. How *old* was she?

"What is happening here?" I asked Lincon, still disconcerted by her being his 'mother.' In whatever way that looked to Lincon.

"Ah, my apologies," he said gentleman-like, but didn't remove his gaze from her. Lincon was wary around her. "This is my mother, Sasha, one of the first-ever created hunters, pre-crafted before your time—you know how it is. Vampires coming to earth, etcetera," he casually rolled out. This was the first I'd heard of anything so elaborate. This time I did side gaze him, and the slip was enough for her to find an edge. Before she could leave her spot, Lincon charmed a wicked smile at her, his gift in use. She shook her head back and forth, easily slipping off his illusion.

She smiled at him, a gut curling vicious smile. And Lincon laughed in response as if they were old friends catching up over a long-reminisced story. His gift worked for only a few seconds on her which possibly meant all mental gifts were ineffective. He was useless opposing her.

The humans who piled out from the buildings noticed us and began to take aim and shoot in their frightful panic. "Lincon, go have some fun," I purred, abhorred at their will to still fight and especially raise a gun at us. "And free the wolves."

Lincon seemed to squirm under his mother's stare. I'd never seen him act like this. And if he had reservations about this confrontation, I wanted him gone. It was better to fight alongside the Lincon I knew than the one who was shifty now. He seemed hesitant until his crazed mind clicked into place, I could see the glaze slide over his eyes as he thought about all the fun he could have.

"Can I kill her?" I asked him as I raked a few fingertips through Fire's fur, trying to comfort and ease her. I was worried she'd act of her own accord, too driven by revenge.

"Have at it, though I've tried to kill her myself hundreds of times. And, Esmore, don't die. I do enjoy our time together." He smiled before taking a step back and then another as if testing if his mother would actually let him go. She only watched with those hollowed black eyes.

"How interesting," she said, crossing her legs as she sat in an absolutely dominant display that she had all the time in the world to chat despite the chaos erupting around us. "A creature of hunter and vampire created organically? My my, sometimes Mother Nature does come up with some interesting things without the will of science behind it. How I would love to take samples."

"You'll have to come and get them," I antagonized, skirting my newfound gift on the edges of my skin. She might be able to resist mental attacks, but flesh-eating was a different kind of special.

"Ah, the arrogance of a hunter," she purred, not at all finding humor in my tone. "They just don't make them like they used to." She gracefully popped up onto her feet. I now noticed the briefcase beside her.

"Why are you helping the humans create the werewolves?" I demanded of her. If I could source it back, maybe I'd find a cure for them.

"Werewolves, you named them?" she enquired, mouthing the word werewolves one more time. Her face crinkled in distaste. "How soft the hunters of this day have become. They are nothing more than experiments. That is all, nothing deserving of a title." Fire growled, and Sasha's face dropped slightly as if noticing her for the first time. Had she had pupils, I imagined she might've focused them on her. "Or is it perhaps because you've become attached to one?" She sniffed the air, her tongue rolling around behind her mighty fangs. "And it would appear there's a mix of vampire venom to keep it interlinked with you. How fascinating."

I was daunted by the sudden intrigue as if she was gripping me with her unforeseeable gaze. I didn't allow her intimidating power that rolled from her in waves, suppress my demand for answers, even if I'd have to fight for them, which instinctually I felt was a bad idea. "I'll repeat my question one more time. Why are you helping the humans?" I asked, and this time I pointed the tip of my sword toward her, more so as a distraction. It wasn't my blade that would strike her. Gaging by her age, her strength and speed would be far superior to mine, so I'd have to rely heavily on my gifts.

"You do know I come from the original hunter bloodline, don't you, dear child? And I have lived for hundreds of years that surpass your measly few. You would be wise not to threaten me," she warned, and I felt perplexed as she effortlessly intimidated me. My vampire relished in the idea of challenging her to test my strength whereas my instinctual tolerance told me to run away from this place and get as far away from her as possible. She didn't feel a part of this world.

Unwisely I relished in the recklessness of my vampire. "And why do you think I care?"

"Stop, Connor, Stop! It's done!" I could hear Balzar outside the wall trying to contain Connor from his frenzy. The gunfire had ceased as Lincon played about with trying to find a way to release the wolves from behind some electric gate.

"Because I thought you should have sufficient knowledge before you dare raise your sword at me twice. You are no match for me. As for the humans, I couldn't care less about working with them. I have no great opinion of their species. I simply care about my work. As you can see, the humans can't contain a simple handful of my experiments. A few get out and boom, perhaps if the pup beside you were wiser, she might've done the same instead of running with tail between her legs and leaving her kind behind."

Everything happened so quickly. Fire snapped as I'd worried she would, and Sasha's speed outmatched hers phenomenally. She was standing in front of Fire from one heartbeat to the next. I lashed my gift out at her with anticipation as to where I thought she might be. My eyes could barely keep up with her movement. I connected before she was able to fatally strike Fire, but she was still thrown back and smashed into one of the cages where another wolf howled. The trail of wolves howling hauntingly followed.

Sasha stared down at her arm that was no longer there, ash flickered away amongst the orange flames coming from the burning building. This compound only had a few more minutes before it was entirely damned. I enforced a push of urgency into Lincon. What was taking him so long?

"Now that is delightfully fresh," she said, unperplexed by the missing limb.

"How do I find a cure?!" I demanded. I could feel Chase tugging on our link. He was tracking our trail. I had to hurry for my answers because I didn't want him anywhere near this woman.

"Dear child, there is no reversal for a creature harvested from science, especially a plague that will take over this world of its own free will. And even if one could be made, *I* will never make it." She flipped back on top of the wall, defying rational gravity, and picked up the suitcase with her only hand. I could sense Kora and Kasey behind her, hovering at the base of the wall as I'd instructed. Now I doubted even their gifts would hold her back. I slammed an urgency into them to run. I could sense Connor and Balzar nearing the hole I'd blasted in the wall. "Not all of us are cut out to live as monsters." She gave a pointed look to the twins who ran into the distance. She'd known they were there the whole time. "Some become the demon and others peril, either of their own accord or because they're hunted for it. So why do you, beautiful little creature, care so much to save them when they're already damned?"

The final gates unlocked, and the wolves broke free, the fire on their tails as they skirted out, avoiding the direction Sasha stood in. Fire growled and snapped at those who came toward me, ensuring none tried to attack. I felt the familiar presence of the one who tormented me in my dreams. She growled as if sensing the exact same thing.

"How did he find me?" she bitterly grumbled. "Send my regards to Lincon and warn him if I see him again, I'll pin him to my wall and experiment on him as if he were a newborn vamp all over again." With that, she flipped over the edge. I ran after her, but a chaotic explosion blew apart the wall where she'd been standing. I was thrown back, calling for the Descendant and grabbing Fire as I flew into the sky and away from the remains of the blast. I had no doubt she'd somehow managed the explosion.

My skin melted and festered with burns, quickly healing as I hovered in the air holding Fire. She'd only been licked with flames on her side, within a day she would heal. I searched for her over the mass of stumped and burnt-out forest. She was nowhere to be seen.

Wolves piled out of the establishment, not all of them having made it. I could sense Chase on the edge of the forest. A blanket of sabers pooled out from the trees, immediately hastening towards the wolves as Deemori came into sight, running toward Connor.

Why did you block me out? Chase demanded as he came into sight and spotted me hovering in the air. I swooped down in front of him, dropping Fire as I landed swiftly. I mind dumped everything that had happened. His face shifted in horror and relief that I was okay. *Please stop leaving by yourself. I might have this thing Fier planted in me, but I'm not an encumbrance. I can help you.*

I know, I said, reaching out to press my hand against his chest. Although his mental security was all I thought about now it wasn't the only reason I'd run off headfirst. *But remember this is who I am—this has always been who I was.*

His shoulders slumped slightly. He'd once called me his willful wife. And that had never, nor could it ever change. I was a huntress who was steadfast on action. Somewhat depleted and irritated he said, *In a time that you are being hunted, please depend on me more.*

"No mark, you're okay," Deemori addressed Connor in her thick accent, assessing him. Her sabers chased off and clashed with the remaining wolves. I gave her an effective look, not at all pleased. There was no point in killing the wolves, they weren't mindless beasts like her sabers. And surprisingly, she called them back, sanctioning them around our group for protection of the wolves, were they to try and attack us— none of who did as they scurried away to escape.

Balzar seemed broody and blood coated. "Okay? We don't have one human captive because you lost control," he scolded Connor. "Cesar's going to have our heads."

Chase looked back toward Lincon. "You!" he snarled.

"Ah ah aaaahhh." Lincon raised his finger, shaking it back and forth as Chase dropped to his knees in a clouded illusion.

"Free him at once!" I snarled, flaring my wings in a show of power. Lincon beamed with a smile as if daydreaming what might happen if I were to punish him. Lincon's attention suddenly dawdled off into the trees, and he sagged depleted, releasing him. No longer thinking rationally, Chase lunged for him again, but I hooked my hand onto the back of his jacket pulling him back. It infuriated Chase that for all his strength, he couldn't strike Lincon. Something he'd wanted to do for a very long time.

"Nothing like a family reunion," Lincon said, kicking up dirt. And I realized he was talking about that familiar presence that crept toward us in New York. "I should've known." But as quickly as he said it the presence vanished.

I pointed at Lincon accusingly. He knew far more than he'd been leading on this whole time. "*You* have some explaining to do."

CHAPTER 34

I SLAMMED LINCON down hard into a chair, he cackled at the manhandling, and I scoffed, disgusted by his arousal. Kora couldn't have seeped further into the painted walls even if she'd tried. Kasey was pivoting herself into a position where she might be able to intervene if she had to. I shot her an intimidating glare to pin her in her spot. I didn't have time for games today. We were in the shared room where we'd once dined together, having kicked the remains of Cesar's coven out, although most of them were already outside training.

Cesar paced back and forth the room brooding with the brothers positioned throughout. Connor stared at the floor as if reliving his horror and shame of having lost control. Balzar was wary to put as much distance between him and Cesar as possible. Yolo was sitting down on a chair, his arms loosely hanging over the back of it, casually. And Tythian looked down his nose at Lincon from the back of the room.

My mother was closest to the door watching Cesar slowly lose his temper. "I knew the moment you scampered in here you'd bring us nothing but issues!"

Lincon scoffed at him, affronted. "Um, Pot. Kettle. Have you seen your current situation that you've created all on your own? Don't be pissy with me just because my parents came to town." Was I the only one missing out on the bigger picture here?

"Tell me why your *mother* is the one behind the virus and werewolves," I demanded, ignoring Cesar. His temper wouldn't hasten the interrogation.

"I didn't know my mother was behind it. But now it kind of makes sense," he articulated thoughtfully. "I didn't know. I haven't seen my mother for sheesh, a couple of hundred years easily."

"And your father?" Cesar growled.

"Still at the bottom of the sea," Lincon said in a sing-song way.

"What am I missing here? It seems like there's more to this than simply the creation of an entirely new species." I barked back tediously as Cesar and Lincon shot daggers at one another.

"Do you believe in folklore, Esmore?" Lincon asked me open-mindedly.

"It was never proven," Cesar grated, crossing his arms.

"Thus the word 'folklore,'" Lincon taunted him. My mother stepped forward to cross the room and stand beside Cesar, ensuring he didn't attack Lincon. Balzar licked his lips, uncomfortable with the tension in the room. He seemed uncertain if Cesar couldn't take his anger out on Lincon now, he'd take it out on him instead.

"You see, little huntress, as the stories were passed down to me by my makers, my parents—I'll tell you the same. Though it's highly irrelevant to our mission now. But I'll always entertain when the room demands it." He fluttered his hand about aloofly and crossed his leg over casually. "It is said that vampires didn't originate in this world. My father and maker, Kyran Klaus, was a prince from a different place consisting of vampires who warred with one another for the sparse land they had and the humans who protected them. Let's just say my father, Kyran, was somewhat known to be a Mad Hatter Prince. His brother reigned over the kingdom, trying to keep the peace until Kyran started another war with Oppollo all because his brother paid attention to Kyran's new plaything.

That plaything was none other than my mother, Sasha Pierce. She was one of the humans who protected their walls. You see there, vampires hadn't yet evolved to be able to walk in the sunlight, and so they depended on the humans for protection just as much as they needed them for a food source. Sasha and a handful of her childhood friends were experimented on by her mother, who crafted the first hunters. You saw those big black eyes, rather gnarly if you ask me. She did have pupils once when she had control of her strength.

It was said during the last war in their world, they followed Oppollo and a few of his men here to Earth. The portal however broke behind them, and they've never been able to return since. Oppollo's objective has and always will be tyranny and monopolization. Since being here he did exactly that. It took him a few hundred years to build an army. Your father, Cesar, being one of those he turned. Then he constructed the Vampire Council as an equal demise so he could take over the human species, which back within their homeland were rather obliging fully aware of their inferiority, but it wasn't so much the case here.

Anyway, besides that's the boring part. So Kyran convinced Sasha what a great idea it would be to raise a child, aka me as a thirty-something-year-old French man who Kyran considered to have a striking resemblance to himself. My father was very vain but clearly had good taste.

They tortured me in their own ways, my mother with her experiments and my father, well perhaps he prepared me for the real-world crafting wit and little stir-crazy methods, but then our happy family broke up when my father turned my mother into a vampire against her will. She eventually tricked him and sunk him to the bottom of the ocean where he hasn't seen the light of day for hundreds of years since. So it's kind of funny because if anyone could outright oppose Oppollo it was probably Kyran, but now no one can find him."

He shrugged, clearing his voice as if trying to step over all the information quickly because it bored him. "He tries to reach out to people with his gift from time to time in their dreams, calling them forth to find him or just playing with them. He likes to torture people." He chuckled as if reminiscing on good times. "His gift enables him to embody or more specifically possess creatures on the surface for a short amount of time. But the most he can take is small animals, though they can be rather menacing when they find you." He was waving his finger around like it was a personal joke. "I can only imagine the pranks he's played on my mother and how furious she must be that he still haunts her."

"Why didn't she just kill him?" Kasey asked. Lincon was charmed that she was eating up his story. We were all engrossed and eyed one another warily. How had this been the first time I'd heard of this. Was this even possible? Lincon was one of the craziest people I'd met, and he was an illusionist. Maybe he'd begun to believe his own lies.

"Kill Kyran?" Lincon snorted. "Well, ask Cesar here how that goes. Oppollo tried to be rid of him for years and townships fell every time due to the devastation that surrounded them while they fought."

Eyes were now on Cesar. He seemed irritated by the shift. "Kyran and Sasha are real. Their story and origins I'm not so sure of. Even we had folklore amongst my people before Oppollo pillaged my village. But that's all it is. Stories. Until I see it with my own eyes, I can't believe it. Know this though, Kyran is best kept at the bottom of the sea. And Sasha would be better off dead too. All three of them."

His narrowmindedness wasn't surprising. But my pragmatic self tried to fathom if I too could believe such an elaborate story.

"Oh, come on now, Cesar, ye old brute!" Lincon toed his feet into a little dance at the edge of his chair. If the story's true, then none of us would've met and had this opportunity to hang out like this! I don't know what are lies and truths when it comes to our origins, and what would I know, I'm just a crazy person." He amped himself up laughing at what he considered a hilarious joke.

Yolo squinted uncomfortably across at him, fiddling with the wooden cross at his chest. "Wow, your family sounds kind of fucked up," Yolo drew out to break the silence.

"I don't think I need to hear that from the likes of anyone in this room thank you very much." Lincon clicked his tongue.

"So, what does this change?" Balzar asked, breaking his own silence. He was daring enough to draw Cesar's attention to him.

"Absolutely nothing," Tythian answered from the corner of the room. "The matter of the *wolves* and Oppollo and the old world are separate matters. We still have a war to attend in two weeks. Humoring ourselves with Lincon's family tree will only cause distraction as the wolves have already done these past few weeks." The way he titled *wolves* was as if they were menacing. They'd become an extruded complication. Had they been mindless creatures like the sabers I wouldn't care less to slaughter them. But these were trapped humans inside, cruelly mutated to appease what, a crazy scientist huntress x vampire gone rogue and the humans who were willing to facilitate her maddening concepts?

"Tythian's right. This changes nothing. But from now on if anyone sees one of those bloody seething haggard dogs they're to be killed on site." Cesar looked at me deadpan.

Chase grabbed my hand, a reminder to keep my flexed power in check as it wanted to act on its own accord. *Esmore, he's protecting his people,* he carefully said. *We should be doing the same.*

I felt slighted by him. I knew we didn't see eye to eye on the subject, but if Cesar allowed them to start killing, then how long would lesser intelligent vampires uphold their truce on Fire and the others within the coven.

Naturally, Tythian seized his opportunity to voice the same question. "And what of the few that Esmore carries around with her like a child with her doll?"

The painting beside him exploded into ash, a warning shot. My vampire sprung to action as he teleported in front of me, shoving me into the wall behind. My feet dragged along the ground from the force, reining a firm stance. Fire snapped and went to bite him. He teleported into the back of the room, Chase was upon him now, a fistful swiping him into a chair and breaking it.

Chase dropped to his knees grunting as Connor used his gift to suppress him. Yolo and Balzar blocked Tythian from advancing on Chase. I raised my hand to Connor, threatening him in the same light. "Don't," my mother warned. I thought she was threatening me, but then I realized she'd shifted herself into a compromising position beside Connor. He side glanced us both with that haunting look in his eye.

"Trinity …" Cesar mumbled. The room was divided. It would be a miracle if we could outlast this tension before we even made it onto the battlefield. Connor dropped his gift, arrogantly raising his nose and looking down on Chase.

"What happened between you two?" Yolo asked Tythian and me sincerely.

"What happened?!" Tythian asked, shaking with rage. He pinned me with his gaze. "When one is there to witness my familiar's throat being sliced open and is then treated as a pedigree dog afterward in my own coven, you might understand my perplexing thoughts about honoring her as an equal, and especially distastefully as my sister. Cesar, you need to rein in control within this coven. We used to be mighty."

"Don't you dare take a tone with me, boy," Cesar warned. Tythian tsked and bit down hard on his lips to avoid speaking. He teleported from the room, the black hole swallowing him whole as he made his dramatic exit.

"Oh my, he really does enjoy making a dramatic exit, doesn't he?!" Lincon laughed and jabbed Kasey in the ribs. Even though this had been an interrogation, the room had mostly turned on Tythian. Everyone looked at me now and then Chase.

Esmore… but I blocked him out. I needed time to be on my own and think. I was being scrutinized for what I felt was the right thing to do. And I didn't even know where to start drawing pieces of Lincon's story and what might've been fathomable.

"I'm done with this place," I said, kicking the broken chair beside me. *And everyone could burn to the ground in it.*

You don't mean that, Chase broke through my defenses and I only snapped them tighter shut. Fire followed behind me. I was tiring of these constricting rules and opinions that so easily went against my own navigation.

CHAPTER 35

T HAT EVENING I took flight. Flying amongst the billowing clouds and letting the moisture in the air strike at my face helped clear my thoughts and all the answers I was trying to unravel. What would I do with Titan and Chris? Fire wasn't even a question, she'd follow me of her own accord, but I had to secure a shelter for the pups. And my ever-looping question of how I could ensure Chase's sanity and safety in this fight no matter what? If we were to fail and Fier was displeased, he'd flick the switch to Chase's humanity forcefully.

As I circled the sky, mindful of Fire below who tracked me, I focused on Dillian and Tori who stalked through the mass of trees. And what would Dillian do? I circled a few more times before descending, ensuring my unkempt emotions from before wouldn't interfere with this conversation that needed to be had. I prepared myself for the vile of his words as he so openly despised me.

By the time I'd circled the area a few more times, Dillian and Tori were nearing the front gate of the institute. I free fell from the sky, enjoying the heart-pumping adrenalin that coursed through me as the thought of not being able to open my wings and break my fall elicited through me. My power skirted around me as if preparing to eat away at the earth itself if I were to realize that vision. I snapped my wings open, shaking the ground as I plummeted feet first.

"Shit!" Tori said, jumping back and through the gates. Dillian didn't so much as look twice, uninterested in my display of strength. It would appear very little unnerved him these days. Fire ran out of the trees toward me, a small rodent hanging from her mouth.

"I need to speak with you," I announced to Dillian.

"I have nothing to say to you." He gave me the cold shoulder and kept walking.

"It's about Julia." That paused his next step. "We might've found a place that can assert security, well in numbers at least amongst her own kind."

"With hunters?" Tori asked regretfully because it had been too late for him. He felt the strain in the air between Dillian and me and found it wiser to pardon himself. "I'll leave you two and go check up on the pups. Fire?" He urged her along. She eyed Dillian as she sauntered past him, her striking blue eyes menacing as if she goaded him to try something.

Dillian skirted around the edges of the fencing to the institute, he stood adjacent from our wing where Julia had all but been imprisoned. All those times he'd stood here pretending to take an interest in the pups training, he'd actually been standing here, to be as close to her as possible. I wondered what he thought if anything at all.

"There's a group of rebel hunters my mother's in associate with. They're willing to take her, but the exchange needs to be made in three days."

"Three days? We can't take her sooner?" he asked. I fell short of what I might say next.

"Do you truly feel nothing for her now?" I found it hard to believe. Even if this was a cold shell of my best friend, I was certain even beyond death, his love for Julia would surpass even that.

"I didn't realize you were such a romantic," he said coldly. "What I feel for her is wanting to lick the salt off her neck and dive my soul-sucking fangs into her flesh. Past any of that intensity, I can think of nothing else." He was rigid and inexcusably cold. "And even if I could remember how to love her." And a part of me felt that he still did. "I'll only hurt her. Should we make it past this period, and I find restraint, I'd then be forced to watch her grow old and die, while I didn't change a bit. Instead of walking that life hand in hand and having children of our own to raise, I can give her nothing now!" His dull eyes struck me savagely. "And she needs to know that the remains of the man she once loved, of who she thinks I am—is lost. So yes, Esmore, send her away and to her own people. That way I won't be a burden on her future any more than she is on me now."

My heart twisted painfully at all that he wasn't saying as if for the first time I was seeing Dillian, my best friend. Slowly, I put my hand on his shoulder. I was certain he'd try to break my arm or seethe vile words not to touch him. He inspected the touch as if it was something new to him, his eyebrows knitting in confusion. But I truly wished and dared to think somewhere deep down in his newly changed form, Dillian was still in there. I just didn't know how many years it might take for it to come back out.

Depleted, his voice cracked. "I don't want to hurt her." Tears pricked at my eyes at my broken best friend before me. Flashbacks and moments came crashing into me as we sat on top of the wall at my Hunter Guild. I always found it so fickle as he tried to draw empathy out of me, and now the roles had reversed. We'd just turned into very different people, not people, creatures.

"I'm sorry for having failed you," I admitted to him, wishing we could go back to the time where we went on missions together, oblivious to the reality of the outside world and its conditioning. Unbeknownst to all the vile plans hatching and the part we might play in them. A time when we had one another's backs and fought gallantly side by side as hunters.

Dillan shook his head, a small laugh splitting from him. "You're not to be blamed any more than we are for not protecting ourselves. I just… never thought this would be my existence. I truly would've preferred dying."

"I'm sorry we couldn't let you go. *I* couldn't let you go."

"And so, you'll understand why I'll always hate you for that." The air sucked out of me as I wriggled my hand from his shoulder. "Tell her for me."

"No." I refused to do that out of respect for Julia at least. I felt my mother's forceful interference adhering that I should speak with Dillian myself. And now I would put the same pressure on him. "We'll help you, so you won't be tempted to attack her. But she needs to hear this from you. You can't hide in the shadows from everything, and especially what is most important." And I had to take heed of my own advice and apologize to Chase.

Dillian caught my hand before I could leave him. His usual cold eyes searched for something. "Is it truly okay for us to live this way, Esmore?"

I considered him seriously. It had been the very same question I'd been asking myself since my vampirism pronounced itself and everything else that happened preceding that event. Sasha's words came rippling back as if anticipating this conversation, '*Not all of us are cut out to live as monsters.*' I patted his hand remorsefully that I'd bound him into the same fate as myself with this never answered question. I didn't know when I'd come to terms with it either … if ever. "We have to find something to fight for." The truth was, besides natural instinct to survive, if we had nothing to protect or live for then we had nothing at all. And that terrified me as I looked into the eyes of someone I loved and had already failed.

"You can't leave me!" Julia cried as she threw what sounded like a pot plant that smashed against the wall. My mother had concealed her scent so as not to tempt Dillian. He'd enforced that we were to stand outside the door at the ready for if he were about to attack. Cruelly, he'd waited for the day she'd be taken away to confront her personally. Every time she'd attempted to bound outside with my mother by her side securing her scent and any vampires daring to get closer, Dillian vacated the premises. And all her effort had been in vain as he avoided her.

Tori and Fire trained with the pups below on the lawn, and I kept a conscious effort on both Dillian's conversation and the few vampires I could sense loitering around them.

"I cannot protect you," he coldly promised. His harsh exterior was back in place, and I wondered if it was a permanent guard or if the Dillian I'd seen slip through the other night was a rarity in itself. Ever since that night, he'd ignored me the same.

Balzar and I now trained alone. Sometimes Yolo would join out of curiosity to watch. After our harsh exchange, Connor had made himself scarce, and I sometimes saw Deemori roaming outside of a night with a handful of her sabers to hunt. But he was never with her. Chase and I had spoken of our indifferences regarding the werewolves, settling to support one another and make a clear decision after this upcoming battle. But we both strongly fought on either side of the line, something that weighed on us heavily. Something that tore at us in equal measure as we respected one another's opinion but couldn't waver our own beliefs. And we'd never expect that from one another, we just didn't know how to come to a compromise and didn't have the time to prioritize it.

"I won't go without you," Julia adamantly challenged. I could hear the quiver in her tone.

"Julia," Dillian crooned. "You know that can't happen."

I felt like they'd been going around in circles. But what I did know was that in the next hour, we were teleporting Julia to the outskirts of New York where we were meeting with Louise as she handled the transaction. Neither my mother nor I had seen her personally since the ambush with the hunters, and I was still suspicious of what 'little involvement' the foreseer proclaimed to have.

As tears and cries tormented the usually quiet Julia, I decided to step toward the balcony, where I could watch them train. I was confident Dillian wouldn't hurt her, but I remained visual on their movements as I'd promised Dillian. It felt too personal of a conversation to listen into considering I felt as if I'd dragged them into this mess in the first place.

If Julia could be pulled away to safety, then what could I manage for the pups? I wondered as I watched over their training in their wolf forms. Titan's fur was jet black, her earthy brown eyes piercing in contrast. Chris was slightly smaller, though in time I imagined he'd grow larger when hormones crept up. Tori and Fire exemplified certain maneuvers. Tori seemed unfazed by the fact that one bite from Fire could destroy him. Fire lunged for him, and Tori demonstrated a swift movement to grab her around the neck and put her into a hold. Very slowly and without biting, Fire showed the pups how they could break out of it.

In the near distance, I could sense Lincon and Kasey. Kora was the only one within my sight. She seemed out of sorts as she blatantly stared toward the direction of the pups. She was completely out of it, her ability to fight coming to a near stop, compared to the warrior she'd once been. Maybe she couldn't handle this life, her instability was cracking to the surface, and no one knew how to help her. This form of illness wasn't something we'd dealt with previously. Instability was a weakness and reckoning within the confines of our upbringing. If anyone might've been inclined to help her, it was Kasey.

And then like a sudden epiphany, I realized Kasey and Kora could shield the pups in a hidden place while we went to war. They had no thirst for blood and no particular interest in harming the wolves. The twins and Lincon had very little interest in the new plagued species. And if Kora fought anything like she had on our last mission, she was nothing but a liability on the battlefield.

"It's done." Dillian curtly nodded as he firmly held the door shut behind him. I could hear Julia scratching and kicking at the door, demanding he let her out and that their conversation wasn't over. Her distraught sobs echoed in the room as she slowly slid down on the other side of the door. Dillian's hand hovered over the door. At first, I thought I might have to pry his hand off it, but slowly he released it, looking downward and never back.

"Dillian—" I reached out to him, but he jumped over the balcony I was leaning against and sped through into the forest. Tori had noticed his exit and looked up at me with a knowing and saddened expression. He excused himself from the pups parlay and followed Dillian if only to make sure he had security in numbers.

"It had to be done," my mother said coolly. Unfortunately, a lot of sacrifices had to be made. I'd just never wished it upon Dillian who'd already sacrificed so much. "I'll make the arrangements, and we'll leave within the hour."

"Do you think he'll come?" I asked after my mother. Could Dillian put himself in that position to truly see her off? To even be so inclined as to who she was being handed over to?

"I think you expect more empathy from him than he's able to produce right now," my mother said, matter-of-factly. I slumped in exhaustion. Everyone who turned changed, and it wasn't until years later that they began shifting back into who they once were, well the mannerisms and behaviors. But for some, maybe it would be too late. Tori, against all odds, seemed to adapt quickly. But Dillian … I worried about how long that might take.

CHAPTER 36

THE WIND AND rain flapped our robes and hoods. The rain pelted against our skin unnaturally like the wild storms we used to bunker down from within our Guild. It was as if the sky was mourning the loss for both Julia and Dillian. She had her suspicions he might've been with us in the way that she continued searching the robed figures behind us. And much to my ease, he had come, if only to see her off and be done with it, but silently in the back where she'd never be able to reach.

Unlike our usual meeting place near the bridge on the outskirts of New York, we met in overgrown shrubbery and woodlands. The grass was thick and vibrant, coming to the height of my shoulder. My mother and I waited with Julia. Tythian and the others guarded our backs as they had done every time we'd met with the hunters. Julia had only a small backpack with her. She was dreary and her face cold. She stared at the ground, tired from crying, and looked as if all the life had been pulled out of her.

She was resistant to come, partly forced, but also there was some part of her deep down that knew this was the best way forward. Her time of housing within covens had come to an end. Had always been at an end, and I worried what future issues harboring her in the darkness for so long might've cost her. As it was, it cost her everything, which was Dillian.

I was surprised by the pair that walked toward us. I was expecting Louise and her usual group. Instead, a foreign man and woman shuffled forward. They, too, wore sooted dark hoods and robes. I was on the ready, though I could sense they were hunters. I kept my hand lazily about my garter in case these imposters were willing to strike. The woman shifted back her hood revealing fluorescent green eyes. Her gaze transfixed more on Julia than anyone else, unflinching from the pelting rain.

"A plant summoner," the woman said, "is very welcome to join our group of rebels." The man with fluorescent blue eyes pulled back his hood as well to show his face. Though my mother and I wouldn't remove our masks, they could see our fluorescent hunter eyes. The hunters before us made a pointed look toward the small group of vampires that flanked us amongst the shrubbery. The man's lip curled slightly, hastened and disgusted as they restrained their natural instinct to fight.

"I was under the assumption Louise would be here to mediate the exchange," my mother said warily. Now Julia did look up, daunted by her future.

"As we would've liked the same." The woman pressed a considerate glance toward the vampires once again. She briefed a curious glance over me before continuing the conversation with my mother. "But Louise has reason to believe few suspicions loiter around their connection with us. And in doing so, we didn't want to risk exposing her, especially when doing a favor to someone she considered a friend."

I was still surprised by the revelation of there being rebel hunters. For how long had they existed? How did they break past their programming to serve and keep the humans alive? How could they learn to prioritize anything else? But in its way, my mother and I had learned to do the same.

"It's tense times, Trinity," the woman said contemplatively. "As I'm sure you're well aware. We mustn't hover around here for too long in case we're spotted. So come, huntress, align with us, and we can keep you safe amongst your own kind," she hurriedly said. Julia now seemed uneasy by the extended hand. I couldn't blame her, she was being pushed into the unknown, and we didn't know them personally. I placed a hand on Julia's shoulder, my grip firm to hold her tight in place.

"Why do it?" I asked, not wanting to hand her over so easily even if time was of the essence. "Why did you create a rebel group? Why do this favor for us?"

The woman considered me and then her partner. From the way she looked at me, I was certain Louise had tipped her some information as to who I might've been. "Firstly, it's not for *you* we do this, but we owe Louise many favors for her blessing us with foresight in situations that might've had our camp up in a blaze.

"As for the reason behind banding together with hunters the same as us, it's rather simple. Because the Guilds have been tarnished. Like everything else in this world, even leaders of our own kind have become corrupt. It's our mission to find a better way, a new way. The way it is now is no longer substantial."

"So, you're an idealist?" I asked, almost mocking.

A small cynical smile twisted. "And are you not? Those who stray onto their own path are often just as much. And people have fought for lesser causes. Let's just hope yours is as great as Louise prophesizes it to be because if it is, our ideals and meeting will come together once again. Until then," she nodded curtly to us both, "I wish you the best in your endeavors and promise to look after this one. And in truth, her gift will benefit our crops greatly. Not every great warrior is shipped off onto the battlegrounds. There is a place for her amongst our kind."

Julia was now looking back between the few shadowy figures behind us, no doubt looking for Dillian. *He will not come,* I thought and willed her to understand. This would be just as hard on him as it was on her. I truly wanted to believe that. I loosened my grip on her. The release startled her, and she sucked in a shaky breath, looking at me with wide eyes. My heartbeat sped up at the thought of what she might spit at me. At the hatred she would seethe me and accuse me of being an accomplice for their end game. I felt no more hidden by the mask, like she was seeing through to me and I hated being so vulnerable. Despite all my strength, her eyes pinned me to the spot, my guilt doing more damage than she might ever be able to do by laying a hand on me.

"I'm scared," she whispered. I let go of the breath I'd been holding. "I know we haven't always seen eye to eye, and this isn't how I wanted it to go. But I wanted him to stay alive just as much as you did." Her voice trembled. I thought tears would streak down her cheeks once again, but looking at the swollen puffs under her eyes, it might've not been physically possible. "Please don't let him be consumed by it. Help him out of the darkness. He can't hear my voice anymore." Her bottom lip trembled.

I hastened to say, "I can't promise that." This was the reality of the world we now dabbled in. Sometimes there was no coming back. Things could not be undone, and some things would never change. No matter how much we willed them to.

A mixture of anger and fear rolled over her expression. "I do not blame you for what's happened, Esmore. I don't know if you care to hear that from someone as weak as me, but I've never blamed you, and neither did he." Tears sprang to my eyes. I needed to hear that more than she would ever know, and though I couldn't agree with her, feeling entirely guilty for it, I thanked her for giving me a piece of Dillian that he would now never show. And in the bottom of my heart, for making me feel not alone for making the decision to let him and Tori turn.

She briefed a glance over at the hunters. "I'm sorry about this, I know it'll make you uncomfortable, but I selfishly need it," she said. She twisted and wrapped her arms around my waist startling every reflex. I ushered my power back as it fretted to attack and push her away. Julia was no threat to me. She never had been.

I uncomfortably lowered my hand onto her back as she hugged me. The other hunters looked away, disgusted by the familiarity and act of affection. Corrupt our kind was indeed. "I hope our paths cross again," she mumbled before straightening herself and walking toward the hunters who extended a hand for her.

And in truth, I hoped our paths never did because she was one of the few who I genuinely believed deserved better than our kind, and I hoped that she would find some kind of peace and safety to live a long and fulfilling life. My mother and I didn't move until the three of them were out of our sight. A sadness and wave of relief overcame me. At least one of us got out.

It was Lincon who whistled up beside me, an irritable noise as he danced to his own tune. "Might I be so loved as to have the right to hug you?" He opened his arms wide, and I pushed him back by his face.

"No," I said, disgusted more so by the act of touching him. The alluring presence of the shadowy figure that haunted my dreams came into range. I swished back and forth in my spot disorientated by how close it felt to me. A small croaking noise alarmed me as I almost stepped on the brown frog at my feet.

Lincon looked at it, delighted. "Oh, Daddy Bear," he said cutely as he collected it and raised it to his eye level. I grimaced in disgust.

"That's your—" I didn't even want to finish the sentence because of how farfetched it sounded. But that terrorizing presence was definitely pinpointed on that creature. If Lincon's story was true, then his father, Kyran, was currently at the bottom of the sea and had possessed this frog.

It tried to jump out of Lincon's grip, but he held it firmly … too firmly. A pop burst between his hands. "Oh, no!" he crooned as he slopped the remains toward the ground. I looked away, disgusted. *That* had been the menacing presence that spooked my dreams?

"Let's go," I dismissed, disgusted. We were mantled by the heavy rain. With no more than a side glance, Tythian teleported us one by one. I waited for everyone else to be teleported and remained with the last vampire who stood amongst the shrubbery peering out to where Julia had been taken. I couldn't see the expression on Dillian's mask-hidden face, and he was unflinching as always. But I felt the need to stay with him, even when it angered Tythian that he too was waiting in the cold rain.

Despite all that had happened between us and since our last violent exchange, Tythian hadn't so much as spoken to me, now was no different, even when he made his irritation clear. Reluctantly, I placed my hand carefully on Dillian's shoulder and then on Tythian's forearm so we could teleport together. I held on tightly to both, scared Tythian might decide to drop us in whatever kind of void this might've been, and scared that Dillian might step away of his own accord.

But when we reappeared in front of the institute, he continued to stare at it as if it was still Julia he was watching after. Slowly, he raised his hand to mine and patted it before walking back toward the forest alone.

You can't help him, Chase consolidated.

I know, and that's what hurts most, I admitted, watching out for him. Chase ran a gentle stroke down our link, and I could envision his touch along my face. I felt selfish for having this when Dillian could not.

CHAPTER 37

THE NEXT FEW days were a blur of training, constant meet-ups within Cesar's room, and executing last-minute changes and plans. Tomorrow would be the day we'd move out. Tythian would teleport Lincon, Connor, Balzar, and me into Tracey's already moving Council, and our mission would begin from there.

We'd all shifted uncomfortably at the acknowledgment that in only a day we'd be divided. I didn't want to leave Chase any more than he wanted to leave my side. But he had a coven to lead, and I had an assassination to execute amidst all the chaos that would soon break loose. I'd still been considering the many ways I could protect Chase from such an outcome if I were unsuccessful. Especially if I were to be killed, I was certain it would tip him off into the instability of being a saber, and I didn't want that to happen. I needed to find a way to prevent that.

I now stood on the outer edge of our territory, the piercing light of dawn breaking through the trees as we saw Titan and Chris off. We'd let them sleep for a few hours before waking them up and piling them with a bagful of our resources, food, and weapons. They were confused as we ushered them in silence, making sure to misdirect many of the vampires' gazes who crept inside to rest and clear out of the rising sun.

Chase stood closely behind me. Although he didn't endorse their species, he'd warmed up to the pups in the same measure as Fire. Jenn was with us as well, and it was I who had to pull *her* back reminding Yolo there were far greater consequences waiting for him from Cesar and his coven if he were to leave with them. As much as I would've preferred that, entrusting them with the twins was my only option. My mother and Fire were with them. The plan as we'd discussed was that Kora and Kasey would guard the younger ones. Kasey wasn't at all interested in what she considered as 'babysitting' while everyone else fought, but Lincon implied a stern talking to, and afterward, she'd reluctantly agreed.

Fire and my mother were with them to find a hiding place, midpoint between here and where the Vampire Council meeting would be hosted so we could find them afterward. My mother would conceal their whereabouts and smell, while Kora and Kasey would assert a wall so no one could step in even if they came across it by chance. After their position was ascertained, my mother and Fire would return. Chase offered four of the gargoyles as protection, enlarging their team in case they came across anything while relocating. The gargoyles were one of few I trusted. They were connected to Jerimiah and Darcy who had only ever shown initiative and loyalty.

By the time they would return and catch up to the rest of the covens who would be on the move, I'd already be gone. I promised to meet Fire and my mother on the front line. Fire was reluctant to leave my side, but the plans were specific as to who would be accepted within Tracey's Council, and the spots were limited for the inner room where their meeting would take place.

It might've been easier to have Tythian teleport them, but we kept this departure in secret, although I suspected Cesar would know about the detail to some extent. A cruel twist in my heart was creeping in as Titan rubbed her eyes, looking about in confusion, it'd been the most innocent she'd looked in weeks. I dropped to one knee, so I was at her eye level and pulled Chris in closer as well.

"Now, you two listen to me. We're going to send you away for a little while with Kora and Kasey, okay? They will protect you, and I'll come and find you again," I said, straightening one of the straps on Chris's shoulder absentmindedly. Just as Julia had found her way out, I wanted to find a way out for these two who should've never been dragged in so deeply.

"Are we not training hard enough?" Chris mumbled in disappointment as Titan went wide-eyed.

"Your training is admirable," I said, trying for a comforting tone that sounded far too regal. "Where we're going isn't safe. There will be a big fight. A lot of people are going to die, and I want to make sure you two are safe."

"But we can fight. We can turn into the wolves and bite everyone!" Chris said more boisterous than usual. I realized he was speaking on behalf of the usual boisterous Titan who was now exchanging glances amongst the adults as if she were being abandoned. Kora and Kasey mortified her, and to a child, I supposed they did look scary, but they'd seen more hideous creatures. That wasn't the problem.

"Hopefully, if we succeed, you'll never have to," I said, and my gaze reluctantly pulled toward Jenn. Though for them, that would never be true. Vampires would hunt them just because of what they were. And I hoped I survived long enough to protect them until they were at least old enough to fend for themselves.

"Please don't leave us," Titan said, throwing herself at me and almost knocking me off my feet. Chase was behind me with a sturdy arm, holding me upright in support. He remained silent, but I could feel his strength and encouragement pool through me. This was the right thing to do. This was the *only* thing to do. "Please don't make us!" She sobbed. "Daddy never came back last time and he'd promised!"

A lump lodged in my throat. No, he'd never come back because of *me*. I felt another push from Chase as he sensed my reluctance.

"Titan, listen to me," I said, pushing her back slightly so she could look me in the eyes. She tried avoiding my gaze, so I lifted her chin. Even then she looked elsewhere. Such a rebellious little thing. "I need you and Chris to look out for one another until I come back."

"Last time we were sent away, *they* came for us." She threw back in my face. It stunned me, my failings thrown at me like a dagger.

"Then you know it's not safe here. We are housing with their kind, Titan. It has never been safe here. This way you can properly be protected. See Kora and Kasey there? They are two of my finest huntresses."

Titan reluctantly looked back up at them, her stare dipping to the enlarged fangs that speared over their chins instead of the coral color of their huntress eyes. "Show me that you can be brave. Go on this mission as I go on mine." I was clutching at anything that might resonate with the little one who was sure to turn into a commendable soldier. Perhaps a little too rebellious for her own good.

"Why hasn't Julia come back?" Chris asked curiously. "Did you send her away too?"

"Yes. Julia is in a safe place, but she can't come with us." If I could've sent them with the hunters, I would've, but their kind would not be welcome, even when they were children. "You need to go. Did you pack your teddy?" I asked Titan, considering the small bear I'd taken from her Human Compound and brought back for her.

She straightened her spine and shoulders. "I'm a warrior, not a child. I don't need a teddy."

It saddened me to see. As children amongst hunters, we were trained to have a lack of innocence, we were purely bred to be soldiers. Titan and Chris were not. This cold-blooded war and trauma had stripped them of that freedom.

I considered her for a moment and acknowledged her strength, no matter how misplaced it was. With a thoughtful sigh, I removed my Barnett crossbow and quiver of arrows.

What are you doing? Chase asked me peculiarly.

I have no need for it anymore if I can implode *someone into ash with my very thoughts.*

"Now, Titan, I'm going to give you something very special. I've had this weapon for as long as I can remember. I want you to keep it safe for me. And when I come and collect it from you afterward, I'll show you how to use it." An odd wave of sentimentality rushed through me as if passing down an heirloom of sorts.

But for her, when she became strong enough to use it, it might protect her life on more than one occasion. She went wide-eyed by the weapon. She'd seen me carry it around more often than not. "And, Chris, I'll make sure to find you a weapon as equally superb."

"I want a sword!" he blatantly requested. I kept the smile from showing.

Fire nudged her head between Titan and me as if to hurry us along. "It's time," Chase said gently from behind. "Before others see." His hand firmed on my shoulder as if hardening his resolve for me.

"No," Titan said defiantly and stomped her foot. Fire offered her a warning growl, but Titan ignored her. "NO! I'm not going!" she screamed, irritating my sensitive ears. I exchanged a nod with my mother who pulled her out of my arms. "NO!" she screamed again and clawed to keep a hold of my arm. Her little nails dragged down, leaving a trace of blood. "NO!" she screamed once more and then fell into a stupor. My mother had put her to sleep. Chris had begun tearing up, my mother dropped her hand on his shoulder, and he dipped toward me, deadweight and asleep as well.

Kasey's lip peeled up in disgust as she collected the small child and threw him over her shoulder not so delicately. Kora absentmindedly collected the Barnett crossbow and quiver. I stood, trying to push down any emotion that dared sabotage my hard resolve. But it was difficult as I stared at the tear-stricken marks on Titan's dirt-tainted face. I felt oddly light without my Barnett crossbow on my back. Now I would only have my sword there.

Before leaving, my mother looked at me. This would be the last time we'd see one another until the battlefield.

"Fight well, my daughter," was all she could manage before she assembled her group. The four gargoyles shifted into their vampire form, fluidly spreading around the small group. Fire nudged my hand demanding my attention. I ruffled my fingers through the fur atop her head as she looked at Chase expectantly as well. He scratched under her chin with a lopsided smile.

"I'll see you soon," I whispered to her. Remembering the few words we'd exchanged the night before. I'd asked her to look out for Chase in my stead until I made it onto the battlefield. That he was to be a priority above all else. She dipped her head and chased after the others.

"Do you think they'll be okay?" Jenn said worriedly with her hands clutched at her chest. She flinched under my effective look. I couldn't think otherwise.

The room felt empty. As soon as I'd returned to our wing, the teddy was the first thing I'd noticed, thrown under the bed as if hidden from prying eyes. I propped it up onto the bed in between pillows as if it would replace where they usually slept. Already the institute felt cold as we prepared to abandon it. There was an eerie silence despite the days of robust noise and clashing of weapons as Tythian continued to teleport in all sorts of arsenal.

I placed my hand on the hilt of my sword, admiring its smooth texture. We'd slain many enemies together. I'd brought this from the Hunter Guild, and it would venture with me into this next battle. Patches of rich-looking dirt sprinkled the floor in the corner where Julia's oddly beautiful plants and vibrant fruits still thrived. The dawn began splintering in.

Chase came behind me, his arms wrapping around, his hands splaying on my stomach as he pulled me in tightly. I had mixed feelings about his hands on my stomach at the thought and discussion of if we ourselves ever wanted children. I entwined my fingers in with his. And especially the thought of everything that was to happen in the coming days. I wanted to stay frozen like this, hiding my face so he couldn't see the fear in my expression.

If I had enough courage, I'd force him away into the opposite direction of the battle, but that wasn't the man or warrior he was. And that was why I had fallen in love with him, besides his brazen attitude in the same light.

"I don't want to let you go," he murmured against my ear as he nipped at it. This would be the last morning we'd spend together, and we couldn't even claim one another in the way that we most wanted, having to pull back on our primal urges so I wouldn't transfer this gift to him. "I'm scared you'll fly off into the sunset and never look back." He pulled me down into his lap on the uncomfortable chair. I remembered the more leisurely times when we'd swing on his hammock that seemed so misplaced in this world.

"I'll always come back to you," I said, though if doing that would keep him safe, I'd consider it.

"I just always feel like you're going to disappear, like ash catching in the wind through my fingers." *And that has more to do with your reckless nature than anything*, his growl melted my insides, creating a heated reaction from me.

I pressed my forehead to his. "And I feel the same way about you, Chase," I admitted. I was so scared to lose him. That this fight might push him over the edge. If I were in danger, he'd fight through thousands of vampires to get to me, but I wondered what the cost for drawing that power might be. I was certain it would be his sanity. And though he might be able to protect me, where would that leave us then if I were to lose him, or the other way around?

Arousal to the side, we sat here just like this, frozen in time, heated with the building anticipation between us. "I don't want to leave your side," I whispered, vulnerable.

"We could run away together," his stormy gray gaze connected with mine. He gave me a sad smile. *I'm not joking.*

I know you're not. I kissed him gently, sending waves of my love and warmth through our connection, wishing it would erode all that had tarnished him. That I could somehow evaporate the disease from his mind. *But we can't run away from this.* There were too many targets on his back and too many on my own. If I didn't kill Oppollo or die trying, Fier would induce Chase's insanity.

"We do this together," I reminded him. He sighed, so downbeat to his usual self. We'd been fighting these last few weeks, disagreeing on so much, but it all seemed irrelevant now as we counted down the hours.

"But we won't be together on the battlefield. You'll be stuck inside, with some of the most powerful vampires in existence and I'll be forced to watch from the sidelines." I pressed a kiss along his cheek and then his brow, adoring all that he was. And everything he meant to me.

"And I will make it out to you. And we will fight side by side, as we should and as is right."

I could tell he didn't believe me entirely. Not because he doubted my skill but because the situation unsettled us. "The moment something changes, I don't care about the others you get out straight away. Promise me."

"Chase, we will—"

Promise me, he said more adamantly, stunning me. I shook my head profusely, hating the tenderness of his vulnerability. It anchored me back to the memory of him, Dillian, and Tori, imprisoned in the cellars. I would make it out to him and prevent that from happening. A tap on the door pulled an irritated growl from Chase.

"Chase," it was Clarissa this time, who rarely visited. "We need you down here."

"I'll be down shortly," he lashed out at the door. I rested my hand on his cheek, so hurt by his stress-free self seemingly backed into a corner. His expression softened under my touch, but the rigidness in his shoulders never vacated. If we could've, I would have him now and claim him as mine once more … in case it would be the last.

"It's urgent," Clarissa said quietly but no less assertive. Before he could snap at her again, I kissed him, biting down on his lip hard. This was who we were. This was the fight we'd signed up for, even if it wasn't initially our own. And of all the chaos that wrapped around us, at least it brought me to him, because I had something to fight for.

His hand stapled over my beating heart, the pulse somewhat calming his nerves. He was equally disconcerted about my vulnerability. A natural one, and I was appreciative that I could no longer defy death in such a way. I placed my fingers through his hair and pulled him in harder.

"Give me a few more minutes and I'll be down," Chase said weakly, and it had nothing to do with him having taken my breath. *Just a few more minutes for us before they take the rest.*

He'd claimed his coven for us and for me. For protection. But right now, as the few minutes we had together were scarce, it felt as if their demand for attention was menacing.

"Go," I whispered, stealing one more kiss and then another. When I tried to let him slip through my fingers, I would pull him in more desperately than the last, my body betraying me. We stayed like this for minutes, trying to find our resolve to part.

"I don't want to leave you," he said shakily, making it more than surreal of the war that was upon us.

I wanted to say, *then don't.* But the huntress within me found a quivering voice. "You must." I found strength in my resolve finally stepping away from him. Clarissa hadn't yet left the other side of the door though she remained silent. Her looming presence was enough of a distraction to fully pull away from Chase.

I admired him as he stood, the muscles in his body flexing like the divine creature he was. I was hungry for him. And if we made it out of this alive, I'd be sure to find a way where we could rekindle our bodies in the way they were meant for one another.

He went to take a step away, but with lightning speed slammed me against the wall, his tongue rolling against mine as his hand snaked down my sides, sending a shiver along my entire body. He bit into my neck, savoring a small taste of me. I moaned at the excitement and heated pleasure. But he pulled away, licking his lips and kissing me one more time, trying to force himself into a safe zone, if there was such a thing for us.

"I love you, Esmore Bourne." I smiled at his additive of last name to my own.

"And I love you, Chase Bourne." He kissed me once more before leaving the room. I followed him out, watching him as he descended the stairs. I hummed after his departure, and it felt like the world would envelop me. Jerimiah and Darcy were in their gargoyle form on either side of me. I stared out into the sunrise, my thoughts idly wandering as to how far the others might've already been. I hoped they were able to find the furthest place from here to hide them, and then tears sprung into my eyes as I considered a very safe place for Chase. A thoughtful plan that might work if this upcoming fight strained his mind too viciously.

"Jerimiah? Darcy?" They shifted from their gargoyle form.

"What is it, Esmore?" Darcy asked. I looked at them both, wanting to gauge their reaction and loyalty to what I was about to suggest.

"If I thought of a plan to ensure Chase's survival would you do it, even if it might betray his wishes?" I didn't want to execute this idea, but I'd only set it into action if Chase truly began to lose control or if someone might hurt him. Perhaps this was the only way I could keep him safe. He would hate me for it. But it was something I was willing to do. As long as he was alive and sane, that's all I cared for.

Jerimiah and Darcy shifted uncomfortably. We'd previously had a similar discussion, but at the same time, I hadn't the slightest idea how I could protect him. But now was different ...

"What did you have in mind?" Jerimiah asked warily. They were as reluctant to betray him as I was. But the importance of Chase surviving was everything. And another tear sprang to my eyes, knowing that I could rely on these two with such an important task.

I would rather beg for forgiveness than permission, knowing all too well that Chase would never agree. But maybe, just maybe it was the only way I could keep him alive and out of Fier's clutches if we were overpowered in this war. I was willing to die for him. And I was certainly willing to piss him off in the process.

Childless Teddy

A childless teddy laid wake in the remains of the hollow halls.

Of what was once a home for hundreds of vampires and the in between monsters that found refuge.

The rooms are cold and abandoned — similar in the way that they were found.

Certain never to return.

And perhaps someone afresh will house in it soon.

If only the survival of their race were to continue after this disastrous war.

And so, a small child left behind her teddy.

Baring her shoulders and thinking herself a young woman instead.

No matter how protected, she will be targeted.

As will all her kind.

The teddy will be forgotten.

Much like the remains of her innocence, stolen by the violence that she had seen.

That is this world.

And that is all it has to offer.I have power.

CHAPTER 38

T HE MOMENT TYTHIAN teleported us to meet with Tracey's small traveling group and Council, Lincon placed an illusion over us to look elegantly fake and perfect, just as her other members were. I scoffed at the changes in Balzar, Lincon, and Connor. They looked nothing like themselves and even when I looked down at my own hand, I was shades darker. I didn't even want to see my reflection.

I wondered if Lincon's gift had a vicinity limit, whether he had to hand blanket his gift individually to his victims or if anyone would simply see us as we were now. But I much preferred that as an option rather than Tracey reaching her tentacle-like hand to permanently shift my appearance.

They'd made a substantial distance on foot. We didn't meet them in the cold isolation of her land and Council and were only two days away by foot from the Council meeting location. The weather was dire and the sky grey. We waltzed out from the decaying treetops conscious of the bow and arrows that were pointed our way the moment we revealed ourselves.

Tracey was expecting us, but they couldn't identify us physically. Considering this was the place we'd agreed upon, I still appreciated their measures. Iris, alongside another two soldiers, walked toward us. I'd forgotten how big he was, and I noticed Balzar's head tilt back as he appreciated his size. He was measuring him in the same way I had when first meeting him. How would we fare in a fight against him? Tythian had already left, disposing the four of us to size up the fifty or so Tracey had brought with her as an entourage.

"I expected it to be a little bigger," I said in way of greeting to Iris. "You know the whole entourage thing. I thought she'd have flags or something sparkly."

"It's good to see you once again, Esmore," he acknowledged. "Though I must admit the sex change confused me some." I looked down at my chest, gaping at the flattened image. Huh. It made sense considering the rest of Tracey's guards were men. "And your companions?"

"Does it matter who is who?" I said, guarded. Just because we were aligning for the sake of agreeing to their terms it didn't mean we had to divulge any more information that might give them a further edge. Before leaving, my mother had shrouded me with her gift of concealment, deterring away from anyone who might smell or hear my heartbeat, and Lincon's gift encroached on that. Though admittedly, Iris was the first test subject.

"I suppose not," he said just as dryly. "You will all stand behind me. Each Council is only allowed to take in seven members, you'll fan out amongst the room. Esmore and I will remain on either side of Tracey as she sits," he instructed. "Now come. Oh, and the moment I suspect something is going awry, I will not hesitate to kill any of you."

"That works both ways, my friend," I threatened. He seemed equally unfazed as we'd been. He led us back toward the group. Iris's bulky shoulders hardly shifted under his thick tight coat. They'd become accustomed to their attire despite it seemingly out of season considering their location. Iris was the only hunter-born vampire I'd met, and it gave me hope that Dillian and Tori would find some resolve and peace no matter where they might find themselves.

As it was now, they were reluctant to stay with Chase and my mother. Though Tori had pledged loyalty toward me, I felt for Dillian it was more necessity of having nowhere to go and wanting to fight for the sake of it. He'd never been much of a fighter, not that he was incapable, but he always sought out other ways to resolve an issue. Long gone were those days.

"Ah, Esmore, or should we start calling you Eli?" Tracey mused to Iris as she looked over me scrumptiously. "So glad you could join us." I was glad to see that her sister, Patricia, wasn't considered an equity in the Vampire Council meeting. I looked her up and down from head to toe, not at all surprised by the lavish attire she wore. It was similar to the style I had last worn when I'd stayed at her Council. It was a green dress stunning comparatively to her mocha skin. A split went up her leg, and I could see the shine of a blade. She wasn't even attempting to hide her weapons. Her hair hung over her shoulders in loose waves, the back of her hair pulled up with two fine-picked ornamental pieces that I wouldn't be surprised if they were daggers too.

"You brought so few of your Council?" I asked inquisitively. I wasn't so sure what the standard protocol was, but Tracey embellished that most Councils would bring half an army if only to flaunt their sheer size. Either Tracey was tactfully making hers seem smaller or she cared to guard her sister and her Council more in case things ended badly for us, and she was overturned as a traitor.

"I'm not like the chauvinist pigs in other Councils who feel the need to show and compare cock size," she replied with a tart smile. Ironic coming from her, who cared about all things vain. "And besides, this will be nothing more than a scuffle. Once the action begins and you rid of Oppollo, my men and I will draw back into the shadows. If others choose to involve themselves then so be it, but we will not have a hand in the aftermath."

"So much for joining forces," I said coldly.

"I have given you more than enough. Would you ask for my hands on a platter as well?" She scoffed. "One day, child, you will appreciate all that I've given you, and hopefully it's not a day too late," she implied my possible upcoming failure. But if she truly thought I would fail she would've never wagered an alliance with us. "Now, shall we move along? This Council meeting will not start of its own accord until our grand appearance has been made." She was as flamboyant as ever as she hurried us along. Begrudgingly, we followed, and I made sure to make a quick assessment of all the obvious and hidden weapons strapped to the men behind us. She might've had no intention to fight, but she came prepared for it no less. And I made sure to keep my gaze forward on Iris. He was the greatest threat during this passing. And from the way the others watched him, they were aware of that as well.

Besides Tracey sometimes evoking small, idle chat with me that consisted of her mainly speaking, there was little change in our formation. We rested twice as we migrated through the change of terrain. Two sabers had stumbled across our group in the woods and were shot down quickly as her men slaughtered them before they could even look at Tracey.

We now approached the meeting of the Vampire Council, I could tell in the way that Tracey straightened her hair, and her nose rose in that superior indignation she held. But Iris seemed more tense than usual, and I could tell we were close. I couldn't sense Chase or any of the others yet, but it wasn't yet night when they'd intended to implement their plan.

An octagonal building came into sight slightly atop a hill, amongst rolling hills of many. The land here was surprisingly green and fertile, and the building looked prestigious compared to most other buildings that descended into rubble over the years. The roof was a stark teal that stuck out in contrast to the grey of the building. There was a lack of fog and a river I could see in the distance that ran through dividing the landscape. Past it, the ground was cracked and dried. This place was like a secret oasis.

"Oppollo had this built in the day humans ignored our existence. This has always been our meeting place. It has a certain regal charm to it, doesn't it? I dare say it's the only thing he had good taste in," she scoffed.

I eyed her and the way she looked at it with admiration. It was either from the power that Oppollo had or the appreciation of architecture she held after being kept in a frozen castle for so many years.

From all sorts of directions, clumps of vampires walked over the rolling hills, all making a beeline for the misplaced building. I wondered if a gift or sorts was used to keep its prestige maintenance and from others stumbling across this place. To think they'd used this for hundreds of years, every time they had their meetings, and no one had found it.

Mixed emotions stirred within me. The time was now, we were heading into the enemy's den, and I would have to find a perfect opportunity to strike Oppollo. Suddenly I did want Chase by my side. I'd never had issues with going into something alone, but with the amounted pressure of having to execute this correctly because it wasn't just my life at risk, I wanted the chance to look at his smiling face one more time. Or listen to one of his stupid, awkward jokes to fill the silence in a room.

Instead, I found myself looking over to Balzar. Despite his changed appearance, I envisioned his face, needing some kind of reassurance that despite our differences and run-ins, we were stepping toward the same fate. As if knowing why I was looking at him, he gave me a grave nod that oddly simmered my nerves. I needed this moment, the last flicker and remains of built-up anxiety, considering how quickly this all came forward so I could focus on the building rise of my power that put me into a new mental state.

My vampire was suggestive as she crawled to the surface, a beam of excitement running through me as if I were sneaking into a fortunate opportunity—a place where I could kill many and challenge my strength. I clenched my fists, a physical reminder to keep my jittery gift contained. My entire body pumped with a wave of adrenaline at all that was about to transpire. Even if I did go down, I would go down with a fight, and that thrilled me more than any lingering feelings about fear or reservation. This was what I had been born to do. This was who I was and everything I had to look forward to. I was a daughter of war, a creature of the night, and a beast untamed. And they would face my wrath and fury like the fine weapon I was.

CHAPTER 39

T HE BUILDING WAS trimmed with gold paint with various ornate gargoyles that adorned the towering two-story-high glass ceiling. How it hadn't managed to break in the unpredictable weather that often rampaged our land was beyond me. There was no path, yet the vampires who were grouped together seemed to know exactly what door to head toward, despite a door central on every wall.

Large groups of vampires huddled on the outside. As Iris had explained, only seven members per Council were permitted to enter. So these small armies waited outside in various places for their leader. Two groups were clumped lazily around the entrance goading one another. They seemed far too nonchalant considering the prestigious event. Evidently, their Council leader was inside, where a further flutter of commotion began.

The moment one dared whistle toward Tracey, Iris's hatchet was unsheathed and barred under the vampire's throat. He sneered at him, a slow smile coming into place as he taunted him. "No blood. You know the rules," the ghastly vampire chided. A few others snickered behind him as if encouraging Iris to try.

"Iris," Tracey said behind him, drawing the attention back on herself. She sidled up toward him, placing a delicate hand on his shoulder. I made sure to follow her, as any loyal guard would. He seemed uncomfortable as he lowered his blade. Her bewitching gaze slowly raked over the lowly vampire who'd whistled at her.

"Do you like what you see?" she purred.

"Very much." He clicked his tongue, looking over her legs with an appreciative glance.

"And you know who I am?" she asked.

"Hot as fuck that's what you are," the vampire said daringly. A small smile spread on Tracey's lips as she waltzed up to him as if drawn in by his pathetic allure. By the size of his fangs, he wasn't a very old vampire, or a smart one.

"And you must be very new. Yes, the laws of this place dictate that no vampire is to kill another on these grounds, or their Council will suffer in consequence. But, dear boy …" she purred as she raised her hand to his face softly. His expression seemed to change slightly as he became uncertain about her approach. But he remained still in case the others mocked him for it. Or perhaps he was dense enough to think she genuinely wanted him. "I do not shed blood." The cruel intent in her eyes was as sharp as a knife as his figure began to contort, and he screamed. His body rumbled with swollen blisters, lumps arousing over his skin and face like a thick cemented skin.

He scurried away, falling back into his comrades. They spilled away from him like he had the plague. Tracey pulled a small handkerchief from between her breasts, much reminding me of how Tythian might act as she wiped at her hand, disgusted she had to touch him. "How Smith's Council lacks in class," she remarked.

I recalled the name. It was one of the marks Cesar had placed on his map that would be ambushed tonight by a coven we'd aligned with. Tracey had confided that she was certain he would be one of the Councils who would rise with Oppollo. By the size of his group here it determined either he brought the majority of them to defend him in case something were to happen or his Council had even more back at their estate.

"You're a crazy bitch!" one of his comrades spat out. Tracey arched an eyebrow. "I know who you are! You're the leader of that Council that's going to vanish into nothing! You mean shit here!" He spat on the ground.

"Oh, my," another woman said. I hadn't even heard her group sneak up behind us. I was unnerved by the number of vampires we were encircled by. "How distasteful these young ones have become." A woman seemingly in her mid-fifties with a group of seven women behind her approached the entrance. From her profile, I gathered this was Anita, the only other female to hold a place on the Vampire Council amongst the twelve members.

"Anita, how long has it been?" Tracey crooned dismissively of the vampire who'd spoken up. She walked over to her, both sharing a kiss on the cheek in a friendly manner. Anita was one of a few who we'd been informed that mostly kept to herself. It was of Tracey's belief that she would neither stand for or against Oppollo's reign. As Tracey had put it, Anita liked to stay out of 'drama.'

"I believe I haven't visited your court for many years and it might be due time for a visit. Perhaps after this meeting, depending on how it bodes." She was beautifully matured in all senses. She was speckled with freckles and a short bob cut of strawberry blonde hair with few strips of grey. Her fair skin and hair coloring seemed unusual considering I'd never seen such a color before, only ever on vampires. It seemed the colored gene faded out over time. Anita was one of few vampires I felt warmth from. It was unnerving considering the cool nature of vampires, and I became further suspicious of her.

The two ignored the various insults and spiteful words from Smith's vampires. The women at Anita's back were proudly just as ignorant. "Shall we go in and see how everyone else fairs?" Anita asked.

"Well, I suppose we don't have a choice, do we?" Tracey remarked, and they both amicably laughed. I exchanged a glance with Iris, he too was uncomfortable by the exchange. And for all the vampire's threats from the group Tracey had just attacked and all their profanity, they didn't step back toward us. I considered how easily it might've been for me to evaporate them into ash, or for Iris to implode them with his lightning.

I kept an eye on Lincon, making sure he wasn't being influenced too easily by the 'excitement.' The last thing I needed was him going on a slaughter rampage and breaking our cover because it felt like fun. But his gaze was trained forward. Evidently, the prize of Oppollo's head and the upcoming fight enticed him more.

Anita and Tracey spoke between themselves, chattering casually as if this was simply a pastime. Tracey had no tells or reservations about the betrayal she'd set upon her own kind. We formed a singular line behind each of our leaders. Iris was first and closest to Tracey, I followed shortly after with Balzar guarding my back.

The two great doors that were opened were pristine, not even weather damage had tarnished the lacquer on its rustic charm. The rest of Tracey's group stayed back, permitting only the seven of us to follow through. The woman who sidled up beside me, following Anita's singular line, briefed an appreciative glance over me. I ignored her. I was starting to think this meeting was only in the context for the leaders to come together for orgies and casual chit-chat.

The inside of the building harbored flickers of orange and pink from the colored tint on the windows above. It eerily felt holistic in the way it'd been built with golden candle holders and relics on display of times and periods I wasn't familiar with. Giant pillars held the building up with a smooth marble edge to them. I hadn't seen a building so beautifully fortified and undamaged.

Velvet green couches were stationed around the edges where vampires lounged casually, chatting. It was a harsh contrast from the reception we'd received at the front. I could quickly decipher who were the leaders amongst their groups. They were circled by their seven. Although everyone spoke with a smile, it was evident the edge beneath was anything but friendly.

The two women guided us around a circular room that was centralized in the building. Before reaching for the doors, a familiar face rounded the corner, speaking with one of the members of his entourage. Fier flamboyantly pointed to one of the art pieces before drawing his attention to our group. My next step faltered as a light shake thrummed through my body. He was here. In front of me now. I could as easily implode him without a second thought and be done with it.

Balzar pushed my back slightly, reminding me to keep walking. I bit down on my lip hard, waking me up from my spell. I could have Fier's life now. Easily. But if I did, I'd ruin our ruse, and furthermore, how would I reverse Chase's disease without him?

"Ah, if it isn't my two favorite women of the Council," he said charmingly.

Anita seemed indifferent to his approach. Tracey, however, took a long sigh and then faked a smile. "What a striking image of your father you've turned into."

Fier's green eyes glowered stormily at her. As if Tracey had twisted a knife in simply by mentioning his father. Iris took a step forward so he was shoulder to shoulder with her. She didn't seem to reprimand him for it. Iris always made his presence known, drawing that condescending attention to himself instead of his leader.

Fier smiled and slowly patted Iris on the chest patronizingly. "Oh, how I wish you'd consider offering me your big oaf. I do have a particular fondness for the previous hunter kinds."

"You wouldn't know what to do with a man such as Iris," Tracey said mildly as she went to place her hand on Fier's wrist to pull him away. But he did so of his own accord, cautious not to let Tracey touch him. A small breeze swept through the room, a vain show of power on Fier's account.

"Oh, but I would. I have many enemies to rid of, I'm certain pointing him in the direction would bring me much delight. Much like throwing a boulder into the masses of an army, I'm sure it would do at least *some* damage."

"I've never met anyone who's made so many enemies in their short time of reign," Anita remarked emotionless. "Your father was amicably fair for the most part."

Fier's cutting gaze fell upon her. "Ah, but not all of us are as efficient as you and your Council, Anita, at being rid of all the covens and Hunter Guilds within your area so you live in a time of peace. One might say such a life lacks in ambition."

"Some of us prioritize our duty as opposed to acquiring personal gain and leisure. From what I've heard, it allows one to be susceptible to spies and traitors wreaking havoc in their court," she said matter-of-factly. I appreciated Anita's quick tongue and wit. A small smile edged on Fier's face, and even in his gaze, one could tell that if it were a different setting, he might've dared lay a finger on her for the underhanded insult. Despite Anita not being one for gossip, she was certainly direct and in the know.

"Perhaps you're right, and I still have much to learn," he waved a fluttery dismissive hand with an air about him as if he were certain one day he would rule, and she was already beneath him. "If you will excuse me, I have matters of … *leisure* to discuss with other members, for those of who are not so tightly wound up." He briefed a glance over our group.

My heart raced with the anticipation that he might recognize me, but he glanced over me as an insignificant subordinate and carried on his merry way.

"A handsome young boy, but far too energetic for my liking," Tracey remarked as he left. Anita didn't comment.

The gold-rimmed wooden doors leading into the central circular room were darker than the rest. My irritated skin was appreciative to finally catch a break from the days of walking in patches of daylight. Even with my heart, the natural irritations and uneasiness of my vampire self remained. Chase and I had even tested the effects of silver, which still prominently burned and weakened me.

The great room was housed with columns and gold rimming, even the inside harbored gray gargoyles, very primitive in contrast to the marble of the flooring. The domed roof was plastered in gold, creating a pristine reflection. I caught sight of myself, a handsome man with harsh cutting features and green eyes. If we were anywhere else, I might've admired the handy work of Lincon's gift. I was handsome.

He was smiling in my direction as if noticing my startled expression. In the center was a large round table with twelve chairs. Only one other leader had entered the room. The silent vampire was seated at the table and looked up from his book, his eyes were a milky white. Blind perhaps? But yet he read a book. I realized then his finger was trailing along raised bumps on the pages. I'd never seen anything like it before. He looked to be in his sixties. He briefed a glance our way before looking back down, engrossed in his book. He was tidily dressed, as were the seven behind him who looked more like scholars than fighters.

Anita and Tracey didn't offer him much attention. If by description alone, I believed this to be Antonio, who was another Tracey said we didn't have to concern ourselves with. Apparently, of all the Councils, she said that his was the meekest and would fall away from a fight as quickly as a newborn vamp were to pounce on a pint of blood. In her words specifically.

Iris pulled out a chair for Tracey, he'd purposely positioned her closest to one of the three doors in the room. I had no doubt this was so she was closest to an escape route. She idly thanked him and then waved her hand dismissing the others. Only Iris and I were to remain standing behind her, shoulder to shoulder, stiff as the soldiers we were. I glanced around the room. Connor and Lincon had positioned themselves adjacent to me and closest to a door. Balzar was directly behind me, standing against the wall. Soon this room would encompass the most powerful vampires who'd lived and terrorized humanity for hundreds of years. And I was shadowing one who casually chatted as if she had no hand to play in the devastation that was about to come.

Chapter 40

THE ROOM BEGAN to swarm with all kinds of members. Some with eccentric taste in fashion, others looking more barbaric, while some looked as if they'd been taken out of a sophisticated society and placed here just so they could openly sneer at one another. These were the groups of the powerful twelve who ran the Vampire Council, coming from all parts of the world.

I hadn't expected them to be so versatile nor did I suspect them to be so unfriendly toward one another. Despite the rules that housed them and the treaty they'd originated those many years ago, it was rather apparent that many of them in the room were sizing one another up in powerful displays. I was certain the only reason they hadn't attacked one another, even outside this meeting was because of Oppollo's loose reign that he would try to fortify today—he who hadn't yet arrived. All but one seat had been taken, and many of them spoke ill of the tardiness. Though I imagined none would be daring enough to say it to his face.

There was no indicator of sunset or time in here, but surely it was already nightfall. I was on edge for every second that ticked by, my hands itching to grab hold of the sword sheathed on my back, just so I felt comforted. Every second was unnerving with ample opportunity for someone to see through our illusion and attack us. I couldn't sense Chase or the others. I would sometimes share a brief glance with the others, as they waited for my signal as to when Chase would reach out to me, letting me know they were in position.

"Ye fiddled with one of me' boys, Tracey?" Smith crooned across the table. He was bald with a few piercings in his face. He wore a bright purple suit as if it was the best attire he had in his grasp.

Tracey rolled her eyes. "If one of your men is so bold as to threaten and also think he could bed me, then yes I gave him what *I* would consider as delightful pleasure."

"It was probably an improvement if it was someone from your Council," another vampire sneered as he looked across the room at Tracey, with a transparent 'I want to fuck you' gaze.

"Ye think this is funny, Yuri?" Smith jumped out of his chair. Yuri didn't flinch, but the members of his seven did. As did Smith's.

"Gentlemen," Fier said, clapping his hands. "Are we not on mutual territory? "Come now, shouldn't we be displaying comradery?"

"Ye can go fuck yeself." Smith threw a hand toward Fier. A whistle of wind blew through the room, displaying Fier's lack of control and a mild threat. "Ye come in as a young blazer wanting to dominate. Ye be long dead before the day ye ever take charge."

"At least I can pronounce *you* because I'm not missing all of my teeth, you disgusting bottom scrape of vermin," Fier articulated ghastly. Tracey arched an eyebrow and nodded as if to agree with his comment. She evidently didn't mind the drama of the meetings.

"I suggest everyone takes their seat if they don't wish to embarrass themselves before Oppollo arrives," Antonio said in a raspy voice. He didn't look up from his book.

"How nice of you to join us for once," Yuri chided, finding a more comfortable position. As if Antoni could sense the oncoming presence, a chill swept through the air. A phantom-like mist materialized across the table from me, and the silhouette of a sturdy figure and face appeared.

A group of seven robed and masked figures stalked into the room. They'd been so silent I hadn't noticed them treading through the hall or opening the door. *Oppollo.* There were no real features to his face or body, it kept shifting in the slightest as he hadn't fully materialized.

Everyone silenced and dropped into their seats. "How pitiful," his voice chastised. "Nothing more than spoiled brats wasting time." No one spoke. My power flexed, wanting to peel across the table and strike him. Could my gift even work on him if he wasn't a physical being? There was a moment, small and brief, that his body seemed to stagnant into the physical. Though it wasn't enough time to make out any physical features, I decided to count between the next shift. If there was a pattern, perhaps I could use it to my advantage.

"Hmmm," he crooned as he looked past Tracey's shoulder and at me. I froze. Did he know? Could he see past Lincon's illusion? "Many new faces." He looked around the room not only at our members but at the greater group. I internally sagged with relief. *Six. Seven. Eight.* His body materialized again for a split second before vaporizing. Each of his seven assassins scattered amongst the room, standing between every second Council. Council leaders shifted uncomfortably, with the targets now at their backs. One stood directly behind me and beside Balzar. He didn't flinch, but I didn't appreciate the close proximity either.

Another stood beside Connor across the room. I had the sneaking suspicion Lincon would be terrorizing himself internally, feeling left out that he didn't have one so close to him to kill when things would go boom. The room was silent and cold. No one dared speak. *Six. Seven. Eight.* Again, he flickered into materialization. I wondered if anyone else had noticed the tick in his power, the tell of what possibly made him vulnerable. The last time I'd encountered him, I hadn't the chance to find a weakness, but now as we stood here, across from one another with him unaware, I had found an advantage.

"It has come to my attention that the covens have been rallying activity more so than usual. It's also come to my awareness that they've been posing as members of my Council by wearing robes and masks. It's disconcerting that their activities have been of course happening in many of your territories. Do your Councils lack in such security that anyone can run amidst nowadays?"

"In all fairness, Oppollo, and I mean no disrespect when I say this, but how are we to know the difference between ye group and theirs by deciphering between hoods and masks," Smith boldly asked. "If we were to openly attack and have that wrong …"

"Perhaps it wouldn't be such an issue if you had already dealt with your coven situation, Smith, instead of now staring at me like a fool. I thought when I built this Council I'd employed intelligent beings. And yet here we are. The only two who have properly cleared their territories are Anita and Antonio. That then leads me to question if the rest of the

Council have slackened? Have you forgotten the duty that binds you because of your own personal desires?"

"Ah, Oppollo, if I may," Fier said, raising his hand casually. "I have significantly cleared the covens and the Hunter Guild which pestered my father's reign. The San Francisco area is mostly cleared of any tyranny or implications."

"Boy, you've only recently been rid of a Hunter Guild because one of your members took in a hunter to be housed under your roof without your knowledge, and you were blessed with the opportunity to follow them back to their Guild like a guided path of breadcrumbs. And even then, you called forth the ill disgrace of sabers to take out their inhabitants instead of using your own people and might. Do you truly think that Guild is vanquished relying on such cheap tricks, or would you say they've simply relocated?" Oppollo ranted layers of Fier's inadequacy. "Your Council is riddled with spies, and even when you thought yourself clever enough to tip me off about Cesar's coven, who I've been hunting down for years, your failings come short once again with only a handful of his members, all because you had a personal grudge against two because they outsmarted and embarrassed you by infiltrating your Council. You brought me to a child's fight." Conveniently, he left out the part where I'd bested him in that *child's fight*. "So, I think it's best you remain silent prior to puffing your chest any higher. You have made no achievement, on the contrary, I find your reign lacking."

Fier ground his teeth, trying his best to hide his fangs so as not to be taken in a threatening manner.

"I'm so baffled by the lack of integrity, and yet you all walk around with so much pride. The humans are still out there not fully at our disposal to be farmed. The covens still conspire against us because they have not yet been vanquished. The hunters still parade as if they seemingly still have a chance to restore humanity as it once was, causing more damage than I'd like to hear of in particular Councils." A few vampires dipped their gaze, guilty. I found some satisfaction with the knowledge that we pestered them in such a way. "And recently it's come to my attention that the *humans,"* he seethed their species, "have had such lucrative time that they've created a subspecies of wolves to attack our kind. Now tell me," his hand slapped on the table as physically as any power. The force of it blew frosty air up at everyone, pushing back their hair, "does that sound like territories are being dealt with? Hmm?

Anyone?" No one dared answer back, and only half the room was willing to meet his gaze.

He peeled away his hand from the circular wooden table. A handprint was left indented in the surface as if it was melted silver bending to his will. *Six. Seven. Eight.* There it was, a smidge of time where he materialized. Every eight seconds, I began to pulse a small wave of anticipation to Lincon, Connor, and Balzar, hoping they'd pick up on the transition, the more of us who knew the better.

Esmore? A wave of relief washed over me as I anchored myself to Chase's familiar voice. I stroked the essence of him, so comforted to hear his voice after so long. *Are you okay?*

Yes, they're all in here. Where are you? He grew silent for a moment. I watched the room carefully as I tried to focus on my conversation with Chase. Why had he gone quiet?

Sorry, we're falling into place. The groups of vampires out here from each Council are scattered. We're identifying groups so we can separate to match whose gifts will work best. Can you stall time?

Stalling time wasn't so much in my control. It was the matter of when I would interrupt to strike. This meeting was either going to be a very long one or very brief depending on Oppollo's mood as he drew the room's attention. What I found oddly disconcerting was Oppollo's mannerism to control a room much reminded me of Cesar's. He might've despised him, but he'd certainly adopted characteristics from his maker.

I hadn't sent the others the signal yet. I was to only send them a wave of alert when the others were in position, and I was about to attack. I waved my mind over theirs. They were on high alert, but Balzar seemed the most on edge, undoubtedly because he would be the first to face one of Oppollo's assassins.

"This brings me to believe that I have no choice but to micromanage your Councils. I gave you ample time, four hundred years to be precise, and yet it seems all for nothing. So, I'll offer you one more chance, a minor favor if you would consider it.

I give you all three months to be rid of all covens, hunters, human governments, and these mongrel mutts in your territory."

Smith's head jarred upward, unable to control his obvious frustration.

"And what will happen to those who do not complete this task within the given timeframe, or disagree with this ruling faction?" Anita asked coolly. There was no lingering impression that she was going to defy

Oppollo, but she was the only one bold enough to question it. Probably because she had no fear of the punishment when she'd already cleared her region.

"They'll find themselves in unfavorable circumstances, for those who fail will stand down as leaders. They will be exiled, shamed, and turned away from the safety of any Council." Meaning they would have no place to go and be hunted down by their own kind.

We're in position. We've circled the area. Send Tythian an image of the room you're in, Chase instructed. I scanned for Tythian distastefully, pushing past the knowledge of Cesar and my mother's concealment in effect. It was only because I'd made previous transactions with Tythian's mind that I located him in the near distance. Reluctantly, I mentally tapped on his mind. And just as disgruntled, he opened it a fraction so I could share with him the image of this place so he would know where to teleport into. The moment I pushed it into his mind, he closed off to me so fast that a pang of pain vibrated through me from whiplash.

Oppollo has a tick, I began to report to Chase. *Every eight seconds—*

"Well, ye are sure of yeself aren't ye, Oppollo. But my Council don't agree to ye terms," Smith purred, showing off his ghastly fangs, and a swell of power resided within him. A blinding light and implosion erupted in the room as a powerful gift exploded in the center of the table, and everything around us combusted to rubble.

CHAPTER 41

S MITH WAS ONE of the handful Tracey had insisted would vouch for Oppollo. But it appeared either she had lied or the thought of power and domination pulled Smith into a delusion of crazy intent. Everyone snapped into commotion seconds before the explosion. The gifted vampires within the room had noticed the threat prior to its combustion, only a few were caught in the explosion, but no one had died from it.

Iris and I dragged Tracey to the floor, a heated singe on our backs as the blast ignited the room. The thick wooden table seemed to take the majority of the impact, and with dramatic flair, it splintered across the room, scattering pieces of wood. An arousal of blood began to stir in the room from quick healing injuries. Three of Anita's assistants had thrown themselves over her, taking the brunt of the explosion. One of them was forced to reef out a piece of wood anchored in her eye, with a low grunt.

The vampires here were some of the oldest, pain had become second nature to them in all the battles and victories they'd survived. Iris and I looked around, eyes blinking as we adjusted from the dotted spots to the chaos that was now erupting in the room. Tracey was fine as she snarled and rose to her feet like a true warrior not letting herself be kept on her back for too long.

I turned to find Balzar awkwardly pinned to the wall, a piece of wood protruding from his shoulder. One-handed, he was trying to pull it out with disgruntled moans of irritation. With lightning speed, I aided him, yanking it out with no warning. His thick black blood trailed the wall. Had it been under other situations, I might've taunted him for being too slow.

Chaos erupted around us, the lightning blast only a distraction as Smith's group roared into action in an attempt to pile onto Oppollo. They didn't even come close as his well-trained cloaked assassins siphoned them off one by one. Oppollo strangled Smith by the throat, raising him above the ground in front of everyone in a display.

A flurry of activity began to stir outside. *No, no, no,* I interjected into Chase's mind. *That wasn't my signal.* But I could sense it was already too late. The explosion had broken parts of the wall, a possible collapse in its wake as sections of the room began to crumble in chunks.

"Let this be an early example," Oppollo said over the top of Smith's spiel of hateful words. Vampires of Smith's Council erupted into the room. Their signal had been given, but it was too late for their leader. With little remorse, Oppollo dove his hand into Smith's chest and reefed out his black unbeating heart. His body sagged into a slump of decay as his members came in with weapons foolishly raised just as quickly being taken out by his members. They never stood a chance. Oppollo looked our way.

My heart stopped, this was my only chance. "It would appear we have some intruders," he purred. I whipped my power out toward him, lashing at him, but he vaporized into nothing in the same manner he entered. The wall behind where he once stood exploded and turned to ash. The roof and building let out an eerie cry as it began to concave. I searched for Oppollo, waiting for the moment he'd manifest in the room if he hadn't already left, but Balzar grabbed hold of my arm. "We need to get out."

Tythian teleported in, long enough for others to see him and begin to sense the commotion that had erupted outside. Indefinitely, Fier's gaze found us across the room with one eyebrow arched as a smug smile began to curve at his lips. Did he really think all of this was happening because he'd expected me to do so?

Darkness flooded as Tythian teleported us out into the cool fresh air of night. Atop the hilltop and one of our many positionings, sabers flooded from the density of the trees sliding down the hills and toward the building I'd just been standing in. Deemori was instructing them silently to advance and take out all vampires who opposed us.

The building we'd once been standing in concaved with the sound of scraping and crashing metal and glass. Vampires piled out of it as they sprung into action the moment they realized they were surrounded. Some of their Council groups were on the outskirts, fighting off the sabers before they crept closer toward the building, or their leaders. It was an all-out war, pockets of fights happening atop every hill, the moon hiding behind clouds as if fearful of illuminating the gruesome bloodshed that was now in action.

The sabers were the first wave. We were next. I could sense Cesar and my mother across from us, so far and yet so close to the commotion. Lincon and Connor were in position on my left with Cesar's elite. And on the right, Yolo and Balzar led the partial second half of Cesar's coven. Sporadically, and in smaller doses were the covens that Cesar had aligned with. Many others would be attacking the majority of the Councils' home bases as Cesar had orchestrated. The Council vampires spilled out in masses. By the looks of it, most had brought the majority of their group whereas, some like Anita, only brought a handful to fight their way out.

"Esmore," Chase said, exasperated, and grabbed me. He pulled me in for a tight hug. I desperately clung to him as I watched the escalation of Cesar's plan. Fire was by his side, growling at the commotion below. Jerimiah, Clarissa, Spungee, and Darcy were at the forefront of his coven, impatiently waiting behind. They were geared in various weapons, and I found a newfound beauty and appreciation as I admired them briefly. On this night and with the lack of light, they looked like death demons. No matter their eye color, they all seemed to dilute into a dark menacing glare as they waited for their signal.

"Chase, I don't know where Oppollo went," I warned Chase in way of greeting as he bundled me.

"You don't have to look too far," a voice appeared out of nowhere behind us. Chase shoved me out of the way as Oppollo materialized between us. Fire leaped for him, but he mystified once again. She dove straight through the spot where he once stood. Chase's coven was geared to fight and then startled as he vanished into nothing.

Chase was at arm's length, but I warily listened out as a wind rustled between us, trying to catch the glimmer of Oppollo.

"And here I thought you were dead," Oppollo's voice echoed. "The beloved daughter of Cesar. I had fantasized about this day in numerous ways and concluded I would face him first, out of personal begrudging more than anything. And yet here I am, sniffing out a rat that was presumed to be dead." His voice was everywhere at once. I tried tracking it, and a flicker of white caught my gaze. *One. Two. Three.* I began to count his tick, and I could sense Chase doing the same. He was taunting us, hovering about to let fear and anxiety creep in.

The moment his tick appeared—and too close to Chase for my liking—I could sense Chase throw a mental hurdle of shock as he sliced his blade through Oppollo's stomach. At the same time, I lashed my gift out, and its precision chewed away at much of Oppollo's arm before he evaporated. I felt my power drop as if the prey it'd caught had freed itself. But the ash remained, splintering toward the battlefield below. We'd finally landed a hit.

Black blood dropped onto the ground from where Chase had sliced him. If it hadn't been for the tick, we might've thought killing Oppollo impossible, but now I realized he was just as killable as any other. Though his wound would heal within seconds, it didn't stop the black blood from giving his position away. Even then, we couldn't physically harm him until that tick reappeared.

After the wound, Oppollo wasn't messing with us anymore, his predatory intent could be felt in the air. With an unnerving sense, I could feel him approach Chase again. I called upon the Descendant and cannonballed myself toward Chase and Fire to knock them out of the way. When they hit the ground, I looked over my shoulder, only the remains of a hand and sword flickering to attention for a mere second could be seen. *One. Two. Three.*

Chase was guarding my back as a robed assassin plunged down a dagger, aiming between my shoulder blades. With grace, he flicked away the man's strength and punctured his sword through his heart. My heart pounded as I noticed all the black robes descend upon us. The hill below was scattered with shriveled black goop and the remains of sabers. They'd already fought through the first wave to reach their master's side.

"Together!" Chase yelled to his coven as they waited for his command. "Let's not wait for the dead!" he roared, confronting another assassin. Fire was guarding my back as my wings shuffled uncomfortably. I could sense Oppollo with an eeriness as if being followed by a predator.

Seven. Eight. I lashed my gift out in the place I was certain he'd be. Only a splinter of ash came from him, and I didn't even know what part.

"An interesting gift you have there, girl," he purred with amusement.

Chase's coven erupted in some wild barbaric scream, hisses, and snarls curving out unnaturally. For all their waiting and all the tension and build-up of being locked in one place, it felt as if it all came down to this moment. The others had already begun to descend into the arrays of Councils that fought through the sabers to get to them. There was only one way out, and that was through us.

An assassin lunged for me, his movement hard to track, but my gift worked of its own accord, reaching out for the figure in an outlandish lash. The figure exploded into ash, cloaking the next who came in behind him. My sword grazed along theirs as I quickly assessed Chase's position. He was fending off two.

I lashed my gift against my adversary, but nothing happened. I tried again, but I could feel the robust wall it splattered against. Whatever his gift was, he was one of few who could counter mine. He shoved me off, taking the moment to strike downward on my chest. I could feel the breeze from it, barely missing. He had me on the defense, and my vampire self erupted savagely as I tried to get closer to Chase and guard his back. And I could feel him doing the same.

My gift sprung out on my left as the invisible presence of Oppollo appeared. My gift silhouetted my side like a preventative shield, acting of its own accord. The blade he'd tried to use on me evaporated into ash. One of the gargoyles attempted to strike him but fell through air where he once stood. They were raised, their feet not able to touch the ground as Oppollo lifted them. They shifted into their gargoyle form and a crack formed in their neck where Oppollo must've tried to behead them.

The assassin jumped on me, my momentary focus on Oppollo compromising my position, but Fire bit his ankle, dragging him back. When he spun to dip his sword into her back, she released and backed away. The hand that'd been holding the sword was sliced off by Chase who appeared behind him, black blood splattered on his face. I kicked the assassin's chest as he tried to swivel out of our trap. Chase speared his sword through from back to front.

On instinct, I lashed out my power to Chase's side, flecks of his hair breaking into ash as I apprehended Oppollo trying for Chase once again.

An array of arrows shot at us from the side, I raised my other hand leading my power like a great wall to eat away at them.

I was working on reflex as we fought through the masses of mixed Councils and assassins fighting through our numbers. I was divided in gifts and magnitude of who was controlling my body as each power had its own temperament, and slowly my hold between my vampire and my recent gift as huntress became unassociated.

Thunder rolled over the hills, a tell that Iris was trying to get Tracey out of the fight. The ground shook from all magnitudes of power being confined to this one battlefield. My gift became an avalanche of walls as it acted on its own accord as Oppollo struck at me from different angles. I couldn't keep up with his pace as my gift worked on impulse in a way it had never done so before, ensuring he couldn't reach me. I would look this way, and then he would strike behind. I was scattered on the offense, trying to keep up with him.

A blast of wind struck at my back, and most of us were thrown forward, both ally and foe. Chase caught me, and we rolled into the gravel together. I arched up over him, my great wings wrapping around us like a shield as I made eye contact with Fier. *Traitor. Of course, he'd feign to support Oppollo.*

Chase rolled me over as another striking wind blasted in a thin line toward where we once laid. It wiped out another handful of vampires.

Another blast on my side as my gift erected a wall against Oppollo. This time it wasn't ashing away, it was solidifying as if hard sand. Chase punched through my wall reaching for the pressing presence beyond with a savage snarl. But nothing was there. Another great wind hurled toward us this time landscaping. I collected Chase, extending my wings into the air and using the Descendant's strength to raise us. A sharp stab pierced into my lower half as my huntress gift was too slow to block the attack.

"Not impossible," Oppollo's voice sneered from his countless attempts that failed. My gut twisted as Chase's knowing stormy gray eyes realized what'd happened.

"Esmore!" I could still feel the blade in my lower back, twisting the balance of my spine. Oppollo tried to strike again, but this time I was focused on him, my mistake being distracted before. My gift shrouded Chase and me in an ash-like barrier. I was finding out more about my gift on the battlefield than in my weeks of training.

I'm okay. I could feel my gift eating away at the blade in my back, the remains of its particles evaporating into nothing so my wound could begin to heal. Another wave of wind washed over us, pushing me and my wings back as I struggled against its force. With the added weight of Chase, I buckled and dropped toward the ground. I pulled my wings up strong, trying my best to control the defense. Chase was first to roll on the ground as I released him. When I hit the ground, my right knee dropped. My wound wasn't fully healed. I quickly shoved my fingers into the sachet at my hip, dipping into my golden claws.

Already a vampire pounced for me. I could feel Chase covering my back as members surrounded us. Obviously, we'd become a priority. I didn't know whose Council the first vampire attacked me came from, but it made no difference. I wanted cold, wet blood on my hands. The thrill of it antagonized my vampire like never before. So many to conquer and kill, losing sight of all else. My body thrummed for it.

I skirted to my left, knocking the vampire's arm away. My wing swept up as I grabbed hold of his wrist. It shattered his shoulder and arm, his hand opening to free the blade. Chase caught it, piercing the blade through his chest and slicing it across the next vampire's throat who tried to attack him from behind. A spray of blood infringed on my wings as I dodged the next vampire easily. They were distracted by the span of my wings, and I drove my hand in through their stomach, shoving up as their ribs clawed at my arm from the inside. I clamped down on their heart and pulled it out with satisfaction as they heaped into a pile of black mush.

I couldn't help but glide my tongue along the taste of their death, disgusted by its tang. But I was too excited by the sheer satisfaction of knowing I could play with all of them. I took another step, only a slight hobble now as my wound in my lower back had almost completely healed.

My link with Chase had never been more in unison, the sheer focus on his face arousing me as we attuned to one another, enjoying this vampire dance. He was like darkness sweeping through them, masses of corpses and decay lay in his wake. An utter badass and he was all *mine.*

Dodging these vampires now seemed indefinitely easy as I let the vampire and beast take control and I purred with delight at its rising reign and arousal. My heart thrummed with excitement, knowing that if any one of them pierced my chest, I could die. The stakes were high, and I wanted to play.

I curled my nails under the jaw of one vampire, folding in my hand to crush his jaw as I threw him over my shoulder face first. My hands were slippery with black blood as I slashed across the face of another, so deep that they cried as one of their eyes splashed across the ground and was stomped on by another who attacked me, though they hesitated as one after another they fell.

I lashed out my gift, an excessive explosion of ash blowing up as the figure incinerated. I began to laugh. This was child's play. I lashed out at another, a blow of ash wiping to the surface. Three daggers were thrown my way, although I could've incinerated them, I decided to neatly catch them one by one with a wicked smile as I anticipated lightning speed itself. The daggers were beautiful, and I could imagine no better spectacle than them stapling into three different skulls. The thought of the sound delighted me so, making my toes curl in anticipation.

I pegged two, hitting my targets. As the third slipped from my fingers, a sharp slice cut into my neck daring to harbor all the way through. Before I knew it, a powerful implosion of crystal ice cloaked and supported the second half of my throat as I gurgled on my own blood, unable to breathe. *What?* Confusion stunned me for a moment as my body slumped back. I fell into Chase's arms, all noise had vanished as I saw the gargoyles break through the vampires with Jerimiah and Darcy's lead.

The iced crystal that kept my head attached to my body, but barely, was connected through a thin iced thread that embedded Cesar's foot to the ground. My eyebrows wrinkled in confusion as the mist of where Oppollo once hovered over me vanished.

I'd become so preoccupied in my bloodlust that I'd forgotten to keep an eye out for his presence—and he'd almost beheaded me. My mother fought through to my side as noise of clashing weapons and breaking bone vacuumed into existence around me. My body was slowly trying to heal, but not fast enough as my mother came to my aid. I gurgled on my own blood, still stunned by what had happened. Everything seemed to slow down as my life faded in and out with Chase's forceful hand keeping me to this world.

Cesar was stuck to his position, and I could hear the wild cackle of Oppollo as he circled us. My mother's gift swept through me like liquid as it began to sew me back together.

Esmore, I could feel the tiny flicker of my link with Chase breaking in and out as the sudden realization that I could die on this battlefield came to fruition. Another spark of lightning erupted across the sky as it shook beneath us. Elements that should only be harnessed by nature were erupting around us chaotically as the sharp smell of blood fermented the air. I realized shockingly that was my blood.

I tried to raise my hand to Chase's cheek so I could wipe away some of the blood that marred his otherwise beautiful face, wanting to remember him in another light. But I had no strength as if it had been sapped from me. My sudden bloodlust swallowed whole as my vampire realized it'd gambled our very lives. Yet there was no regret, if only because I might be leaving him. I couldn't move even if I chose to, that crystalized ice holding my right side into position.

Chase, my thought was a mere whisper as I tried to hold onto that link, too scared to yet peak into the darkness that was hovering. He was on the other side, grabbing for me, holding on tightly so I couldn't go anywhere.

"Your ideal of family has always made you weak, Cesar," Oppollo announced, though it sounded sheepish in all its forms. I let my eyes roll so I could see from my peripheral as Oppollo manifested smugly and approached Cesar who was trapped with his entire leg in crystalized ice. I tried to call out to him, to warn the others, but felt the wet bubble of my blood choke out of me. In the distance, Fire ran, leading Balzar and Yolo toward us.

They were blown away in a blast of wind as Fier announced himself once again, many of Chase's coven behind him unflinching on the ground.

I slammed a wave of panic into my mother, only giving her enough time to turn and witness as Cesar raised his sword and began to fight for his life. But it was already too late as Oppollo vanished into mist. I choked with an attempt to raise my hand to lash my gift out to strike Oppollo. But it wasn't in time with his tick. And it was already too late.

CHAPTER 42

M Y MOTHER SCREAMED, the sound defiling my ears. I'd never heard my mother scream. But she twisted her gaze, panicked as she reapplied her focus on reattaching the remains of my neck. Behind her, Cesar transcended into black goop, concaving over the crystal ice that still didn't break. I watched despairingly as I realized he'd given his life for mine. I'd despised him for so much, and yet I felt a tear glide down my cheek at his sacrifice and the truth of his care.

My mind churned into despair as a harsh and brazen presence crept up on me, the link threading between Chase and I turning into a violent torpedo—Chase was turning. I shifted my gaze, willing my mother's craft to work sooner so I could reach out and pull him back to me. But it was already too late, I felt the turn and revolt of his mind. Powerful black wings sprouted from his back as he snarled, and my mother was forced to dip back.

Chase, I weakly tried to call to him, but it was a calamity of lost space and prickly vines. Jerimiah stuck his sword between us, fending Chase off so he wouldn't attack my mother and me. Instead of turning on his gargoyle allies, he shot for the sky.

Balzar and Yolo screamed in painful rage as they reached where Cesar had last stood. They struck out blindly as dread filled my core and I realized Oppollo would kill them next. For what felt like the first time, I took in a huge affirmative breath and then recoiled as I tried to cough up more blood.

Tears streamed down my mother's cheeks as she continued the last of her gifts threading, reviving me where I should've fallen. She could've tried to intervene against Oppollo, but instead, as she'd promised, both Cesar's and her aim were to protect me. Nothing I could do would make amends for my life being traded with Cesar's, but if I could only avenge him and finally be rid of Oppollo as promised, maybe that would take away some of my mother's pain, and my guilt. My gaze fixated on the tick of manifestation I might see from Oppollo.

Chase's figure descended from the sky once again, dropping to meet with where I calculated Oppollo might be. It was nothing but blind instinct that drove Chase as he dove headfirst toward the ground. Balzar and Yolo bounced back toward us, breaking away from the ground imploding beneath them by the sheer force of Chase's strength.

My wings wanted to take flight, as if his power and twin gift was calling to me, imagining we should take to the sky together. To fight together. I could feel his mind spiraling into madness as he tried his hardest to focus on only Oppollo. But even that was slipping, and soon, those thorny bushes would pull apart the link we shared, breaking me away from his thoughts once again.

Meekly, my body pumped with life, my mouth still full and tasting of my own blood. I took a rattling breath as my mother subsided all injuries. I felt so weak and lethargic, but I had to muster the strength to end this, once and for all.

I ambushed my mother's mind with the encouragement of sufficient force to shove her back. There was enough distance between us as I sharpened my gift to eat away at the crystal ice that acted as a brace only moments ago. As soon as I was freed from it, I rose, my wings rolling ensuring they were still functional.

Chase, I tried to reach out to him, but he was already too far gone. He dodged, his wings flattening low, but a trickle of blood still appeared across his cheek before healing. Oppollo was taking him seriously. Fire was by my side now, inspecting my weak frame. I dismissed her when I saw Anita and Fier come into view. At first, I considered the way they looked at one another, that they might take this opportunity to disembowel each other, but instead they turned their two separate Councils who followed them toward us. Despite Anita's lack of members, the women I'd seen earlier in the day were still alive. *Superior warriors*, I considered. But I didn't have time to entertain them, my priority laid elsewhere.

"We can handle this," Clarissa said, coming up my side, unnerved. "Help him. Bring him back to us." Her usual monotone had a little more urgency in it. Despite my prelude of Clarissa avoiding a fight because of Spungee, it seemed they had a mystified connection, much like Fire and I did, in the way they fought together. Jerimiah and Darcy flanked her as they squared off the new adversaries. If Anita was now here, I realized with certainty that it meant they'd broken through one of our lines. Where Anita and her Council might've been able to run, instead, they came looking for the fight.

Behind them was a massacre and mounds of thick sludge as vampires decayed over the terrain. There was more black sludge than green grass. Masses of vampires still fought, but there was definitely a silence from where the other covens had joined us. And there must've been many sacrifices for Cesar and my mother to make their way here.

I called to Chase, trying to coo him back to calmness, but it was hopeless. The moment I approached his mind, I was defiled and pricked by that thorny bush Fier tampered him with. That disease that at any time Fier could click his fingers and turn him into a saber or now even worse, Chase might spiral into that state of his own accord.

I'd become too reckless, thriving in the bloodlust and let my guard down. I didn't have time to think about what had just transpired and that I'd almost died. He was acting like a bird, swooping on prey, and it offered me a guide as to where Oppollo was positioned. I swept into the sky, much like Chase, but close enough to Oppollo where I could watch out for his tick. The moment I saw the flicker of his hand. I began to count.

Chase stop! I thought as he descended once again. Much like myself before, he wasn't thinking clearly. He was going to get himself killed. His timing was off, he wasn't thinking strategically anymore, and he'd leave himself wide open for Oppollo's attack.

I tsked, frustrated that I had to change course. Chase was and had always been my priority. Oppollo I'd have to deal with later. I swooped up toward Chase, colliding with him. Chase and I crashed in the sky like ravaging beasts. He clawed at me with blunt nails, striking me across the cheek as I tried to smash waves of calmness into him. We spiraled through the sky as we clung to one another.

Chase! I tried to reach him, coherently conscious that this was how he felt all those times reaching through to me, but I hadn't listened, and now … Chase's wings were larger than mine as he sprawled them out to try and tear out of my grip. He was so beautiful and deadly, and I was apologetic that he couldn't yet use it within his control. *I'm sorry to use cheap tricks, my love,* I flickered out a little of my power, only letting it eat away enough to damage his wing so he couldn't fly properly.

His body sagged with the uneven weight and I caught hold of him, my hands sliding down his arms from the mass of blood on them. "Chase, you're going to have to trust me," I gritted out as I tried to steady our descent. A figure appeared behind him as we fell. I lashed out my gift, protecting his back as the assassin tried to strike him. A startled scream cried out as ash flicked away pieces of her hand, and she vanished again. It had been the same presence that'd attacked me on the night we ambushed the hunters. *But who?*

Chase's grip firmed around my throat as I became distracted. Had it been any other time, I would've charmed a seductive and willing smile, but this time I knew he was only focused on the kill. I gripped his wrist, willing that my piercing nail would be enough to deter him, but it wasn't. The figure reappeared again, and this time, I slammed my wings to a halt as Chase and I defied gravity. It gave me enough of a glimpse to see a familiar face of someone who should've been dead. Blonde hair rippled in the air as she dropped away from us with an ugly snarl on her face— one with fangs and cruel, wicked eyes.

"Whitney?" I choked out, once again aware of Chase's imprisoning grip. She vanished. My thoughts fumbled. *Whitney was alive? Tythian's familiar was alive …*

Acute awareness struck me. I slammed a wave of alertness into Darcy and Jerimiah as they fought stoically against the many vampires that evenly matched us in numbers. I needed them to attend to Chase while I defeated Oppollo, and then I had a certain brother to confront. I tried to reach out to Chase once more, but his mind was completely cut off to me with those choking vines.

An avalanche of realizations dawned on me as I watched Tori and Dillian fight through the masses of numbers to reach our post. Lightening boomed like a stifling cry from the sky, and I could feel the sense of grief bolster from its direction. Iris ... which meant ... something had happened to Tracey.

Tracey's perfumed scent greeted me before the shadowy figure of Tythian. We'd been set up, and that meant Chase was more vulnerable than I'd ever known. *I'm sorry, my love,* I chided to Chase before letting the wisps of my power eat away at his hand, enough that he'd be forced to let go and plummet to the ground. Jerimiah and Darcy could contain him, and his hand would regenerate, but now I faced an all-new opponent that was ominously despicable. Tythian teleported as if trying to surprise me. But I could already smell the scent and blood of his last prey. Iris was mourning the loss of Tracey because Tythian had killed her.

Tythian appeared from nowhere on my left, freefalling as I did. He struck out daggers, each of which ashed into thin air as my gift defended me. And then a sword. He was throwing things at me as I dove for the ground adjacent to the direction I'd left Chase. I had to warn the others of his treachery. I wouldn't die up here, letting him get away with what he'd done.

All of it made sense now. A car appeared in the sky as it dropped over my head, groaning as the abnormal drop splintered off scrap pieces. I lashed my gift, taking satisfaction as it exploded, and held onto my breath as the remnants of its remains coated me. I twisted and landed as gracefully as a cat on the ground.

"You just won't die, will you?" Tythian's voice cooed over the wind. "The darling daughter of Cesar. Oh, so powerful, and now not so immortal." He was sneering as he teleported to stand across from me. He was admiring the dry blood along my throat longingly as if he'd wished the wound were fatal.

"Why?" Was all I could manage as I stalled time for the others to be within hearing range. I wanted them to hear his admission. My instinct hadn't been fraught. Jerimiah and Darcy had sprung into action, and now Balzar and Yolo were close enough to witness and hear the truth behind their brother's betrayal. "This whole time, the traitor was you."

"Not all," Tythian confessed. "But enough to keep you running rampant and spiraling your dearly beloved into mayhem."

"Tythian?" Yolo said, confused as he came into sight and overheard the last part.

Tythian stared at his brother, and then Balzar who followed. There was only a moment of grief before he caught my gaze again, ignoring them. That cool, calculating stare despising me openly. "I only ever wanted power, and Cesar had become stuck in his ways. He was so short-sighted and only wanted to be rid of Oppollo because he killed his mangy family hundreds of years ago. Why when he could gain so much more? And if he wouldn't then I would.

I thought he and Oppollo were my only challenge. But then I met Chase as I infiltrated and aligned with Fier. That Descendant holds more power than you'll ever realize, and if he learns to control it … to put simply that's a problem for me. And by using you as a token of this oncoming war, you who couldn't control your bloodlust, vengeance, and notion to protect everyone would see him come undone. You made it all too easy to distract away from anything I might've been concocting on the side."

"You bastard!" Balzar said without hesitation and flicked his sword, dismissing the amounted blood on it. He still wore his preferred knuckle spiked gloves which were just as bloody.

"I would stop there. I don't want to kill you, but I will," Tythian said, raising his hand. "You all followed Cesar so blindly. He was a losing power, but because we at one time shared comradery as brothers I offer you to join me, or I will let you walk away alive at least. But if you test me and become an obstacle, I will not think twice about removing you from my path."

"We would never join you!" Balzar seethed.

"Balzar," Yolo said quietly, trying to pull his brother back. They'd just witnessed Cesar's murder. Yolo feared losing another loved one today. Balzar was riled, his fangs snarling as he was twisted and torn from the betrayal and unexpected death of their leader and maker. In some ways, their father. *My father,* a small remorseful part of me considered. I'd now lost two. I couldn't lose anyone else … and if Chase was their primary target, Tythian would try to plow through me to get to him, especially while he was spiraling out of control.

I slammed another urge into Jerimiah and Darcy. I didn't want to depend on this plan, but if this was the only way I could assure his sanity and protection, then I would play the villain in this role. If Tythian was working with Fier, then this was all to their advantage and ploy while pretending to work with Oppollo. They were hoping to wipe out their competition during this war.

Whitney was alive, more specifically, a vampire. I'd watched her throat be slit in front of me, after being told she could never be turned because of the disease she'd endured after being experimented on by her brother within the Human Compound. But all of that had been a lie. From the very start when Fier slit her throat, it'd been for theatrics. All of this had been a set up from the start.

And that meant … the only other person who knew of Dillian, the hunter, and wolves' location before they'd been attacked was Tythian. Clarity engulfed me, transfused into an unsettling rage as I thought of Tori's recollection of there being two attackers that seemed to come out of thin air. Tythian and Whitney because if she'd been turned and they were familiars, she'd have the gift of teleportation too. Tythian had been with us, but plausibly he'd been with her for the first allotments of killings. Titan and Chris getting away was perhaps an oversite or lack of Whitney's ability to capture them. "You killed them!" I snarled as savagely unbound as I'd been when I'd almost been killed moments before.

I could no longer hesitate. I lashed my gift out at him, he teleported out. Another familiar presence crept upon me, this time Oppollo had reared his ugly head. I burst my wings into action, pulling me back hard. Balzar and Yolo were caught off guard as I heeded them to stay away.

An ambush of vampires crept our way, distracting me from my ability to focus purely on Oppollo. My hands itched to tear off each of their limbs, my impulse to savor in the bloodshed once again narrowing my sights. I painfully gripped onto the tranquility of my huntress self, keeping form and notion to stay in control so I wouldn't risk exposure like before.

My gift danced about me beautifully, lashing out at multiple vampires at once. I saw a flicker of Oppollo once again and began my count. *One.* He had killed my father. *Two.* He'd brought so much chaos and pain to our covens. I elbowed one of the vampires in the face, long enough to startle them as they took a step back. My gift billowed around them, eating away slowly in torture so I could hear his scream. *Three.* I'd never heard my mother scream like that before.

My power swelled within me, growing like vines that wanted to explode out of me. *Four.* This was a never-ending war if he survived. I let the gift consume me as it had, losing my grip of control. It felt wet and slippery as it slithered within me, bundling into its own maddening chaos. *Five.* I stood in one spot, no longer fighting, superiorly aware that no one could touch me as I was now. *Six.* My power was like an ominous purple haze seeping out of me, blossoming as it welled and I apathetically searched for the figure I would tear apart. *Seven.* I had to protect Chase, no matter the costs, and Oppollo was standing in my way. And then I would face Tythian with no remorse in the way I would strip away the flesh off his bones.

Eight. I let my power explode, eating away at the grassland as it transmuted with lightning speed and wrapped around Oppollo's millisecond of appearance, but it was enough. That second felt like a lifetime as I stared into the eyes of my prey, the struggle and surprise as he stood just before me, having been ready to strike the moment he thought I'd dropped my guard. My power ate away at him, filled with jittery compulsion to chew through him and continue further on. Past him and all this land because Oppollo was insignificant. A vampire who'd reached his time and pathetic reign.

He, who was once known as a phantom, erupted into a torturous death as I chewed out his life support as if I were gripping him with my very own hands. A calculating pleasure gripped me as I felt the power and feat. Flicks of ash rose from the ground and flicked in the air as if I'd torched him myself.

Oppollo's death wasn't all that had been caught in my wicked mass. Vampires surrounding me were eaten alive, and my gift only wanted to stretch further, to continue eating away at all this pathetic world had to offer. I glazed in the ideal of a new world, of banishing all those who lived in this and controlling the next.

I felt a yank on my line. Not that of Chase who mirrored my own undoing, a startling bark snapped me out of my maddening thoughts. Fire was reaching out to me, dancing along the lines of where my gift continued to sweep out as death itself. Others had begun running, both allies and foes as my power swept out of me like a cool branch decaying the land.

Her howl, a cry for help pulled at me again as she pondered along the border, not running so close as to be harmed but not running for safety as the others did either. I stared in her direction, my purple haze mesmerized by the beauty that unfolded. I was like a blossoming flower of death. And all of them deserved it.

Suddenly, a sharp pain dropped me to my knees as Connor's gift pierced into my mind like raking talons. I screamed and clutched my head, trying to will the infringement away. I blocked the pain from Chase so he couldn't harbor any of what I was dealing with. I only cared for him. I tried to push back on Connor, but my gift tired as it crawled back in, exhausted from its stretch that might've continued forever if I hadn't been stopped. It was like a cold snap back into reality.

The pain was lifted and replaced by a maniacal cackle. "I finally get to kill you!" Lincon purred delightedly as he advanced on Connor. I had no time to think, only enough exertion to jump back and away from Tythian who teleported to my side, thrusting his blade toward where I once cowered over myself.

Sabers erupted from the trees as Deemori desperately wielded them to take out anyone who came between her and Connor. Balzar and Yolo were forced to fend them off, once allies, now enemies. Lincon only rolled his eyes as sabers scattered around him, disarrayed by whatever malicious torture he was impending on them.

I could feel the link between Chase and I slowly disintegrate as the cool serum that Jerimiah and Darcy injected him with pulled him into a dormant sleep. My heart ached as I used such a cheap trick on him to use the syringe Yolo had given me. I grasped onto his thorny-like mind that began to detangle and recede as he was put to sleep. I reached out for him, the light of our link flickering as he slipped out of my grasp.

I'd made this request, and yet it didn't hurt any less as my familiar went cold and dormant, barely reachable. Tythian teleported out and then back to collect Connor. Whether Connor knew about Tythian's alliance or not, when he dropped from Lincon's clutches and reappeared at his side, finding sanity once again, I realized he'd stand by him. The sabers rounded, guarding them against the front as Deemori stood between us and them.

A divide in the siblings. Lincon sauntered up to me, coated in blood as his delicate fingers marred his jaw as if he were doing some bizarre face painting with the blood. "Well, isn't this an interesting turn of events?" I didn't want to wound Deemori, but she was in my way. As she stood by her familiar, I would stand to protect mine.

I lashed my gift out, stretching its bounds again, giving myself enough time to distract them as Jerimiah and Darcy fled with Chase. Sabers in a line toward where Tythian and Connor stood erupted into ash. Where Deemori had once stubbornly stood was also gone, but not by my gift dispelling her. Whitney had teleported in to save her.

A harrowing line of wind swept against us, knocking us back as Fier tentatively walked toward us. Whatever his personal battles, he looked as exhausted as the rest of us. We might've had the strength and stamina of monsters, but when pitted against one another, with every calculating blow, we were definitely going to be inflicted one way or another.

I could no longer lock on the location of Chase, Jerimiah and Darcy having taken him so far away as planned that not even I would be able to trace him, even though I knew exactly where they were taking him, as promised. I wouldn't go there until I was rid of Fier and Tythian. I would not be the one to lead them to his sanctuary where he would now be safe. A pang of guilt evoked me. I had betrayed Chase in every sense, and I shouldered the reality that he may never forgive me. But I had no regrets when this was the only way I could protect him. Even if I weren't to make it … he would. This way, I would be their only target.

Spurts of lightning postponed their advance as Iris's bulky form came into view in the distance who was indefinitely on a hunt for the murdered of his maker—Tythian.

"How could you do this to our family?!" Yolo called out to Tythian, upset more than the outrage Balzar openly displayed. For the first time, Connor seemed uncomfortable, and I suspected he hadn't known about any of this prior and perhaps there was more to be said. But he didn't deliberate or move from Tythian's side.

"Family is a weak notion," Fier called out for his partner in crime. "Power is the only thing to be respected in this world. At least one of Cesar's spawn was able to realize that," he said smugly. Tythian smacked away Fier's outstretched hand that dared to rest on his shoulder. Though they might've been in alliance, it didn't seem under friendly terms.

"Now my, little golden bird," Fier purred in his righteous tone with a smug smile. "I believe you have held up your bargain and disposed of Oppollo. I thank you for that. You've served your purpose, but I'm afraid I can't hold up my end of the deal." He raised his fingers. My heart lurched as he betrayed our deal. My gift slowly and exhaustedly jittered across the ground to implode him, but a gush of air seemed to hold my power back. He seemed smug as the definite click of his fingers seemed to echo.

I reached for Chase and our link, unable to feel the pulse of its life. It hadn't changed. Fier furrowed in confusion and clicked his fingers, and a wave of relief swept over me as I realized my plan had worked. Fier couldn't activate the disease in Chase's mind if Chase himself wasn't active. Neither living nor dead, a place in between. There was no brain activity for the disease to fester on, it lay dormant just as he did.

"My, my, ever the clever girl," Fier snarled with disdain. "What cheap trick did you muster?"

Another shot of lightning exploded beside them, and they teleported away. Fier was left on his own, though he held his ground, dodging it narrowly.

Everyone burst into action as Connor and Tythian reappeared, this time armed. In their way, Lincon, Balzar, and Yolo stood. A clear divide. A line in the sand.

Tythian flicked in and out from portal to portal. It was only on blind instinct that his brothers could match his sword that came down on them. Lincon charmed a wicked smile toward Connor. In a playful measure Lincon raised out his hands. "Shall we fight like men? No tricks or mind games?" It was a mockery toward Connor because he was already at a disadvantage, but Lincon like always, simply wanted to play.

Another gust of wind swarmed for me as I flew high, dodging it and swooping toward Fier as I let my gift sluggishly reach out to him. It was too slow, recharging from my uncontrolled expansion from before. If I'd had more time to train, if I'd learned how to control it properly, perhaps my limit wouldn't be so immediate.

Fier dodged my attack, not before another bolt of lightning crashed before him, throwing him off guard. Iris, with his oversized hatchet was playing monster's advocate as he swept it down over Fier. Whitney teleported in, grabbing him and then teleporting him out from the spot that might've been his grave. Iris snarled in frustration, turning his gaze toward Tythian who was still fighting his brothers.

Suddenly, a portal opened behind me, and a gush of air struck me in the back. I was harpooned toward the ground, spiraling as I thrust my wings so harshly that I barely hovered above the ground before dangling my feet to delicately touch it.

The chaos that was erupting around us was dwindling in figures as they killed one another off. Anita and her members were slicing through Chase's coven like they were easy prey. I locked eyes with Tythian and willed my power to strike him like a powerful force. His hand that held a sword and went to strike Fire as she snapped at him disintegrated into ash. I'd finally got him.

Time suspended as I struck him with the mental challenge of being shocked, pinning him into place. I thrust my gift out again, narrowing it to his core. Whitney teleported in, her face, hair, and flowery misplaced dress unmistakable. But instead of the warmth that was once in her delicate eyes, nothing but cool hatred and resolve remained. She teleported Tythian out before my attack reached. I snarled, stepping toward them. One second it was Tythian by himself, the next, they were gone. She reappeared behind Yolo with a twisted smile, looking over his shoulder as she smugly stared at Balzar and me.

We reacted the same, our voices not reaching Yolo in time. He didn't even have time to twist and fend her off. They might've been used to Tythian's presence and scent, blindly knowing where he might next appear, but Whitney's they were not.

A hideously sized dagger pierced through his back and through his chest. Blood dribbled down his front as he shifted into Jenn.

"YOLO!!!" Balzar screamed and fought viciously against the sabers that now bombarded him as he tried to fight through to his brother. I torpedo through them, my wings circling around me, focused only on reaching Yolo's side. Fire snapped and attacked the sabers that tried to jump on him.

I caught Jenn before she fell, perplexed by the blade that protruded through her chest but not close enough to the heart for the kill. I wrapped my hand around the handle of the blade, but she choked out a startling cry. "Stop!" Red blood erupted from her mouth. I was confused by the very human resemblance. Yolo was a vampire and bled rotten black blood. Not … this …

"Yolo, you need to shift back, this can be healed," I reasoned. I'd already thought I'd lost him once. I wasn't willing to let him go a second time.

"Please don't," she said as we dipped further to the ground, her head now on my knees with the blade awkwardly poking from her back. Fire took down sabers that advanced on us. My gift meekly revolved around us if any dared to get close enough. "Did you get Chase away safely?" Jenn asked, having caught onto my scheme. I was perplexed by the change in tone. If he would just let me pull this blade out, but I'd never seen Jenn's face look so at peace. Red seeped onto my leather pants.

I nodded, scared of his judgment for what I'd done, but realized he'd probably given me those syringes with such a thing in mind. I just had to figure it out for myself. Always two steps ahead.

I nodded. "Yes."

She nodded, satisfied with that answer. And it was a mingle of Yolo and Jenn's mannerisms as one. "Good, look after him. If I had the chance to do anything to protect Jenn, I would've. I've lived with that regret, and now I can finally be free and reunited with her."

"I don't understand. Change back, you can rejuvenate, Yolo!" I reached for the blade again, but she twisted awkwardly out of the way, more blood spluttering from her wound and mouth. It defied all logic.

A small smile pressed on Jenn's delicate face as blood oozed from her wound. "Esmore," she gasped. "I've lived over three hundred years. I'm tired. A life without her … has been meaningless no matter how hard I've tried to move on. I should've died to reunite with her a long time ago. And now I realize I can have that. *Finally*. I will not change back if this is the most human death I can endure."

I realized this had been why Yolo hesitated to defend himself against the werewolf within the Human Compound because if it had bitten him, he might've been able to die then as well. The mournful oppression was too relative to my own recent thoughts.

"This death is normal. And here you said you didn't like vampires." She tried to laugh, but more blood bubbled out. Her hand clutched at the wooden cross, the only thing Yolo kept of himself. "But I'm scared," she admitted. "I've been told vampires don't see the afterlife because we're all bad. Do you think I'll still get to see her, or I'll simply vanish?" She clutched to that wooden cross with desperation, with an old faith Yolo had once admitted he'd long abandoned. Now it seemed like everything to him. Balzar skirted and dropped to his knees, and I enabled the last of my strength to surround us like a blizzard so no one could intervene or hurt us. Any sabers who tried to plow through splintered into ashes. Fire nudged under my arm, her mouth mewed in sickening black blood.

I didn't know what I believed in when it came to the afterlife, but I lied convincingly, clutching my hand over his. "You'll see her. She's been waiting for you for the longest of times."

"Shift back!" Balzar roared, grabbing for the weapon and pulling at it. Balzar began pushing me out of the way, desperately clutching for his brother. "You said we were in this together, you liar!" The moment he pulled out the blade a tremendous amount of blood pooled out. "Shift back!" he cried angrily at Jenn who looked at him with sad eyes.

She raised her hand to her brother's cheek, the warm eyes a mix of hers and Yolo's expression as that cheesy grin appeared. "This is what I want, Balzar. If I choose any time, it's now."

"Don't leave me alone!" Balzar gritted out desperately, and tears pooled from his eyes as he rocked Jenn back and forth taking her from my lap. "You can't go too." Amongst all the death and treachery, Balzar only had Yolo left on his side and even he chose death.

I could sense the disappearance of the others, one by one being teleported out and leaving the sabers behind. The hundreds that remained now attacked not only the Council members on the battlefield but us as well.

"Bury me, please," Jenn said with a sad smile as her eyes scanned the sky above us into the night, and I hoped she saw some kind of light and peace in the afterlife. That Yolo would be reunited with his love, something he'd wished for hundreds of years, only made me yearn for Chase as he disappeared from my senses completely. The sabers only continued to grow in numbers, breaking out of the woodland, and I could hear Iris fighting them off alongside Chase's coven to get to us—to get to me. If only they'd known of the betrayal I'd laid before them and on their master, they wouldn't so desperately try to reach me.

"We have to get out of here," I said to Balzar, clutching onto his shoulder. He brushed me off placing his forehead to Jenn's. "Balzar, we're being overrun by sabers."

"Then I'll kill them all," Balzar savagely rasped. "I need to bury him."

I looked down at Jenn's hollowed eyes, all life devoid. One startling factor being that she didn't slump into the compost of black mush like a vampire, that somehow, Yolo had been granted his wish and died a human death. Looking at her still, I only wanted to slump further into mourning alongside Balzar. But as Yolo died for his love, I had to fight my way out so I could save mine.

"Be safe, Balzar," I said, lingering my hand for a moment longer before nuzzling my fingers through Fire's fur. "We need to retreat." I sucked my gift back in, not surprised that Lincon was cackling as he sliced through sabers with adamant joy. They weren't even kill shots, just anything that made his hands and skin filthy with blood.

"Where's Chase?" Clarissa came into view with only a few remaining members of the coven. The remains of the Council were cornering us. Though they'd taken a mighty hit and Oppollo had been killed, their numbers were still outweighing us. Both sides had taken losses today.

"He's safe," I growled out, not in the right temperament to deal with further questions.

"*Where?*" she tentatively asked, dipping her gaze to Jenn dismissively. A saber leaped for Spungee behind her. I lashed my gift out protecting him from the rear. I danced through a few of the sabers that crept closer to Balzar as he shuffled with Jenn's light weight over one shoulder.

"Esmore!" Tori glided through them just the same, all his training paying off as I found a settling proud moment for the apprentice. "They took him! Tythian took Dillian!"

"What?!" I snarled, watching the masses of Council members collide with the sabers now. Deemori was no longer here, and yet they still fought, the thirst so great as maddening beasts. They had once been humans, then vampires, and once their humanity had been lost, they turned into this.

"He went of his own accord," Tori gushed, confused. "They came to kill us. But Dillian insisted he go with them because Tythian was his creator. It gave me enough time to escape, but they still took him."

My eyes widened. Did he sacrifice himself or feel a form of allegiance with Tythian? Lightning struck at multiple sabers within our vicinity. I pushed my thoughts away only focusing on action. We needed to retreat before we were overrun or anyone could follow us. Our objective had changed, and now I had a new enemy to face. And while they were scattered and retreated themselves, I needed to do the same.

"We need to go," I told him, relieved when I saw my mother running toward us. We were slowly regrouping.

"You're retreating?" Iris irked over my shoulder.

"Tythian and the others have retreated. You should go too," I warned. I circled and tipped my blade toward his throat, armed and suspicious of his motives. If Tythian was gone, maybe he'd turn his weapon against us.

"I'll come with you," he asserted indifferently with the blade to his throat.

"It's invite only," I snarled, and in doing so Fire did the same, her hackles rising. His lightning struck from the sky, skirting along the edges and frying sabers one by one. Screams from vampires erupted as I realized he was killing off members of the Council.

"I can give you enough time for a distraction. But I'm coming. He killed Tracey. I will not rest until I have his head."

I made a rash decision. Iris was an asset and could be used in this very moment as we broke away from the war. If he became an issue later, then I'd deal with him personally.

I watched as Balzar retreated in his own direction, a few of Cesar's coven following him as he slaughtered through his enemies one-handed, with Jenn still over his shoulder. I wanted to be with him to bury Yolo like we'd done within the Hunter Guild to show our respects. But this was a battlefield, and the most I could do was make sure the others remained alive.

"*Where is he?*" Clarissa snarled once again. Tori poked his sword toward her, in warning not to step any closer.

"*Safe,*" I declared once again. "Retreat and regroup elsewhere, Clarissa. We go our separate ways here unless we're to meet again, and only, under Chase's order."

"You did something to him?!" she snarled, livelier than ever before. Fire snapped and snarled as she stepped forward. It was a far greater threat than Tori's blade. She didn't move, begrudgingly staring down at the wolf who could kill her with one bite.

"It's time," I said, briefing a glance over at my mother who was saturated in various elements and blood but otherwise unharmed. A jagged bite mark was festering on her shoulder but seemed to otherwise heal slowly.

I led my small group away, allowing Lincon to be the greatest distraction of all as he maliciously cut through the others, his wildest dreams coming true as he crazily slaughtered by the masses. I'd exhausted my gifts, and even my vampire counterpart felt tedious from the strain. My small group looked relinquished as they carried forth and I ensured we fled with one intent in mind.

We'd been betrayed. Oppollo was dead. Now I had a greater enemy and one that would target Chase until the end of time, but not if they couldn't find him, and not if I kept it that way. Though I wanted to check on him and ensure Jerimiah and Darcy upheld their end of the deal, I felt instinctively they had and that our plan had been a success. But a lurching coldness was in the core of my stomach, understanding it might be some time until I could free him. That I would have to regroup and kill Tythian and Fier before their reign became a problem. However, above all else, as long as their target was on my back and not Chase's, I felt contentment in knowing I'd evened the battlefield in some way.

So, I ran harder than ever before with the remains of my small group. Intent that I would free my love one day from the cold binds and sanctuary he bed in. Frozen in time until I could eradicate our enemies who so quickly tried to turn him into a monster where he could never return. Even if he hated me for it, I did what I thought was right, knowing that he would've died trying to protect me. And I took that right away from him, inducting myself as the protector instead.

Until death would we part. I would create an army to protect him.

EPILOGUE

T HE SWIRLS OF magic glittered around me in an array of colors, blinding me from making out anything in particular. I huffed in irritation, it had been the first night in weeks I'd actually attempted to get any rest and here it was, being defiled by that all paradoxical presence.

"Will you continue to hide behind your games, Kyran?" I asked with an edgy tone. I dipped my hand into the paint-like substance, the color rippling over me and splintering into plastered cracks revealing a long-ago abandoned room. It much reminded me of being back in the institute. Isolated and cold.

A small slow clap began as I felt his presence grow on me. "And here I thought we could play some more," a smooth voice edged. It was compelling as much as it was disconcerting. Purposeful slow steps came toward the jarred open door. A shadow fell over the opening. The creak of the door slowly edged open. I expected to see a monster or perhaps some vile-looking bunny rabbit. Instead, a handsome man with piercing blue eyes walked in. Striking in fact. Eyes that could transfix and consume anything that he desired. The world at his fingertips. A slow smile drew across his face. I realized in an instant, that Oppollo and Kyran might've originated from the same place, but they were two completely different monsters.

Oppollo wanted to conquer the world and its inhabitants. Whereas, Kyran would light the world on fire just to see what would happen.

He raised one delicate finger as if to shh me. "You're thinking about how handsome I am, aren't you? Or perhaps how stunning it might be to watch me paint this room with the blood of our enemies, or I could always fall short and use yours."

I had to push myself to speak, his presence saturating me with an unnerving submission. He was all-consuming and lethal. "I was just thinking about how uncanny the resemblance between you and Lincon is," I chided, trying to find sass and power. I wasn't the biggest monster in this room, and though this might be a dream, I dreaded that instead of his games and treating me as some mere toy, he would snap his fangs down on me, even in this dream and no trace of me would remain. That was the power he emanated.

"Ah, my dear son." He cocked his head as if listening out for him. Or something else. I wasn't sure. It was highly probable more than one conversation inhabited his mind. He was, as far as I'd been told, trapped in the bottom of the sea. As if he weren't already mad enough to start with. "How does he fare? Still killing in the fashion I taught him?"

"I dare say he's stepped out of your shadow and become something quite extraordinary himself." I tried to find a way out of the dream, to will myself to wake but I was trapped here.

Kyran seemed to consider this with a delightful smile. He was in every sense, beautiful. But in the same way a blade was finely crafted. And right now, I felt as if he were tipped toward my throat.

"Well now, I'll have to see about that myself. Will you come find me, dear little queen of wolves?"

I frowned at his nickname, but was more perplexed by his insinuation that I should prioritize finding him. I had other matters to resolve. I had to exile Fier and Tythian so I could bring Chase back. So he would be safe, and we could find a place in this new world we would build together. If he would still have me after what I'd done to him, that was. "Finding you, Kyran, has and never will be a priority."

I expected an outburst and consequence, but he only chuckled at my resentment as I said his name. "I could give you anything you want."

"What I want right now is not something you can give me, but only something I must earn myself." *And besides, the world is a better place without you*, I thought.

He cackled this time, throwing his head back in a monstrous laugh that all too reminded me of Lincon. A few moments passed until he finally collected himself, theatrically wiping tears away from his eyes. "You do not want to make an enemy of me, *girl*. I've been watching you from the moment my son took an interest in you."

"Goodie," I said dryly. Was that the only reason he'd become attached to me and haunted me in my dreams?

"Let it be known you are not the only person I have spoken to nor will you be the last. And even they have shortcomings," he gritted out, irritated. "But I like you, you have that certain craze in your eyes that tells me you're a woman who could get the job done as opposed to those who you now call enemy."

My gaze locked with his. "Are you speaking about Fier and Tythian?"

A smile crawled over his beautiful face once again. I took a step forward, reaching out to him in an attempt to fling my gift at him, but he burst into swirls of golden paint. His laugh echoed around me.

"If you will not help me. You will learn to regret your decision. It might not be now, and maybe even ten years, perhaps one hundred until someone digs me out. But let it be known, I will hunt you and all that lays in your wake."

My eyes burst open as I shuffled uncomfortably on the bed without sheets and blanket. Fire's head propped up at the end of my bed. The two pups were curled around her in their wolf forms as well. I dipped my feet over the edge of the bed, a mixture of thoughts consuming me. So Kyran had been speaking with Tythian and Fier as well? How much had their actions been puppeteered? I felt tense and needed to go for a walk.

"Esmore." Tori was standing at my door. I brushed my hand through my hair trying to wash away the impending doom that I felt loomed over me. I looked over at the headboard where flickers of ash remained. I called my power back in, assuring myself that the others hadn't been hurt by it. My muscles ached as I flexed my shoulders and wings back and forth.

Since the battle, I hadn't called the Descendant back in. The weight of its power on my back was a constant reminder of all that I was capable of and would accomplish in due time. I could see dawn breaking through the windows of the deplorable remains of the castle we'd taken sanctuary in.

Iris had brought us here, encouraging that this was one of the locations Tracey had considered relocating her Council to. It would do for now. It was a safe base. In parting my mother used her gift to conceal its location much like the security of the institute and covens. Though, I couldn't convince her to stay. After Cesar's death she was convinced for now we had our own paths, and she'd find her way to the rebel hunters to rectify the damage that had been done and ready to protect ourselves from the changes in the Council that would stir.

I pushed off the bed, embedding my hatred and rage for Tythian and Fier and the hand they'd forced upon us. I should've seen it coming and should've predicted a way around it. But I was just as much a fool as everyone else who had been blinded by their antics.

"What is it, Tori?" I asked coolly, trying not to take my anger out on him. He reminded me too much of Dillian. The loss and the betrayal but now they just mounted up one on top of another. Did he really go of his own accord? Did he look toward Tythian as if he could offer him more than what I could? Or did he do it simply to exchange his life for Tori's?

"Some wolves linger at the edge of the walls trying to get in. Iris is holding them back right now, but they don't seem vicious," he skeptically said. Fire's ears pricked up and she jumped off the bed, stirring the two young pups awake. Fortunately, they were quick to find warmth with one another and squirmed back to sleep.

"Wolves?" I said incredulously. With my mother's gift, nothing should've been able to make it through, but as we were learning perhaps the werewolves sense of smell was more specifically heightened than vampires and hunters combined.

"I thought it might be best that you come out before Lincon returns after his hunt," Tori sheepishly said. Because if Lincon returned without instruction he'd slaughter them just for fun.

Fire's nails clicked along the uneven cemented flooring as we walked through the castle. It was dark, dusty, and mostly broken. There was a consistent drip from a leak somewhere that irritated my senses. My wings curled into me as if the sheer touch of one of the walls might leave grime on their immaculate coloring and shine.

As I encroached on the degrading outer walls that were meant to be a form of security, I could sense a small group of wolves loitering and mostly snarling amongst one another. Fire didn't seem stressed by their presence, and so I took that as an indicator that they didn't come here looking for a fight.

Iris was peering down on them atop of the wall, his long hatchet unsheathed, ready if any might change behavior.

"They've been down here for a while trying to find a way in," he detailed. It was still peculiar having him at my side, and I wasn't entirely sure if I could trust him, that could only be earned in time. But if our last fight had been any indicator, I would at least give the former hunter a chance. I needed all the power I could obtain to strike at Tythian and Fier.

The gates were open, but they didn't dare cross the invisible line that I was certain Iris created with his firing gaze. I walked through it. I didn't have my sword strapped to my back but wouldn't need it. I could evaporate them into ash within seconds if they so much as looked at me wrong.

"Shift," I commanded of the one who seemed to be leading the pack of twelve. They looked at one another uncomfortably. I couldn't understand their way of communication, but I noticed the hesitation. Good. They saw me as a threat. A pale wolf shifted into an even paler naked man. Three others behind him shifted, but most of them remained in their wolf form.

"We've been searching for you," the man timidly said. Surprisingly Fire shifted, standing at my side and speaking on my behalf as if it were some honor to speak with me directly.

"For what reason would you seek her out?" she asked, wary of the wolves behind them.

"You saved us from the camps, and you work alongside one of our own." He played about with his fingers meekly. This was no warrior, though the few behind him seemed stronger and younger.

"I am an exception," Fire said, pointing her nose in the air.

"I have no need for more deaths on my hands," I remarked. The others might've been right. I'd become so fixated on the werewolves that I might've missed vital detail about Tythian's betrayal.

"We do not plan to be a burden. All that we ask is for space where we can build our strength, and if that is under your command to rise against those who did this to us, then so be it."

"I have no intention of facing the humans," I irked. The humans had done plenty wrong. But I was only focused on Fier and Tythian as they would now focus on me. I was their target, and I would monopolize that, so they didn't have the chance to search for Chase.

I could sense Titan and Chris walking out in their human form. I looked out from my peripheral where Chris yawned and rubbed his eyes. Titan was warier. Since retrieving them and the twins, Titan seemed slightly more stubborn than usual because I'd forced her to leave. I couldn't help but find humor in the single bow she carried alongside my Barnett crossbow I'd gifted her. It still looked far too big for her, and I was uncertain as to what she thought she'd manage bringing it out here. But at least she had the heart of a warrior. Tori stepped in front of them, not letting them venture any closer toward the wall or unknown wolves.

"It's not only the humans we begrudge, but the vampires have dwindled our numbers in our search to find you simply because of what we are. They'll kill us all unless we have a place to regroup and build our numbers. We can help one another. I heard you lost your lover in the past war with the Vampire Council and want to avenge his death?"

I looked at him incredulously. How they'd heard of such things already hastened my resolve to cure Chase sooner. But better a rumor of his demise than the reality that he was still alive, though it still riled me to hear such a thing come from a stranger's mouth.

"Please, there's a reason why you saved us that day. Though I might not be certain what you are," he said, rolling his hand in the air to exasperate over my wings, showing fangs and fluorescent purple huntress eyes. "You are our only chance of survival. And much like us, you're a misfit. And by coming together, I'm sure we can help one another out. Just please, give my people a chance."

I narrowed my gaze on him and his ideal that we were the same, that we were misfitted creatures of this world, a part of the same coin. And it irked me so greatly because I had once come to the same conclusion. But I had also let their kind become a distraction to me. I had fought against Chase in the opinion of their right to live and thrive. But what if they were the very army I needed to build to protect him?

What if in its wicked sense, this was why I had been so begrudging to the idea of killing them. I'd seen them as a source of power from the start, and maybe that was the greater gain I needed now to employ an army.

"If not for yourself then let us help protect the children," one of the women said. My gaze intimidatingly dipped to her and then the smaller wolf at her side. Not a child as young as Titan and Chris but perhaps a teenager.

I could sense Lincon and the twins encroaching on our territory, returning from a fresh hunt. "Having numbers isn't a bad idea," Iris announced from behind. Fire's gaze snapped on him.

"And who are you to give unsolicited advice, soldier from a Council of all things," she seethed the savageness in her tone as gripping as her growl in wolf form.

"I'm a realist, no matter what way you look at it. Fier and Tythian have an army, and we have a group of bandits at best."

"Fire," I distracted her and flexed my wings slightly, enjoying the slight breeze that nurtured their nerve endings, "what do you think of these people?"

Fire had once made it known she felt no personal attachment to their kind. After all, they were all humans experimented on. But aligned, perhaps they could be something greater. Something menacing.

"I don't necessarily like the idea, but if we were to stay true with your focus and intent, then this might be a starting place," she confirmed. We'd fallen short the last two weeks of how we could create an army that would measure Fier's. I considered going in with my handful of warriors, but the disadvantage was too great. Especially now that the Council hadn't been disbanded into total ruin and it was highly probable Fier would direct their attention toward me.

Little Queen of Wolves, Kyran had called me. I begrudged him for predicting such a thing and even now, I doubted it might work, but I had only something to gain. This could be the start to build my army around Chase, no matter how maverick a group. This could be the start of the world as we know it coming to an end. Because my enemies know no wrath or fury like my own. For all that they had done to those I loved, and for being the reason I was separated from my love.

I furled my fingers around the lock of Chase's hair in my pocket. I would inevitably destroy them and took glee in the idea of the war to come because now it was truly of my own. They'd pissed off the wrong monster.

Thank you so much for reading my book. If you enjoyed this book, I'd love to hear your honest thoughts in way of a review. It not only helps support my writing but also gives me important feedback on how you felt and connected with the world and characters. I love connecting with my readers and would appreciate if you could take two minutes to leave a review or rating. Thank you so much and I hope you are having a wonderful day!

About the Author

Kia grew up in the Darling Downs Region in Queensland, Australia. Graduating High School, she pursued a career in freelance journalism. In 2014, having always had a passion for writing fiction, she decided to follow her dream of becoming an accomplished author.

Now living on the Gold Coast, Australia and travelling every spare minute she gets, Kia is constantly searching for new inspiration for her writing and filling her heart with adventure, one country at a time.

Other Books By Kia Carrington-Russell

Mad Hatter Vampire Prince:

A PREQUEL NOVELLA TO THE TOKEN HUNTRESS SERIES. CAN ALSO BE READ AS A STANDALONE.

Kyran Klaus is the prince of Grand Klaus, his reputation honoring him the title of the Mad Hatter Vampire Prince. Crazy, deadly, lustful, and utterly bored with life.

Sasha Pierce is one of a kind. Having been experimented on by her mother as a child, she's become a human weapon who's looking for answers beyond the walls where her kind aren't enslaved to vampires.

When the Mad Hatter Prince takes a sudden interest in Sasha and her work, she scarcely begins to cover her tracks and hide her secrets. What she doesn't anticipate is being a pawn in his most sinister performance yet.

Disturbingly Wicked! This novella is not for the fainthearted. Lust, Gore, Wit, and Malicious Humor. Prepare to be deliciously tainted.

Token Huntress

Being born a hunter, Esmore has been raised with one purpose, to hunt and kill the vampire race that destroyed the world as it was known. At eighteen, Esmore's a Token Huntress in her Guild, surpassing her mentor's expectations of her, despite having no magical ability, like all hunters before her.

During a raid in the once iconic San Fransisco, Esmore's team is ambushed, and a mysterious vampire that she is drawn to captures and takes her to the Vampire Council as a prisoner. Her captor- Chase, a lethal, immortal, sexy, and charming vampire who will stop at nothing to claim her as his familiar.

While in captivity, Esmore learns information that makes her question everything she's been taught.

Now in the year 2341, Esmore fights for her survival. But who exactly is she fighting against? The very people who nurtured her, or the evil she's supposed to hate?

The Shadow Minds Journal:

In this world, there are creatures lurking in the shadows. As a child, I once played with them. As a teenager, I began to fear them and became victim to their attacks. As an adult, I now realize that no matter how much I try to escape the grasp of this world, I was inevitably born into it.

Now reborn as a Guardian in the year of 2986, Vivian Lair must uphold the treaty between Angels and Demons on the human world and city of Shabeah. Contracted to seven demons who she can shift into while taking direct orders from the Underworld Lord, Haymen, it wasn't exactly her ideal rebirth. Involving herself with the Angel of War, Gabe is even worse.

Still fighting those who try to possess her during her sleep, Vivian must now record and try to hunt the Volv through the Shadow Minds Journal. Now stuck between the hatred and lust of two of the most powerful entities in all worlds, Vivian is involved inevitably in the upcoming conflict.

Blood. Lust. War. She must kill before being killed.

My Escort Collection:

A collection of the Best Selling contemporary series that includes: My Escort, My Exception and My Expectation. Clover is personal assistant to Debra Coorman, the merciless boss of Candice fashion magazine. The bright lights of New York are dim for Clover, who is tormented by a work schedule like no other. Debra is relentless in her determination to demean Clover. For once, Clover dares to play Debra's games, and intends to prove her wrong at the next glittering event. With mixed emotions, Clover contacts a male escort, Damon. If his velvet voice over the phone is anything to go by, Clover knows her money will be well spent. But when Damon appears at her door, something unexpected happens. The taunts and the games begin. Who is truly going to win at this game?

Aroused: Taming Himself

"Remember my name because you will be begging me for more. This is my promise to you."

Meet Hayden Zilch: entrepreneur, sports manager, investor. Cocky, tantalizing, and an utter womanizer. He is a man who loves pleasuring women. He can show you a world you have only fantasied about.

So what happens when this sex-mad womanizer decides to finally find The One?

Starting off with a list of five women, Hayden sets out to learn the difference between lust and love. His adventures have him laughing, crying in pain, and begging on his knees as he battles to tame himself. Can Hayden really control himself around these five beautiful temptresses?

Taming Himself is the first in this five-book series which tells the story of Hayden's search for both love and pleasure.

Phantom Wolf

A book that is so dynamic and can pull my emotions free so easily is a 5 star novel.
★★★★★ *- Paranormal Trance Reviews*

Sia is a Phantom Wolf. Neither dead nor alive--and rotting from the inside--she is on the edge of her curse. Once a Phantom Wolf has been created, they hunt their blood pack and slaughter all their loved ones. Except for Sia, who woke years after her death to find herself rampaging through the land on a lonely path.

She continues to run from the rival pack that hunts her because she is a Phantom Wolf. Attracted to a scent, Sia finds her old best friend, who is now a grown woman. Having once saved Keeley, Sia takes the role of protector yet again, despite Keeley's involvement with the mysterious Alpha, Kiba, and his kin brother, Saith. An ambush separates the pack and the four of them blindly fight the new warriors that attack them: desperately needing to find out where the attacks are coming from, as Sia has vowed to protect Keeley. But at what cost?

Now being chased, Sia finds herself conflicted by the mortal and spirit world while trying to protect her kin. Sia must confront her fears, as well as the human lover who killed her many years before. It is not only survival Sia contends with, but her own façade that must be broken so that she may find peace within herself once more.

The Three Immortal Blades

Contains the entire Award Winning Collection. Karla Gray is an ordinary young woman that is taken from her mundane life into a world of blood lust as she begins to struggle with a unique ability. Karla is a Shielder; an exceptional fighter born with the rare ability to project a Shield for protection. However, Shielders are not the only kind that possesses such a talent. The Shielders battle a war that has been raging for centuries against Starkorfs, who harvest humans and Shielders alike to obtain a near immortality. Alongside the charming Lucas and selfless Paul, Karla must unravel the purpose of her curse and battle an unknown presence manipulating her thoughts; a mysterious woman who may be dormant for now, but has every intention of possessing Karla- mind, body, and soul. Within this new reality that Karla faces the search for the Three Immortal Blades begins.